live your dream

B.B. MILLER & LESLIE CARSON

Cover Design by:
Jada D'Lee Designs

Cover Image by:
iStock Photo

Editing by:
Lauren Schmelz, Write Divas

Interior Design & Formatting by:
Christine Borgford, Type A Formatting

chapter one

matt

A DULL JACKHAMMER BEATS RELENTLESSLY in my head as I slowly become aware of frenzied movement beside the bed. I can't even imagine trying to open my eyes. The thought is painful. Why did I let the Brit talk me into tequila? You would think I'd have learned by now.

"You're a stupid fuck. . . . Too dumb to remember to come home on time."

I squeeze my eyes tighter, trying to drown out the memory of my mother's shrill voice. No amount of time seems to let me forget my childhood. It's always there, lurking in nightmares and twisted memories.

"Shit . . ." It's a whispered curse from a panicked female voice, bringing me back to the torture of the morning. I turn my head in her direction and groan, trying to put together what happened the night before.

Redfall, my band, had played a concert in support of the What's Your Dream Foundation. There's no way I'll ever forget it; Parker Jensen, an eleven-year-old kid fighting leukemia, had his dream fulfilled by spending a day with his idol, our front man and one of my best friends, Kennedy Lane.

We came close to losing Kennedy to the demons he's battled since an accident took his sister's life a few years ago. But being involved in something like What's Your Dream changed him and made him look at life in a different way. I don't think Parker will ever know that he's the one who did the saving when it came to Kennedy.

Yesterday's concert will stay with me for a long time. The rest of the night, though? A bit of a hazy mystery. I remember Kennedy heading off with Abby to their own private celebration, and Sean Murphy, our borderline insane drummer, dragging Cameron Chapman (or Three, as Sean likes to call him), our rhythm guitarist, and a group of us out to celebrate.

It started in the limo with a few members of the charity foundation's team, including the delectable but equally infuriating Tessa Baker. I've never met a woman like her. Long black hair, curves that drive me insane, and a sarcastic mouth on her I'd like to put to better use. She's challenged me since the moment we met in the lead-up to the concert for Parker. Questioning nearly every word that came out of my mouth, taunting me with her delicious curves and sharp wit. There's no denying we get under each other's skin. A more frustrating woman I have yet to meet. She seems to know every button to push to get a reaction out of me.

The limo cruised the steep streets of San Fran as we indulged in expensive champagne before Sean demanded that we stop outside a gentleman's club. Cue the ensuing battle of wills with Tess where she accused us of setting the women's movement back a few decades.

Snippets of the alcohol-induced rant rush back to me.

"We love women, all of them, don't we, Grasshopper?" Sean was always so helpful.

"Come in and see it for yourself before you pass your high-and-mighty judgment." And she did. Tess marched her sweet ass right up to the doors and demanded entry from the linebacker-sized bouncers.

I wonder if there's anything she'll back down from.

Being famous comes with a few perks I'll never complain about, and one of them is getting in anywhere, anytime, no questions asked. So, our little entourage, already half shit-faced, spilled into the high-end club so that Tess could see for herself that the women weren't being forced to do anything they didn't want to.

That particular club was one Sean and I have been to a few times. It catered to the elite, to the rich, to the ones who needed and demanded confidentiality. You could get a five-star meal and the best liquor money can buy while enjoying top industry DJs, a high-quality burlesque show, and uber-exclusive lounge areas.

Tess probably expected sticky floors and drunken frat boys catcalling women chained to stripper poles. What she saw rendered her speechless, and what a fucking sight that was. It may be the one and only time in the couple of days I've known her that I've seen her at a loss for words.

Once we were safely tucked into one of the white leather VIP booths, we broke into the Tres Quatro Cinco. Sean had opened up a tab to pay for a few bottles of the expensive tequila, and rounds of whatever poisons anyone wanted. Everything after that point was a blur—a nasty, pinpricking, and painful blur.

I have bits and pieces here and there of hushed, wicked words whispered close to Tess's ear, the touch of her hand against my thigh, her twirling beneath a lamppost under a cable car sign. But the blanks between are greater than the rest of the foggy picture.

I have no idea how we made it back to the Fairmont. I run a shaky hand over my face, hearing more rustling from beside the bed. "Where is it?"

My mouth feels like it's full of cotton. Something definitely happened last night. I get snapshots of Tess practically pouncing on me in the elevator, and drunken, uncoordinated limbs grabbing at my shirt while the pair of us stumbled into the hotel room.

I can smell her on my fingers, still taste her on my tongue, and feel her hand clumsily reaching into my jeans.

"So stupid . . ." It's the last thing I hear before the door clicks shut.

"GRASSHOPPER!" IT'S SEAN BEATING ON the door. I ignore him and throw a pillow over my head. I'm used to lack of sleep. Lack of sleep and a hangover from hell, though I could do without. "Open up, Matty!" He bangs some more. He won't give up. He never does.

"For fuck's sake." I roll my sorry ass out of bed, shuffling across the floor as he knocks out a continuous rhythm on the door. I find my jeans in a pile on the floor and tug them on. "Enough!" As I whip the door open, Sean's there filling the space, his ridiculous blue hair styled up to perfection. It's tempting to stick something in it just to piss him off. He tries to peer over my shoulder into the room. Always so fucking intrusive.

"You alone?"

I grip the door, trying weakly to push him out of my face.

"Christ, yes. I'm fucking alone."

Sean barrels past me, and I shut the door behind him, leaning against it.

"It smells like sex in here."

I try to shake off the lingering effects of the alcohol swimming in my veins, and the memories that seem to haunt me. Everyone has their own demons. Kennedy's rest in the bottle and guilt. Sean and Cameron's have been the most convenient drugs of choice. Mine are dark and twisted memories I can't escape. "Tell me again why you're here?"

"I'm hungry, and we have shopping to do." He turns to size me up, shaking his head as he takes in my half-dressed state. "You fuck her?"

"Again. Why are you here?" I meet his stern look with one of my own.

"You heard me."

"Since when are you so interested in my sex life? You not get any lately?"

He laughs and moves to one of the windows across the room, tearing back the curtains to reveal a cloudless, blue sky. Another stellar San Fran morning. The room floods with the harsh light, doing nothing to dull my headache. The Brit sinks down into one of the leather chairs by the window, making himself at home.

"I get plenty, mate. And I'm interested because, for once, *she's* not a random."

"Fuck off."

"No, you fuck off. She works with Abby. If things go sideways with you two, it could make it uncomfortable between Abby and Kennedy, and we just got him back." I cringe. Sean's right. Kennedy's just found the love of his life with Abby Walker, the director of What's Your Dream, and Tess's boss.

"I mean, have I not taught you anything?" he rants, jabbing a finger at me. "Law Number 27—don't shit where you eat." Since his last name is Murphy, Sean's developed a hideously long list of his own brand of 'Murphy's Laws' that he's constantly exhorting us to follow. Not that we listen much.

I shake my head. It was one night. No more, no less.

"There's nothing to go sideways, Dr. Phil. Get over your fucking laws."

He lets out a laugh, leaning forward to pick something up from the floor, leveling me a knowing look as he swings a bright pink lace bra from his fingers. "This doesn't look like nothing."

Another fragment of the night comes back to me. Tess, swaying her hips to some music heard only in her head, reaching around to unclasp her bra.

"Fuck." I can feel her full, heavy breasts filling my hands, my tongue piercing rolling over her hardened nipples.

"You did fuck her. You asshole," he rants in an accusatory tone.

"No. I didn't."

"You sure?" He lifts his brow before starting in on his inspection of the bra. "Damn. Forty double D. You are the luckiest fuck on the planet."

"I think I'd remember fucking someone like Tess."

"I sure as hell would." He twirls the pink lace around his finger.

"Hey. Watch it."

"Mhmm. Nothing happened, my ass." He tosses the bra on the rumpled sheets of the bed. "Look at you, all defensive . . . protective even."

Pushing away from the door, I start for the bathroom and grumble under my breath, "I'm taking a shower."

"Make it quick. I'm hungry."

He gets a door slam for an answer.

"Look at this place. Are you always such a pig?" he hollers from the other room. I switch on the shower, trying to drown out his voice. As the water warms and the room fills with steam, I lean against the counter and avoid looking at the sorry fuck in the mirror.

Yesterday, everything was so different. Being with Parker, seeing the kind of support he has, was both inspiring and a reminder that I never had any support—not until the damage had already been done. I know I can't change my past. And, somehow, despite the clusterfuck of my childhood, I've made it. That doesn't mean I've forgotten.

Some scars never really heal.

Sean's voice booms through the door, preventing another unwelcome trip down memory lane. "It looks like a gale went through here. No wonder she left you before the morning."

That's the thing about women. They always leave.

"YOU GUYS WERE LIKE, SO hot up there." This glowing review comes from the run-of-the-mill, half-dressed groupie we find lingering outside a diner with her equally enthusiastic friend. At least we got to eat breakfast in peace.

We tend to garner more attention when we're out with Kennedy, since he's our front man and a favorite of the paparazzi and their associated trashy magazines. It's not unusual for us to get noticed without him, especially after a concert like the one we put on last night. It's moments like this that I think about how different my life used to be.

Everyone has issues, baggage, or whatever buzzword of the day. Having no idea which of my mother's clients was my sperm donor, and living on the streets between foster homes after mom ended her own life when I was twelve, is mine.

I was more than a handful in those early teenage years after her suicide, so I don't blame the foster system or the families who had all the good intentions in the world. But I've learned hell is paved with good intentions. When it comes right down to it, people will disappoint you, so now I keep my expectations low. I expect nothing. Nothing is what I get and what I deserve.

I finally found a bit of normalcy—or my version of it—when I was sixteen. I thought I was old enough to be on my own. The reality was I had no idea what the hell I was doing. I had a chip on my shoulder, angry at everything and everyone.

And then Tom Logan found me.

I had been trying to hotwire his vintage Shelby—an initiation ritual for a gang of thugs I had no business being involved with. I should've been enjoying high school, dating some nice girl, maybe figuring out what college to go to, but somewhere between tenth and eleventh grade I dropped out—not just out of school, but out of life. I was living on the streets at the age of fifteen.

Learning to stay alive as a homeless teenager in the seedy neighborhoods of LA made you grow up pretty damn fast. It's survival of the fittest where every day is a fight for food, for shelter, for the right to take a breath.

By the time I found the gang with its vague promises to keep me safe, I had been to twelve different schools, a handful of group homes, been arrested for more petty thefts than I could count, and was introduced to the fine art of dealing drugs.

I had become somewhat of an expert at sneaking into dodgy hotels and rundown stairwells of apartment buildings to sleep—if you could call it that. "Always sleep with one eye open" is the only piece of good advice I got from a dude named Hades, the self-proclaimed badass leader of the gang.

I learned early on that the only person I could count on was myself. Hades and his gang of equally lost souls scattered like the rats they were, back to the underbelly of LA when Tom confronted me in front of his Mustang.

This initiation ritual wasn't random. Tom was targeted. He worked at one of the local group homes for teens and at one time had kicked Hades out for his continual disregard for the rules. This was payback.

"You don't want to do this." Those were the first words Tom ever spoke to me, and I'd be lying if I said I wasn't terrified. If I were arrested again, I'd likely be doing some serious time in juvy. And, while a solid roof over my head and three squares a day was wildly tempting, even I didn't want something like a prison sentence following me around.

Tom was an imposing man next to my rail-thin, sixteen-year-old form. At least six five, he was obviously in love with the gym. He was bald with a thick goatee and dressed entirely in black. In the nearly empty parking lot, he was like something out of a bad dream.

Tom took a step toward me, and my back pressed against the car. Trapped with nowhere to go seemed to have become commonplace for me. "I can help you."

"Fuck off." It was the only response to his words. On the street, "help" could mean a thousand different scenarios, some of which were a one-way ticket to an early grave. I looked around frantically for Hades, for anyone to have my back like they promised they would. Only the faint echoes of shoes hitting the pavement greeted me. Alone again.

"When was the last time you ate? Slept in a bed?" Tom leaned forward, getting into my space, and I could see the hard lines on his face, a thick scar next to his mouth, a nose that had obviously been broken a few times. But more than that, it was his eyes that I noticed. There wasn't any judgment there, no ill-placed sympathy, no look of disgust or shame, all things you get used to seeing from strangers once they realize you're homeless.

"Why do you care?"

"Because I was you once. And I know what it feels like."

We stared at each other for a while as LA continued around us. A police siren squealed in the distance, car doors were opened and closed, a bus sped by the parking garage. "Get in the car . . . please."

It was the first time I had heard that word in a very long time, and he sounded sincere. Now, Tom could've just as easily been a serial killer or some sick fuck who preyed on kids like me. Maybe I was incredibly stupid and naive to get into a complete stranger's car that night, but I did, and that changed everything.

"Grasshopper?" Sean waves his hand in front of my face, bringing me back to the present. "The gorgeous Danielle here would like an autograph." A Sharpie is thrust into my hand, and I blindly sign my name on her barely there Redfall tank top.

"Does it look good?" Danielle asks, practically sticking her tits into my face.

Leaning back, I nod with a grin. "It looks great." Her friend beside her jumps up and down, letting out an ear-shattering squeal.

Sean tries his best to quiet them down, his voice dropping. "If you could keep where you saw us to yourself, just for a while, we'd really appreciate it."

Danielle nods so fast, I'm afraid her extensions are going to fall out.

"Thank you, darling." Sean winks at them before we pose for a few more pictures, and we're on our way once more.

"I think the days of you shopping at the mall are coming to

an end." Sean scoffs at my statement, leading us down the street.

"It'll die down, Matty. It's always mental right after a show."

"And yet you want to go buy sunglasses today of all days. Why not just order them online like everyone else?"

"Because I'm not like everyone else."

I let out a laugh. "No shit."

He throws his arm around my neck as we duck into the next store. "You love me, Grasshopper. Think about how dull and boring your life would be without me in it."

The thing is, he's right. Not that I'd ever tell him that.

"YOU WANNA GET HIGH?" IT'S Hades's voice, taunting me from his perch high atop the swing set in the park. I'm curled up inside the faded orange tube slide, trying to keep warm. Gunfire in the distance reminds me just how far away from the days of playing at the park I really am.

Despite me dealing drugs, I don't do them. Hades and his crew use me to get them, though. And even with promises of food to eat when I score their meth, I eat dinner out of a garbage can.

I try to sneak away from the park when I think they're asleep, but one of them catches me. I can't get away, no matter how hard I try, and they drag me back under the swings to beat the living shit out of me.

Bolting up in the bed, I'm drenched in sweat, the sheets tangled around my legs. My heart races as I reach over to find the light on the nightstand. A warm glow blankets me while I search for my cigarettes and try to shake off the nightmare.

With shaking hands, it's a struggle to get a cigarette out and light the damn thing, but that first drag seeps in and slowly starts to calm me. I wonder if there's ever going to be a time when I don't think about the years of neglect, of living on the streets, of feeling unworthy.

Glancing out at the darkened sky, it's easy to imagine myself still out there—running from the cops, seeking shelter under a freeway bridge, always being bone-tired. I sometimes have to remind myself that's not me anymore. But my success is still something I'm not sure I really deserve.

Blowing out a long puff of smoke, I finally push off the bed and stumble to the bathroom. Flushing the cigarette, I fill a glass with water. I down it quickly, repeating the process a few times before dragging myself back into the suite, knowing I'll be up now for hours. Insomnia, one of my best friends, is also a bitch.

The bright pink lace of Tess's bra catches my eye. The cleaning crew has folded it neatly, setting it on the computer desk by the window.

Quietly, it taunts me, begs me to pick it up, so I do. It smells like her, fresh and crisp. The lace is silky against my rough hand. Being with her last night helped me forget, at least for a little while.

Turning the bra over, I see the tag on the inside, and before I know it, I'm typing *Wacoal* into the search engine on my phone.

Rows and rows of images flood the screen, none of them as enticing as the hazy memories of Tess. I'm fully aware there are a million things that could go wrong with what I'm about to do, not the least of which is what Sean said this morning. This could blow up in my face and cause tension within the band at a time when we're just hitting our stride again.

I can't seem to stop myself. At the very least, Tess deserves to have her tempting piece of lace returned, and maybe just a few more items added to her lingerie collection that she might enjoy. I know this is a distraction, a way for me to try to keep the memories buried.

Typically, I'd head out to the nearest club, or hell, even just downstairs to the bar, and get distracted by some nameless woman who would be all too willing to fulfill her rock-and-roll fantasy. That's been my blueprint for as long as I can remember. For once, I don't want a nameless woman. For once, I know exactly what I want, and Tess Baker doesn't have a fucking clue what she's in for.

Tessa

WHAT THE HELL WAS I thinking?

Shaking my head, I put the kettle on and tug my robe closer as I continue my mental berating. I never drink so much that I can't remember what happened. Never. Of course, I never drink tequila either—not since that unfortunate night that resulted in me skipping naked across the field at Stanford Stadium at two in the morning with the rest of the debate team. Senor Tequila and I are not friends.

It's not as if I'm a prude. I've had my fair share of one-night stands and have lived to tell about them. But this time . . . I rub a hand over my face in despair. The walk of shame felt even more shameful yesterday morning as I slunk my way out of the Fairmont and down to the transit station to catch the M line home. To hook up with *him*, of all people . . . that scruffy, egotistical asshat.

I'm smarter than that, damn it! I'm a freaking Stanford grad, for Christ's sake!

I can't deny that I'm attracted to him, despite the current state of his hair. Why on earth he ever thought a Mohawk was a good idea, I'll never know. Tall and broad-shouldered, with classically blond hair and blazing blue eyes that see right into my soul, Matthew Logan is the epitome of bad-boy hot. Even more, there's this . . . *something* . . . a determination and beauty in his movements that captivates me. And the way he plays on stage—he's amazing. Fingers flying over the strings while he stalks around the stage, he is an equal and integral part of the juggernaut that is Redfall.

When he snarled at me in the boardroom before the show, he was so *infuriating*! Infuriating and provocative, and so damn full of himself. He practically dared me to go with him after Parker's concert, so of course I couldn't back down.

Damn my pride.

Squeezing my eyes shut, I will myself to remember. The limo ride is clear—mostly—and the visit to the club. Who would've expected that behind that nondescript front door not far from Fisherman's Wharf was a place like that? I've been down that street a dozen times, and I've never noticed there was a strip club there, which I guess is the point.

The rest is fuzzy. I can remember looking out a window at the city lights upside down as my head hung over the edge of . . . something. A couch, maybe? I cringe, thinking of the spent condom wrappers I had to step over in my rush to leave the suite before he woke up. Disgusting. At least we were safe. I just wish I could remember!

I groan and pluck the whistling kettle off the gas burner to pour myself a steaming cup. Quickly dunking the tea bag several times, I breathe deeply as the distinctive scent of Darjeeling permeates the air. Tea has always been comforting to me, and I need some comfort this morning.

Enjoying the warmth of the cup in my hands, I curl up in a corner of the sofa, staring out at Lake Merced, just visible through the fog. I love my home. Nestled between the San Francisco State University campus and the San Fran Golf Club, it's my little piece of heaven. The door opens and I look over in surprise. "Did you go running or something?"

"I wish. A server block decided to crash. Just the way I like to start a Monday," my roommate explains with a grimace. At almost six feet tall with a glowing, coffee-colored complexion, Jada Harris is a striking woman. A mutual friend introduced us about a year ago. Jada, an IT network engineer for SFSU, owns our condo and had been looking for a roommate to offset expenses. We hit it off over coffee, and I moved in the next week.

"The water should be still hot if you'd like tea," I offer, and she smiles gratefully and heads into our open kitchen. "I thought you normally worked remotely on stuff like that outside of business hours."

"Normally I do, but . . ." She sighs and busies herself with tea making. "Tito panicked and called me in. It's a long story. My plan is to go back to bed for a few hours and go in around ten." She steps around the breakfast bar and gives me a curious look. "Aren't you going in to work? You're normally in the shower already by now."

"Yep. Just moving a little slow this morning," I say, plastering on a smile and standing. "Are we still on for the movie tonight?" We'd been planning on going to that new period drama with James McAvoy for weeks.

"Wouldn't miss it!" She smiles tiredly. "But for now, I'm hitting the sack. Have a good day!" With a little wave, she disappears into her bedroom. Knowing I've got to get moving, I retreat to my own room and head to the bathroom. One of the awesome things about Jada's two-bedroom condo is that we each have a full bathroom.

Looking balefully in the mirror, I gingerly prod one of the myriad of hickeys that pepper my throat, chest, and boobs. Jesus, I look like I went ten rounds with a hungry pit bull and lost. Fuck. What kind of a psycho leaves marks like that? I'm going to have to wear a turtleneck, and I hate turtlenecks.

Closing my eyes, I get a sudden memory of a pair of intense blue eyes hovering over me, with silky blond hair flopping over a broad forehead. I suck in a sharp breath as a shudder of desire racks my body. My mind may not remember everything, buy my body obviously does. Damn it.

I turn on the shower and take a deep breath. It's just another day, Tess. Pull yourself together.

TWO HOURS LATER, I PASTE a bright smile on my face and say hello to everyone as usual, as I make my way down the hall and to my desk. I fire up my computer and let my morning routine lull me. Thank God Abby, my boss, is taking a few days off. She'd take one look at me and want to know everything.

However, because she's not here, I probably won't be hearing about my job application anytime soon.

Abby Walker, executive director of What's Your Dream, has never treated me as just an assistant, and it's something I love about working with her. She's always included me in her decisions, and I know as much about our dream fulfillments as anyone else on the team. With Abby's encouragement, I threw my hat in the ring for the open position of giving director. It's a stretch for me, but, damn it . . . I want it.

With a shudder, I recall the conversation I overheard where Kennedy Lane had handed our former giving director, Nadia Baskov, her ass, calling her out on her unprofessional behavior. Following that was the board meeting during which Nadia had thought she was going to expose Abby's relationship with Kennedy but only managed to make a fool of herself. No one was sorry when she handed in her resignation, but it left What's Your Dream in a lurch.

I want to fill her spot. I'll miss working so closely with Abby, but I'm ready for more responsibility. And she'd certainly never have to worry about *me* using some poor kid's dream as a chance to hop in the sack with a client.

I slump with the reminder; no, apparently I sleep with them only *after* the dream has been fulfilled. Brilliant.

"You look nice." I look up to see April Morrison, communications director, peering at me over her stylish glasses.

"Thanks," I say, my smile faltering. To hide my hickeys, I paired my one and only turtleneck—black—with a matching skirt, belt, and heels. With my black hair and dark eyes, I probably look like a dominatrix.

I need to go shopping at lunch.

"Since Abby is out, how would you like to sit in on my meeting with Nintendo at ten thirty?" She looks at her iPad and taps something. "I could use some backup."

"Sure." I look at her in surprise. "This is for the Jacobson dream?" Mary Jacobson is a thirteen-year-old from Sacramento with Hodgkin's lymphoma. Her only way of relaxing during her chemo treatments is to play video games, and her dream is to work with Nintendo on an idea she had for a game.

April nods, smiling a secret smile. "Yep. And Ralph will be dropping by for lunch afterward. You should join us."

"Okay. Thanks." I cock my head at her unsubtle dropping of the chairman of the board's name. "What's going on?"

"Nothing," she says innocently, which only makes me more suspicious. April doesn't do innocent. "See you at ten thirty."

I FIND OUT WHAT SHE was hiding about three hours later. Our

Human Resources manager asked to see me and offered me the giving director position. Effective immediately! Breathlessly, I float down the hallway to my desk, my face aching from my perma-grin.

My smile gets impossibly wider when I see the giant bouquet of flowers on my desk. Eagerly, I check the card and laugh. Abby! She knew exactly what was happening, of course. Smiling fondly, I stick my nose in a blossom and inhale the delicate fragrance. I feel like I could open a window and soar across the city like Tinkerbell . . . or like Tinkerbell's evil twin, considering my all-black apparel today.

Just when I thought the day couldn't get much better, the meeting with Nintendo had gone swimmingly. Thanks to my obsessive note-taking in every meeting I attend with Abby, I was completely up to speed with everything that had been proposed already and could participate as an equal. Lunch with April and Ralph Shepherd, chairman of the board of directors, had been interesting. He's a lovely man, but I felt like I was being evaluated. Now I know why.

"Hi, Tess. Nice flowers." I look up to see Jeff from the mailroom standing in front of my desk with an enthusiastic smile on his face and holding a large rectangular box. "I've got a special delivery for you."

"Thanks!" I take the box and eagerly look to see who sent it. FedEx overnight delivery? I bet it's from my parents—Abby probably gave them a heads up. This is likely one of those inspirational posters my mother's so fond of.

Absently, I flip the package over, looking for the pull tab on the box, as Jeff chatters away. "Actually, I'm glad I was on call when this came in. I've been looking for an excuse to talk to you."

"Really?" I finally find the tab and rip it down the side of the box. I glance up, surprised to see Jeff still standing there, shuffling his feet like an excited puppy.

"Do you think you'd want to go get some coffee sometime?"

"Oh, um, sure. That would be great," I say, distracted by the mystery of the box. I finally loosen the lid and lift it so I can peer inside.

Holy shit!

Quickly slapping the lid back down in alarm, I clutch the large box to my chest awkwardly and look up to meet Jeff's curious gaze. "Uh, thanks a lot, Jeff. This is really for Abby, so I'll just put it in her office," I stammer, backing away from him and into Abby's empty office. I say from the doorway, "Coffee would be great sometime. Thanks!" Giving him a bright smile, I quickly close the door and retreat to my boss's sofa, placing the box on her coffee table. Slowly opening the lid again, I sift through the contents with growing dismay and anger. This definitely isn't from my parents.

Underneath a layer of fancy tissue paper lies more lingerie than I could wear in a week. Lacy bras, silky underwear, and even a satin nightgown that looks like it would feel glorious against the skin, all in my size. And right on top is a replica of my favorite hot-pink lace bra, the one I left behind in my haste to escape Matt's suite.

"That . . . that . . . presumptive ass!" I finally sputter. What in the flaming hell? Who does he think he is? And he delivered all this to me *at work*? Where anyone walking by could've seen what was in it? What if the obliging Jeff had decided to be helpful by opening the damn box for me? God!

I stare at the contents, mystified. We had one night together—one! That's it. Done. Finito. Why would he do this?

A spot of plain grey cotton nestled amongst the lace and ruffles catches my eye, and I tug it free. A Redfall T-shirt—of course. But it's the note that flutters to my lap that makes me laugh in spite of myself.

Thought you could use this. It's far more fashionable than that rag you wore the other night.

To provoke him, I'd purposefully worn a Landon Ravine shirt at Parker's concert. It worked. Matt's eyes had almost bugged out of his head when he'd seen it, and he griped about it all night. He despises Ravine.

I drum my fingers on the box lid while I contemplate my next move. He obviously thinks he's won our war of wills, and this is his way of flaunting his victory . . . like spiking the ball in the end zone.

Well.

With a huff, I close up the box and pull my cell phone out of my pocket. If he thinks I'm going to let him have the last word, he's sorely mistaken.

Game on, buddy.

chapter two

matt

MY VICTORY MOTORCYCLE IS KEEPING me busy, and I need that right now. My thoughts over the past few days keep drifting back to Tess—her smooth silky skin, her sarcastic mouth, and the delicious curve of her spine. It's fucking torture.

Wiping my hands on the greasy towel hanging from my back pocket, I look up from the motorcycle, grinning at Tom Logan as he stands with his arms folded across his wide chest. It's a welcome break from my brain that won't turn off.

Dressed entirely in black as he typically is, his leather vest is open to reveal a well-worn Redfall T-shirt. Before we made it big, it would've been Zeppelin or Pink Floyd. It's hard not to feel a surge of pride seeing him wearing it.

My garage is a far cry from my adopted father's modest one on the outskirts of South Central LA, where he taught me everything

I know about bikes. As a teenager, I thought it was torture. What I know now is that Tom was saving me, hour by hour, day by day, bike by bike.

He didn't have to do it. He could've just as easily left me on the streets and forgotten about me. Worse, he could've turned me into the cops.

For whatever reason, he didn't do any of those things.

That night when he found me trying to steal his Shelby, he took me to the group home he worked at, and he didn't leave my side. He stayed up with me all night as I bitched and complained.

He did something no one else had ever done up to that point. He actually listened to me. He didn't pass judgment, didn't tell me all the ways I was screwing up my life. He didn't feed me lines about wanting to change me, or paint some all-American-family picture where I'd fit in, with cozy dinners around a table every night, and people who actually gave a shit about me. I think that's how eventually, over the next several years, he grew to be the first adult I actually respected.

It wasn't easy. I've lost count of the number of times he dragged me back to the group home from the streets after curfew. I had finally found someone as stubborn as I was.

On one of those nights, after a back-alley fight that left me with a scar on my ribs, he took me back to his small garage. I was in pain, and the last place I wanted to be was around anyone. But when he opened that door, I was awestruck. I stood there gaping at the monster of a bike in the middle of the dimly lit garage, and at the rows of tools all neatly aligned on the beaten-down tables that bordered the space.

"Grab a torque wrench," was all he said. When I passed him the wrong tool, he didn't laugh at me or give me a slap across the face—both things I was used to receiving from adults. He just nodded his head to the table, and said, "The other one there."

We worked well into the night on that bike, losing track of time. One night. That's all it took and I was hooked. Finally, I was productive and doing something other than worrying about where my next meal was coming from or wondering if I was going to get stabbed for sleeping somewhere I shouldn't.

Over the next year we fell into a routine of sorts. A few times a week we'd end up at his garage, and we'd work until night fell. He'd order pizza, or we'd sit in the garage with bowls of his famous homemade stew. When my mother was alive, meals were an afterthought. I'd be lucky to dip some stale crackers into a half-empty jar of peanut butter for dinner.

I started looking forward to the days he worked at the group home. Then one day a few months before my eighteenth birthday, everything changed. We had finished up working on another bike, and he asked me to come inside so he could show me something.

I only went into his house to take a piss in the small bathroom. I never ventured any farther. Didn't think I was welcome to, so his suggestion we go inside was something new, and it made me nervous.

"Relax, Matt. There's nothing to be scared of."

"I'm not scared of anything." It was a lie, and Tom of all people knew it.

But he just strode to the door that led to his house. "Mhmm."

Hands clenched into fists, I followed him down a short, carpeted hallway and into a basic kitchen. The place was old but clean, and I could smell the stew of his cooking away in the Crock-Pot on the counter. My stomach growled. He nodded to the round table and a single beige envelope that sat in the middle.

"Have a seat."

"I'm good here." Living in fear most of your life did things to you. Protective mode was instinct. But this was Tom and, up to this point, he'd done nothing but save my sorry ass more times than I could count.

"You're going to be eighteen soon," he said.

"An adult," I added. Although where I would end up once I reached that particular milestone was a mystery. Too old for a group home, no foster family in sight, my gut told me I'd be back on the streets within a month of my birthday.

He let out a low laugh. "Jury's still out on that one." He passed me the envelope. "I've been doing some research," he started, his typical hard exterior softening.

"Research?"

"Into adoption." The world, my heart, everything just stopped. My knees buckled, and I had to grab hold of one of the chairs to keep from falling down. The big intimidating man just stood staring at me. This man I had come to respect, who had bailed me out of a hundred different situations, wanted to do something I never even dreamed was possible. Nothing could've prepared me for this. I didn't know how to process the wildly conflicting emotions raging through me. No one had ever done anything like this for me. I didn't think I deserved it. Didn't understand why anyone would want to adopt a fuckup like me.

"If you'd be interested . . ." Tom stumbled over his words. Something he never did. "I'd like to start on the paperwork to adopt you officially."

Finally, I found my voice. "But why would you . . . I mean, I'm just another fucking homeless kid."

"You're wrong. You're much more than that, and Matty, you've got to know by now that I already think of you as my son." He eased the envelope toward me, and I looked at it like it might burst into flames.

"What would this mean?" My voice was small, quiet. His wasn't.

"It would mean you'd always have a place to call home. A roof over your head, food to eat, your own room."

My eyes snapped up from the envelope and met his. "My own room?"

"Ah. Got your attention now, hmm?" He grinned at me before moving back to the hall. "I'll show you."

It seemed to take a year to get down that narrow hallway. My heart hammering, he pushed open a door to the right, and stepped into the room. I lingered on the threshold, terrified, blown away, and caught somewhere between suspicion and relief.

He looked nervous as he rubbed his big hand against the back of his neck and flicked on a light. "It's not much, but it's yours."

The smell of fresh paint hit me hard and fast, and I tentatively craned my neck into the room. It was small, but there was an open window that faced a line of trees that ran the side of Tom's yard, letting light into the room. The walls had been painted dark blue, a big Harley-Davidson sign hanging on one wall, a tiny wooden desk with a black lamp in the corner.

My eyes fell to the single bed with the blue-checked comforter, and I swallowed back the lump in my throat.

"I know you like bikes." He moved to the corner where a guitar rested against the wall. "And what kid doesn't like music?"

"You mean adult," I managed, afraid to take that step into the room. I knew this was big. Maybe the biggest moment of my life to date. Somehow, as soon as I stepped foot into that room, everything I knew, and everything I had been told about what a disappointment I was would change.

He grinned, lifted the guitar up, and placed it gently on the bed. "Not quite an adult, but you're getting there."

Setting his hand on my shoulder, he waited, but I had nothing. "Got the guitar from a buddy of mine who used to be in a band back in the day. Said he'd show you how to play if you want."

I just stared at him in shock, and like he always did, like he always still does, he said the things I needed to hear. The message simple, always from the heart. "This is up to you, Matt. No matter what you decide, it's not going to change how I feel about you. Now, there'll be rules." I narrowed my eyes, but he pressed on. "Curfew, keeping your room clean, helping around here, and staying away from people who make bad decisions. But you'll always have a home, and I'll always want what's best for you."

I could feel something brewing behind my eyes, and I bit the inside of my cheek to keep it from happening, deciding to focus on the guitar on the bed. It was sleek and black, and it was something to ground me, to keep me focused so I didn't lose my shit.

Tom patted my shoulder and squeezed past me. "I'll be in the garage."

I waited and listened to every single creak of the house as Tom moved through it. The whole time I lingered in the doorway, staring at that guitar, studying it, learning every curve and edge it had. It held me, it captivated me, and it calmed me at a time when my entire world had just been turned upside down.

It was a promise, a potential opportunity in an otherwise fucked-up existence. I didn't know it then, but outside of Tom—and eventually, many years later, the band—that guitar would become the only thing I could count on in my life.

"You've upgraded the garage," Tom notes, drawing me out of my memories. He moves to the chrome tool cabinet and inspects it as only he can.

"Thought it was time."

"Thanks for the delivery last week, by the way. Nothing like restoring a vintage Harley to pass the time away."

I try to suppress a grin, but it's hard. I haven't found anything as satisfying as giving back to Tom. It's the least I can do after everything he's done for me. "I thought you might like that one. It had your name on it."

"Can't wait to ride it."

"I'll be right there with you."

He glances my way with a familiar slow smile. "I know. And I'm sorry for disappearing after the charity concert. I didn't get a chance to talk to you. There was an incident at the center. New kid taking a beating from the old-timers. You know how it goes."

I know all too well how it goes. I've been on both sides of that particular nightmare. "You don't have to explain it to me. I'm glad you were able to make it to the show."

He slowly circles the bike. "I don't even know how to describe it. It was amazing to watch you up there."

"As long as you enjoyed it."

"I did. The group home also enjoyed another anonymous donation a couple of weeks back." He gives me a knowing look. "You wouldn't happen to know anything about that, now, would you?"

"I haven't got a clue what you're talking about."

"Matty . . ."

"I could use some help on the intake manifold." I focus on my latest bike rather than him. "It's been giving me trouble. Make yourself useful, old man."

His big, warm hand rests on my shoulder. "You don't have to give us such big donations all the time, you know. You don't owe us anything."

I meet his steady gaze. "You taught me to give back. That's what I'm doing. And I owe you everything. Case closed."

With a nod of agreement, we get to work.

♪ ♩ ♪ ♩

"EARTH TO GRASSHOPPER!" I FEEL one of Sean's drumsticks hitting my back.

"That fucking hurt." I bend over to pick the stick off the floor, firing it back at him. He ducks as it sails over his head.

"Where'd you go there?" Kennedy stares at me like I have three heads.

We've been rehearsing in Kennedy's studio at his place in Bodega Bay on and off for the last few days, getting ready for the Australian leg of the tour.

Unfortunately, I've zoned out. I'm distracted, my mind taking me back to the night I spent with Tess—the parts I can remember anyway. Slowly it's becoming clearer, like the pieces of an erotic puzzle that shouldn't fit together but somehow do.

Still nothing from her on my FedEx delivery a few days ago. I should know better than to expect anything from anyone, but I would've thought it at least warranted a reaction of some kind.

Maybe she has no sense of humor. Maybe she just had her fun and wants nothing more to do with me. Fuck knows it wouldn't be the first time.

"Sorry, man. I think I need coffee."

Cameron adjusts his guitar around his shoulder. "You mean another pot to go with the four you've already had. Rough night of it last night?"

"Something like that," I mumble. Setting my guitar on a nearby stand, I head to the drink table. Wildly changed from even six months ago, instead of alcohol the table is lined with energy drinks, a smoothie machine, and organic snacks brought in by our head of security, Tucker Pearson.

We've all grown over the last few months. Losing Brodie Dixon, our tour manager, and almost losing Kennedy was a blow to us all. Seeing Cameron go through another round of rehab, and then spending time with Parker, has made us all take a step back and look at what we're doing with our lives. A reset of priorities, if you will.

"You said you didn't fuck her." Sean rounds his drum kit and gets in my face.

I push the annoying Brit out of the way. "Not now," I practically growl at him.

"Fuck who?" Cam asks, his smirk firmly in place.

"No one."

"Tess. He fucked her." Sean always knows how to silence a room.

"Jesus." Kennedy lets out a sigh of frustration before leveling me a stern glance. "If you screw this up, so help me . . ."

"Enough. All of you." I slam the energy drink down on the table a little harder than I should. "I'm a grown man, not a child."

"Tess? Really, Matt? There were thousands of women there that night and you had to pick Tess?" Kennedy asks, his face disapproving.

"You know what? I'm out of here." I take the stairs two at time, needing some air.

Sadly, alone time is a rare thing with this group. It doesn't take long for Cameron to find me. "You're a lot faster than you look." Cameron's voice drifts to me, and from my prime location on an otherwise empty stretch of beach, I scowl at him.

He sinks down to the sand beside me as I take a much-needed drag from the cigarette. I know it's a bad habit. I'll try to break it, eventually.

"You draw the short straw?" I ask, unimpressed by his sudden appearance. I knew it was coming. This is what we do. One of us is always pulling another back into the fold, keeping the peace. We've been through a lot together over the years, and that kind of comradery, well, it's nothing short of a brotherhood.

It took a long time for me to trust the guys, but after this long together, I know now that any one of them would take a bullet for me, and I'd do the same in a heartbeat. Coming from the place I did, that in and of itself is a bit of a miracle.

Cam steals the cigarette from my fingers, inhaling slowly with a nod. "Must have either been one hell of a night or she's one hell of a woman."

"Bit of both, I think."

"Hmm." We both look out to the surf pounding against the shore. "Thought so. You typically love 'em and leave 'em. She's different, then?"

"I don't know. I wish I could remember more of it." I shake my head. "Maybe that's why I can't stop thinking about it, because it's a bit of a blur."

"The mystery of it all?"

"Something like that," I admit, pushing up from the sand.

Cam joins me, tossing the cigarette down, and crushing it under his boot. "Well, maybe you should do something about it. I mean if she's got you thinking about her, why the hell not see where it goes?"

"I haven't exactly had a whole lot of luck in this area," I start as we head back down the beach.

"Yeah, but you haven't exactly tried now, have you?"

"LET ME SEE IT!" THERE'S no escaping the excitement in Sean's voice as Cameron and I step back into Kennedy's living room.

"You're like a child," Kennedy complains, trying to push Sean away from the counter.

"I don't want either one of you touching it. It could be any-thing. Lord knows some of your fans are mental." Tucker's voice of reason booms above them both. "And it's not for either one of you."

"What the hell is going on now?" Cam asks as we amble our way to the kitchen.

Kennedy glances over at me. "We good?" I give him a nod in reply, stepping up to the counter.

"Grasshopper! It's for you," Sean announces as he tries unsuc-cessfully to steal the large courier box away from Tucker.

"You order something?" Tucker asks, creating a physical barrier between us and the box on the counter.

I shake my head, narrowing my eyes. "No. Nothing."

"Fuck," Tucker mumbles, starting in on his inspection of the mystery package. "Just stay back a bit. It looks harmless, but you never know."

"Open it!" Sean bounces with excitement. He clearly needs a hobby.

"Did you not get enough presents as a child?" Kennedy nudges Sean in the shoulder.

"Return address is from What's Your Dream." Tucker glances over at me. "Did you ask them to send you anything?"

"No, but—" Sean's triumphant cheer interrupts me as he manages to swipe the box away from Tucker and tears it open.

"Ha!" Sean tosses a handful of packing material to the floor, lifting out a sheet of paper and cracking up as he reads it to himself.

"Oh, this is brilliant!" he shouts when his laughter subsides. Tucker snags the box back from him. "Gather 'round now, gents, and listen up." A feeling of unease washes over me. I didn't ask for the foundation to send me anything. There's only one person this can be from.

"Dearest Asshole," Sean begins, unable to hide his smirk. He pauses before continuing, "Understanding that your time here is short, and you might not get a chance to restock, I thought I'd help you out. The enclosed should aid you in your continuing quest to fuck your way across the planet. Enjoy."

Tucker's laugh fills the room as he tugs out a smaller box from the package, holding it up for us to see. A fucking case of condoms. Kennedy and Cam burst out laughing when Tucker opens the box, lifting out a strip of them, and dangling it in front of me.

Sean grabs the strip from Tucker and turns it over, unable to stop laughing. "Is there something you want to tell us, Matty?" He gives a mock shake of his head. "You need extra-small condoms? Really?"

I'm never going to live this down. Ever. There's a lifetime of condom-related gag gifts in my future. Cameron plucks out another box of the damn things and waves it at me. "At least you know she's thinking of you, even if it is in some extra-small way."

I'm barely able to hold back my growl as I collect the keys to my bike from the counter. I waste no time striding to the door. Clearly, Miss Baker and I need to have a serious discussion. "Aw, come on now, Grasshopper," Sean starts. "Don't go off half-cocked."

The door slamming behind me is the only thing drowning out their laughter.

tessa

A LIGHT KNOCK AT MY new office door surprises me; turning

around, I smile to see April leaning against the doorframe. "Hey there, new executive type," she teases with a grin. "Getting settled in?"

"Yep. It's nice to have a window of my own." Sitting back from the box I was unloading on my desk, I sigh with satisfaction and look out toward the stately old building next door. I still haven't come down from the high after getting my promotion.

"It is indeed." She walks over and sits in one of my chairs. "I thought I'd stop by before I left for the night. Ready for tomorrow?" Abby doesn't know it yet, but she's not accompanying us to San Diego tomorrow to work on another dream. Instead, her boyfriend, Kennedy Lane, is whisking her off on a surprise trip before he and the rest of his band resume their world tour. I frown for a second as I think about a certain arrogant bassist. He'll be leaving then, too. I'm not sure how I feel about that.

Reaching over, I tap a file on my new desk. "Yep. I'm all up to speed on both dreams, in case we have a chance to meet with the Chargers, too."

"I expected nothing less," she replies, giving me another grin before turning serious. "You can do this, Tess. It's natural to be nervous, but we all have confidence in you."

"Thanks," I say with a hint of relief. "Knowing you and Abby have my back means more than I can say." As much as I've loved being Abby's assistant, I know I'm ready for more. I'll have to work hard to develop the kind of contacts that Nadia had, but having Ralph, Abby, and April's support is a godsend.

"Of course we do!" She stands briskly and gives me a bright smile. "We're a team, after all." Just before she walks back out, she pauses and looks out at the darkening sky. "Hey, don't stay too late, okay? I'll bring the lattes in the morning. I can't wait to see Abby's face when she realizes what he's up to—it must be nice to date a rock star!"

Her good-natured laughter echoes down the hall behind her as my answering smile fades a little. April is only teasing—she's as happy for Abby as I am. Abby and Kennedy are made for each other. Her comment draws my thoughts again to the exasperating Matt Logan.

My memory of that night is now mostly restored. Suppressing a shiver, I absently toy with the scarf at my neck. The marks he left on me have finally faded enough that I've graduated to scarves instead of turtlenecks. I don't think he did it intentionally, but I'm still pissed.

Smirking to myself, I try to imagine his expression when he opens up my little delivery. That should knock that massive ego down a peg or two. Not that he'd ever actually be able to use any-thing that small, except maybe as a water balloon. I groan reflexively when I remember how I felt the morning after. The guy must be packing a howitzer in his pants based on how difficult it was for me to walk the next day. Do they make howitzer-sized condoms?

Snorting in amusement, I turn back to my box, pull out the photos of my parents and family, and place them on my desk. Mom was so proud of me when I called them with my news last night. I think they probably heard her squeal in the next state.

It wasn't easy raising a large family, but they managed. A for-mer chief petty officer in the Navy, my dad, Ron, now works as a security guard at Oakland Coliseum. He'd found a way to buff his hard edges when he'd met my mom, Julie. Mom is one of those premier seamstresses who specialize in duplicating the latest red carpet fashions for half the cost. I smile at the photo—it's one of my favorites. Dad, tall, barrel-chested, and squeezed into a tux, while Mom looked incredible in one of her own creations based off a vintage Dior. They beamed at the camera, surrounded by my siblings and me. It had been their silver wedding anniversary and they were so happy. I swallow heavily, knowing that just a month later they had received news of my sister Paula's diagnosis.

It had been hard to find anything to smile about for months afterward.

Turning back to my work, I bend over to open another box and freeze when I hear a low whistle. "My, my, my . . . it's almost like you were expecting me."

Whipping around, I straighten and grasp my chair for support. "What the hell are you doing here?" I gape at the sight of Matt Logan stalking into my office and closing the door.

"Now, is that nice? I think I much prefer the sight of your sweet ass sticking up in the air . . . kind of like a welcome-home banner."

I scowl at his handsome, smirking face. "Are you going to answer my question?"

He ignores me. Instead, I find myself scrambling backward as he takes two quick steps toward me. "Nice office," he comments, his voice a rough purr. "I heard that congratulations are in order."

"Thank you." I stand up straighter, refusing to be pushed around in my own damn office. "Message delivered. You may leave now."

Instead, he chuckles lowly and peruses my new space. He stares at my Stanford coffee mug, and then his gaze settles on my family photos for a second, his brow furrowing in . . . concern? Or maybe in disapproval? "Big family. You look like you'd fit in just fine with Cameron's ilk."

"What?" All I know about Cameron is that he just got out of rehab. And if that's what he meant . . ."The best thing about this office is that it has a door. Use it."

"But I just got here." He sits on the corner of my desk and runs his finger along the edge of the light-colored wood. "Look, I didn't come here to be pissy."

I cross my arms. "Why did you come here?"

"I just wanted to . . ." He frowns in frustration. "Um, what do you remember about that night? After the concert?"

My cheeks heat at the memory of his strong hands gripping my hips as I rode him that night. "It was fuzzy at first." I take a deep breath and face him. "I remember almost everything now."

He huffs and rubs the back of his neck. "I wish I did," he mumbles, frowning at his knees. I'm not sure whether to be disappointed or relieved. But before I can process that, he looks up at me, his eyes glinting with something fierce and predatory. "But what I *do* remember was good. *Very* good."

"Oh." I repress a shiver. "Yes, it was. Very good." I close my eyes and take a calming breath. Having him so close to me again is confusing. I remember the feel of his hot breath against my neck as he surged within me. I also remember the outrage in his eyes when I argued with him about Landon Ravine's band during the concert.

Both memories feel good.

He stands abruptly, startling me. "What if I said I wanted more?"

I blink. "More what?" He can't be saying what I think he's saying, can he? It was one night. From what I know of his reputation, he isn't one for repeats.

And neither am I.

He steps closer and runs a hand down my arm. "More very good." He slips his hand in mine, and my heart begins to pound. It was supposed to be easy. It was just a one-night stand after a night of drinking too much—that's it. Why is he doing this?

The words fly out of my mouth before I can stop them.

"Did you get my delivery?" I'm rewarded by the sudden flush on his face.

He chuckles, but there's no humor in the sound. "Oh yes, I think it's safe to say I got it," he retorts. "Do you have any fucking idea of the crap I'm going to get for *years* to come from that gift?" he complains, his eyes glittering with ire. "I'm never going to live it down."

I yank my hand free and wave it in agitation. "Let me guess. The same type of crap someone might get if she happened to open a package of *underwear* in the middle of a professional office, where *anyone* from the mail boy to the president of the board could walk by and see? Something like that, perhaps?"

He freezes, confusion crossing his face. "I just thought . . . This is the only address I have for you! How was I supposed to know you'd open it here?"

"Why wouldn't I open it here? How was I supposed to know you were going to flaunt my stupidity in my face?" I mentally curse the tremor in my voice. "Wasn't it enough that you won?"

He looks at me with a mix of concern and frustration. "You think that night was about winning?"

"Wasn't it?"

We stare searchingly, warily, at each other for a beat, and I hold my breath as he cups my cheek. "No, it wasn't. Not for me. And I hope not for you." Then his lips cover mine.

It's like my heart stops. His other hand comes up to rest lightly on my neck as he hums against my lips. The luscious scent of warm leather combined with a hint of machine oil swirls around me, reminding me of all things dangerous and fast. It's a complete contrast to this kiss; he takes his time, sweetly reacquainting himself with my lips. Heat rushes through me and I can't help myself—my hands fly to his head to pull him closer, and I lament the loss of most of his hair. Fucking Mohawk!

Too soon, the pressure lessens, and he pulls away. My breath catches as I stare into those beautiful blue eyes. His lips quirk in satisfaction; my scarf has slipped and my skin tingles under his rough fingertips. "You couldn't have been too upset about my gift," he notes, brushing the edge of my new pale-blue lace bra, courtesy of his care package. "Are you wearing the matching panties, too?"

I smash my lips together in a thin line. Smug bastard.

He chuckles, his eyes twinkling with mirth. "Go out with me. Please?"

"Why?" I step away from him, needing space to clear my head.

"Because I want to get to know you better," he says simply. "Tomorrow night. Let me take you to dinner."

I swallow down my conflicting emotions. "I can't tomorrow. I have to fly to San Diego overnight."

"That only leaves a couple days after that before I have to finish the tour." He frowns and then nods to himself. "That's fucking it. Come on then; get your purse or whatever," he says with determination and grabs my hand.

"What?" I ask in surprise. "Why?"

"Because we're not wasting one more fucking minute."

chapter three

matt

I'D LIKE TO HAVE A picture of her deep brown eyes widening in surprise as I shut her office door. Something tells me Tess Baker isn't surprised too often. I like that I'm the one to do that, but the thought is also a bit unsettling.

I try to think about the last time I had any real interest in getting to know a woman outside of the few hours or minutes we have together as the case may be. Tess is definitely not shallow, no glimpses of the vapid string of women who exist simply to sleep their way through every band in existence.

This thing with Tess is a dangerous mix of want and annoyance. I don't know what the hell is wrong with me. Women being as ready and willing as they seem to be for any rock star with a pulse isn't something I've ever complained about. I've enjoyed myself, and so have they. It's convenient and keeps me distracted from my past that wants to creep up and swallow me whole some days.

But the pull between us is off the charts. I can't remember the last time I felt this way . . . *if* I've felt this way. Tess's gaze follows the path of my tongue darting out to wet my lips, and I'm desperate to taste her again. One kiss and all I want is more.

Her hand tightens around mine, giving me a glimmer of hope that's quickly dashed as she tugs me back, stopping my forward motion. "I can't just leave because you want to talk. Whatever that means in your world." Her words drip with indignation, but I can't resist, pressing my torso against her devastating curves. An involuntary groan vibrates from deep in my chest as my hands frame her face, and her lips meet mine.

"Fuck, what is that?" I mumble against her lips.

"Wha—"

I let my tongue piercing roll across her tempting bottom lip once more. "Your lips taste like—"

"Cherry almond," she says through a breathless whisper.

I'm consumed with this insane desire to devour her whole. Fucking hell.

"Cherry fucking almond." It's a growl under my breath, and my hand slips through the thickness of her hair, tightening against her scalp.

"I have a bunch of different flavors," she adds absentmindedly.

"There're more of them?"

"There's a bourbon one and—" My lips crash back to hers, and she meets every wet desperate kiss with one of her own. She turns her head, exposing the sweet curve of her neck to me, and I rake my teeth against her smooth skin, tasting, wanting more.

"Do you remember this, hmm?" I rasp under her ear, feeling her hands glide up my arms against the worn leather of my jacket.

"God," she whimpers so quietly I can barely hear. "Yes. I

remember that. Your piercing." I can't help but smile against her lips. "You didn't taste like an ashtray, though."

Brushing the pad of my thumb over her cheek, her panted little breaths fan my face. "It's a bad habit I'm trying to break." My voice is rough, thick with want, the blood surging hot and dangerous through me.

"Is that what I'm going to be? A bad habit you try to break?" I frown at her, taking a step back at her brutal honesty. She always seems to know exactly what to say to put me in my place.

"I hope not." It's as candid as I can be. The fact is, I haven't got a clue what I want, except more time with her. That's a bit of a revelation right there.

"Despite what happened the other night, I'm not interested in being another one of your convenient fucks. I don't want to be someone you'll forget as soon as you're done with me." She might as well just slap me in the face. Unfortunately, I know there's a lot of truth to what she's saying. I don't exactly have a stellar reputation.

Women are never around long enough to stick, and neither am I. I've preferred it that way, and despite what Kennedy thinks about me always trying to find the love of my life, it's more like the love of tonight.

This whole thing with Tess, though? It feels different. It's been a long time since I've even thought twice about a woman once she left my bed, let alone had her playing on repeat in my head for days.

I meet her darkened eyes that seem to see right through me and hit her with the truth. "You, Tess Baker, could never be forgettable." Her breathing stops and I love her reaction to me; my gaze draws to the fading reddened marks that scatter her neck.

Slowly, I trace my fingers along her smooth skin. I love her curves—they drive me insane—and her long naturally black thick hair is gorgeous. It sets her apart from a lot of the bone-thin, shallow models that tend to follow us around. Her mouth drops open as I sweep my index finger along one of the lingering bites just beneath her collarbone. "I like seeing these on you."

She seems to fight back a shiver, bracing both her hands on the edge of the desk behind her, like she doesn't quite trust herself. "You're an animal."

I fiddle with both ends of the silk scarf draped around her neck, lowering it around her waist and tugging her forward. The feel of her breasts pressing against me does more than test my patience. She's the picture of a seductive dream in her office-appropriate outfit. It makes me want to bend her over the desk and fuck her until she forgets her name. Judging from her palm that's traveled up to curl into a fist against my jacket, I'd say I'm not alone on that. "You have no idea." Leaning forward, I brush my lips under her ear, breathing her in. "It's almost five—you couldn't have much more work today. Come with me."

A sharp knock at the door, and the spell is broken. "Tess?" An annoying male voice filters into the room, causing my guard to snap back into place. "I've got a delivery, and I wanted to check if we're still on for coffee, you know? Our date?"

I bite back the bitter sting of disappointment and lean away from her. Still fisting my leather jacket, Tess's gaze darts to the closed door, and I see it right there as plain as day.

Guilt.

Caught in the act before we even get started. So fucking typical. "Seems like someone's been busy." My voice is hard, bristling with anger.

"It's not like—"

"Tess?" The door swings open and her hand drops from my jacket like she's just received an electric shock. "Oh, sorry, I didn't know you were busy."

"She's not." My jaw clenches with pent-up rage, and I lock eyes on hers. "I was just leaving. Enjoy your date." It's hard not to size up the delivery guy as I move past him. Eager, excitable, maybe a bit intimidated sums him up. And short—well beneath my six-three height. I've never been happier to inherit something from my mother in my life.

Jeff, according to the little silver name tag dutifully placed on the pocket of his shirt, looks as if he might pass out. His eyes are the size of saucers as he gives me a panicked once-over, lingering on my neck tattoo like so many others do.

Looking down on him is easy, and it's wildly tempting to use my size against him, but I'd just be giving her what she wants—yet another excuse not to see me. She's probably got a pros-and-cons list going already. I don't need to do anything to add to the flaws I already know are there.

"Matt." My name is an exasperated sound falling from Tess's lips. Without another word, I storm down the hallway, ignoring the hushed whispers aimed at me. I've gotten used to that over the years, although it's never been because of a woman. Cameron was right. I do love 'em and leave 'em. The sudden appearance of a date Tess conveniently failed to mention is a harsh reminder of why.

Stabbing at the elevator button, I can feel the tension rise and the walls closing in. I don't know what the hell I was thinking coming here, or why I give a shit about who she's dating. I'm not sure if I'm more disappointed in her or myself.

The elevator doors finally open, and I step inside, pushing the lobby button, glaring straight ahead at the light spilling out of her office. I can hear a flurry of activity from down the hall, and then she's there, darting out of her office, hurrying in my direction.

She blows my mind. Just the sight of her makes my heart do things it's not used to, and it almost makes me stop the doors from shutting. Almost.

"Wait!" she calls out, picking up the pace, although it's difficult given those boots she's wearing.

My eyes lock to hers and my heart drops seeing regret staring back at me. But because I'm an ass, I don't bother to stop the doors as they close.

Straddling my motorcycle outside of the office building, I look up to the sky in frustration. Of course, it picks now not to start. Damn thing. I thought Tom and I fixed it the other night.

A mess of black hair from inside the revolving door catches my eye, and I try to start the bike once more. "Fucking hell," I mutter under my breath, watching as Tess wildly scans the street in both directions before zeroing in on her target.

Down the steps she marches. If she could breathe fire, I swear she would. The wind picks up, swirling her hair about her shoulders, some strands getting in her face before she stops at the curb beside the bike.

"What the hell was that?" she rants, both hands balled into fists at her gloriously rounded hips.

"That was me leaving you to your date."

"What are you, sixteen?" Her arms flail as she unloads on me. "We're not in high school, idiot. You don't just go stomping off like some Neanderthal. It wasn't a date, and had you stayed five seconds to hear me out, you would've known that," she snaps.

"You sure he knows that? Because I'm pretty sure Jeffrey-boy there used the word date."

She throws her hands up. "You are the most frustrating person on the planet!"

"Right back at you, sweetheart." We're drawing a bit of a crowd. People are gawking in that way they do when something upsets their otherwise mundane day. I try the bike once more, a wave of relief rolling through me when the engine turns over. At least I can count on something.

She narrows her eyes at me before reaching for the key to the bike and, in a bold move, turns it swiftly, tugging it from the ignition. I'm not sure if I should be amused or irritated. "Did you just steal my key?" There's a dangerous tone to my voice, but she completely ignores it.

Instead, she waves the key at me before taking a step away from the bike. "What is this, anyway?" She motions to the motorcycle, scanning it with interest.

"It's a Victory custom," I grind out.

"I've never seen anything like it," she murmurs almost in awe.

"I built it. That's why."

Her delicious mouth drops open, and she stares at me in disbelief. "You built this?"

"Guilty as charged." I lean back in the custom leather seat, folding my arms across my chest. Score one for me. "Surprised?"

She nods slowly, her gaze sweeping appreciatively over the black and chrome frame. I feel a strange twinge of pride wash over me. Tom and I worked for countless hours on this bike. It's one of a kind, like all the bikes we've built together over the years. "I had no idea."

"You'd be shocked what you don't know about me."

That seems to snap her back to her fine assertive self, and she levels me with an annoyed look. "Right back at you, *sweetheart*," she fires back at me.

The air is thick with a heady mix of tension, desire, and frustration as we stare at each other in a silent standoff. The world could fall apart around us, and I don't think either one of us would notice.

"He your boyfriend?" I ask finally, glad to be grounded to the seat of the bike. I don't trust myself right now.

Her expression softens, and she shakes her head. "God no. You think I would've spent the night with you if I had a boyfriend?"

"Wouldn't be the first time."

She rolls her eyes. "That's supposed to make me feel better? And maybe you should try raising your standards just a little." I lift a brow in response. "You know this is pretty hypocritical coming from you, Mr. Fuck-my-way-through-the-female-population. God! You're with a different woman every single time I turn around."

"When's the last time you saw some picture of me with a woman?" I challenge, knowing I'm treading on thin ice. There're pictures out there, loads of them. Probably entire sites dedicated to Redfall and our various hookups over the years. We've been more careful lately, with the concert for Parker in mind, but cell phones coupled with the dreaded paparazzi means pictures are bound to get out. And let's face it; none of us are in line for sainthood.

Still, she seems to consider my question for a minute before answering. "Before the concert for Parker, I guess."

"Mhmm. Exactly."

She lets out a hard laugh. "So, a couple of weeks and you're some reformed dark angel all of a sudden? Forgive me if I find that very hard to believe."

"And forgive me if I didn't realize you had a hot date tonight."

"You don't have any claim on me!" she yells, and I give her a slow nod.

"No. I sure don't. That's pretty clear."

That shuts her up. Her mouth mashes into a firm line, the tension evident in her body, like she's fighting some internal battle with herself. "If you'll just give me my key. I'll be out of your hair."

Holding her gaze, I extend my hand and wait. I feel the cool metal drop into my palm, and I can't resist closing my hand around her fingers, tugging her forward against the frame of the bike.

She takes a surprised breath in, her eyes widening as I lean towards her, my mouth hovering just shy of hers. "God, I want to—"

"So do I," she interrupts, her voice uneasy.

Needing some distance, I lean back against the seat, my heart pounding with an unfamiliar beat. "How about a ride first? Extra helmet's in the saddlebag."

She blinks, giving the bike a wary scan, and I can almost hear the internal war she's waging. "It's a pretty easy yes or no answer. You either want a ride or don't. Choice is yours, Tess. It always will be."

Tessa

MY HEART RACES AS I stare at him in astonishment. His chin lifts in challenge as he smirks at me, but there's a glint of resignation in his eyes. As if he's fully expecting me to go back inside and fail this test, which is exactly what this feels like—a test.

"I don't have my purse, or even my coat," I say, stalling. My eyes flicker over the bike once more. It's gorgeous, but not exactly made for demure riding. He purses his lips, considering, and then silently removes his leather jacket and offers it.

"You don't need your purse for where we're going."

I eye him warily. "And where is that, pray tell?"

"Climb on and find out."

Without any further thought, I take his offered coat and slip it on, pretending not to notice the surprise on his face. The worn leather hangs below my ass, and I have to shove the sleeves up so I can use my hands.

Popping the catch on the saddlebag, I pull out the black helmet and slam the lid again. I catch him stifling a smile as I toss my hair over my shoulder and step up, easily slinging my leg over the bike. Thank God, I wore tights with my ankle boots this morning. My skirt rides up to my upper thigh, and I gasp when I feel his hand on my knee.

"Put on your helmet and hang on, sweetheart," he purrs before tugging on his own black helmet. I hastily follow suit and wrap my arms around his waist. My breath catches in my throat at the feel of his hard torso through his simple black T-shirt. He reaches back and tugs at my knee, urging me closer, so I snug up tighter, fully pressing my chest to his back. He rumbles something that sounds like, "That's better," and then we're off.

IT'S BEEN YEARS SINCE I rode on a motorcycle, and I've forgotten how exhilarating it is to fly through the city with nothing between you and the surrounding traffic. The powerful vibrations surge through me, making it hard to think about anything besides hanging on. The frustration I felt before drains away, and I can't stop the laugh that bubbles up. For a few thrilling minutes, I can forget the confusing desire and irritation I feel for him and just let myself enjoy the moment. Between the warmth of his jacket and the heat emanating from his body, I feel like I'm in a sauna. It's pure heaven.

Twenty minutes later, we're nearing the wharf. He turns down an alley off Stockton and stops in front of a gated driveway. He punches a code into a tiny, beat-up keypad, and the gate slowly rolls up, making a god-awful noise as it goes.

"Jesus," I observe mildly, and I can hear his laughter.

"Beats having an alarm system," he grunts. We pull into a

garage that's much larger than I expected to find, based on the small entrance. It's also a biker's idea of heaven.

We park next to three other bikes: a Ducati, a classic Harley, and something else that's in pieces. He shuts the motor off and the sudden silence seems surreal. Doffing my helmet, I grip it in one hand and steady myself against his shoulder with my other as I climb off. He casually pulls his helmet off and runs a hand through the remains of his savaged hair, watching me as I survey the space.

It's neat as a pin, from the large selection of hand tools perfectly arrayed on the wall above a well-used workbench, to the tidy coil of extension cords next to the professional bike lift. Impressive. I turn and am surprised to see a gorgeous, old glossy-black Camaro off to the side, almost like a forgotten toy.

"Is that a '67?"

He gapes at me for a second before slamming his mouth shut. "Sixty-eight. How did you know that?"

"Oh, I've picked up a thing or two over the years." He frowns, and I hate to think what's running through that head of his now. "My dad had one when I was little," I explain, putting him out of his misery.

"Oh." Taking a deep breath, he looks relieved and holds his hand out to me; I automatically place mine in his much larger one. He slowly rubs his calloused thumb over my knuckles, the action somehow more intimate than the passionate kiss he gave me in my office. "Come on," he murmurs, and leads me toward a doorway at the back of the garage.

The heat that had been boiling over between us earlier has calmed to a simmer, and I can feel his nerves as he leads me up a long flight of stairs. When we reach the second landing, I pause, trying not to pant. These are killer stairs. "Where the hell are you taking me?"

"My place," he says shortly, tugging at my hand. "We're almost there."

"Jeez, it's like climbing the Filbert Street steps. Do you haul groceries up all these steps?" It's not something I would ever picture him doing.

"Nah. The stairs are just to the private garage. There's an elevator that leads down to a central lobby in the front for stuff like that." He finally stops at the top, opens a door, and gestures for me to walk ahead of him. "Here we are."

Feeling a bit like the fly to his spider, I step into a large open space that looks like a converted warehouse. The walls are a rough brick and the ceiling has exposed beams and air ducts. From where I stand, I can see pale leather sofas and several guitars on display. In another corner are a dining set and a sleek kitchen. In the remaining corner is a spiral staircase; it leads up to an open loft edged with low walls so I can't see what's up there, but I'm guessing it's his bedroom.

It looks comfortable, but rugged and eminently masculine . . . just like its owner.

"Nice place," I say, strolling along one wall. I can feel his eyes on me as I walk. It's unnerving.

He steps over and sets the helmet he'd been carrying on the dining table and turns to lean against a chair. "Thanks." He points toward a large steel sliding door suspended from two wheels on a long bar. "That's the main door that leads to the elevator."

"The women you bring here must love this." I gesture to the gas fireplace and try to appear unaffected. I could easily imagine him curled up on the couch with some faceless bimbo in front of the fire, doing all those things that keep haunting my dreams.

"I don't bring women here," he says, his voice clipped.

I look at him skeptically. "But you brought me here."

"I did." He frowns down at his feet and doesn't elaborate, so I continue my tour. It's a feeble attempt to stall whatever is coming next, but it's all I've got right now.

"If you live this close, why did you stay at the Fairmont after the concert?" A series of rough-hewn boards serve as shelves— they're perched on long spikes driven into one wall. I peer closely at one photo nestled among several shots of the band. It's a photo of a teenaged Matt standing proudly with a classic Harley and a tall, imposing older man with an impressive walrus moustache. The man is wearing a faded Led Zeppelin T-shirt, and his bulging biceps are covered with tattoos. The photos are the only homey touches in the otherwise spartan room.

"Sean and Cam were staying there," he replies with a shrug. "It's easier."

Two large, arched windows dominate the wall by the kitchen. They're filthy, but I can see across the rooftops next door to the bay. My fingers brush against the tuning pegs of a guitar in its stand. All of the instruments are gorgeous. It seems he prefers natural wood colors, although one of them is a deep, glossy blood red.

His voice comes from right behind me and I jump. Damn, he's quiet, despite wearing heavy boots. He stares into my eyes, and my stomach flutters with nerves. I don't know what I'm doing here. Why the hell did I get on his bike?

Stepping quickly, I put a sofa between us. It's hard to think when he's so close.

"Matt, why am I here?" I search his eyes, trying to tamp down the hope bubbling up in me. This man attracts me like no one else I've ever met. He's infuriating, stubborn, and petulant, but he can also be kind, generous, and loyal. I saw that side of him when he and the band played at the hospital for Parker and the other sick kids on the cancer ward. Parker was the little boy whose dream had started all of this—the boy who had brought Redfall into all of our lives.

"I told you before." His soft voice contains a determined note that makes me look up. "I want to get to know you. Tess, that night . . ." He shakes his head and runs a hand nervously over his ragged hair. "I haven't been able to get you out of my mind, as clichéd as that may sound. And I want a chance to . . . Well, I want a chance. With you."

I blink in surprise, feeling my jaw go slack. Could it be true? To give myself time, I look down at the couch and adjust one of the pillows. "But you said you don't remember much from that night. What if the rest of me doesn't meet with your expectations?"

He steps swiftly around the sofa and gently takes my chin between his fingers. "Tessa Baker, I honestly don't think that's possible." His lips descend in a sweet kiss, and everything seems to disappear except him. My hands automatically slide up his firm chest, and one slips around his neck to hold him against me. His mouth moves gently against mine, until the tip of his tongue teases my lips to open.

That simmering passion between us boils over again, and my heart hammers in my chest. From my chin, his hand moves to the side of my face, while his other cups the back of my head, his fingers tangling in my hair. I cling to his shirt, holding him close as he kisses the breath out of me. When he finally pulls away, I can barely see straight.

"I just wanted to talk tonight." His nose skims my jawline, making me shiver. "I want to get to know you better. All of you. But I swear to Christ, Tess, when I kiss you . . . feel that sweet body of yours . . . talking is the last thing I want to do."

I run my hand over his hair and thread my fingers through his floppy center strip, tugging gently. "We can talk later," I breathe.

"Because I feel the same way."

He groans and presses his lips to mine, his hands moving to my shoulders. "You want to know what I remember about that night?" His voice is low with barely restrained passion. "This." He kisses me again, his fingers trailing down my shoulders, and completely catches me off guard when he rips open my blouse. Delicate buttons fly as his face descends to nuzzle my chest. "I remember these, too," he grunts, kneading and squeezing my breasts with his large hands. I gasp when he deftly scoops each breast out of the top of my bra and suckles me hard. "So fucking round, and firm, and *real*."

I can't help the mewling noises escaping me, and I clutch his shoulders for support. Desire burns hot like a wildfire, and I feel like I'm about to explode. It may be a mistake, but I can't deny it—I want him. Now.

His lips reclaim mine and he scrambles to push my skirt up as I struggle to unbutton his jeans. Suddenly he looks down and scowls. "How the fuck . . ."

He tugs at my tights, and I giggle at his befuddled expression. "They're tights," I taunt, unable to help myself. "Too much of a challenge for you?" His eyes narrow and he spins me to the right; in a flash, I'm bent over the dining table, and he pulls down my tights and panties in one swift move. I feel the cool air on my ass.

An open wallet hits the table next to my face, startling me, but a hand against my back holds me in place. His fingers slip between my legs. Holy mother of . . . In and out, stroking me, stoking the fire within until I can barely stand it. "I remember this, too." He's breathing hard and his voice is rough. "So smooth, and tight, and wet. You're fucking *perfect*."

Then his touch is gone, leaving me squirming; the silence is punctuated by the sound of panting, both his and mine, and a quiet rip and rustling behind me. Before I can stand up, he grips my hips and I feel a nudge.

A cry escapes me as he pushes inside. It's not painful, but holy fucking Christ! Now I know why I felt like I'd been split in two the morning after. Howitzer doesn't feel like an exaggeration.

His chest presses against my back, and I can feel his hot breath against my ear. "And I remember *this*." He thrusts again to emphasize his words. "Don't you?"

"Yes!" I wail, my hands scrambling against the smooth surface of the table as he begins moving in earnest. He feels so good . . . so, so good . . . and so much better than my memories. The strength conveyed by his thrusts and his hold on me sends thrills running down my spine. The table is cold and hard against my skin, a delicious contrast with the heat coursing through me. He's hitting every one of my spots, and my climax quickly builds, teeters tantalizingly on the edge, and then spills over spectacularly, tearing another cry from my throat. I see spots before my eyes, and I can't catch my breath. His movements become choppy, and I hear a chorus of guttural cursing above me before he slams in one more time and stills.

My breath is knocked out of me again when he collapses against my back. His hands find mine on the table, and he links our fingers as we lay there a moment, letting our racing hearts calm. "Holy fuck," he rasps, and then chuckles weakly. "You're going to kill me, woman."

"If you don't let me breathe, I'm the one who'll be in trouble," I wheeze. The closeness is nice, but I'm beginning to lose circulation in my legs.

"Oh, shit, I'm sorry," he blurts. He helps me to stand, but my legs give away, and we sink to the floor in a tangle of limbs and loose clothing. Our laughter trails off as he takes my face between his rough hands. He's smiling gently, but it's the vulnerability in his blue eyes that touches my heart.

"*That* is what I remember about that night," he whispers. "This—" He gently taps my forehead. "—is what I want to learn more about. If you're willing."

I nod, feeling like I'm stepping off a cliff, and his breath leaves him in a whoosh. "Yeah?" He looks as if he doesn't quite believe me.

"Only if we can get off this floor," I say solemnly, but with a smile playing around my lips. "And you have to let me borrow a shirt." My stomach growls. "Oh, and if you feed me."

He chuckles. "I'll see what I can do. I have a couple restaurants on speed dial," he says with a smirk that makes my heart skip a beat.

What am I getting myself into?

chapter four

matt

THE FIRST TIME I SAW Lexi Shaw I knew I was in trouble. I was nineteen, still trying to figure out who the hell I was, and failing miserably. On the days when I wasn't helping Tom in the garage, I was with his buddy, Fletcher Reid, who had supplied Tom with my first bass guitar.

Fletcher had spent his life immersed in rock and roll. He was a virtual encyclopedia of knowledge and experience, and he was a gifted musician. I didn't appreciate any of those things at the time and didn't realize Fletcher was teaching me things that would stick with me for my entire life.

The only thing I could appreciate about spending time in his tiny apartment was that he had a niece. A twenty-year-old hot-as-hell blond niece with long legs and tight little cutoff jean shorts that taunted me endlessly.

She was the best kind of temptation—visiting for the summer from Virginia, with plump, glossy lips that were a prominent feature in all my teenaged dreams, and absolutely, positively off-limits. Which meant, of course, I wanted her even more. Try telling a hotheaded kid like me he couldn't have something and watch what happened.

It was the best kind of summer fling, even if it left me with a broken heart. When Lexi went back to Virginia, I fell into the kind of funk that only happened when you lose that first love.

I haven't thought about Lexi in a long time, but now, as I stand in my closet and debate what shirt to give the delicious Tess to wear, an unfamiliar feeling churns in my gut. I think Tess Baker has the potential to do a whole lot more than break my heart.

♪ ♩ ♪ ♩

I STIFLE A GROAN AT the sight of Tess half-dressed and inspecting the picture frames on the shelf in the living room. Her now destroyed shirt flares open, revealing just enough of that smooth skin to drive me out of my mind. Now that I know how she tastes, I only want more.

As if she can sense my presence, she wraps her arms around her waist, turning in my direction. For a few torturous seconds, we stare at each other, the undeniable heat radiating between us, as she looks her fill of me, and I do the same.

My throat is dry, and my cock aches even though I've just had her. I hold up the two shirts with a shrug. "Vintage Harley or a dress shirt." Her brows lift in surprise. "Seems I'm fresh out of Landon Ravine and Vandal T-shirts."

I could get addicted to the playfulness in her eyes, and she doesn't disappoint. "Well, lucky for you, I have a bunch of them," she fires back at me.

"I do have to say this look . . ." I nod in her direction. " . . . I like a lot."

She tugs on either side of the shirt, trying to cover her ample breasts. "I loved this shirt," she announces with a hint of annoyance.

"I can get you another one."

"No." There's defiance in her voice I don't like.

I narrow my eyes. "Why not?"

"Because I don't want to owe you anything."

Another slap to the face. "Is that what you think?" Crossing the room, I hold both shirts out to her, her eyes widening as I lean forward, the thin thread I'm holding onto dangerously close to breaking. "I have no expectations. None. You don't owe me a damn thing."

Pressing the shirts toward her, I wait until she takes them before putting some much-needed distance between us. The kitchen is safer. Much safer. Hauling open the junk drawer, I rifle through the takeout menus, trying not to steal a glance at her as she tugs the T-shirt over her head.

"Is this your dad?" My hands still on a Mexican menu, and I slowly meet her gaze. My heart hammers in my chest, and I fight the voice in my head that has always told me not to get too close. The less they know, the better. It's been my mantra for as long as I can remember, and it's served me well. But Tess does things to me. Things that make me want to silence the nagging voices.

"Essentially. Yes."

Her lips tighten and she sets the picture frame gently back onto the shelf. "Essentially?"

The silence drifts between us as I struggle to find a way to explain something I don't share with many people, least of all with a woman. It's not as if I advertise this part of my life. It tends to bring up nasty memories I'd like to keep dead and buried.

Gripping the edge of the counter, I give her the truth. "He adopted me."

She can't hide the shock on her face, and she stumbles over her words. "I'm sorry, I didn't know."

"Don't be sorry," I interrupt her quickly. "Tom Logan is the only reason I'm standing here and not six feet under or worse."

Fiddling with the ends of her dark hair, she looks lost for words. "There are worse things than being dead?" she finally asks, her voice tentative.

I feel the tension in my jaw ratchet up a notch. She probably hasn't got a clue what it's like to live like I have, Stanford grad that she is. Judging from the pictures of her family in her office, I'd hazard to guess she's lived a pretty sheltered life. Not that I would wish my childhood on anyone, least of all Tess. "A lot of things are worse."

"What happened?" She shakes her head, heat blooming over her cheeks as she stares at the fascination of the area rug. "Never mind."

"I don't know who my biological father is, and I don't want to know," I blurt out. "The woman who gave birth to me killed herself when I was twelve." She glances back at me, her pretty mouth dropping open slightly. "I was in and out of a few foster families, and I lived on the streets in LA for a while. Then Tom found me."

She takes a few steps in the direction of the kitchen as I continue. "I was sixteen, living day to day, and involved in shit you don't want to know about. Gangs, fights, petty theft." I shake my head, cursing the memories that are always lurking. "If Tom hadn't brought me to the group home, hadn't taken a chance on me, I don't know where I'd be. Not here with you, that's for sure."

I can see the telltale signs of sympathy that I loathe, and I can't help closing the distance between us, taking her face between my hands. "Don't feel sorry for me. Not you. I didn't tell you so you'd look at me like I'm a charity case."

"Then why did you tell me?" She takes hold of both of my wrists. The intensity in her eyes just about does me in.

"Because I don't want secrets. They have a way of ruining everything."

Brushing the pad of my thumb over her cheek, she leans into my touch, closing her eyes. "No secrets seems like a good rule," she breathes, leaning against my torso, her hands tightening around my wrists like a lifeline.

Resting my forehead against hers, I let my eyes slide shut, feeling like the weight of the world lifted from my shoulders. "It's a good place to start."

An hour later, sinking back against the cushions of the sofa, I let out a satisfied groan. The weathered coffee table is strewn with the remains of the Mexican feast we've decimated. The conversation flowed easily and stayed far away from the minefield of my past. She's more interested in hearing me play and listening to me talk about the places the band has traveled, and I'm happy to indulge her. Even with the insanity that surrounds Redfall, it's a much safer conversation for me to have.

I didn't expect playing for Tess would hit me like it did. There's something powerful and intimate about picking up my guitar and playing only for her. Letting her see a side of me that isn't drowned out by screaming fans and harsh lights. It's just me and the bass—raw and focused solely on her.

"I think I ate my weight in nachos." Tess stretches her legs out beside me, a barrier of pillows strategically placed between us. Once the food arrived, she seemed to make a concentrated effort to put some distance between us. I don't like it, but I think that's part of the reason she did it. At least I know I'm not the only one affected. Her not-so-subtle display of licking salsa verde from her fingers is something that will stay with me for a long time.

"Almost as good as Mexico City."

"Jerk."

"And the shrimp *aguachile ceviche* at this hole-in the-wall café in Puerto Morelos . . . Man." It doesn't take long before a pillow hits my head. Leaning up, I hold her gaze, stuffing the pillow behind my head to get more comfortable.

"Now you're just bragging. Is there any place you haven't been, world traveler?"

"Lots of places, and enough about me. Let's talk about you, Cardinal. Where have you been?" Her eyes widen a bit, and I like that I can shock her just a little too much. "What? Surprised the guy who only has a GED knows anything about Stanford?"

"You know cardinal is the color not the—"

"Not the bird. I know." I shake my head, settling back against the pillows.

"You know, sometimes you look at me like I amuse you."

"Is that right?"

She twists her long hair back, the Harley T-shirt stretched across her plump tits, giving me a perfect view. "The little smirk of yours, don't think I don't see that."

"Never said a thing, did I?"

Leaning forward, I reach for one of the water bottles on the table, drawing in a shaky breath as her fingers graze unexpectedly over my heated skin. "What's this one for?" I know which tat she's tracing, a matrix of black double-sided arrows inked on the inside of my wrist.

I turn to face her, holding her curious gaze. "Why don't you tell me what you think it's for?"

"You don't really like to talk about yourself, do you?" She tilts her head.

"Right back at you. Don't think I didn't see the butterfly."

"You saw that?" Her voice gets softer and her eyes grow wide as she traces her fingers in an aching temptation over my skin.

"Hiding. Under all that gorgeous hair. Why go to the trouble to get a tat if you're not going to show it off?"

She swallows hard, as if she's trying to rein in some emotion that's lingering just under the surface. The last thing I want to do is make her uncomfortable, but I want to know more—her secrets, her fears—so I tell her about the tat.

Linking my fingers with hers, I trace over the lines of ink. "This one is a reminder that everything is connected. The past affects the present and the future." She breaks my gaze with a subtle nod, her eyes tracking over my arm. "Tell me about the butterfly."

Glancing at me once more, her eyes glass over, brimming with unshed tears. "It's for my sister."

"You lost her?" She doesn't need to answer. I recognize that look. Seen it too many times over the years. Haunting memories that fade but never really leave you in peace. The light brush of her fingers continues to fire across my skin, and she centers back on the chaos of ink on my arm.

Even though I know she's avoiding the question, I focus on the feel of her soft fingers against my skin, a hungry need growing with each stroke. "We don't have to talk about it." While she continues her exploration of my tattoos, I take in the curve of her neck, those lips I want to taste again, and the sway of her jet-black hair framing her face.

I wonder if she can hear my heart hammering, if she realizes how fucking beautiful she is. "You've got a butterfly too?" She's clearly amused at the bright tat that rests beneath a series of music notes on my bicep. "There's got to be a story there."

"That's just pure stupidity. Lost a bet with Cam." She looks at me like I'm crazy, and I shrug.

"And he actually made you get it?"

"Can't go back on a bet. And see? We have something in common."

That smile of hers grips my heart. "You guys are pretty close, aren't you?"

"Goes with the territory. You can't spend as much time as we do together and not be."

I can't resist reaching to cup her cheek and tracing the pad of my thumb along her jaw. Heat replaces the amused look in her eyes, saying what words can't. Her mouth drops open and her breathing becoming deeper. I want her mouth on me, tasting and teasing, exploring.

Her fingers dig into my arm. My cock presses against the zipper of my jeans, and it would be so easy just to take her again. "Matt . . ." It's a needy little whimper, and I swallow back a groan, leaning away from temptation. As strong as this pull is between us, I don't want it to be all there is.

Letting out a slow breath, I let my hand drop from the curve of her cheek. "We should get you back."

"HEY," HE WHISPERS AS I push up from the couch. Strong arms wrap around my waist and gently pull me back against his chest. "It has been a long day for both of us. It would be too easy to just carry you upstairs and not let you out of bed for a week. But I don't want to do things that way with you. I don't want to screw this up—whatever *this* is."

Closing my eyes, I let myself relax into his embrace. "I don't want to screw this up either." I take a deep breath to center myself. "I just feel like I'm flying blind here. I don't understand why this is so hard," I admit, surprising myself. I feel off-kilter. One touch from him and I'm on fire. If I don't find some balance, I could lose myself.

He chuckles. "Baby, I haven't understood anything since I woke up after the concert. Maybe even before that." He turns me around gently in his arms until I'm facing him. "But I want to figure it out."

The vulnerability in his eyes makes my heart twinge, and I gently press my lips to his. "Me, too." Another soft kiss later, and this time I'm the one pulling away when I feel his fingers begin to grip my hips more firmly. It restores my confidence. Maybe I'm not the only one who is feeling a little out of control. "Can you call me a cab?"

"Are you kidding?" he scoffs, stepping away with a wry smirk. "You think I'm just going to shove you in a cab and send you on your way?" He steps over to where some coats are hanging on pegs that jut out from the brick wall and selects a worn jean jacket.

"Here. It's going to be colder out there now." He offers me the jacket, and I slip it on; the flannel lining is soft and smells nicely of him, some spicy woodsy scent. I wait until he turns around and take a deep whiff of the collar. Mmmm . . .

"Ready?" He's wearing his leather jacket and looking at me with a confused smile. Shit, I hope I didn't moan out loud.

"Yep. Let's go."

We descend the killer stairs, and he stops me from getting on his bike again. "No, we'll take this." He gestures toward the glossy black Camaro. Once ensconced in the soft black leather seats, my grin widens at the sound of the engine.

"You said your dad had one of these?" He glances over at me while we wait for the creaky gate to open.

"Yeah. It was his pride and joy. He used to take my sister Rachel and me out for ice cream when he was home," I say with a fond smile. "We used to pretend we were famous movie stars or something in a hot car and would wave to people as we drove by."

"That's a nice memory." He turns onto Powell, heading in the direction of my office, when his grin suddenly turns into a frown. "Wait, what do you mean, 'when he was home'? He didn't skip out on you, did he?"

"Oh, God, no!" I realize that with what Matt has said about his background, he probably assumed the worst. "He was in the Navy—a chief petty officer. He was only on shore a few months at a time before he had to ship out again. He served in the first Gulf War on the Eisenhower when I was little. But he was—is—a great dad."

"Oh." He averts his face and clears his throat. "Um, you said he sold it, why?"

My smile fades. "He didn't want to, but they needed the money." I rub the smooth upholstery absently. "He had just retired, and he and Mom were looking forward to spending more time together and with us kids. But my sister got sick."

When I fall silent, lost in my memories, he looks at me hesitantly. "Rachel?"

"No, Paula. She was my oldest sister." I sigh and look out at a line of people waiting to get into a corner restaurant. I hate talking about it. It was the first time anyone close to me died. The feel of his hand closing over mine draws my attention back to see his eyes. His look is encouraging and comfortable, and I start talking.

"It's funny that you said your mom died when you were

twelve—not funny, but an odd coincidence," I amend swiftly. "I had just turned twelve when Paula started complaining of head-aches. She had graduated from UCLA and, after a few false starts, had started her dream job with an interior design firm. At first, we thought it was just the stress of work getting to her. Mom imme-diately wanted her to move back home so she could baby her, but Paula was an independent cuss. There was no way she was going to crawl back to her parents' house just because of a little stress."

"Independent, huh? Must run in the family."

"You have no idea," I joke, but my levity fades. "Anyway, after a few months she finally went to the doctor. Eventually she was diagnosed; she had an inoperable brain tumor."

"Holy shit." His whisper drifts in the silence, and he squeezes my hand.

I take a deep breath as my office building comes into view. "She didn't have health care, and she wasn't a dependent on Dad's policy anymore. Dad was able to cover her again, but the VA moves so slowly." I shrug. "That's why he sold his car, to help pay for some of her chemo treatments. But it was fruitless. She died before I turned thirteen."

He finds a spot to park, and we sit in the darkness for a few moments with my hand in his. Visions of sterile hospitals, stern nurses, and my parents inconsolable during the funeral flood my memory. It had been a confusing and terrifying time. I hated see-ing my parents' sorrow and desperation while my sister wasted away in a hospital bed while the VA dragged its feet because of her "preexisting condition." Their depression and grief following the inevitable end was even more difficult to cope with, considering I was in the midst of my own grief.

"I've avoided hospitals ever since. Don't know what I'll do if I ever have to visit someone in one." I manage a wry smile and shake my head. "Well, thanks for the ride—" I begin, but his soft grunt cuts me off.

"I'm walking you to your office." He gets out, leaving no room for argument, and stalks around the car to open my door. Joining him on the sidewalk, I give him a wry grin.

"You're used to getting your own way, aren't you?"

Chuckling, he takes my elbow and steers me toward the building. "Not often enough, in my opinion."

The revolving doors are locked at this time of night, so I lead him to a side door and swipe my badge, the only ID I have with me. On the way up in the elevator, he holds my hand firmly; it should feel awkward, considering how long I've known him, but it doesn't. We're quiet, lost in our own thoughts, until the elevator pings and the doors open on my floor.

"So," he begins hesitantly, gesturing for me to go first. He falls into step beside me. "Your tattoo is for your sister?"

"Yes. She loved them. This time of year, I like to drive down to Pacific Grove to see the monarch sanctuary. She loved that place." I remember the smile of wonder that would always light her face when she saw the colorful little things flitting around like dozens of airborne flowers.

"Butterflies have sanctuaries?"

Arriving at my office, I chuckle at his surprised expression. "They do. It's amazing to see so many in one spot."

"Huh. That would be cool to see."

"Um, this will just take me a second," I mutter, grabbing the stack of files I'd set aside for my trip tomorrow and shoving them in my messenger bag. I'm aware of his intense stare while I rummage through the bag to ensure I've got everything. It feels like years since we were in here. In just a few short hours, he's managed to turn my world on end.

I straighten and look at him warily. "So, what happens now?"

"What do you mean?" He looks genuinely confused until I gesture between us.

"Us. You and me." I try to shrug off my nervousness. Although I want to believe him when he says he wants to pursue something with me, I can't help but remember all the loose talk I heard during the concert. "I mean, I know what you said, but you'll be gone for a few weeks. I've heard about what happens on tour. I know I can't expect you to . . . you know . . . um, *abstain* from . . ." I trail off when his face darkens, and he reaches for me.

"Damn it, Tess." He wraps his arm around me, his expression a combination of frustration and hurt. "I know I don't have a stellar reputation." He pauses, studying me cautiously. "What exactly *have* you heard about what happens on tour?"

I purse my lips. "Sean and Cameron were talking between sets at Parker's concert. Something about the three of you hooking up with triplets in Sydney." He groans in exasperation, and I instantly wish I'd kept my mouth shut. To be honest, I hadn't heard the *whole* conversation, but come on. If you hear rock stars talking about partying with *triplets*, what else could it mean?

"Aw, Jesus. Look, who knows what Sean was thinking. The guy's a maniac."

"I'm just saying—" His mouth on mine cuts off my rambling. His lips are warm and firm, and they move against mine with urgency that sparks the same in me. I'm left gasping for air when he breaks away just as abruptly.

"And just because those two idiots were talking about hookups doesn't mean that I'm necessarily included." He huffs impatiently. "Okay, it doesn't mean that I'd be included *now*. They can do whatever the fuck they want. Doesn't mean I'm going to go along with it."

He plants a hand on my hip and pulls me closer, the energy between us shifting. *"Tess."* My name is a rough purr between us. "Don't think about the tour. How long are you going to be in San Diego?"

"Just overnight." I hate how breathy I sound, but I can't friggin' help it when he's holding me like this.

"That gives us one more night before I leave. Text me your flight info, and I'll pick you up at the airport."

"And then?"

"I'll do my best to convince you that I'm a man of my word." I grip the long, floppy strands of his Mohawk as his lips descend once more, this time for a long, languorous kiss. A moan escapes me as his hand travels slowly from my hip to skim my breast. I snake my leg around his thigh as he moves me to sit on the edge of my desk, our breathing ragged. Just as his other hand shifts to move up under my skirt, we both freeze when the hallway light snaps on brighter. His eyes shoot open at the sound of a vacuum firing up in the distance somewhere.

"It's the cleaning crew," I announce unnecessarily, trying to rein in my raging hormones. The speed with which he can take me from zero to sixty is frightening. Nervously pushing my hair behind my ear, I try and fail to look unaffected. Holy God—was I really going to let him take me right here on my desk?

Yes, yes I was.

He takes a shaky breath, mixed with a chuckle. "Jesus, what you do to me, woman."

BACK DOWNSTAIRS, HE PULLS ME to a stop in the lobby. "Where are you parked?"

"Oh, I take transit," I say with a shrug and offer him a smile. "Thanks for driving me back so I could fetch my things. I'll text you the details for my flight, if you still want me to."

"Of course I want you to." He rolls his eyes. "But you don't mean you're going to take a bus now, do you? Where do you live?"

"Over by SFSU. And no, I take the train." I'm not sure what the problem is, but he's obviously not happy. "Matt, I do this all the time. I'm perfectly fine, I promise."

"It's late, though." He frowns and runs a hand over his hair. "I'll drive you."

"No!" I take a calming breath and repeat more normally, "No, thank you. You've done enough, really." I don't want to offend him, but, damn it. I can take care of myself.

He looks baffled by my refusal. "Tess . . ." He looks to the sky, as if seeking divine intervention. "At least take a cab, okay?"

"Fine, okay." I hold a hand up. It will cost a fortune, thanks to all the freaking taxes they pile on, but if it makes Mr. Grumpy-pants happy . . .

Grumbling to himself, he leaves me trailing behind him while he flags down a taxi. He leans down and says something to the driver before I reach him. He opens the door for me but pulls me close before I get in. "Have a good trip tomorrow," he says gruffly. He gives me a lingering kiss, making me a little light-headed. "I'll see you soon."

I can't help myself; I cup his cheek, letting my fingers scratch his scruff lightly. His sigh is barely audible as he leans into my touch. "I look forward to it," I whisper, and then turn and climb into the cab. Matt closes the door with a solid thunk. Looking out the back window, I see him watching and standing as still as a statue, a tall figure clad in black leather and denim that disappears when we turn the corner.

"Your boyfriend really loves you," the driver comments in a heavy accent after I give him my address.

"Oh, he's not my—"

"He's paid for your ride," he continues, flashing me a friendly smile in the rearview mirror. "You're all set!"

I groan at the intractability of certain bass players and lean my head back against the seat before breaking into a soft chuckle.

chapter five

matt

IT TOOK EVERYTHING IN ME to put her in that cab and watch her drive away. Some dangerous, base-level instinct has kicked in. The word "mine" repeats over and over in my head. An intense, constant, addictive beat threatening to unhinge everything I've come to know and believe about myself.

An actual relationship is new territory for me. The line of women who want to fuck a musician is long. The line that really wants to get to know one seems nonexistent.

The longest relationship I've had lasted a grand total of four months with a backup singer for one of our warm-up bands. It came to a screeching halt when I found her in a threesome on one of the other tour buses. It was a jagged pill to swallow, to be made to feel like a fool on your own tour.

Since then, what Cam said to me is right. I haven't exactly

put in an effort in this area. I haven't had to, or cared to until now.

I'm also aware that time isn't on my side here. I've got less than three days with Tess before we'll head to Australia for the final tour dates. Tomorrow is a write-off, given her trip to San Diego, which means the clock is ticking.

I don't like being under the gun like this. I want to take my time with Tess and savor the experience. I was an idiot to suggest we leave my loft. I want her plump lips on me and her endless curves spread out like a meal on my bed. I'm aching to fill my hands with her soft, full breasts, and have her fall asleep in my arms. I want to see that dark flash of heat in her eyes over and over again.

But it's more than that.

I need to learn why her independent streak is such a fucking turn-on. I think I can listen to her voice and never get tired of hearing it. Even when she's challenging me. *Especially* when she's challenging me.

Her intoxicating scent lingers on my jacket. I can still feel her in the room even though it's been hours, and I'll never be able to look at that table the same way again. She fucking ruined me, and I don't think she has a clue.

This is why I've been so careful about letting women get too close. And now, within a very short period of time, Tess knows things about me that fewer than a handful of people know. I don't know if that's a good thing or not.

Restless, I haul my faithful black bass from the stand, slinging the strap over my shoulder, and let the curves ground me like they always have. It's something I can count on, something I can trust. It's never failed me before, but when I close my eyes and my fingers start in on Kennedy's latest masterpiece, all I can see, all I can feel, is her.

The feel of her pussy clenching around me, milking me dry.

Her thick, raven hair spilling over the table in a long cascading wave. A groan of frustration rolls through me, and uncharacteristically, my fingers falter clumsily, a string breaking.

My eyes snap open, heart hammering relentlessly, and I stare down at the neck of the bass in disbelief.

Everything disappoints you eventually.

"IS EVERYTHING OKAY?" TUCKER'S TIRED VOICE grumbles through the phone, and I can't help but laugh. He's usually so intense and regimented all the time, it's amusing to catch him off guard.

"Everything's fine. Did I wake you up, sleeping beauty?"

He pauses before I hear him huff. "What do you think?"

I glance at the vintage clock on the exposed brick wall. "I think it's not even twelve yet. The night is still young." I take a final drag from my cigarette, heading to toss it out in the kitchen. I really need to look into those patches.

"Yeah, but I'm not. The four of you have aged me thirty years, I'm sure."

"You love it, and you know it."

"Some days I wonder." His voice trails off, and for a minute I wonder if he's nodded off on me. "There a reason you're calling, or did you just miss me?"

"I need a favor."

"Anything for you, Matty." Tucker's loyalty still floors me. I know how lucky we are to have him in our corner. It's something I'll never take for granted.

"Just like that?" That gnawing voice is back, annoying me, making me question whether this is a good idea. "No questions?"

"You never ask for anything, so whatever it is must be important to you."

The silence gapes between us as Tucker waits. He knows I'm stalling, but the man has the patience of a saint when it comes to us. "If we could just keep this between us, I'd appreciate it."

He actually sounds slightly offended when he fires back at me. "Of course. I know it's hard for you, but you can trust me, Matt. You'd be amazed the shit I know that I keep from all of you."

"That right?"

"You guys are worse than a soap opera sometimes, I swear. Hit me. What do you need?"

"Can you get me an address?"

He lets out a low laugh. "Let me guess. Tess?"

Running my hand across the back of my neck, I glance out the window. "Am I that obvious?"

"Do you really want me to answer that? Normally, I'd advise against stalking a woman to get her attention, but something tells me she'd be surprised if you didn't show up uninvited."

"I don't really know what I'm doing." It's a dark admission I wouldn't make to too many people.

"That's usually the way it goes. She the real deal?"

I watch a taxi speed down the street, which only makes me think of Tess driving away. My skin prickles at the feeling. "She could be."

After a moment, he asks, "Want me to do a background on her?"

I bristle in annoyance. "What? No. Jesus, Tucker."

"Just throwing it out there. Everyone has a skeleton or two they don't want to share. It's been my experience the more you know now, the better." His honesty has always slayed me, and this is no different.

The thing is, he's got a point, but if Tess ever found out, I don't want to think about the wrath. "No. You hear me?"

"Loud and clear. But I'll throw out a different offer."

"I'm listening."

"I've got Lane on a pretty tight schedule with working out now. You're welcome to join us when we're down under."

I scowl, opening up the fridge. "You think I need to work out?" I ask, slightly annoyed. I've never really had to hit the weights, and seem to have the metabolism to eat like a linebacker and never have to worry about it. I shake my head at the thought. Clearly my genetics, which I know next to nothing about, are at play there.

"I think it helps Lane keep his mind off the things that tempt him." There's no mistaking his message here. He's seen enough of me, of all of us, to know our bad habits, women being mine. "We're going to be gone for a couple of weeks. Just think about it."

Pulling a takeout container from the fridge, I slam it on the counter with more force than necessary. "I will."

"Do I need to go over the security protocol with you?"

"What protocol?" What the hell is he talking about?

"Jesus. You're such an amateur," he says after a dark laugh. "No sex videos on your phone. No X-rated Snapchat pictures, because no matter what they say, once that shit hits the Net, it's out there, and I've got better things to do than to spend hours trying to bury photos of your junk."

"Not to worry. I'm more of a hands-on type of guy."

"Fuck you, Logan. I did not need to hear that. Give me twenty and you'll have your address."

I open the takeout box, cradling the phone between my shoulder and ear. "It's going to take you that long? You're slipping, Tucker."

"Shut up. I'm half asleep or you'd have it sooner."

Less than twenty minutes later, after I've demolished the rest of the Mexican leftovers, my phone pings with a text.

I grin when I see the address and apartment number, complete with directions from my place to hers. It's followed quickly by another message.

Tuck: FYI—She's got a roommate. Keep that in mind when you're stalking.

Shaking my head, I toss the containers into the trash. How he found out that piece of information at this time of night, I'm pretty sure I don't want to know.

Thanks, man. I owe you.

Tuck: You don't even want to know how much. Be careful.

Always am.

Tuck: Famous last words.

IT'S AMAZING HOW EASY IT is to slip back into old, dangerous habits. Instinct kicks in, and you remember things you should have forgotten and never should have learned. Living on the street, I had become somewhat of an expert in breaking into buildings. It came in handy more times than I want to think about.

The skill doesn't fail me now as I easily pry open the side door to Tess's building, annoyance creeping in. She lives in a pretty safe neighborhood bordering Lake Merced, but if I can break into the building this easily, anyone can. The thought is unsettling.

No security camera in the stairwell is another red flag, although Tucker won't have to worry about video of me breaking the law. I'm well aware that this crosses the line of desperation. Sean would probably call me pathetic for pulling a stunt like this. One of his famous Murphy's laws—let the women come to you—is about to be broken.

Quietly, I push open the door at the second level and step into the bright hallway. Holding the door to prevent any unnecessary noise as it closes behind me slips back to me like second nature. Being a smaller building, there are only two doors on each side and an open alcove at the end of one hall with light spilling out. Experience tells me it's probably the laundry room. I tamp down the memories that threaten to pull me back to darker places. Memories of sleeping in dirty laundry rooms for a few hours of warmth and safety, only to be kicked back out to the dangers of the street once more.

A new goal in mind, I search out her door and make my way down the hall, my senses honed to every sound around me. The muted hum of a dryer grows louder, the smell of clean linen drifting down the hall, confirming my initial suspicion.

I catch her number on the last door on the left and stop in my tracks. I'm fucking crazy for doing this. I'm a thirty-six-year-old man, not some teenager with a stupid crush. I rake my hand through my hair, feeling the stiff bristles scrape my palm. How has she managed to unnerve me?

My head snaps back to the laundry room and off-key lyrics belting above the sound of the dryer.

"When the time comes, I'll remind you of all the things we didn't say."

I'd recognize those words anywhere. They're Kennedy's lyrics, one of our biggest hits to date. He won the Grammy for song of the year for that, and even though Kennedy always claims awards are popularity contests, I know this one actually meant a lot to him.

I'd also recognize that voice anywhere. Even singing off key, it's sultry, sinking into my veins and driving me out of my mind as I approach the alcove.

Tess's round ass is poured into black yoga pants and she's swaying in front of the dryer. She arches her back and grinds away to the sexually charged beat playing in her headphones, obliterating every thought in my head.

Her long, dark hair is wet and piled up into a messy bun on top of her head, revealing the erotic curve of her neck and the wings of the butterfly tattoo on her shoulder that peek out of my vintage Harley shirt. She's still got it on. My heart stutters at the visual.

She's unfiltered and perfect. This is the Tess I want to get to know in every and any way I can. And if that makes me a weaker man, then so be it.

I can't stop looking her over; lust and a predatory fire burn through me. She bends over to open the dryer and the rhythmic sound of the machine stops abruptly as she guides the clothes into the hamper on the floor.

My mouth goes dry, my voice sounding raw and needy even though she can't hear me. "Tess."

I close the distance between us in the small space, wrapping my arm around her waist from behind, and tugging her back against me. I hear her take a sharp breath in, and I pull one of her earbuds out, sliding my palm up over her mouth, whispering in her ear. "Shh . . . It's me. Matt."

Panicked, dark eyes meet mine as she turns her head to glare at me, struggling against my hold. I loosen my grip around her waist, lifting my palm from her perfect mouth, and she turns, pushing against my chest, sending me stumbling back. "What the fuck are you doing?" she screeches. "Are you crazy?"

"Starting to look that way, isn't it?"

I let my eyes fall over my shirt stretched taut across the round swells of her heaving breasts. Sweet Christ, she's not wearing a bra. "You nearly gave me a heart attack! What the hell are you doing here?" Her hands are balled into fists at her hips.

Her eyes light with that addictive heat I've been craving since I put her in the cab, fear morphing quickly to desire as she waits. "Well?"

I take a step forward, desperate to touch her, and she doesn't stop me. "I couldn't stop thinking about you."

"Yeah?" She looks shocked. Maybe pleased? I can't really tell. "Well, there's this thing called a phone. You could've called, texted."

"I wanted to see you. I don't want to wait until you're back from your trip. Time isn't a luxury I have." It's a harsh realization. She could turn me away right now, and this would be over. I know how rare it is to find a person who is willing to put up with the demands of a musician's lifestyle. I'm willing to put it all out there to find out because she's worth it. She's worth the humiliation of sneaking around in the middle of the night and the risk of being told to go to hell. She could easily become my addiction; hell, I'm already halfway there.

Her lips part in surprise at my words, and I wonder if they taste like cherry almond again, or something equally mind blowing. She blinks as if she can't quite believe I'm here.

"We're not having sex." She lifts her chin.

"You feel better getting that out there for everyone to hear?" She bites back a grin, and I gently cup her face, watching as her eyes close to my touch, her dark lashes brushing her creamy skin only for a moment. This is her: real, soft, and supple in my arms, not an ounce of makeup on her, and, fuck, she slays me. "I didn't come here just to have sex," I whisper once her eyes meet mine again.

"You didn't?" she breathes out on a sigh, her tongue darting out to wet her bottom lip.

"Let me in, Tess. Show me who you really are."

♪ ♩ ♪ ♩

Tessa

"WHAT IF YOU DON'T LIKE it?"

The words escape me before I realize it and my cheeks heat. I can't believe he's standing here, in the flesh. He's rattled me so thoroughly falling asleep was impossible. So I'd decided to get a few things washed for my trip while I knew I'd have the laundry room to myself. Even then, I couldn't stop thinking about him, so I scrolled down to one of my favorite Redfall playlists, just so I could listen to Matt's distinctive basslines. The man is as talented as he is gorgeous.

A gentle smile curls his lips, and I feel the featherlight touch of his rough fingertips across my face as he traces my blush. "I can't see how that would be possible," he murmurs. "You're the most fascinating person I've met in a long, long time."

His sincerity strikes a chord, and my shoulders relax marginally despite the ridiculousness of his claim. The guy knows a million people—major league musicians, for crying out loud. "I find that hard to believe."

While still holding my face, he leans down to give me a soft, sweet kiss. His lips are warm and firm, and they move gently with mine, making my heart race. I expect him to deepen the kiss, but instead he pulls away and gives me three pecks before straightening. "Believe it."

He releases me but doesn't move far. Between the heat from the dryer and his own natural furnace, the room is suddenly stifling. "Matt, what are you doing here, really? It's almost midnight." I ask again, frowning. "And how on earth did you get in the building?"

Embarrassment tinges his low chuckle. "It wasn't hard to get inside. I used the side door," he says, ignoring my first question. Then his expression turns severe. "And you should complain to the property manager about the lack of security. Any-fucking-body could get in here. It's pathetic."

I stick out my chin. "This building is perfectly safe. I've lived here for a year and never had a problem with people breaking and entering until now."

"You've just been lucky, apparently," he shoots back.

"Hey," I say softly, reaching out to touch his hand in a conciliatory gesture. "Since you came all this way, let me wrap this up and we can talk inside. Okay?"

He nods stiffly, and I turn quickly to bend and scoop out my remaining clothes from the dryer. I hear a weird strangled groan behind me, and glance over my shoulder. He's staring at the ceiling and muttering fervently to himself. No doubt second-guessing whatever he had planned, I'm sure.

My task completed, I lift my full basket and try to step past him. He takes the basket from me, his eyebrow raised as if daring me to contradict him. "Thanks," I murmur and lead him down the hall. See? I can be cooperative.

"Be quiet." I shoot him a look as I let us in. "Jada is asleep. She gets up at an ungodly hour."

"Who's Jada?"

"My roommate. It's her condo." I roll my eyes at his satisfied grunt and lock the door behind us.

"What's she do?" he whispers.

"She's an IT guru for SFSU." I look around the darkened condo nervously. Jada and I aren't slobs, but I've been helping her sort through some boxes of stuff her grandmother sent her and things are stacked all over the living room. There really isn't anywhere to sit.

I quickly lead him down the hall past Jada's door to my bedroom at the end. I'm not sure why, but it feels like I'm back in high school and sneaking my boyfriend in past my parents' room. I flick on my bedside light and close the door before taking the basket from him and placing it on the floor next to my closet.

"I'm sorry, but things are a bit of a mess in the living room right now." I shrug self-consciously and gesture to the one chair I have in my bedroom. "I'm afraid this will have to do."

He holds back a grin and watches me shift from foot to foot. "Works for me," he drawls. He drags his leather jacket off and, before I can ask him what he's doing, he kicks off his boots and stretches out on my bed. I glare at him as he puts his arms casually behind his head and grins up at me.

"I said that we weren't having sex."

His grin grows. "I remember. As you can see, I'm still fully dressed," he says, low and sultry. "But I'm not having a conversation with you sitting in that hard chair when there's this nice soft bed right here."

"A conversation?" I look at him with trepidation, feeling that now-familiar push and pull between us. He looks disturbingly at home stretched out on my bed.

He exhales deeply, looking a little lost. "Tessa, I meant what I said. I just wanted to see you and maybe talk a little. I didn't want to wait until you got back."

God, he's been nothing but sweet and I can't turn off my inner bitch. Taking my hair down swiftly—I hate lying down with a bun on the back of my head—I move to sit on the edge of the bed, but he quickly reaches out and grabs my wrist. With a gentle tug, he pulls me down beside him, slipping an arm around my waist to hold me loosely against him. "Okay?" he asks, playing with my hair that's draped over my bicep.

I answer by placing my head on his shoulder. It feels both odd and wonderfully natural to be with him like this. The frightening truth is that everything with him has felt that way. A man has never gotten under my skin like Matt has, and the speed with which it's happened is even scarier. I've only known him a few weeks, since the crunch time before Parker's benefit concert began, but it's made no difference.

I let myself melt into his warmth. "Sorry I'm being such a bit—"

"Stop right there. I've known more than my share of bitches and believe me, you are *nothing* like them." He looks down at his feet. "You just don't trust me yet."

I wish I could contradict him, but I can't. As right as it feels to lie here with him, there's something in me that won't let me relax completely.

"When I told you about Paula, I left a few things out," I begin, and I can feel his attention on me. "What happened to her was as awful as awful can get, but I was so young. I didn't understand the science of it or the financial hardships my parents went through until I was older. What I did understand was the emotion. The feeling of losing something that was so very important with nothing I could do about it."

He hums in encouragement and I continue, "Paula was engaged to a sweet guy named Erik. They'd dated forever, and he was part of the family. When she was diagnosed, it was a shock to all of us, but Erik was amazing. He wanted to marry her immediately, but he didn't have insurance, and the VA wouldn't let Dad put her back on his policy unless she was a dependent." I shake my head bitterly, hating how cold and impersonal bureaucracy can be.

"So, what, did he leave her?" Matt asks, bringing me back.

I shake my head. "God, no. He was always with her, taking her to appointments and staying with her during chemo. He was her rock. In one way, it was almost too much for Paula; she was so independent, but she needed him to get through all of it. She hated leaning on him but also loved that she could. I think now that it made her hate the disease even more, because of how it affected everyone around her. She hated that it made him *have* to be strong for her, that it put him in that position. Do you know what I mean?"

"I think so." He lets out a deep breath. "And I think I have an inkling as to how she felt."

"Erik was strong right up until the day she left us, and then he crumpled like a lost little boy." I swallow back the emotion that always bubbles up when I think of Paula and Erik's tragic love story. "He made it through the funeral, and then a few weeks later, he disappeared. He quit his job, moved out of the apartment he and Paula had shared, and drove off without a word, not even to his own parents. They were devastated. It was as if he couldn't bear to see any of us anymore. Losing him made everything about that awful situation twice as bad. It's like I lost a sister *and* a brother at the same time."

"Have you ever heard from him again?" he asks, with a puzzled frown.

"No. It made a huge impact on me." I pull at a loose thread on my sleeve. "That someone who was so in love, so *committed*, could just disappear without a word."

This is why the pull I feel toward Matt is scaring the hell out of me. As much as I try to tell myself that history doesn't have to repeat itself, I'd be a liar if I said Paula and Erik's story doesn't play into my current attitudes toward dating. Why open yourself up to that type of pain when you can have a few months or nights of fun with no expectations? Most guys are relieved when they realize I'm not dreaming of rings and shared bank accounts. When the occasional guy does get clingy, I usually send him off with my well wishes and a spectacular blowjob.

I've discovered that good head tends to soften the blow.

Matt pulls me closer, and I feel his lips against my hair. "Thank you for sharing that with me. That would've been hard for anyone to go through, much less a twelve-year-old."

"I wonder whatever happened to him sometimes. My brother thought he saw him a few years ago getting into a cab in Chicago, but he was gone before he could make sure."

"Your brother? I thought you had a sister."

"I do. Rachel is my sister, and I have twin brothers who are the oldest, now that Paula is gone."

"Big family," he grunts, and I can't tell if that's approval or not. He runs his hand down my arm. "Do you *have* to go to San Diego?" he asks wistfully.

"Yes, I do. Especially since Abby isn't going."

"Why isn't she going?" He sounds puzzled and I prop myself up on an elbow to look at him incredulously.

"Don't you actually talk to your bandmates?" I ask with a touch of exasperation. "Kennedy is spiriting her off to some remote romantic location for a few days before he meets you guys in Australia. Didn't he tell you?"

His eyes light up with understanding. "Um, he may have mentioned it," he mumbles. "I've been a little distracted lately."

"It's a big surprise. I can't wait to see her face." I grin, thinking of her expression. She does so much for everyone else; it's about time someone does something special for her. "Anyway, I've only had this job for two days, and it's important to me. I want to do well, to show her that she made the right decision. I mean, how did you feel the first time you took the stage with Kennedy?"

Surprise flickers across his handsome face, and then his eyes become thoughtful. "Like I was on top of the world, and I wanted to prove I deserved to be there." He places a kiss at my temple. "Tess, you're going to be great. Not just because you know the job, but because you *care*. That's the key, I think."

"Thanks." I glance up at him. "So, um, do you want me to call you when I get back?"

He huffs a laugh. "What do you think? Of course I do. I drove all the way over here, broke in even, because I didn't want to waste a minute with you."

A thrill runs through me. "When's the last time you spent the night simply sleeping with a woman?"

"No comment," he growls dryly and tightens his arm around me. I let him be, and after a few minutes, I realize that his breathing has become deep and regular. Risking a look at him, I see he's indeed asleep, his face relaxed and peaceful. His long eyelashes brush his high cheekbones, and my heart skips a beat. Good God, he's pretty.

I tug my fleece bedspread, flip it over our fully clothed bodies, and snuggle in beside him. Tomorrow should be interesting.

chapter six

matt

WAKING UP WITH LAYERS OF thick, black hair draped over me like a blanket does things to me that I wasn't expecting. A few fitful hours of restless sleep are normal for me. Normal however, seems to have gone out the window since Tess blazed into my life.

Even though it's still dark outside, I've slept like a rock. Uninterrupted and nightmare free. I could get used to this feeling, despite it being a bit of a foreign concept to me. I'm surrounded by a warm, sleepy woman, her scent permanently planted in my brain. Something uniquely Tess that I can't quite put my finger on, but it's snuck under my skin.

Her cheek is pressed to my chest like she's done it a thousand times before. My heart pounds faster, my hand seeming to have a mind of its own as my palm gently glides into her hair, the strands silky against my fingers. I can't stop running a circuit over the generous curve of her hip. My palm fits like it was made to be there, and I feel her burrow impossibly closer against my side.

I can feel her heart beating a slow and rhythmic bassline against me, stirring something deep inside to the surface. Contentment isn't something I'm used to. I don't remember falling asleep last night, and it pisses me off because I had plans. Plans that involved getting to know Tess and what makes her tick. Passing out before I even got started was not part of the plan.

Her hand drifts lazily and seriously low across my hips, setting every nerve ending on fire, and I'm still fully clothed. The taunting memory of just how good skin on skin feels with Tess is torture. It would be easy. So damn easy to strip the barriers of our clothes away, sink into her, and hear those sultry little groans I'm not even sure she knows she makes.

Breathing her in is dangerous, but I do it anyway as the muted light from the street lamp peeks through the sheer curtains in her bedroom. It's predawn and unnaturally quiet, another first. My life is lived loud and to the extreme on most days. I exist in a constant state of noise and chaos: interviews, meetings, rehearsals, concerts, screaming, die-hard fans, the electric buzz of backstage before and after we've played. Even my dreams are loud and abrasive.

But, here, surrounded by the cloud-like softness of her sheets, and her body curled around mine, everything is different. It's still and calm. I know I'm flying blind here, and if I'm not careful, I'll crash and burn. We both might.

The realization does nothing for my racing thoughts. The truth is life would be a hell of a lot easier if I just left Tess alone. If I had never come here tonight, if I hadn't sought her out in her office, shared my past with her.

As if she can sense my mind working overtime, she mumbles something against my chest and shifts away, turning her back to me. Maybe that says it all.

"I MUST BE DREAMING." IT'S a groggy statement that makes me grin as I flip the pancakes.

Even leaning against the stool as if she doesn't trust her legs to hold her, I can tell Tess's roommate is tall. Tall and exhausted as she blinks the sleep out of her eyes. She's in quite a state, looking like she just rolled out of bed, with puffy brown eyes and a rumpled, oversized SFSU hoodie hanging off her shoulders.

She gives me a wary once-over as I fill a mug of coffee.

"You must be Jada. I've heard a lot about you. I'm Matt."

"Funny, I've heard nothing about you."

"Ouch." I grimace and try to push back the sting of her biting statement, sliding the mug over to her. "Coffee?"

She narrows her eyes, but hauls the stool out from under the counter, sinking down. "Don't think I don't know what you're trying to do here." Her critical tone rings through the kitchen. I ignore it.

"Cream?" She shakes her head, taking the mug between her hands, and blows gently over the top, her eyes fixed to mine.

"It's really you, right? I mean, I've dreamed of rock stars before. Not you specifically, of course."

"Of course. Pancakes?"

"Got to be a dream," she mumbles into the mug while I busy myself with plating the pancakes.

"I'm not sure what this bullshit is." I set a bottle of mystery syrup down beside the plate. Navigating Tess's kitchen after I reluctantly left her bed was eye-opening. Despite the cabinets being almost overflowing with baking ingredients, judging by the price tags still on the pots and pans I found, I don't think either one of them actually cooks often.

"Maple syrup?" She pours about half the bottle over the stack of pancakes.

"No. Real maple syrup, the good stuff, is from Canada, and it's awesome."

"Yeah? Well, this was on sale for a dollar ninety-nine and it works just fine."

Her fork cuts easily through the stack. This is the one meal I know how to make. Tom made sure of it. He said pancakes would work for any meal, and he's not wrong.

Jada closes her eyes and moans. "Of course they would have to be this good. I didn't hear you guys last night," she starts after inhaling another bite. "Typically, I hear when Tess has company."

I try to get a handle on the pang of jealousy that rips through me. "Does she have company often?"

Jada shrugs before tackling the pancakes once more. "My lips are sealed." I let the quiet drift between us while she cleans the plate. I think she would've licked the excess syrup off if I hadn't been in the room. "Just so you know, regardless of the fact that you make the best pancakes I've ever had, I know people who can make it so your body is never found."

Leaning against the counter across from her, I lift my mug in a silent salute. "Good to know."

"YOU MADE THIS?" TESS LETS out a groan of appreciation as she takes a bite, causing my dick to press against my jeans with impatient need. Tess emerged from her room, sleepy and sexy as hell, shortly after Jada left for work, the sight of her destroying a few more of my brain cells in the process.

There were a few moments of awkwardness, her cheeks heating as she sought me out in the kitchen, looking at me like she couldn't quite believe I was actually there. I could almost feel her meticulously laying down the bricks on the wall to put some distance between us.

I know it's up to me to knock that wall down, brick by painstaking brick. If life has taught me anything, it's not to give up. Somewhere in the back of my mind, I wonder if the challenge is part of the reason I'm so wildly attracted to Tess. I'm used to women throwing themselves at me, at the entire band, to the point where I'm embarrassed for them sometimes.

As I watch her devour the pancakes like they're the best thing she's ever eaten, I know it's more than a challenge. She doesn't care that she's still in the shirt—*my* shirt—that she slept in last night, or that her long hair has been hastily pulled back into a messy ponytail. She couldn't look less put together or more beautiful than she does right now.

"Don't look so surprised, Cardinal. I'm a man of many talents."

She stops mid-chew, her gaze drifting over my torso, turning slightly dazed in the process. "Mmmm." I let her look her fill, the blood heating in my veins at her blatant gawking. I want her to remember this while she's in San Diego. How it felt to have me in her kitchen, to share breakfast, to breathe in the same space. It's all I want her to think about.

"I met Jada. She's quite protective of you."

Her eyes widen and she peers over my shoulder in the direction of the stove, clearly looking for more pancakes. "You were up that early?"

Nodding, I lift her now empty plate and turn back to slide the last of the pancakes on for her. "Sleep and I don't really see eye to eye most of the time." She nods but says nothing.

"Women must love this breakfast." She stabs into the fluffy goodness on her plate.

"I've only made it for the guys."

She lifts her gaze to me, and it's like she can see right to my soul. "You're joking? This is gold. Make this and they'd never want to leave."

"That's what I'm counting on."

She takes a deliberate lick of the fork before setting it down. "I'm going to take a shower."

It's a tempting invitation.

"Then I'll leave you to it."

Her brow knits together and she parts her plump lips. Stunned speechless looks good on Tess.

"Do you love your job, Cardinal?" I ask, not so gently tugging her hair free from the elastic, pulling my fingers through the thick strands.

"I just . . . wha . . ."

"Do you love your job?" I repeat the question, unable to resist tracing my thumb over her bottom lip.

She just blinks at me with a quick nod before nipping at the pad of my thumb. "Then I'm going to leave you to your shower, because if I stay, you'll never get to work on time, and probably not at all. I don't want to be the reason you lose something you love."

OPENING UP THAT DOOR TO leave was harder than it should have been. Everything in me screamed to stay, that I was where I was supposed to be. And now I'm kicking myself for leaving her even though it's the right thing to do.

With Kennedy on his way to some tropical paradise, and Sean and Cameron MIA, my options to fill the gap of time yawn in front of me. I'm restless and agitated. I've tried to distract myself with the guitar for a couple of hours, and then with the bike. The things that would normally hold my interest aren't doing the job this time.

Which is how I find myself knocking on Tom's office door at the group home. My presence is met with surprise. It's not like I've never been here. The visits are just few and far between.

"Matty. Didn't expect to see you." Tom looks up from a stack of papers on his desk. I know he hates this part of the job. "Everything all right?"

He rounds the desk, leaning against the front, eyeing me with that parental concern I've only ever seen from him.

"Yeah. I've got some time before we head out to Australia. Thought I'd see if you need any help." I spot a black-and-white picture on his wall that makes me smile. It's the two of us leaning against his Mustang fastback off to the side of the road on the PCH, the Pacific rolling in the background. It was taken about five years ago when we had finally gotten the car back in pristine condition only to have it break down about twenty miles into the journey.

"We can always use help," Tom says. "Was just going to take one of the boys through a lesson on the Harley."

"Sounds perfect."

"A LITTLE MORE ELBOW GREASE there, Beck."

The seventeen-year-old scowls and grumbles, "Does it really matter?" Typical response from Beckett, one of the obvious leaders in the house. It didn't take long for me to figure out the pecking order. The scene is too familiar, which stirs up all sorts of haunting memories.

Having been in more than my fair share of group homes, I know the boys here have it good. The house is always pristine, they're never lacking for food, and Tom ensures there're a wide variety of activities for them to pass the time. For a lot of these kids, free time isn't a good thing. It tends to lead to risky or worse, illegal activities that only serve to get you in deeper.

I know Tom's put the money I've donated over the years to good use. There's an entire room dedicated to music, tricked out with the latest instruments and recording equipment, and this garage is something else, a real mechanic's dream. The rest of the money is used to fund educational programs that will help these kids long after they're gone from here. There's no way Tom would be able to afford it all with the inadequate funding provided by the state.

"Course it matters. That polishing compound will make the covers look awesome."

"We're supposed to be working on the engine, not spending all of our time fucking cleaning," Beck complains.

"Hey. Watch your mouth." Beck glances up at me with a sheepish smile. "And this is all part of it. When this bike is done, you'll want it to look its best."

"Whatever," he complains, but he flops down to one of the stools across from the bike and gets to work on the task. The tables turned entirely, I can start to understand now why Tom worked so hard to gain my trust, and why he tried when no one else did. I see a lot of myself in Beckett. We have the same cocky attitude, but buried underneath all the bravado there's a desire to get out of the shithole situation he's found himself in. And while I don't know the details of what brought Beckett to the group home, I do know he wouldn't be here if it weren't bad.

We work for the next half hour or so, the comfortable silence broken by the sound of Beckett methodically polishing the engine cover blending with the occasional clink of tools as I tend to the exhaust. How many hours did Tom and I spend just like this? There's something about it that grounds me and shakes away the anxious itch that's been rioting through me since leaving Tess this morning.

"So," he says, passing over the cover for inspection. "Must be cool to be in a band." He tries to sound like he couldn't care less.

Turning the cover in my hands, I give him a nod. "It is."

"When did you learn to play?" He stays focused on his scruffy boot pawing at the garage floor.

"When I was about your age."

His head whips up, his eyes wide. "Really?"

"True story."

"I could learn then. I mean, it's not too late?"

With a grin, I hand him back the cover. "You did a really good job on this." Beck's eyes widen at the compliment. Something tells me he hasn't heard too many lately. "And it's never too late, Beck."

♪ ♩ ♪ ♩

"YOU BETTER WATCH HIM," I mumble to Tom as we work in the kitchen, finishing off a pot of his famous stew to feed to the boys. I cast a quick look at Beck, and Tom chuckles, giving me a nudge in the shoulder.

"You think I don't know who I need to keep an eye on?"

With a shake of my head, I start filling up the bowls with mouthwatering stew. The hearty scent brings another round of memories, good ones this time. We had a lot of conversations around his stew and countless hours spent in the garage that bonded us together for life. "I'm sorry. Of course you know."

"Kind of reminds you of someone, hmm?" He grins at me and cuts through a thick slice of crusty bread.

"Just a little."

"Beck's a good kid. If I can keep him away from that one," he adds, lifting his chin to one of the tall, lanky teens currently slouched back in one of the chairs, his boots up on the dining room table, barking orders at some of the other kids. He's wearing a baseball hat backwards over his scruffy brown hair, an old gray T-shirt hanging loosely off his thin frame, and a few tattoos clearly done by someone who didn't know what the hell they were doing dotted along his forearm. I've seen dozens like him over the years.

"Name's Zach. Been here for a couple of months now. Trying his hand at dealing crystal meth these days." Tom shakes his head, wiping his hands on a dish towel hung over his shoulder. "It's not getting any easier. Some of the shit these kids are into would make even your head spin." I see that familiar stern look taking over Tom's face before he raises his voice so they can hear us in the dining room. "Zach. Feet down. Time to set the table."

Zach meets Tom's hard gaze with one of his own before slowly dropping one foot then the other to the floor, and rising to give him a mock salute. "Dish duty for you later, it is," Tom announces before focusing back on the bread.

"Do you need more staff around here? I'd be happy to get you some more help—"

"Stop right there," he interrupts as only Tom can. "You donate more than you keep for yourself already, I'm sure, Matt. Throwing more people at it isn't going to work; you know that. They have to want to change or they won't. Simple as that."

"I seem to remember some tough love helping out."

"That, I've got loads of. Getting them to listen is the problem."

"So, you come to see the animals in the zoo." This from Zach who has wandered in to collect the plates for the table. Seems even he can follow instructions.

"Not at all. Just here to help," I fire back at him.

"Right. Camera crew on the way or something? Is this your charity case for the month? Good photo op and all that." I meet Zach's bloodshot eyes, and I can see the crushing pain. You'd have to be blind not to.

"That's enough," Tom says. That tone still has the ability to grab my attention, and judging from Zach's shoulders that have dropped a few inches as a result, he feels it, too.

"No camera crew. Just me."

Zach lets out a rough laugh. "Right. Well, it's not every day we get a real bona fide celebrity in here. We should be honored by your presence, really."

"I said that's enough. You'll treat him with the respect you give me and everyone else who works in this house. Are we clear?"

At Tom's words, Zach wisely shuts his mouth, his lips mashing into a grim line, before lowering his eyes to the floor, muttering, "Crystal."

"Thank you," Tom adds, earning him a nod from Zach. He strides quickly back to the dining room, setting the table as instructed.

"Maybe coming here wasn't such a great idea."

"Are you kidding me?" Tom grabs the basket of bread before turning for the dining room. "It's the best idea you've had in a long time."

LATER, AFTER THE BOYS ARE stuffed from dinner and working away on the Harley, a booming crash echoes from the garage.

Panicked shouting follows quickly and has Tom and me moving in the direction of the sound. "Call the cops!" I think it's Aaron Crawford's voice I hear, bellowing above the clang of tools hitting the garage floor. Aaron is another member of Tom's staff, and even though he's the size of a redwood, he's starting to lose the battle of separating Beck and Zach.

The Harley lies on its side on the floor of the garage as Zach screams his idiotic teenage head off, barely held back by a couple of scrawny members of his gang, brandishing a tire iron over his head. "I'll fucking kill you, asshole!"

"I'd like to see you try," Beck spits back, blood gushing from his nose as Aaron shoves his arm between them, coaxing Beck away from Zach.

"Enough!" My voice rises as I push away the two teens holding Zach, while Tom helps Aaron with Beck. It doesn't take much to yank Zach's arm behind his back, forcing him quickly to the floor of the garage. The tire iron falls from his grasp, landing with an almighty clank.

Zach growls, trying to look over his shoulder, his muscles coiled in tension. I push my knee against the middle of his back, ensuring he won't be going anywhere. "Did you hear me? Enough."

Hope can be dangerous. It was Zach's suggestion that they keep working on the Harley after dinner, and I thought it was a positive sign. But, just when I think Zach might be making progress, chaos explodes.

"Get the fuck off me," Zach hisses, trying unsuccessfully to squirm away. I know getting taken down in front of the other kids has got to be killing Zach. Talk about a blow to his inflated ego.

"What's one of the main rules here?" I ask as Zach lets out a staggered breath beneath my steady hold.

Nothing from any of the teens. The kids in Zach's gang just

stare, eyes wide, mouths open like they can't quite believe their fearless leader has been rendered useless.

"No fighting," I grind out.

"You calling the cops?" Zach hollers, a slight panic in his voice as he flails on the garage floor. "You son of a bitch. You better watch your fucking back."

I lift my gaze to Aaron as he loosens his grip on Beck. Kid looks like he's gone a few rounds with a prizefighter. Swollen lips, left eye blackening as we speak. "You know the rules. Cops get called after your third fight," Tom says.

"Fuck," Zach mutters.

"You want to press charges?" Aaron asks Beck as he sits him in a chair. "Your nose is probably broken."

Beck lifts his shirt up to his face, trying to stop the bleeding. He glances warily in Zach's direction as I haul him up from the floor. "No. Let's just say you owe me now." Beck and Zach glare at each other, a silent exchange we can all hear clearly. This isn't done between them. Not even remotely.

"DO YOU KNOW WHAT SET it off?" Tom asks as Aaron and I sit in his office. An afternoon dealing with the cops and the fallout from the fight has us all keyed up. With Beck deciding not to press charges, they both got off with a warning, but not after getting an earful from the officers on duty.

An uneasy quiet has now settled over the home. I can't help but feel like it's the calm before the next shit storm. Judging by the death glares I've been getting from Zach, I think he'll be glad to see me leave.

Aaron shakes his head. "Not a clue. One minute they were

fine, changing the tire. I turn my back for five seconds, and Zach is practically jumping the bike to try to get Beck."

"You think he was on anything?"

"You know I'd never let anyone in the garage who was high," Aaron answers defensively. "And you saw him at dinner. He wasn't on anything."

Tom holds his hands up. "I know, I know. I'm sorry. I had to ask. You know what Zach's been doing."

"You think it's time to start thinking about—"

Tom leans forward in his chair. "Don't finish that sentence, Aaron. I don't give up on these kids, and neither do you. That's what every single person has done to Zach and a million kids like him. Give up. We're not doing that. Not now. Not ever."

My heart tightens at the conviction of Tom's words. He's the reason I'm still here. The reason hundreds of other kids are, too. I'm not sure he even realizes the kind of effect his has on a kid who has lost everything.

"I know that. It's just frustrating. Zach's a smart kid. And he's good with the bike, when he's not being a pain in the ass," Aaron admits. He leans back in the chair, raking his hands through his hair in annoyance.

"Then we keep working with him until he realizes that. No matter how long it takes."

AN HOUR OF PLAYING THE bass has done nothing for my mood. I've been all over the map today. The time at the group home took me back to places I didn't necessarily want to go. No matter how hard I try to bury that part of my life, it has a way of sneaking back in. Seeing those kids today, knowing their struggles are similar to what mine were or worse, tears my heart out.

And there, throughout the day, running a constant circuit through my brain is Tess. She's the one I want to talk to, and I'm annoyed that she's in San Diego while the clock ticks away.

Abandoning the guitar, I stare at the phone taunting me from the coffee table. I'm ready to cave, but it turns out I don't have to. The chime of a new text coming in brings an immediate smile to my face.

Cardinal: I got off in the shower thinking of you this morning. How was your day?

Tessa

I WAIT NERVOUSLY FOR HIS reply, curling my legs up under me in the armchair. The quiet of my hotel room is a welcome respite after a day of constant motion.

Abigail's face was a picture of shock and excitement this morning when Kennedy greeted us on the tarmac. April and I had driven her to the airport under the guise of all three of us coming to San Diego. She abandoned her responsibility surprisingly fast, however, when Kennedy presented her with a not-to-be-refused offer of four days on a mystery island.

After seeing her off, April and I had just enough time to make our own flight. San Diego always seems even more sprawling than LA to me. It took forever to get to our first meeting, and then it was nonstop from there. It all went well, and I'm elated that my first efforts as giving director have been so successful. We've secured dream fulfillments for three deserving children, and the knowledge I'm able to help is both humbling and rewarding. The best part will be when we see the hope and excitement in those little faces when they receive their hearts' desires, just like we saw in Parker's face. It's the reason I love working for What's Your Dream.

April was ecstatic when we got back to the hotel. We went over her ideas for promotion and toasted our good deeds at the bar downstairs until the awkward attentions of a group of businessmen drove us to our rooms. Before Matt burst into my life, I might have considered one of their invitations for a cozy drink, but now . . . I could barely muster up a polite smile as we fled, which is vaguely troubling. What's more troubling is that even with all the activity today, he hasn't been far from my thoughts. The sight of him making himself at home in my kitchen, his beautifully decorated skin and muscular arms on full display, has haunted me all day. He moved with an unconscious grace that rendered me speechless. Then he denied me! I mean, what am I supposed to think? No one turns down shower sex, especially in such an incredibly sweet and considerate way. He comes over in the dead of night—breaking into the building, mind you—just so he can dazzle me with his pancake-making skills and gallantry the next morning?

Nibbling on my thumbnail, I stare at my phone, willing him to answer me. I have a few more things to review tonight, but I couldn't help myself—I had to text him. Actually, I wanted to hear his voice, but I chickened out. I thought I had Matt all figured out. I succumbed to his hotness after the concert, we had some fun, and that was supposed to be that. I was going to recover my dignity and move on. Instead, he wriggled under my defenses with caring words and gestures that I never saw coming. Oh, and let's not forget the reminder of just how hot sex with him can be.

My phone chimes and I grab it eagerly, only to laugh when I see a photo of a white sand beach with the message, *"Thank you, girls! I'm having a mojito in your honor."* I smile fondly, remembering

Abby's flustered eagerness this morning. She and Kennedy are clearly nuts about each other. It's wonderful to see. If anyone deserves the love of a good man, it's Abby. And the sheer adoration in Kennedy's eyes when he looks at her . . . I swoon a little on my boss's behalf. It's a wonder she doesn't turn into a pile of goo every time they're together.

It shocks me when I realize that I've seen a glimmer of the same thing in the eyes of a certain bassist. A frisson of fear and excitement runs through me. I feel like I'm on the upward slope of a roller coaster, just before cresting the apex and plunging to . . .

Ding! I jerk at the sound of my phone chiming.

Matt: Nothing about my day could compete with that image. Except maybe seeing you in my arms this morning.

I blink at the phone in surprise and then groan, feeling another chink in my armor open. Where does he come up with swoon-worthy stuff like that?

I'll take your word for it.

Matt: You should. When do you get back? Flight #?

I smirk, and quickly send my travel details, along with a question about what he has planned.

Matt: Not sure yet, but I only have one night left to spend with you before I have to leave. I don't want to waste it.

Every muscle in my body clenches with anticipation.

Sounds promising.

Matt: Well, I aim to please.

Pleasing me didn't seem like a problem for him, at least in one respect. Closing my eyes, I shiver as I recall the intensity of his blue-eyed gaze as he peeled my clothes off in his loft. It felt like he could see right through me, which was as disconcerting as it was intriguing.

We'll see. Don't get too cocky, mister.

Matt: I think I like that. You should call me Mr. Logan all the time.

I snort out a laugh as my fingers fly over my phone.

Don't tell me you're one of those kinky bastards that like riding crops, handcuffs, and making women call you 'Sir.'

I can't help but squirm at the thought of Matt and me in his bed, naked, with a couple of silk scarves. There's a long enough pause in his reply to make me nervous I've gone too far.

Matt: Jesus, woman. You should come with a warning label. I just sprayed beer all over my couch.

I burst out laughing at the thought of him having to mop up; I also can't believe he actually admitted it.

You'll live, I'm sure.

Matt: I will, but my Rickenbacker might not. It's soaked.

Okay, now I feel a little guilty.

Matt: You should. It's one of my favorites. I know how you can make it up to me, though.

Smirking, I let my fingers fly, not willing to let him win this round.

I said I only felt a little guilty . . . and it's passed now. Missed your chance.

Matt: I hope not.

My breath catches, and I stare at the phone that suddenly weighs heavy in my hand. As unbelievable as it seems, Matt has been clear about what he wants, and I know his words mean more than our playful banter. What the hell am I thinking? I'm finally considering a serious relationship for the first time, and I choose a world-famous manwhore?

Shaking my head at myself, I quickly type out a response.

Time will tell. I need to finish up a few things here before I hit the sack. I'll call you when I'm back or something. Okay?

Matt: Or something. See you tomorrow. Oh, and Tess?

Yes?

Matt: I'll never turn down a shower with you again.

"WHAT IS GOING ON WITH you today?" April asks in exasperation as I almost topple a little old man with my carry-on. I apologize profusely, but he mutters something in German and walks away scowling. I can't blame him. He's the second person I've accidently smacked with my bag.

"Just a little distracted, I guess." I shrug, trying to ignore her piercing gaze.

"Distracted. Right," she scoffs, and cocks her head at me. "Your distraction doesn't have anything to do with a certain tattooed musician, does it?"

I gape at her. "What?" I answer dumbly, and she smirks triumphantly.

"Please. I have eyes, you know. The way you two were going at each other during Parker's concert prep, it was only a matter of time."

"I don't know what you're talking about." I hitch my bag strap higher on my shoulder and try to look unconcerned, but she laughs softly.

"I also have a snitch that tells me you had an office visitor a couple days ago."

I narrow my eyes. "Jeff." That weasel. There'll be no coffee dates for him now.

"Among others." She smiles fondly at me as we weave our way through the throng. "Tessa, don't worry about it. If it can work for Abby, why wouldn't it work for you?"

"It's not like that," I huff. "We're just having some fun."

She nods thoughtfully. "And that's okay. It's equally okay if it turns out to be more."

"It's complicated."

"No doubt." She gently bumps her shoulder to mine. "Don't sweat it. Enjoy it and see what happens. You know that Abby won't mind; hell, she'll be ecstatic for you. You two can commiserate when Redfall hits the tour again."

My stomach flutters nervously at the reminder. He'll be gone for three weeks. Plenty of time for him to sow a few oats, plenty of women willing to help him.

My phone rings, and April tells me to go ahead while she retrieves the bag she'd checked from the baggage carousel. Stepping into an out-of-the-way corner, I answer.

"Mom?"

"Tessa! Sweetie, are you sure you can't join us at your brother's on Christmas? Your dad said he'd get your ticket for you."

I stifle a groan. My brother's wife can't travel until after the birth of my newest nephew, so my parents and Rachel are flying to Seattle. They aren't leaving until Christmas morning so we can have dinner together Christmas Eve. "I can afford my own ticket, Mom. But I can't afford to take that much time off right now. You know I just got that promotion, and there's a ton of stuff that's just been sitting since Nadia left."

"You work too hard," she grumbles, but continues before I can say anything. "All right. We'll see you this Sunday for lunch, yes?"

"Yes, Momma," I reply patiently. "I'll be there." Which means I won't need to eat for three days afterward; for my mom, there's no "off" switch in the amount of food she prepares for holidays or when guests are over. If he didn't stick to his military workouts, my dad would look like a small mountain.

"Wonderful! Well, Ms. Fonk is coming over for a fitting, so I have to get ready. And Tessa, as much as I wish you could join us in Seattle, I *am* proud of you, dear," she states, and I can almost hear her smile.

"Thanks, Momma." April is returning with her bag in hand, so I say my goodbyes to my mother and quickly tuck my phone away. We make our way to the taxi lane, and my mouth drops open. Parked at the end of the lane is the shiny black Camaro with Matt standing tall next to it. You could knock me over with a feather.

April laughs next to me. "Go on," she says, nudging me to life. "It's too late to get much more done at the office today anyway. I'll see you tomorrow."

In a daze, I walk down to where he's waiting, a smug smirk spread across his face. "I thought I'd save you from the fucking taxi surcharges and give you a lift." He reaches out and takes my bag from me, snapping me out of my haze. He's right—the exorbitant cab tax surcharges in our fair city are outrageous.

"Well, since you've offered." I give him a mocking curtsy and he shifts, as if to hug me, but casts a wary gaze at the people swirling around, some of whom are beginning to gawk. Instead, he helps me in the car, and within minutes we're speeding toward town.

"Do you have to go back to work?" he asks, shooting me an indecipherable look. I shake my head.

"Nope. I'm free for the night."

"Good." He hums in satisfaction and takes my hand, twining our fingers together. It's an intimate gesture that sends shock waves through me.

"I thought we'd get some drinks and a little dinner and go back to my place." He shoots me a playful look. "*I* don't have a nosy roommate."

Uh-oh. "What did Jada say to you? She only told me she'd met you and to warn her next time when a shirtless man was likely to be making breakfast." She'd also said that he was fuck-hot, but I don't see a reason to inflate his ego any further.

"Not much." He changes lanes and glances over at me. "She seems a little protective."

"Her bark is worse than her bite." I squeeze his hand, but he doesn't look convinced.

"Hmmm. So, what are you in the mood for? Mexican again? Italian?"

A weird feeling hits me; it feels surreal to be sitting here with him, having a normal conversation about normal things like a normal couple. I'm not even sure we're a couple yet. Is this what's ahead? Picking each other up from the airport, going home for dinner, and housework, and pets, and mortgages, and taking out the trash?

"I don't understand what you're doing with me," I blurt and am instantly irritated with myself. I hate sounding needy, because I'm not. But I'm honestly confused. Based on what I overheard Cameron and Sean talking about during the concert, it sounds like Matt loves life on the road. He's had women all over the world—twice—and I know how voracious his appetite is from personal experience. Why would he want to settle for just one? Because if he was with me, it would be *only* me—or he'd find himself with one of his guitars permanently implanted in a piece of his anatomy designed for exits only.

"Well, let me see." He rubs his chin with mock seriousness. "Besides being one of the most gorgeous women I've ever seen, you're smart, loyal, and kind. I saw how you worked with those kids who attended Parker's concert; you care, Tess. That kind of compassion can't be faked. You love your job and you're committed to helping them. Why wouldn't I want to be with you?"

"Yes, yes, I'm awesome," I snap with a dismissive wave of my hand, barely able to refrain from rolling my eyes. "I'm serious."

"So am I." He frowns and pins me with a steely gaze. "Why is it so hard to believe that I'd want you? Yes, I'm no angel. I've never claimed to be one. But is it that hard to believe that I want something real?"

Night has already fallen and the city lights twinkle as Matt navigates the city streets toward the embarcadero. We come to a stop at a red light, and I gasp when he slips a hand around my head and pulls me in for a fierce kiss that leaves me panting. "And you, Tessa Baker, are the most *real* woman I've ever met."

Real, huh. My heart beats a little faster, recognizing the sincerity in his voice, and I feel myself melt a little. I look at him thoughtfully, wondering just how much reality he can handle. "When do you get back from the tour?"

He blinks at my sudden switch of topic. "Um, I'll have to check. Why?"

"How would you like to have dinner with me and my family on Christmas Eve?"

chapter seven

matt

MY GRIP TIGHTENS AROUND THE steering wheel at the words Christmas and family. Two things I'm not all that experienced with. I push the Camaro harder, hearing the engine purr in response, and feeling the tension in my jaw ratchet up a notch. "Christmas Eve, hmm?"

"Yes!" I steal a quick glance at her and it ties me up in knots as usual. Seeing her in the crowd outside the airport almost made me speechless. The sight of her long black hair a little messed from the flight, and her plump lips parted in disbelief when she saw me, will stay with me for a long time. The knowledge that I'm leaving in what could be the worst-timed concert tour in history only seems to add to my amped-up state. The things I want to do to and with Tess can't begin to be covered in a twenty-four-hour period.

"It's a tradition! We all have dinner, and my mom makes

enough to feed a small army, which I guess we kind of are in a way. Dad makes this candy cane hot chocolate that is amazing, although now it's not kid friendly. I think he puts more booze in it than anything." I smile at her rambling.

"Sounds pretty cozy."

Leaning back against the seat, she lets out a happy sigh. "It is. What's your favorite Christmas tradition?"

An unwelcome pain in my chest joins my immediate frown, an awkward silence greeting her question. Slipping into the passing lane, I weave through the traffic like a man possessed. She would have to ask about the one thing I hate most to talk about. I'm reminded again of my fucked-up past and just how different Tess and I are. "I guess it would be the first year I was with Tom. Everything before that is not worth talking about." My voice sounds rough, clipped, and a little angry.

"I'm so sorry, I didn't mean to pry."

"You asked, Tess. So I'll tell you. No secrets, right?" My eyes cut to hers, and I try to rein in the mounting anger. None of this is her fault. She's just curious. And isn't this what people do who are trying to get to know each other? "It wasn't something my mother celebrated."

"She wasn't religious?" She's quiet, almost as if she's afraid to speak.

"She wasn't there, is more like it."

"Oh, Matt." I can feel her gaze on me, fueling the tension firing through me.

"I was the kid with the clothes from last year that didn't fit him. The hand-me-downs from all the rich kids' parents who were doing their good deed with their donations to the secondhand store. The same ones who would cross the street to avoid a homeless person." I know I should stop. I don't share this kind of information.

Opening up like this, releasing the demons of the past, has a way of binding people together, and until now, that's the last thing I've wanted. Turns out, everything I thought I wanted doesn't mean shit when it comes to Tess. It's like the floodgates have opened, and I can't do a thing to shut them.

"Tom made a big deal about that first Christmas. Went out to get a tree and everything. He took me down to one of the tree lots and probably pulled out every single one they had to show me. I thought he was crazy. I kept telling him it wasn't a big deal, because for me it wasn't." She takes a sharp breath in, like she can't believe what I'm saying. "Anyway, we got pretty much the biggest tree they had and strapped it to the top of his Mustang. We could barely see out the windshield on the drive home." I shake my head and smile at the memory, taking the next exit off the highway.

"He had all these mismatched ornaments. He handled them like they belonged in a museum. Anyway, we decorated the tree, and he bought me a motorcycle ornament, had me hang it near the top. Even put out cookies and milk for Santa on Christmas Eve. I told him he'd lost his mind."

She touches my arm lightly as I idle at the light. It's a gentle reminder of everything that's good and right. It's Tess telling me it's okay, that she understands even if there's no way she can. My throat feels thick, and thank fuck the light changes, snapping me back into action.

I rev the engine in the Camaro, pulling away from the rest of the traffic, racing away from the past. "I didn't really have money to buy Tom anything, but I was getting pretty good with the guitar by then, and Fletcher, one of Tom's friends who was teaching me how to play, set up a recording session. I made him a CD of me playing his favorite songs."

"That's so sweet."

Seeing our destination ahead, I pull into the nearly empty lot. Shoving the car into park, I keep both hands on the steering wheel, needing something to ground me. "Christmas morning, I had a stocking by the tree with my name on it. It didn't have a lot in it; Tom's job at the group home didn't pay much, but it was the first stocking I ever had. That he would do something like that for me, it blew me away. No one had done anything like that for me before. Not even my own mother."

"Matt—"

I squeeze the steering wheel harder. "Don't, okay? I'm telling you because families and holidays aren't things I'm really comfortable with. I don't want to ruin your holiday because I'm too stuck in my head to appreciate it. I'm just trying to tell you like it is. No sugarcoating."

"What about recently? You spend time with Tom? With the band?" she asks gently.

I frown, finally turning to meet her eyes. The lot lights cast a warm glow over her face, highlighting the curve of her cheek. She's so fucking beautiful, she doesn't even seem real right now.

"Yeah," I start after a beat. "I mean, I'm with the guys twenty-four seven when we're touring, and I see Tom when I can."

"Then I think you're a lot better with families than you give yourself credit for." I start to protest, but her fingers press over my lips. "They're your family. The band and Tom."

I take hold of her wrist, lifting her hand away from my mouth to lace my fingers with hers. "It's where I know I can be myself."

"I'd never ask you to be anything else."

"I CAN'T BELIEVE YOU BROUGHT me here," Tess says in awe as

we stand inside the glass dome of the rain forest exhibit. The humid air is thick with colorful butterflies, the sweet intoxicating scents of the flowers heightened as we slowly move through the exhibit.

It's almost deserted, with the exception of a couple of families with small children shouting in excitement up ahead. Tess called the place magical. I can't disagree, but I think that has more to do with her than anything else.

"I thought you were taking me to dinner." She nudges me in the shoulder as a yellow butterfly lands on her arm.

"I am. Thought maybe you'd like to stop here first." I steer her around another curve, stopping to watch a few blue butterflies line the flowering plants along the waterfall.

"I don't like it. I love it." She leans forward against the railing, and I can't resist setting my hands on either side of her, lowering to press a kiss against her neck. She leans against me, her back settling against my chest.

It's peaceful. In stark contrast to the whirlwind tour I'm about to go on. For once, the lure of the stage isn't holding the appeal it usually does. It's terrifying that my happiness could be tied to something other than being in the band. It's all I've known for so long.

"Good. I'm glad."

She glances up at me and whispers, "You might just get lucky later."

"That's a bonus."

She giggles. The sound inches its way into my heart as a butterfly lands on her shoulder, close to where I know her one and only tattoo is inked into her skin. "Thank you for bringing me here."

Her eyes dart to my mouth, and I can feel the pull, the intense heat between us. "You're welcome."

"You want to get out of here?" she asks, all breathy.

"In a few minutes." I tighten my arms around her, glancing

up to the waterfall. "Let's just stay here a while." Here, where it's perfect and nothing can change that.

"IS THIS WHAT ALL OF your dates are like?" Tess asks as I punch the code into the keypad at the gate. You can learn a lot about someone in a short drive. The closer we got to my loft, the more tension I could feel coming off Tess. She's fidgety, nervous, probably questioning what the hell she's doing.

"I don't typically date."

She laughs. "Sure you don't." The gate grinds away as it opens, and I turn to face her. I thought maybe we were past this, but apparently not. "Right, because you just fuck them and leave them."

"Can't change my past. That doesn't mean I don't want something different now."

She folds her arms across her chest, setting her shoulders, and challenging me once more. "And what is it exactly that you want now?"

I meet her judgmental gaze. I don't want there to be any doubt—no worry, and no question about what I want. I promised her I'd always be honest with her. No games. No hidden agendas, and sure as hell no regrets. "You. All of you."

THE HONESTY RINGING IN HIS voice echoes in his eyes, and it shakes me to my core. I take a shaky breath as the car glides forward. The clang of the gate closing behind us feels final.

My heart is racing, and I startle when my door opens and he reaches down to take my hand. I hadn't realized he'd gotten out of the car.

"I haven't had that before," I admit, standing before him in the garage.

He looks skeptical, and places his hands on my waist. "Someone who wants all of you? I find that hard to believe."

"It's true," I whisper, fiddling nervously with the collar of his shirt. "I'm sorry; I don't mean to be so difficult. I just panicked." He cocks an eyebrow in disbelief, and I rush to try to explain, "It's not that there hasn't been anyone who wanted more. There have been plenty of guys—"

He gently presses his lips to mine, cutting me off, and just like that—bam! Desire ignites, incinerating all my hesitations. Grabbing fistfuls of his shirt, I pull him closer, and he groans into my mouth. "Fuck, Tess," he mutters, and before I can react, he bends and slings me over his shoulder, knocking the breath out of me.

His large hands caress my thighs and ass as he jogs up the stairs. It's turning me on, despite the fact I'm afraid I'm going to bounce off his shoulder. I cling to his belt loops with one hand and struggle to untuck his shirt with the other, desperate to touch bare skin. He doesn't pause when we reach his loft; he continues to his bedroom that hangs over a corner of the living area bordered by a low wall. I see a dresser in the moonlight streaming through the window, and then I'm falling and bouncing as I land in the middle of a giant bed.

He's on me in an instant. We're a tangle of lips and limbs as we tug at each other's clothing. I arch my back, pushing my bare breasts into his eager hands, and purr when he buries his face between them. "So fucking perfect," his muffled voice reaches my ears, and I giggle.

"Shirt *off*." I tug at his collar. Not bothering to unbutton it, I reach down to pull it up over his shoulders, pleased when he ducks his head to make it easier. It suddenly hits me that this is the first time I've seen him shirtless since that drunken night after the concert, and a wave of emotion hits me.

He's so damn *beautiful*. I float my fingertips over the lines of ink on his chest that swirl into a phoenix on his neck. He's a masterpiece. Although I've only scratched the surface, I've seen he's even more beautiful inside. Even if he doesn't recognize it himself.

He doesn't give me time to appreciate it. After flicking the button at my waistband, he tugs my pants off and tosses them on the floor with his own. The delicate lace of my panties doesn't stand a chance—again. "What is it with you and my underwear?" I grumble as he settles himself between my knees.

"Stop wearing them, then." He chuckles and then he dives between my thighs.

"Holy shit!" I suck in a startled breath and convulsively clutch at his head as he devours me like his last meal. Most guys I've been with treat it like a chore, something to check off the list before they can move on to the main attraction. But not Matt. My hips automatically buck against him, pleasure surging through me at the feel of his tongue piercing. He's incredibly good at this. Unwanted thoughts of how much practice he's had over the years flit through my mind like annoying flies, and I bat them away. I refuse to go down that road now.

Sounds drifting up to us from the traffic below provide a backdrop for the moans and occasional curse word echoing in the room. Within minutes, I'm teetering on the edge. It only takes a well-timed swipe of his thumb and grunted encouragement to make me see stars.

A siren sounds in the distance, coming steadily closer until it stops somewhere nearby. But, instead of breaking the mood, it seems to spur Matt on, as if he's afraid someone is coming to stop us. He rises up, a desperate possessiveness in his eyes, as he swiftly positions himself and drives into me with one smooth stroke. "Ah!" The shock of his sudden invasion quickly fades, replaced with an all-encompassing bliss. Just like the last time, it takes me a few thrusts to get used to his sheer size, but then I'm ready for anything. I cling to him like a limpet as he sets a quick pace. Everything fades away—the siren outside the window, the women in his past, and my fear of losing myself. I'm enthralled by this man. He kisses me passionately, never faltering in his rhythm, making my heart race. In this moment, I can't remember ever needing a man like I need Matt. And that realization both terrifies and thrills me beyond belief.

"Can't . . . can't stop," he mumbles against my lips and grabs my knee, bending it to his will. My gasp echoes off the walls—holy hell, I can't breathe—the intensity is mind-blowing.

The tsunami building inside me peaks. Just as I think I'm going to fly apart with the force, he lets out his own guttural cry. Collapsing together, I feel like I'm floating, adrift on a vast ocean, as we gradually come back to ourselves. "Jesus . . . sorry." He heaves himself off me with an embarrassed chuckle. "I hope I didn't crush you."

I snuggle into his side and place a kiss on his shoulder, savoring the salty sweetness of his skin. "Never."

He hums in satisfaction and pulls me even closer. "Good."

"You didn't use a condom." I suppose I should be upset that he didn't ask me, but I can't bring myself to care. Weird. Normally, I'd be panicking and pissed.

"Um, sorry about that." He squirms next to me. "I, uh, I kind of lost my head there for a second. I don't know what happened;

I've never gone bare with anyone. Ever."

"Don't worry. I've got us covered. As long as you're clean."

He relaxes minutely. "I'm clean. I swear."

"Okay, then."

The minutes tick by. I wait for the inevitable awkwardness to set in, but it doesn't. I feel only warmth, calm, and replete, as if I'm supposed to be here. Matt gently traces a tendril of my hair across my collarbone and over the swell of a breast, making me giggle. I can hear his smile in his voice.

"I can't help it. I can't stop touching you." He playfully flicks a nipple, making me yelp. "Besides, I think your tits are my new happy place."

I laugh. "I thought you were happiest on stage."

"That was before I met you."

Tears spring to my eyes at the sincerity in his voice. He's laid it all out and has been nothing but honest with me. If we're going to have a chance, I need to return the favor.

"Matt, I owe you an apology."

"How do you figure?"

"I haven't been completely honest with you." He looks at me sharply, and I close my eyes as I continue, "I've been acting like you are the only one with . . . er, experience. But I haven't been much better."

"Not that I want to hear details, but I doubt your numbers could compete with mine." His voice is laced with regret, and I place a gentle hand on his chest.

"Probably not. Believe me I don't want details either." I wince, mentally blocking out the tales of debauchery I heard Sean and Cameron allude to backstage at the benefit concert. "But I'm trying to explain something. I'm trying to explain me."

He takes a deep breath and covers my hand with his own. The

silence stretches between us as I try to formulate my thoughts. "I've never been serious about anyone before. While my friends in high school and college were dating and falling in love, and later were getting married and having babies, I never did. I had my fun, but I never let it get any further than that. I didn't let anyone in. The longest relationship I've ever had, if you could call them that, was three or four months, tops. Whenever a man starts to want more, to bring families into it, or talks about moving in together, I end it."

The siren is no longer wailing outside the window, and I wonder absently when it stopped. I think the building could've fallen down around us without my noticing. Matt shifts and the rustling of the sheets seems loud.

"Is that . . ." He clears his throat. "Is that because of your sister?"

I nod, although I'm not sure he can see me; the San Francisco fog has obscured the moon, plunging us in darkness. "Yes, but more about Erik, her fiancé. I told you how he disappeared after she died."

"Yeah, but Tess, you were only twelve when all that happened," he argues softly. "You're . . . How old are you, anyway?"

"I'll be twenty-nine in a couple months." I tilt my head at him. "Are you saying that I should know better by now? That the trauma I experienced when I was twelve should be a distant memory by now?" I ask rhetorically, letting the irony of his supposition seep into my voice. Kettle, meet pot. He lets out a quiet "humph," but doesn't respond.

"All I'm saying is that whatever we have between us is as big a deal for me as it is for you. I've never had this before. I've never *wanted* it before. It hasn't been worth it to me. But you . . ." I take a quivering breath. "You *are* worth it. So, if you're willing to try, then so will I."

He slides a hand around my waist and pulls me closer, holding me tight for several minutes. I wonder if he can feel my heart hammering in my chest. "Does that mean you'll stop biting my head off?" he finally asks, his voice sounding a bit rough.

"I'll try to keep a better rein on my inner bitch."

"I don't want you to change, Tessa," he murmurs against my lips. "I just don't want you to doubt me." I lay my head on his shoulder and nod, relishing the feel of his body against mine. There's nothing quite like the feeling of being naked in his arms. "You really haven't introduced a guy to your family before?"

"Never." I laugh lightly. "It will be quite a shock when I show up with you on Christmas Eve."

"Are you sure you want to do that?" He sounds worried, and this time, I silence him with a kiss.

"Of course I'm sure. In fact, the more I think about it, I can't wait to see you with my dad. He's going to love you. Do you want to bring Tom, too?"

He startles. "Oh, um, he's usually busy at the home on Christmas."

"Oh." Disappointment washes over me, but I try not to let it affect my voice. "Well, if he's expecting you . . ."

"No!" he blurts. "I, uh, I want to be with you." He chuckles wickedly. "Besides, since this is the first time you've had a guest, what better way to break the ice than with a tatted-up, scruffy musician with a tongue piercing?"

I rub my thighs together, remembering how that piercing felt on my soft places. Jesus.

He laughs when I suddenly roll him over and straddle his hips. "Right, then. No more talk about parents now."

IT IS ONE OF THE best nights of my life. Pausing only when Matt retrieved my carry-on from the car, we've spent the time wrapped up in each other. We've talked about our lives; he told me a little more about Tom, and I talked about my siblings. I know he's a little intimidated by the size of my family, but he seems to be looking forward to meeting them.

At some point, I wake to feel his hands on my breasts as he grinds against my ass. Gently, he lifts my leg just enough to allow him to claim me again. He moves with great care, but also with a passion that leaves me breathless. "Fuckin' perfection," he whispers hoarsely in my ear, sending a shiver down my spine. "What am I going to do without you for three weeks?"

I'm not sure he expects an answer. And I have the same question. He's leaving at the crack of dawn for the last leg of Redfall's world tour. They have dates in Australia, before playing a few shows in Canada and the US after the holidays. I hate that now we've finally reached a détente, so to speak, we have to separate. Maybe it's a good thing.

My throat closes up and sudden tears prick my eyes. Moving against him more vigorously, I reach behind me to hold him as best I can, for however long I can.

IT'S STILL DARK OUT WHEN an incessant banging wakes me. Groggily raising my head from the pillow, I realize someone is pounding on the steel door below. "Fucking hell, Matty," a deep male voice yells from out on the landing. "Are you in there? Answer your damn phone!"

"Matt," I hiss, pushing urgently at his shoulder. "Get up! Someone's here."

He grumbles unintelligibly and burrows his nose into the crook of my neck. "Wake up!" My frantic whisper is drowned out by a crashing sound against the door below that finally brings Matt bolt upright. He looks around in panic and snatches his phone off the nightstand to look at the time.

"Fuck! I should've been at the airport by now." He scrambles for his jeans on the floor and pulls them on. "Put something on." He snaps me out of my shock. I jump up and dive for my carry-on while he stumbles around, cursing and tripping over things in the dark. He takes the stairs down to the main floor, swearing under his breath. A light snaps on, bathing the loft in a soft glow. The rhythmic banging picks up again, accompanied by a weird howling.

"Shut the fuck up! I'm not the only one on this floor, you know," I hear Matt snarl as he slides the industrial steel door aside. It's surprisingly quiet for the door being so big. After donning some jeans and a hoodie from my case, I peek over the railing to see Sean and Tucker, Redfall's chief security guy, enter.

"Your neighbor should be used to the company you keep by now, Matty," Sean quips, before turning to him with a reproachful look. "You—out of all of us—are always on time. When you didn't show up, we thought you were dead or something."

"Or something," Tucker scoffs, looking accusingly at Sean. "The *or something* is what this one was especially curious about. He wouldn't stay behind."

Sean bats his eyes at Matt innocently, and then he casts a sly look around the loft. "I was merely concerned as to what could've been keeping you . . . Aha!" He grins manically, having caught me peering over the bedroom railing. With a squeak, I drop back down out of sight. "Why, isn't it the lovely Tess," Sean purrs with wicked glee. "Come down and join us, gorgeous!"

"Fuck off," Matt growls. "Just give me a second and we can

go. Make yourself useful and pack my Rickenbacker and the three Gibsons."

"Am I your personal errand boy now?" Sean starts to complain.

"We're out of time. Just do it," Tucker interjects, as I hear Matt stomp back up to the bedroom. When he reaches the top, he grabs my hand and hauls me up from where I've been cowering. He pulls me into the adjoining bathroom, the only area up here where we can have privacy, and shuts the door.

"I'm so sorry, Cardinal." He sighs, pulling me into a tight hug. He buries his face in my messy hair, inhaling deeply. "This isn't how I wanted this to happen."

"It's okay." I rest my forehead on his shoulder. "You'd better get going. Do you need help packing?"

He pulls back and flashes me a crooked smile. "No, but I appreciate the offer. Just stay with me while I fill a bag?"

"Of course." He kisses me gently, and my heart skips a beat. Giving me a squeeze, he reopens the door to the bedroom and flies into action. He's a whir as he grabs shirts, jeans, a shaving kit, and other essentials, and stuffs them into a duffel, all the while muttering to himself. It's kind of fascinating to watch. Since the rest of his home is neat and uncluttered, I wonder if he's usually a fastidious packer as well.

He's finished in mere minutes, and I make sure my carry-on is ready to go as well. But he stops me from picking it up. "Here." He plunks a key into my palm. "Take as long as you need. Go back to sleep, take a shower, whatever. You can lock up when you leave. In fact . . ." He looks at me nervously. "You can use this place while I'm gone, if you want."

My eyes shoot open. "It's closer to your office than your apartment is," he says in a rush, the tips of his ears turning red. "If you have a late meeting or something, it might be more convenient."

I smile gently, knowing that this is huge for him. Hell, it's huge for me, too. "Are you sure?"

"I wouldn't have suggested it if I wasn't." He pulls me in tight, shuffling us away from the edge of the platform and out of sight. "I like the idea of you being here," he adds gruffly.

We jump at the sound of someone slapping a wall downstairs. "Come on, Matty," Sean yells. "Kiss your girl and move your arse!"

"Just wait a fucking minute!" Matt bellows over his shoulder at them. He looks at me sheepishly, as I giggle and loop my arms around his neck. "Pricks. I have to go. Code for the gate is 1984."

I arch an eyebrow.

"You know? The Van Halen album," he murmurs against my lips.

"Go. Have fun." I lean back, holding his gaze. "But not *too* much fun."

He gives my ass a smack before he lets me go. "That goes for you, too, ya know." He laughs at my startled look and gives me one last kiss before he jogs down the stairs. Tucker calls again for him to hurry. I step over to the railing and face the amused looks of Sean and Tucker, and stick my chin out defiantly.

"You boys play nice and stay out of trouble, now," I call mockingly, to which Tucker laughs. "No bar fights or bordellos, you hear?"

"Yes, Mother." Sean gives me a cheeky salute, before Tucker pushes him out the door. The hulking security guard is next, followed by Matt, who turns and gives me one last longing look before shutting and locking the door behind him.

The silence is deafening. I sit down on the edge of the bed, feeling exhausted and alone. It's four in the morning, and I wonder if I should just go in to work.

Fuck it. I set my phone alarm, curl up around his pillow, and drift off, his scent surrounding me.

Work can wait.

chapter eight

matt

"WELL, WELL, WELL. LOOK WHAT the Brit dragged in." Cam smirks at me from his prime location on the private jet. He's already settled in for the marathon flight, legs outstretched on the expensive leather seat in front of him, guitar close by. "Too busy to join your own tour?"

"Our Grasshopper was otherwise occupied, Three," Sean chimes in as I make my way into the jet. I've already had to sit through almost half an hour of endless teasing on the drive to the airport. I don't need more of this shit, especially this early in the morning.

"This have anything to do with a certain dark-haired, feisty beauty with an ass to die for?" Cameron asks.

"Mmm. And those tits, man. She looked good enough to eat this morning," Sean adds. I try not to let their typical banter bother me, but the thought of either of them, of anyone, being even remotely interested in Tess doesn't sit well.

Narrowing my eyes at Sean, I sink down into one of the empty seats after giving him a shove. "She's off limits. You hear me?"

"You've never minded sharing before," Cameron starts, nursing a large mug of coffee. Cam is starting to look better. This latest stint in rehab has been good for him. It's scary to watch someone you've known for so long, someone you consider to be your brother, go off the rails. It seems like the band has been through hell and back over the last couple of years. Sean once said we'd always be a work in progress, but it feels like we're finally through the worst of it.

"Yeah? Well, I mind now." I shrug out of my jacket and try to get settled.

"They seemed pretty cozy there this morning at Matty's place. You should've seen our boy here. All flustered and racing around like a bloody idiot."

"Sorry I missed that. I was too busy being on time and everything," Cam takes another shot at me, and I flip him off. It's not like we've never waited for him before.

"You sure you know what you're doing there?" Sean asks quietly, shoving his red cowboy hat onto my head and tugging the brim over my eyes.

"I don't have a clue."

He laughs, dropping into the seat beside me. "That's my life on a daily basis, my friend. It's also part of the fun, yeah?"

I try to ignore him, and tug my phone from my pocket, switching it on only to have it yanked from my hands by Sean. "Don't." There's a warning in his voice that doesn't get by me.

"Give me back my phone."

"This is for your own good. You don't want to text or call her right now, trust me. Let it simmer. Let her think about you for a while, maybe even miss you a little." He holds his arm high up, waving the phone away from me.

"You mean miss his extra-small dick?" Cam asks through a laugh.

"That, too," Sean answers. "It's all about the buildup, the anticipation."

"Not another one of your laws, Murphy. Not this time." I try to wrestle his arm down, but he twists away and darts into the row in front of me. Damn drummer is a pain in the ass.

"You love me and my laws. When have they ever steered us wrong before?" Sean challenges.

"You want a list?"

He taps on the screen of my phone as Tucker boards the plane and grabs a seat near the door. I'm going to have to change the code on my phone again. "Seems the lovely Tess is not too anxious to text you. Though there is one from a Candee spelled with two Es." He pauses to lift a brow at me and shake his head before continuing. "She's sent you some borderline X-rated texts."

"Damn. I thought I had blocked her." I sink back to the seat, giving up the fight. There's no point really. Once the Brit has something in that thick head of his, there's no stopping him.

"Oh hell! There're photos as well. Candee's into role-playing." He scans my phone with interest before shrugging. "She's going all 'stranger in a trench coat and nothing else' on you. Been there, done that. And these types are never really gone, Matty. You know that. Like an annoying fungus that you can't really get rid of."

"Or an STD," Cam chimes in.

"I've never once had an STD, I'll have you know," Sean announces. "Wrap it. That's the key. Sometimes twice. You're doing that, yeah, Grasshopper? I mean Tessa is brilliant in every way, but you never know."

"You need to shut up now, and I want my phone back," I growl. He continues to hold the phone above his head.

"I'll give you back your phone if you promise me you're being safe."

"I'm being safe," I deadpan.

"I don't believe you. Your eye twitched. Telltale sign of a liar," he rants, pointing his finger at me.

"My eye twitched because you're being an idiot."

"I'm surprised it doesn't twitch all the time," Cam offers.

The sound of the door to the plane being closed by the attendant puts a halt to Sean's ridiculous antics, and he returns to the seat beside me, tossing me the phone. "Big of you. Thanks, and I'm keeping this hat, by the way," I say, relaxing back into the seat.

"It is pretty awesome," he agrees, pounding out a beat on the brim. "I'll allow one text before we take off."

"You'll allow it, hmm?" I shake my head, deleting the text from Candee, whom I only spent a couple of hours with over a year ago at a meet and greet in Philly last year. How she got my number in the first place, I'm not sure. I block her number. Psycho fans are one thing I can live without.

The attendant, a scrawny twentysomething hipster with dark glasses and a man-bun, moves to the front of the plane, clearing his throat to get our attention. He gives us detailed instructions on safety procedures that none of us really bother listening to before he moves to his seat for takeoff. In days gone by, when Brodie was alive and managing us, I'm positive most of our flight attendants were hired from an escort agency. I feel a twinge of guilt about being glad there's not a woman in a barely-there outfit onboard to tempt me.

Brodie was toxic. I know that now. None of us could see just how far gone he was. How he was taking us along with him on a ride that ultimately ended with him taking his own life. Brodie was always there with booze, drugs—which I stayed away from—and of course, women. My weakness.

The thought is a harsh reminder of my past and the sheer number of forgettable women I've been with. This thing with Tess is so new, so different, it's a little unnerving, and I curse the timing of this tour again.

Staring at my phone and our last text exchange, I wonder if Sean is right. There's something to be said about anticipation. Hell, we're driven by it every single time we get ready for a concert. That shot of pure adrenaline just before you take the stage, having to wait until the lights dim and the crowd ignites, is addictive.

There's probably a million things I could text to Tess: how I miss her already, how I'm terrified that I'll screw this up, how I wish for once in my life I wasn't in a band with demands that take me halfway around the world. Instead, I just leave her with this:

I can still taste you on my tongue.

THE SYDNEY AIRPORT IS PURE mayhem. I think Tucker is close to having an aneurism when we get through customs and he sees the crowds. It's more insane with every venue we play. More incessant flashes from the paparazzi, the pulse of the frenzied crowd screaming our names and demanding our attention.

We indulge them, much to Tucker's horror. Our fans are insanely loyal, and it's something I hope we never take for granted. We would be nothing without the fan base. A lot of musicians try to avoid this kind of chaos, but we thrive on it. We sign more autographs and pose for more pictures in a twenty-minute period than we can count before Tucker navigates us to a waiting SUV outside the terminal.

"That's what I'm talking about!" Sean hollers once we're secured and whisked away from the airport.

"I'm going to have to hire more security," Tucker grumbles, shaking his head.

"Get over here, mate." Sean tugs on Tucker's arm as he tries to crowd us all in the back of the SUV to take the traditional picture that will end up on Instagram.

"But Lane's not here," Cam starts as Sean takes a series of photos.

"We'll take another one when Romeo arrives. When's he due to make an appearance, anyway?"

"I'm picking him up in the morning," Tucker replies, shifting back into his seat as we wind our way into the light traffic. Time changes suck, and not in a good way. I'm beyond exhausted, having gotten little to no sleep on the plane. Sleep is never easy for me, and the last thing I need is to have a nightmare when we're thirty thousand feet in the air. It's happened a couple of times before, and the results haven't been pretty, so I try to stay awake as much as I can.

Having posted our arrival in the land down under on Instagram, Sean's now on his cell while I'm trying to resist the temptation of my own.

"Syd! We're in your city!" he hollers into the phone. I can hear annoyed shrieking from Sean's twin sister on the other end of the phone as he tugs it away from his ear with a grimace.

"I'm sorry, Syd. You know how I am with time zones," he says once her ranting dies down. "I didn't even think about what time it would be there. But we're in Sydney! You know I always call when we get here."

As Sean babbles to Sydney, I reach for my own phone, switching it on. It chimes with a number of texts and voice mails that I don't bother with. There's only one I'm interested in, and when I finally see it, it's like I can breathe a bit easier.

Cardinal: *I can still feel you between my legs.*

"THAT WAS BRILLIANT," SEAN ANNOUNCES from behind his drum kit as we take a much-needed break. We're currently in hour three of rehearsals with the Sydney Symphony Orchestra at the historic Opera House, something arranged by Cameron's parents' connections.

With the release of our latest album that features Redfall joining forces with some unlikely musicians, we're starting to be known even more now for pushing the boundaries of our traditional hard rock sound. Playing with the world-class musicians of the Sydney Symphony is going to raise some eyebrows.

We probably would've gotten to play with them regardless of Cameron's family's influence, but I think it happened a lot sooner than it would've otherwise. It's easy sometimes to forget that Cameron comes from a line of billionaires all with their own charities and personal interests. His parents are based in Boston and spend a lot of their time supporting the arts. And while Cam tries to distance himself from their suffocating influence, I know that he's on board with their charitable side.

Today, we're practicing with the symphony and several gifted child prodigies who are here on an exchange from Boston, funded completely by the Chapmans. The kind of money his parents have is staggering, and it would be very easy for Cam to become jaded and develop an elitist attitude. He spent the better part of his life trying to break free from the chains that tie him down, to make a name for himself that isn't connected to the expectations of his bloodline.

Tonight, he's doing just that, playing alongside some of the most gifted musicians I've ever heard in my life, and never missing a step along the way. Cameron grins at me as Kennedy pushes back from the piano and moves to talk to the conductor.

I sling my bass behind my back and flex my fingers. They actually hurt from playing so much, and it feels good. This grueling practice provides a much-needed distraction from my wandering thoughts.

No further texts from Tess has me confused. I'm glad she doesn't feel the need to text me on the regular, but another part of me is annoyed I haven't heard from her. I guess that sums up our relationship pretty well: a constant dichotomy. I never really know what to expect, and that's both exciting and terrifying.

"That was insane. Who would've thought 'Rough Love' could sound like that?" Cam asks almost in awe as he joins me by the refreshment table.

"You almost forget it's a song about fucking a stranger in an alley," I add. He laughs and opens up a sports drink. Kennedy has officially banned all alcohol when we're practicing. It's probably something that should've happened a long time ago. Maybe if it did, we wouldn't have lost Brodie. Maybe a lot of things wouldn't have happened, but I learned a long time ago that you can't change the past as much as you might want to.

The smug smile that Kennedy has been sporting since Tucker picked him up from the airport shows no signs of going away. He saunters over to us and picks up a bottle of water. He looks tanned, relaxed, and at ease with himself. It's something I haven't seen in a very long time. This mini vacation of his was obviously needed.

"That was . . ." His voice trails as he twists the cap off the bottle and takes a long swig. "I don't even know what that was."

"Inspired, mate," Sean suggests, slinging his arm around Kennedy's shoulder.

"That'll work. How was the flight over?" Kennedy asks. We haven't exactly had time to catch up since he got here. Practice started as soon as Kennedy and Tucker got to the Opera House, and Kennedy has played like a man possessed for the last three hours.

"Boring as hell. I hate those long flights," Cam complains. "I still don't really know what day it is."

"Aw." Kennedy nudges Cameron in the shoulder. "I missed you, too."

"Sure you did. I bet you thought about us every day while you were sunning yourself on some private beach and fucking like you may never get a chance to again." Sean helps himself to a drink from the table.

"It was a good few days."

"Fuck. Please do not tell me the next album is going to be all sappy love songs," Sean almost whines.

"There may be a couple on there." Kennedy pops a grape into his mouth and pats Sean on the back before heading to the stage.

Mini break over. Time to get lost in the music again.

Cardinal: Hypothetically speaking: Do you use a specific body shop?
I SQUINT, TRYING TO WAKE the hell up. I have no idea what time it is. Too fucking early would be my guess, but I can't ignore Tess. It's been too long since I heard from her. If Sean ever found out I was sleeping with my phone beside me just in case she tried to get a hold of me, I'd never hear the end of it. I'm sure that breaks more than one of our drummer's infamous Murphy's Laws.

As in for cars or my actual body? Your mind in the gutter, Cardinal?

Cardinal: Ha. Your ego is the size of Australia. For cars, smartass.

Why do you need a body shop? And you think my ego is bad, spend a few minutes with the Brit.

Cardinal: Pawning me off on your bandmates already? And I said it was a hypothetical question. For research purposes only.

Warning bells go off immediately. As far as I know, Tess doesn't own a car. She wouldn't dare touch the Camaro, would she?

Did you drive my car?!?

Cardinal: Oh, look at that! A meeting! Must go.

If that car is scratched . . .

Cardinal: If that car is scratched what, big guy?

Thought you had a meeting.

Cardinal: I'm curious . . .

Curiosity can get you into trouble.

Cardinal: That's what I'm counting on.

You really have a meeting?

Leaning back against the pillows, I stare at the screen in the darkness of the hotel room and wait. She's driving me fucking crazy, but the feeling doesn't appear to be mutual. Another twenty minutes go by and it becomes obvious that she's done with me for now.

Tessa

I DROP MY PHONE ON my desk as if it burns me, my guilt and panic overriding my need to flirt. The one time—*one time*—I've ever borrowed a car without permission and look what happens. I groan, rest my elbows on my desk, and drop my face into my hands.

He's going to kill me. And then dump me. And then kill me again.

It had all started innocently enough. After indulging in Matt's ginormous shower, I all but skipped down to his kitchen, loving every pleasurable ache he'd given me. I was on a Matthew Logan high, and I reveled in it.

After taking a last scan around the loft to make sure I didn't forget anything, I spied the keys to the Camaro sitting on the kitchen table. My fingers twitched and all thoughts of hailing a cab flew out of my head.

The next thing I knew, I was running down the massive staircase to his garage. The glossy black paint, smooth leather seats, and deep throaty engine called to me. He gave me the key to the loft. Surely, he wouldn't mind if I borrowed the Camaro, would he? Okay, maybe he would, but I couldn't help myself.

I grin and look out my office window, remembering the thrill of turning the key the first time. That car is a freaking dream to drive. No wonder it's Matt's pride and joy. And now it's been mutilated because of me.

With another groan, I flop back in my chair and stare at the ceiling, my grin vanishing and my blood beginning to boil again. I'd been in sheer bliss behind the wheel, until I'd realized I was being tailgated by someone on a beat-up dirt bike that looked shockingly out of place amongst the San Francisco traffic. It was impossible to tell gender through the rider's black visor, but something about the way the person sat on the bike made me think it was a guy. It had been so long since I'd driven, he was making me uneasy, especially when he zoomed around me, almost scraping the bumper. The next block I found him behind me again, and I was getting seriously pissed.

By the time I reached my office, he was gone, so I put the jerk out of mind and went on with my day. I pulled into the basement-level parking garage for the first time ever and found a visitor's spot I could use for the day. But I started feeling a little guilty around midday and resolved to return the dream machine to Matt's during my lunch hour. And *that's* when I discovered the long, ugly streak marring the sleek surface from the front wheel to the back. I don't think the word has been invented to describe the sound that erupted from me at that moment. It was somewhere between a shriek, a growl, and a gurgle . . . a shorgle? Whatever. I think I almost gave the security guard a heart attack.

So here I sit, simultaneously wanting to hear Matt's voice and dreading the inevitability of telling him I got his car keyed. The security footage showed that skinny little motorcycle shit cruising the lot before parking and walking suspiciously close to the driver's side of the car, still wearing his damn helmet. I don't know what I did to piss him—or her—off, but the asshole obviously carries a grudge.

Well. There's no use crying about it now. I'll just have to get it repaired before Matt gets back. He's so finicky about his vehicles; he must have a particular body shop that he trusts. But when he replied to my text, I panicked and fell back on my usual snark. I hate that I won't see him for three weeks, but I'll need that time to get the repairs done, so maybe it's a good thing.

My calendar chimes, reminding me that I really *do* have a meeting, so I gather what I need and get to work.

ABBY HAS RETURNED FROM HER getaway with Kennedy and looks tanned, serene, and blissfully happy. It seems that nothing can fluster her this morning. The same can't be said for me, especially when she fixes me with an appraising eye after our staff meeting.

She waits until everyone except April has left, and then pounces.

"So, how is every little thing here?" she asks, a small smile gracing her lips. "I hear you've been expanding your musical tastes lately, Tess."

Crap. I flip my hair over my shoulder and try for nonchalance. "Oh, you know. A little of this, a little of that."

"Hmmm, right. Spill it, Baker." Abby leans forward, looking like the cat that caught the canary. "A little birdie told me you're seeing a certain bass player."

April grins. "What happened after he picked you up at the airport?"

"We went to dinner." I tap my pen against the table. "Look, it's not like I'm keeping it a secret, it's just that it's new. And we don't really know what we're doing. We just want to see where it goes." I bite my lip, knowing that I may have screwed up everything with one rash decision. I wonder what my boss would think if she knew I've added grand theft auto to my resume.

"He looked like he knew exactly what he wanted to do the other night," April observes with thinly veiled amusement.

I squirm in my seat, my thighs rubbing together. "Looks can be deceiving."

Abby finally takes pity on me. "Okay, okay. Believe me; I understand how complicated it can be. Kennedy says Matt's pretty tight-lipped about his past, but also that he's one of his best friends. He seems like a really nice guy, Tess. And the chemistry I saw between you two during Parker's concert is off the charts."

"The chemistry isn't the problem." I grimace. "I know I usually blab all about my private life, probably too much. But this is different. I need to work a few things out in my head, you know?"

"I do know." Abby glances out the window, a secret smile on her face. She turns back to us. "Okay, then. Let me know if you want to get together to watch any of their streaming concerts coming up." I know this is her way of telling me she's available any time I feel the need to talk. Which I appreciate, but I have something else I need to do first.

AFTER ANOTHER ROUND OF MIDDAY meetings, I retreat to the quiet of my office. I've barely had two minutes to myself since I texted Matt. I haven't heard from him since then, a fact I'm trying not to read too much into. I need to get this car thing fixed—now. I slap a stack of dream request folders on my desk, grab my cell phone, and quickly pull up Conner's number. He should have the information I need.

"Conner Baker," he answers, his rich baritone echoing down the line.

"How's the Emerald City this fine afternoon?" I smile. "Is my newest nephew behaving himself?"

My brother chuckles. "Rainy. And yes, he seems to be, although he's making Vi crave sweets. Do you know she ate an entire apple pie last night *by herself*? One minute she's lamenting that she's gonna look like a beach ball after he's born, and the next she's asking for ice cream to go with the pie."

"I'm assuming you don't point that out to her, though." Vivian, my sister-in-law, is usually one of the sweetest women on the planet. But pregnancy hormones can make her turn from a Disney princess to Attila the Hun in a heartbeat. Scary doesn't do her justice.

"Hell no." I can almost hear his shudder through the phone. "I like my balls where they are, thank you."

"I'm sorry I can't be there on Christmas Day," I say wistfully. The baby had just started to kick when I saw them last.

"It's okay. I know how it is with new jobs. It wouldn't be an issue if we could fly down, but Vi doesn't want to be that far from her doctor if Junior decides to come early. You better be available for my freak-out call when she goes into labor, though."

"I promise. But it's not like you haven't done this before, you know," I reply. "Just make sure you have someone ready to catch you this time." When Lacey was born, Conner had made it through the delivery like a champ, and then promptly passed out just when a nurse was going to hand the baby to him. He'd made quite an impression on the hospital staff.

"Very funny. So, to what do I owe the pleasure?"

"What was the name of the shop Dad used when he was restoring the Camaro?"

"Chet's on Elm in Oakland," Conner answers readily. "Chet is the owner. It's still there, although I think Chet only works part-time now. His son is taking over. Why?"

"I have a friend who needs a repair on a classic Chevy. I couldn't remember Chet's name, but I knew he was good."

"One of the best." I can hear papers shuffling in the background. "He costs a pretty penny, but he's worth it."

"Thanks. I've got to go, though. Love you. Kiss Vi and Lacey for me."

"Will do. See ya, sis."

CHET IS JUST AS I remember him from the times Dad used to take me with him when I was a kid. Short, round, and gruff, but with a supreme appreciation of beautiful classic cars. He assures me that the scratch isn't as deep as I feared, and that he can easily have it back in shape before Matt returns. My brother was right, it won't be cheap, but I can trust Chet to treat the car as dearly as Matt would treat it himself.

I swing open the door and toss my keys on the kitchen counter. Since I've spent the last few nights at Matt's, I'm at home tonight in the hope I can spend some time with Jada. However, the silence in the apartment tells me that plan is a bust. A note on the counter confirms it. She's in the middle of a major server upgrade and is stuck with her fellow computer geeks. Ah, well. I guess it'll just be some crap TV and the laundry machine tonight.

I spend the next few hours cleaning clothes and watching C-list celebrities try to dance. But what I'm really doing is stalling. I was shocked that Matt gave me a spare key to his place. I am more shocked at how much I love staying there, being around his things, and sleeping in his giant bed. The effect this man has on me . . . it's disconcerting as much as it's exciting. I've never felt this way about a man before, but I'm not going to fight it anymore. The thought is liberating.

Assuming he'll still speak to me after I tell him about his car.

Looking at the clock, I realize it's time to stop postponing the inevitable. It's around dinnertime tomorrow in Australia, so hopefully I'll reach him. I nervously tap out a text.

I have something to confess.

Minutes pass. I'm about to give up for now and roll over when my phone chimes softly.

Matt: Does this have something to do with your sudden interest in body shops?

In my defense, my judgement was impaired by all the sexing you did to me before you left.

Matt: Cardinal . . .

I take a deep breath and let my fingers fly before I can stop myself.

I borrowed the Camaro. I couldn't help myself. Someone keyed the driver's side while it was parked in my office's garage.

There's nothing from him for a full two minutes, so I keep going, trying not to imagine him punching holes in a wall or something equally ragey.

Not to worry, though. I've already taken it to my dad's trusted body shop. It will be as good as new before you return, I promise. And I'm sorry for being so presumptuous. I never should've borrowed it.

Matt: What body shop? Exactly how much is your little joyride going to cost me?

My eyes shoot open. *That's* what he thinks? Without thinking, I hit the call button.

"Joyride?"

"Tess . . ."

I snap as soon as I hear him rumble my name. "Is that what you think? Look, buddy, I know I shouldn't have borrowed your precious car. And I'm sorry. You probably won't believe me, but I've never done something like that before. However, it wasn't my fault that some little asshole keyed it."

"Tess."

"And making you pay for it never crossed my mind. My parents taught me responsibility, believe it or not, and that mistakes come with consequences. I will be paying for my little 'joyride,' don't you worry, probably in ways I can't imagine."

"You don't have to pay for it," he says quickly, but I barrel on.

"Of course I'll pay for it. I'm responsible."

"You just said it wasn't your fault that someone keyed it."

"I'm the one who took it without permission."

His soft chuckle inflames me, and what little grasp I have on my internal filter evaporates. "I know you probably think I'm one of those desperate groupies that immediately leap on any opportunity to take advantage of rich rock stars, but I'm not. Yes, I fucked up. But it's my responsibility, and I'll pay for it. I'm an independent woman who is perfectly capable of fixing my own problems. I didn't tell you so you would pay for it, you idiot. I could've simply fixed it, returned it to your garage, and you'd never be the wiser. I told you because it was the right thing to do."

"You know, as irritated as I am right now, I kinda want to fuck you into next week."

All my breath leaves me in a whoosh. My indignation vanishes and my heart skips a beat. "You do?"

"You have no idea." His voice is like warm honey that I want to drizzle all over myself. "Tess, I know you wouldn't take advantage of me. I was trying to make a joke. I should know better than to try to be funny via text. It loses something in translation."

"Sorry," I say sheepishly, regretting my outburst. "You accidently hit one of my buttons. I hate it when people, especially men, think I need to be rescued, as if I'm incapable of righting my own wrongs."

"I will never make that mistake." He clicks his tongue. "We seem to do a good job of pushing each other's buttons."

"That we do." I take a deep breath, remembering the longing in his eyes as he held me before he left. "I miss you."

I smile at his soft groan. "Miss you, too. I wish I had more time right now."

"Where are you? Did I interrupt?" I ask, finally registering the background noise on his end. It sounds like he's in a lobby or something.

"Nah. We're done for the day. Sean is dragging us to some extreme restaurant he heard about. They serve stuff like ants and crickets and other shit I'm sure I don't want to imagine. I think Cam will kill him if he can't get a burger or something."

My nose wrinkles. "Sounds fascinating."

"So, you borrowed my car. Have you been staying at my place, too?"

He sounds hopeful, so I admit it. "I'm kinda in love with your shower."

"Oh, yeah?" I can hear the smile in his voice. "Just the shower?" he asks, sounding too casual, so I can't help but mess with him a little.

"And your Cuisinart one-shot. That's pretty cool, too. But I used all your little coffee pods, so I had to come home."

"I'll arrange for a delivery."

"Well, I'd hate for you to think I'm taking advantage of you," I tease. There's a loud crash in the background, and I recognize Sean's booming voice. "Sounds like you need to go."

"Yeah," he agrees, sounding reluctant. "It's probably getting late for you anyway." I can hear more commotion on his end. "Tess?"

"Yes?"

There's a pause, and his voice lowers to a husky rumble that liquefies my insides. "Take advantage."

chapter nine

matt

"WHAT IN THE HELL IS this?" The look on Cam's face? Damn priceless. He reaches for his glass of water, downing it quickly. "Christ, Sean. Are you trying to kill us all?"

"What? I like it." Sean takes a loud, crunchy bite of the mystery stew. "A bit on the nutty side, yeah?"

"That describes you perfectly, moron." Cam tosses a balled-up napkin at him, as Kennedy takes another picture of our unidentified meals on his phone.

"And it's garlic roasted cricket stew with ox heart." The Brit winks at Cam before chewing another bite.

"This is going up on Instagram," Kennedy mutters.

"Food shouldn't make this sound," I add, pushing a congealed bowl of I don't even want to know away from me. "It's all squishy."

"At least they have fortune cookies," Kennedy says, pocketing his phone, and reaching for one from the tray.

"Careful. They might be made from worm larvae or worse." Tucker leans back against the vinyl booth. He's as relaxed as he can be given we're out in public.

We're in the middle of Sydney's Chinatown in a hole-in-the-wall restaurant, indulging Sean on his birthday, a celebration that has lasted the entire week. Not a soul has recognized us, and that's been a welcome change from the sheer insanity that waited for us outside the Opera House at our last performance.

As expected, having the symphony perform with us at the concert has created a buzz. Nicole Hays, our PR manager, is having a hard time keeping up with the additional requests rolling in from other orchestras around the globe. While I'm sure we'll be playing with a symphony again at some point, I also know we won't get into a habit of doing it. That's one of the things we all love about the band. We're always looking to push the boundaries.

"What say we head to the Barfly next?" Sean stretches his arm across the back of the booth, looking like he owns the place. "There's a medieval-themed burlesque show on. Sort of a Cirque du Soleil meets King Arthur."

Kennedy shakes his head. "How do you find this shit out?"

"I have my sources."

Kennedy scowls at Sean. "I'll pass, thanks."

"Aw, did the lovely Abby put the kibosh on your extracurricular activities?" Sean nudges him in the shoulder.

"No. I can do whatever the hell I want." Kennedy tries to push Sean away.

"Mhmm. Sure you can." Nothing like stirring the pot, and Sean does it better than anyone.

"This wouldn't by any chance be a nude show, would it?" Kennedy asks, his interest now piqued.

"It's the Barfly, genius," Cameron chimes in. "What do you think?"

"Come on now. It's not a bloody brothel. It's a critically acclaimed show. All artistic and everything. You may get inspired to write a new song."

Kennedy scowls. "By medieval acrobats? What, something like 'I'm not your knight in shining in armor, but I'll slay your dragons anyway'?"

Cameron laughs, motioning to the waitress for our check.

"See?" Sean grins. "You're already inspired." Then he narrows his eyes at Kennedy in warning. "I put up with all of your shit every damn day." He slaps his palm on the table, causing the plates to rattle. "It's my birthday and we're going, so suck it up."

"HOLY SHIT, HE WASN'T KIDDING," Cameron mumbles as we're escorted into the darkened bar area by a tall, pencil-thin blonde decked out in a sequined armor plate who calls herself Lady Inverness. Trumpets herald our arrival.

Lady Inverness motions to a table near the crescent-shaped stage where two women wearing next to nothing are suspended and spinning on wisps of sheer fabric that hang from the ceiling. Kind of reminds me of the footage I've seen of Pink's last concert in a naughtier sort of way.

Sean plants himself in a chair that looks like a throne at the head of the table. "Did you know about this?" Kennedy asks Tucker, who folds his arms across his chest.

"Not much goes on with you guys that I don't know about."

"What I wouldn't give to know some of your secrets." Cameron slaps Tucker on the shoulder and sinks down into a chair near Sean.

A round of drinks arrives by a waitress whose outfit resembles Maid Marion if she were a porn star. She seems a little starstruck by the group of us, giggling away at everything Sean and Cameron say. With a shaky hand, she lowers a different glass with two straws in front of Kennedy. He leans back from the table as if it's about to burst into flames, glancing at Tucker with concern.

Sometimes, it's easy to forget that this will always be a fight for Kennedy. Going to bars and watching everyone drink can't be easy, especially when it was our norm for so many years. "It's okay, mate. I got you and Three virgins," Sean announces, and Kennedy visibly relaxes. "You can thank me later." Sean raises his goblet, and Cam chimes in with a toast.

"To the annoying Brit. You don't turn thirty-seven every day, but apparently this week is an exception. May the next thirty-seven be even half as interesting as the first."

"GRASSHOPPER? HELLLOOO?" SEAN TUGS THE chair out from under my outstretched legs, bringing me back to reality. We're on the stage, taking a break from sound checks, and my focus has been all over the place. In addition to missing Tess, Tom mentioned yesterday that he had to get locks installed on his office at the group home because someone had rifled through some of the staff and volunteer files. He doesn't know who did it, but I'd be lying if Zach wasn't top of mind.

"Sorry, what?" I give my head a shake and find the rest of the band looking at me like I've gone crazy. It feels like I have in a way. I'm lucky if I've had a couple of hours sleep over the past few days, aided by the nightmares that seem to be back with a vengeance.

I've also picked the worst time in the world to try to quit smoking. I absently rub the patch on my arm. Damn thing.

"What the hell is wrong with you?" Sean twirls his drumsticks in front of my face.

"It's the time zones."

"Mhmm. Would this be the Tess Zone? Anyone else been deep in that particular zone?" Sean teases.

"Can't say that I have, but it looks to be a very nice zone indeed." Cameron lifts his guitar over his shoulder. "Although why she wants your extra-small kind of attention, I'll never know." It's been like this for a couple of days. I know now I'm never living down that box of extra-small condoms she sent me. I thought maybe they had forgotten about it, but then it started.

A couple of nights ago, a pack of extra-small Spiderman underwear in my hotel room with a note from the Brit: *Thought you could use these.* Then on stage, Cameron announced to the Melbourne audience that they were taking up a collection of extra-small condoms for me. Next concert, I spent most of the time dodging foil packets from the crowd. Fuckers. It would be funny if it weren't directed at me.

"You can all fuck off. What were we talking about?"

"Encore for tonight," Kennedy answers. "Paying tribute to Australian rock and roll royalty?"

"AC/DC. See? I was totally paying attention, Gramps."

Sean heads with Cam and one of the roadies back to his drum kit. "When's the last time you talked to her?" Kennedy asks, taking one of the chairs beside me.

"Yesterday. Not for long though." I rub the back of my neck, looking out to the empty stadium.

"It's not easy. I get it, Matty. These other two don't have a fucking clue, though."

"And I'm awful with time zones. Half the time, I feel like I'm waking her up or something."

Kennedy pulls his phone out and taps the screen. "Nic set me up with an app. So I'll always know what time it is in San Fran."

"Shit. I need that." I lean over, taking a look at his phone.

"It's seven thirty at night yesterday if it helps. Sounds like a good time to call her." He takes a long pull from his energy drink.

I've never really thought about time before, how it can fuck with your head. It's *yesterday* where Tess is. "How do you do it? Seriously. She feels a million miles away." And now, I'm sulking.

"Well, she kind of is."

I scowl. "Not helping."

"I send Abby stuff, deliveries of shit she's not expecting, videos of places we go. We Skype, Facetime, text. My phone bill is insane, but it's worth it. I don't want her to feel like I'm drifting, you know? It's hard work, but if you think she's worth it, you'll do the work, man."

A few hours later, I'm pacing like a caged animal backstage, my heart thundering a frantic bassline against my ribs, listening to ring after ring. My calls went to voicemail earlier, and the sound of her cheery voice only notched the growing ache in my chest higher.

Where the fuck is she? I should know better than to have expectations. We never set any times in stone when we'd connect. I highly doubt that she's waiting around for my call, nor should she be, but that doesn't stop worst-case scenarios from flying through my mind.

"Matt?" Finally, I hear her voice, soft and filling up the empty spaces in my heart, and I can breathe again.

"Tessa."

"I was going to call but—"

"But what?" I lean against the wall. Roadies dart around me as they prepare for the concert.

"I don't want to bother you."

"You could never be a bother. Thought I made that pretty clear."

"I know." Unbearable, awkward silence is all we're giving each other in the place of all the things we want to say.

"It's weird, right? I don't want it to be weird," I say quietly.

"I don't either. It's just hard when you're there."

I bite back a groan. "You don't know the half of it." She laughs, and I grab onto the glimmer of hope.

"You're hard, are you?" Her voice lowers as if she doesn't want anyone in earshot to hear what she's saying.

"All the damn time. But just because I miss you."

"I miss you, too," she admits, and I shut my eyes, letting the words sink in.

"Can't wait to see you. Taste you again. Fuck, I need that." I clutch the phone tighter, hearing her breath hitch. "Cherry fucking almond, right?"

She laughs. "It's bourbon flavored today."

"Fuck. I'm already drunk thinking about it," I grumble. "It's only a couple of weeks, and I'll be back. Think you can wait that long for me?"

"I'll see what I can do." I can hear the teasing tone of her voice.

"The concert is streaming tonight. You gonna watch?"

"Yeah," she breathes.

"Good. 'Cause I'm playing for you."

♪ ♩ ♪ ♩

Tessa

MY PHONE ALARM BLARES FROM the bedside table in Abby's guest room. She and Kennedy are looking for somewhere in the city to move into together, but for now, she's still in her old apartment. I grope wildly and silence the damn thing, my nerves jangling and body protesting. It's two a.m. and too freaking early. I smile to myself as I hear Abby's grumbling from her bedroom down the hall. Glad to know I'm not the only one who's having trouble waking up. But I know neither one of us would miss the only streaming concert Redfall has on this leg of the tour.

"Hey." She yawns. "I'll get the coffee started if you fire up the laptop." I nod, and she staggers into her small kitchen as I head to her living room. As I log in to my laptop, I find that excitement is quickly replacing my tiredness. How can I sleep when I know he's playing for me?

A grin eclipses my face when I think about his sultry promise. God, how can just a few words from him, the sound of his voice, give me such a thrill? It's incredible to think that this man, this frustratingly complex and brilliantly talented man, is thinking of me somewhere on the opposite side of the globe.

I hope he knows I'm thinking about him, too.

"Here you go." Abby joins me on the couch and hands me a steaming cup. I thank her and eagerly take a sip, savoring the heavenly aroma. "I'd like to say this is the last time I'll ever get up at such a godawful time to watch one of Kennedy's shows, but it would be a lie," she says with a wry grin. "Thank God the rest of the tour will be in better time zones."

"No kidding." It's been hard to wrap my head around the fact that not only is it tomorrow night where Matt is, but it's also summertime. I've been bundled up in sweaters and he's wearing T-shirts.

She observes me over the rim of her mug. "They're lucky we love them."

I snort and cough through my mouthful of hot coffee, barely

able to keep from spewing it across my computer. "I don't love him . . . them . . . whoever." Ignoring the way my heart suddenly pounds, I busy myself with typing in the website for the concert stream and try to appear unaffected. I fail miserably.

"Right," she drawls, unconvinced. "You're just up with me in the wee hours, sacrificing a good night's sleep and job productivity for the sheer fun of it, not because you're missing your man and want to see him do his thing for thousands of people."

I sigh in resignation. "Okay, I'll concede to the missing him part because, well, it's pretty obvious. But as for the rest." I fiddle with the power cable to give myself something to do. Loving Matt isn't something I really want to think about right now. I'm still getting used to being in an actual relationship. "Can we just watch the show?"

"Sorry." She nudges my elbow. "It's just that you've been different since you met Matt. I mean, I know some of it is that you're putting a lot of energy into your new job, but it's more than that. I don't think a job alone could make a person glow like you have been lately, no matter how good a job it is. It's nice to see, that's all. I'm happy for you."

Smiling shyly, I glance up at her. "Thanks. I'm still not quite sure what I'm doing with him, but I'm not going to waste any more time questioning it and just see where it takes me."

"That's all any of us can do, I think." Her wistful smile speaks volumes as the camera pans across the packed concert hall, the fans chanting for the show to start. "It'll be easier when he's closer to home. Kennedy wants me to join him for the Canadian shows after Christmas."

"Really?" I quickly go over the upcoming schedule in my head. "Do you think you can swing it?"

She shrugs. "Probably. If I can, I'll see if there are some donors

I can connect with while I'm there. If not, I'll take vacation days. The place can survive without me for a couple days."

Not long ago, it never would've occurred to my boss to take a few days off for her own enjoyment. Abby's work ethic is legendary around the office for a reason. That was before she started dating Kennedy Lane. She certainly isn't slacking now, but it's nice to see her relax and enjoy life more.

"You should think about coming with me," she suggests, but before I can answer, she hops a little on the sofa and waves excitedly at the screen. "Oh! Here we go! Turn it up."

I gasp when the band takes the stage. "Matt cut his hair!" Instead of the floppy grown-out Mohawk he'd been sporting when he left, the result of an ill-conceived bet he'd lost with Cameron, his blond locks are now close-cropped. It makes his lickable jawline more prominent. He looks good. Really good. Like, good enough that I want to—

"Oh, for the love of," Abby mutters, snapping me out of my lustful thoughts. "I should've known he took it." I glance over to see her biting her lip and staring hungrily at the screen. Kennedy is wearing a long red silk scarf looped loosely around his neck that I swear I've seen Abby wear in the office.

Based on the look on her face, I don't think I want to know where that scarf has been.

The concert is fantastic, as expected. It's amazing to hear them with the symphony backing them up; the sound is brilliantly rich and full. The guys are on fire and have the crowd eating out of their hands. It feels strange to watch such a spectacle on a seventeen-inch screen.

I can barely take my eyes off Matt. He's wearing tight, faded blue jeans and a black shirt with the sleeves rolled up to expose the intricate swirls of ink on his forearms. Whenever the camera cuts away from him to show another member of the band, I catch myself leaning forward with my fists clenched, willing the shot to return to him. The intensity in his eyes as he looks straight into the camera during his close-ups takes my breath away. He positively owns his section of the stage and sometimes strolls over to interact with either Kennedy or Cameron. The energy between them is palpable.

And then it's over. After the second encore, the guys take a final bow and head backstage, waving to the crowd. Abby and I both slouch back against the cushions as if someone cut our strings. "Holy shit," she murmurs. "I'm as tired as if I was on stage with him." I hum in agreement.

"Hey! Let's send them something. Come 'ere." She grabs her phone and we snuggle together to take a photo. I laugh when I see it; we're a couple of tousled bedheads with not a speck of makeup, wearing the oversized Redfall tees we slept in, slivers of skin showing here and there, and grinning like idiots. Glamazons, we're not.

When I receive it from her, I quickly send it to Matt with a caption: *Just a couple of groupies here.*

"Okay, let's hit the sack. Morning will be here too soon," she says decisively, and I shut down the laptop. Just before we part ways, her phone chimes with a message that makes her blush. "Uh, sleep well!" She gives me a little wave and a goofy grin before shutting herself in her bedroom.

Back in the guest room, I stare at my phone for a while, until it's obvious he's not responding. Or, maybe he just doesn't keep his phone with him like Kennedy does. I settle down under the covers with a sigh. Just as I'm about to drop off, my phone, which I discover is still clutched in my hand, chimes with a message.

Matt: No groupie has ever looked as good as you. I miss you.

I miss you too. You guys were incredible tonight.

Matt: It felt pretty incredible, too. I'm glad you liked it. It's late there, baby. Go to sleep.

I grin at the screen. *Do you really want me to?*

Matt: No, but I'm surrounded by people and can't get away to do what I want to do with you. So, sleep.

Fine, I'll go to sleep. I add a little pouty face.

Matt: You'd better, gorgeous, cuz you won't be sleeping much when I get home.

Thanks to that enticing promise, sleep doesn't come easy.

THE FOLLOWING MORNING, ABBY AND I bear April's teasing about our mutual bleariness with grace and a few shared smug looks. After a meeting with my team, I stop back in my office just in time to grab my ringing phone.

"Tessa?" My eyes pop open at hearing my father's deep voice. "I heard the darnedest thing today. Care to guess what it was?"

"Um . . ."

"I heard that you're in the market for some repairs on a pretty fancy car. A car that does not belong to you. Does any of this ring a bell?"

I grimace, hating how my father can make me, even at twenty-eight, feel like a toddler caught stealing a cookie. "Uh."

"Whose car is it, Tessa? Chet said it belongs to a guy. Don't tell me some bum has conned you into paying for his car repairs."

"Of course not, Dad." I drum my fingers on my desk. "I borrowed a friend's car while he's out of town and someone keyed it. So I'm taking care of it." Responsibility is a big thing for my dad, and I hope that will soothe him. He's been wary of boys trying to take advantage since Paula, Rachel, and I began dating.

"A friend? Must be a pretty good friend if he loaned you a

showroom-ready '68 Camaro," he grumbles. I roll my eyes at how well informed my father is. Chet was the body shop guy my dad turned to when he was restoring his own classic Camaro when I was a kid, and I knew I could trust him to fix Matt's car. However, I apparently can't trust him to keep his mouth shut.

"Yes, a friend," I retort, before continuing delicately, "Ah, a friend I'm bringing to Christmas Eve dinner."

"Really?" He sounds shocked, not that I can blame him. I think my parents have given up on me ever bringing a man to meet my family. "Er, okay. Here, talk to your mother," he mutters, clearly uncomfortable with the direction our conversation has taken. Cars are one thing, but emotions are quite another.

"Hi, honey." I smile at my mother's clear voice although she's sounding a little shocked, too, now. "Did I hear you say you're bringing someone to Christmas Eve dinner? A man?"

"Yes, if that's okay." I swallow my sudden nerves and plow on quickly. "His name is Matt Logan and he's a musician."

"A musician?"

"Yes, he plays bass guitar for Redfall." I'm not sure if that will mean anything to her or not. She only listens to classical. "They're a rock band, but they just did a series of shows with the Sydney Symphony Orchestra in Australia."

"Oh! You said Redford?"

"Red*fall*, Mom. They're world-famous. Ask Rachel the next time you talk to her." I smirk to myself; my sister is going to come unglued when she meets Matt.

"Are they the ones who do that car commercial?"

I stifle a laugh. I can only imagine Matt's face if she asks him that. "No, Mom, that's The Rolling Stones. So, you don't mind if I bring him, do you?"

"Of course not! It would be lovely to meet him," she says, her voice full of wonder, as if she'd just seen a unicorn. "I just never thought . . . Tessa, are you serious about this boy?"

"We just started dating," I reply hesitantly, my heart skipping a beat as I picture Matt's face. "But, I like him, Mom. A lot."

"I would guess so, if you're bringing him here." She takes a deep breath. "Well, Mrs. Hutton is here for her fitting, dear, so I need to go. We'll talk more later, okay?"

"Okay." I hang up and sit down in my chair, relieved. Step one, complete.

The rest of the week goes quickly, although I'm missing Matt like crazy. We catch each other when we can, but it's not easy with the time difference and our work obligations. I can't wait to see him. It's pathetic, but I've even stayed at his house a few nights, just to be near his things. Chet called to say the Camaro will be ready this weekend. My plan is to take it straight back to Matt's and lock it up, safe and sound. No detours.

"Good afternoon, Tess." I look up to see Jeff the Mailroom Guy standing in my doorway, holding a big box. "I've got an overseas delivery for you from a Mr. Logan."

I perk up and try to suppress my grin, remembering what happened the last time Mr. Logan sent me a boxful of something. Discreetly, I smooth my hand over my hip and the lace boyshorts that lie under my pants. "Great, Jeff. Thanks." He sets it on my desk and stands awkwardly as I eagerly begin to open the box. "I'll take it from here," I add, and glance at the door, hoping he'll take the hint.

He doesn't.

"Tess, I was wondering, we never did get that cup of coffee." He smiles hopefully at me, and I realize what I need to do.

"I wouldn't mind some coffee, but I'm seeing someone, Jeff," I say gently, as the light in his eyes dims.

"Oh, I see." He finally takes a step backward toward my office door, looking dejected. "Well, maybe later, then."

I nod as he leaves and then tear into the box—and burst out laughing. A large stuffed toy kangaroo is smiling up at me from the cardboard container, surrounded by packets of Tim Tams and something called Violet Crumble. How sweet is this man? Still chuckling, I snatch a note that I see peeking out of the kangaroo's pouch. My chuckles die with a gasp and all my muscles south of the border clench.

Thought you could use something to snuggle with until I get back. The candy tastes almost as sweet as you—almost. I'm looking forward to revisiting that in person. Soon.

Oh, me too, Mr. Logan. Me, too.

chapter ten

matt

THE RAIN POUNDS AGAINST THE metal Dumpster, dripping in a constant, steady rhythm. It's melodic and hypnotizing, dulling the hunger pains that roll through me. It's well past midnight, the streets never really silent, but quieter now that most of the bars have closed for the night.

I watch the shallow puddle at my feet fill with the dirty runoff from the Dumpster. I'm shivering from the cold, feeling dampness in my bones. I reek of the streets, of sweat and blood, and days without a roof over my head.

I'm desperate to close my eyes. Exhaustion threatens to take over, but I can't let it. I won't make that mistake again. The last time I did, I woke up to a stranger hovering over me with a dull, dirty knife at my throat.

Pulling my knees up to my chest, I scan the alleyway once more, and with shaking hands fish out the stale, rock-hard crust of bread I've been *carrying around for the last couple of days.*

Primed to every single sound on the street, I stare into the darkness and tear off a bite of bread, chewing slowly. In the distance, the sound of hurried footsteps echoes, my heart beats faster against my ribs. A trio of voices gets louder, closer, inching toward my safe haven. Of course, you're never really safe out here.

I hold my breath and cower closer to the Dumpster, but it's too late.

"What do we have here, boys?"

I'm jolted awake, my arms flailing. Disoriented, my heart pounds out a frantic bassline, thanks to my latest nightmare.

"Jesus, watch it." I turn to the sound of Cam's voice. From his seat beside me, he narrows his eyes, shoving my arm away from him. "Your left hook needs some work."

"Sorry, man." Pushing up in the seat, I glance out the window of the plane to the darkened sky. It's not enough that the nightmares keep coming; now my bandmates have to witness them.

"Another nightmare, hmm?" Cam keeps his voice low, and I take a sweep of the plane. In a rare sight, Tucker is passed out, snoring away on one of the couches. Kennedy and Sean are huddled together, sharing a set of headphones, deep into composing some masterpiece I'm sure we'll be playing soon.

"Something like that."

"You know I hated rehab." I glance back at Cameron. He hasn't really talked to us about his time in rehab, and none of us have pushed him.

"It couldn't have been easy."

"It wasn't. It was fucking hell." He stretches his legs out, his eyes darting up to the front of the plane before he continues. "Those first few days were awful. I'd wake up with night sweats, shaking, fucking cursing everything and everyone. And the nightmares?" He shakes his head as if he can will the memory away. "I know this isn't drug-related for you. But it's something."

My jaw sets as I look back at him. "I know you don't like to talk about shit, but talking in rehab for me helped. You get it out and it's done. It's not eating you alive anymore."

My grip tightens on the armrest. I was an idiot thinking I could hide anything from these guys. "Just know that I'm here if you want to vent." He nods to the front of the plane. "We all are. And if it's not us you want to talk to, I've got the names of a few therapists."

I scoff at that and he hits me in the arm. "Fuck knows Tess has got enough to put up with, what with your extra-small package and everything. She doesn't need to deal with you flailing around in your sleep, too."

I groan. "I'm never going to live that extra-small shit down, am I?"

He shakes his head before settling back in the seat, closing his eyes. "Never."

♪ ♩ ♪ ♩

Tessa

"ARE YOU SURE HE'S COMING?"

I fix Jada with a baleful eye. "He would've been in town already, but he had to do something for Cameron." It's Christmas Eve, and I'm trying to control my nerves. Matt's thirty minutes late to pick me up to go to my parents' house, and I'm a basket case. Jada's censorious looks aren't helping.

Since I pulled my head out of my ass, things have been better between Matt and me—as good as things can be when there's been a literal ocean between us. Texting has proved more reliable due to the time zone differences, but we have been able to squeeze in a few phone calls and one incredibly hot bout of Facetime sex. Jesus, if he can get me that worked up over video conferencing, I'm going to self-combust when he lays hands on me in person.

Jada huffs and arranges a platter of antipasto. While I'm at my folks' this evening, she's hosting a get-together here for her coworkers who don't have anywhere else to go for the holiday. Catered, of course. Neither of us can make much beyond ramen or spaghetti sauce out of a jar. "Must have been important." She hasn't come right out and said it, but I can tell that she's just waiting for him to fuck up.

"It was. He had some kind of a family emergency and Matt volunteered to help." I adjust an ornament on our fake Christmas tree in the corner. Whatever it was that happened with Cam, Matt was the only band member left to deal with it. Kennedy and Abby flew to be with his folks in Minnesota, and Sean was on his way to England to spend the holiday with his sister. The guys are close—more like brothers, really—and Matt couldn't bail on him. His loyalty is one of the things I admire about him, so I'm not going to get all pissy when things don't go my way. "Look, I get that you don't like him," I continue, lifting my chin in defiance.

"I never said that I don't like him." She frowns. "It's just that I haven't seen you like this before. You're all moony and swoony, distinctly un-Tess. And he didn't look like the swooniest guy when I saw him, no matter how well he can flip a pancake."

"Looks can be deceiving." I smile wryly. "And it's worse than that. I'm falling in love with him."

It snuck up on me. I bolted awake a couple nights ago after dreaming of him, struck with the realization that no matter how I twisted and turned, I had to admit what was staring me in the face. I want him. I want to be with Matt more than I've ever wanted to be with any man in my life. He challenges me and makes me think about myself differently. Not only does he respect me, he trusts me—which is huge. The circle of people Matt trusts isn't just small, it's tiny.

I shift on the sofa, letting my epiphany wash over me once more. It's more than respect and trust and desire and passion, as important as all that is. He fills an empty space in my heart I didn't know I had.

It's *love.*

She stares at me, her dark brown eyes incredulous. "You're . . . wow." She looks away, shaking her head, and chuckles. "Wow, okay. Didn't see that coming, but okay."

I purse my lips. "Well, thanks, friend." I didn't see it coming either, but her words still sting.

"I'm sorry," she says quickly, instantly contrite, and comes to drag me to sit on our sofa. Andy Williams is crooning about silver bells from the iPod dock. "I didn't think it was that serious. You guys haven't been together that long. Does he feel the same?"

"I'm not sure; we haven't talked about it. You said it your-self—I only met him a couple months ago. It sounds ludicrous." Although we've shared some momentous things about our pasts, things we never discuss with anyone else, we've still barely scratched the surface. I look down at my hands folded in my lap and take a calming breath. "But I can't help it. I know how I feel." And I can't pretend I don't anymore.

I smooth my hair back. "He obviously cares for me, but I don't know how deep it goes. He keeps things pretty close to the vest. And there are so many demands on his time. The band, all the shows, the fans, the press." I glance at her, trying to find the words. "That's partly why I haven't said anything. I don't want to be another demand. Something else he has to deal with. Does that make sense?"

"Yes." She toys with one of her earrings. "But who says you would fall in that category? I think it would be pretty freakin' great if someone told me he loved me."

I slump back into the cushions and look at the ceiling. "It's easier said than done."

"Tess," she says with a touch of exasperation. "If you love him, tell him, for heaven's sake. Don't worry about what I may or may not think. Go with what feels right for *you*." She looks at the clock in the kitchen. "But it would help if he'd get his ass here so you can."

There's a knock, and my heart leaps. Ignoring Jada's teasing laugh, I jump to my feet and race to the door, stopping only to smooth my dark red sweater over my short skirt and take a deep breath. I swing the door open and try not to let my disappointment show; it's Jada's friends from work. Mustering a bright smile, I usher them in and help with their coats, exchanging holiday greetings and good wishes. I carry their proffered bottles of wine and plates of Christmas cookies to the kitchen while they greet their hostess with enthusiastic hugs. Someone starts singing along with Bing Crosby. Their exuberance is infectious, and I feel a pang of longing.

I fire off a quick text to Matt, telling him that I'll call later. I can't delay any longer; I have to get going or my mom is going to have a cow. Grabbing my coat and purse, I carry them to the door, waving my goodbyes to Jada. She's already embroiled in conversation, so I don't want to interrupt. I open the door and freeze.

Matt is standing on the threshold, his hand raised to knock. His blue eyes seem even brighter than I remember. His short blond hair is a mess, as if he's been running his fingers through it. He's wearing a black dress shirt and pants under his worn leather jacket and looks like he just stepped off the cover of *GQ*. I want to eat him alive.

"Tess." He lunges at me at the same time I drop everything in my hands and leap into his arms. And then his mouth is on mine, plundering, claiming, and igniting the fire in me. He tastes like cinnamon toothpaste and smells like heaven. He grunts as I pull at his soft hair, and I moan into his mouth. His hand is under my skirt, squeezing my ass as he presses me against the wall. "Fuck, I missed you," he mumbles against my lips, and I hum in agreement. Time has stopped.

Until a throat clears from somewhere nearby.

We freeze and slowly look to the side, where there's a roomful of computer nerds gawking at us. Jada looks like she's about to burst out laughing; she may hurt herself. Matt slowly puts me down, ensuring that no one gets a look at my ass. A light blush covers his cheeks; he's adorable.

"Uh, hi, everyone. Merry Christmas." He gives an awkward wave. There are a few giggles and awkward waves back. "We'll just be going now."

"Too bad," Jada says, grinning at me. "I was getting ready to sell tickets."

Matt looks at me in desperation, and I take his hand after retrieving my coat and purse from the floor. As our fingers interlock, my nerves vanish. "Come on, tiger," I say with a grin. "Time for the real show."

"YOU FLEW TO BOSTON?" I look at him, startled. No wonder he was late. I knew he was with Cameron, but I didn't know that included shuttling him across country.

Matt's pensive frown is visible in the streetlights. We're exiting the Bay Bridge on the way to my parents' house in Oakland.

"It wasn't my first choice. He got some bad news. His dad had a heart attack."

"Oh my God! Is he going to be okay?"

"Yeah, he had to have surgery, but he'll be okay. Cam kinda freaked out. We wanted to make sure he got back there in one piece, and I volunteered."

Nodding, I let it go, remembering Cam's recent trip to rehab. The guys were probably worried the stress would trigger old habits. Reaching across the smooth leather seat, I take Matt's hand and give it a squeeze. "It's good that he has friends like you."

He squeezes back. "I'm sorry I was late. Did you get my texts?"

"No, just the one where you said you were stopping to see Tom. Oh, turn right here, and then a left at the stop sign."

He obeys smoothly. "He's looking forward to meeting you. He wants me to bring you around tomorrow, if that's okay."

"Okay." My stomach flips over. "First, we have to survive tonight."

He swallows. "Right. Give me the rundown again?"

"My brother Casey is a veterinarian. He's divorced and has custody of his two kids, Mason and Lily. Mason is nine and Lily is six. Rachel's husband, Jim, is a lawyer, too, and their daughter Janey is four."

"Wait, I thought your brother was Conner?"

"Conner is Casey's twin. He's the one in Seattle. Mom and Dad are flying to see him and his family tomorrow and will spend a few days."

"That's a lot of names to remember." Matt grips the steering wheel a little tighter.

"Don't worry, we'll ease you in." I indicate another turn and point to the house on the corner. "And here we are."

It's a typical family house built in the early '70s, but the upper rooms have a partial view of the bay. Mom and Dad bought it when he retired from the Navy, and they couldn't be happier. There's room for Mom's sewing business and for all the grandkids to stay overnight, and that's enough for them.

The deep, rumbling purr of the Camaro ceases, and the street is silent once again. Before he gets out of the car, he slides a hand behind my head and pulls me in for a kiss. "Just in case I can't do this again for a few hours," he murmurs, pressing his lips to mine. It's soft and sweet, and I melt into his embrace. We haven't had nearly enough time to reacquaint ourselves.

"I'm sorry; I should've canceled so we could go back to your place." He gives me one more peck and leans back to look in my eyes.

"No, you shouldn't have. Your family is important to you. We would've had more time together if I hadn't gone with Cam."

I lean my forehead against his. "You were being a good friend. It's okay. We can wait a few more hours."

"Not sure about that. I might have to drag you into a closet or something." He gives me a wolfish grin before getting out. After helping me join him on the sidewalk, he holds my hand tightly as I lead him up the walk to the side door. It's cold enough to see my breath, and I tug the collar of my coat. The glow from the kitchen pierces the darkness, and I grin automatically at the sounds that reach my ears from the open window. Mom's kitchen is the hub of all life in the Baker household, and tonight is no exception.

We step up on the porch and I reach for the doorknob, pausing when I hear Casey's voice. "Where's Tessa? She's usually the first one here."

"She texted to say she'd be a little late. She's bringing someone."

A clang of something being dropped. "No shit?" my brother asks in disbelief.

"Casey, language. It's Christmas."

"Who's she bringing? We're talking about a guy, right?"

"Matthew Somebody, and he's a musician. He works for someone named Redford; to be honest, I was too stunned to listen to much more."

"Redford? Like Robert Redford, maybe?" Rachel chimes in, and I hear my mother huff.

"I don't know, but I figure we'll have plenty of time to get to know him over dinner. If she's bringing him to Christmas Eve dinner, it must serious, so I expect you to be on your best behavior, Casey."

"Mom, I'm not ten anymore," my brother whines—like a ten-year-old. "What kind of musician?"

"I don't know. Rachel, get the potatoes, please." There's a clatter of dishes as my mother continues, "She had that work project with the symphony last year. Maybe she met him there?"

"Whoever he is, he's as tall as Dad," my sister's voice sounds, silencing all other voices. I spot her eagerly peering at us through the window, and I know our time is up. Matt stiffens, and I give him an encouraging smile just as the door swings open.

"Get in here before you guys freeze to death. Why didn't you bring him to the front door?" My sister is grinning like crazy as she takes in the tall, handsome man at my side. "Hi! You must be Matt. I'm Rachel."

My sister is a force of nature, and there's no stopping her once she gets started. She ushers us into the warm room, taking our coats and slinging them over a kitchen chair, flittering about and making the rest of the introductions before I can get a word in edgewise. "This is our mom, Julie, and our brother, Casey. My husband is in the living room, trying to get the fire started." My brother nods to Matt, peering at him like he's not sure where he's seen him before. The kids race into the room to see what's going on and come to a screeching halt. Lily and Janey giggle when Matt winks at them, and Mason stares at him like he's a god. There's no doubt that my nephew recognizes him.

For his part, Matt looks a little shell-shocked. I mentally chastise myself for not using the front door. Oh, who am I kidding? There's no good way to ease him into this.

Then all conversation stops when my dad steps in the room.

"Matt, is it? Ron Baker," my dad rumbles, straightening his shoulders. Even though he no longer wears a uniform, he can still command a room with his mere presence. He takes in Matt's closely cropped hair, strong jaw, and the tendrils of ink on his neck peeking out of his collar. Matt easily matches my dad's six-foot-three, and I have to give him credit; he meets the steely gaze directed at him straight on, never flinching.

"Matt Logan, sir," he says respectfully and extends his hand in greeting. "Tess has told me a lot about you."

Dad's lips twitch as he shoots a reproachful glance at me. "I wish I could say the same." They shake hands, my dad continuing his parental intimidation glare, until Mom approaches and taps him on the shoulder. She's a tiny thing, but she has my dad wrapped around her little finger.

"At ease, Chief." She gives him a wry smirk and steps up to Matt next. Her small hand disappears in his. "It's a pleasure to meet you, Matthew. Merry Christmas," she says with a warm smile, her gray eyes sparkling. "What a lovely, old name. Is your family Catholic, by any chance?"

Matt freezes and I fear he's thinking of his own mother. "Mom," I warn, but before I can come up with something more to say, Matt takes my hand.

"Er, I think Tom, my dad, might be Episcopalian," he offers

in that shy tone that always melts my heart; it apparently has the same effect on my mother.

"Close enough." Beaming at him, she steps up to his other side and slips her arm in his to lead him into the dining room. "You're just in time. Let's eat."

chapter eleven

matt

IT'S SUDDENLY HOTTER—WAY HOTTER THAN it should be. While Tess's family seems nice—very all-American as they politely pass dishes around the large dining room table—I can't help but feel that I'm about to be cross-examined and found lacking. I'm not going to lie; her father is intimidating as hell.

I've played for stadiums full of screaming, frenzied fans, can manage personal and often intrusive interview questions with the best of them, and can hold my own with a room full of famous people. All that seems like nothing compared to this. The last time I was this nervous, I was auditioning for the band. Somehow, it seems there's a lot more to lose now.

Fine china filled with a home-cooked feast I would normally want to devour turns my stomach. Tension rolls through me, and I sit with my back ramrod straight in the chair, unsure of where I should look or what I should say. The feeling is unsettling. I tug at the collar of my shirt as Tess fills up the wine glass in front of me.

"Where did you go to school, Matt?" And so it begins.

Ron Baker's firm and commanding voice seems to bellow through the room. All heads turn from the menacing man at the head of the table to me. Waiting, watching with bated breath.

I meet his steady gaze, my hands clenching under the table. "I didn't finish high school, sir. I got my GED later, but I didn't go to college."

He lifts a brow. That's all he has to do and I know what he thinks. Five words and he knows I'll never be good enough for his daughter.

So many eyes on me. Silence around the room that was just buzzing with noise and chaos. I can feel them all assessing, forming their own scenarios of why I didn't attend Stanford or some other school.

Fuck it. He's not the only one who can ask questions. "Where did you go to school?"

"The US Navy." I swallow back the lump in my throat. Of course he did. There's no comeback to rival that kind of greatness. The man is a retired Navy vet for fuck's sake.

"What does your father do?" If I'm not worthy, maybe Tom will be.

"He runs a group home for teens." A nod of approval or maybe minimal acceptance from Ron.

"What's a group home?" Lily, I think Tess said her name was, chirps from the kids' table beside us. Maybe I should've sat over there. It's wildly appealing at the moment. My mouth twitches as I look over to them. The anarchy of the kids' table. I'd definitely fit in better.

"It's a place where kids can go when they get into trouble,"

I explain.

"Dad just sends us to our room when we get into trouble," Mason chimes in around a forkful of mashed potatoes.

"Some kids aren't lucky enough to have rooms." Brutal honesty. Maybe Ron will appreciate it.

Lily's eyes widen. "No rooms? No Xbox, either?" As if this is the worst thing in the world.

"Afraid not." More awkward glances amongst the close-knit family around the table. Unclenching my fists, I tentatively pick up my fork.

"Tess mentioned you're in a band." Julie shifts the conversation. Probably better if I don't eat. I abandon the fork. "Redford, I think?"

"It's Redfall, Grandma," Mason adds, rolling his eyes. "They have, like, the number one album right now."

"Oh! I had no idea. What kind of music is it?" Julie smiles. Tess said she hasn't brought a guy home before, but they're all looking at me like I'm a six-headed alien from another planet. Still, this I can handle. Just talk about the band and what I love. Stay far away from my fucked-up childhood that no one needs to hear about.

"Rock music."

"Oh! Like the Rolling Stones in that car commercial?" she asks excitedly, making me chuckle.

"A little bit. But we mix it up, too. On this last tour, we played with the Sydney Orchestra." Julie looks impressed, at least. Ron, not so much. He stabs his way roughly through a piece of turkey on his plate. I reach for the wine, scowling as the cuff of my sleeve slides up to expose more of the ink on my wrist. I'm going to need something stronger to get through this. A shot of whiskey or a cigarette. Fuck, that would be good right now.

"That sounds ambitious," Casey, Tess's brother, cuts in.

I give him a nod, setting the glass back down without spilling it all over the table. "It was. They're a talented group of musicians. It was quite an experience."

"What instruments do you play?" This from Rachel who appears to be interested in the answer.

"Bass, but I can play a few other instruments, too." I feel Tess's hand slide along my thigh, giving a squeeze. A move that does nothing for my nerves. I'm electrified anytime she touches me, but now? After weeks of not seeing her, when she's wearing that tempting, tight red sweater that hugs every perfect curve she has? Under the naval inquisition? I think I jump a foot in my seat.

"You can play other instruments?" Tess asks, the sound of her voice calming me slightly.

I grin at her with a nod and turn to meet her dark eyes. "Told you there was a lot you don't know about me." Her seductive lips curl into a knowing grin at my answer, a faint flush blooming over her cheeks.

"Do you play piano at all?" Julie asks, her voice suddenly quiet.

The jarring sound of forks hitting plates echoes through the dining room, and I wonder what minefield I've stepped into this time. All eyes are turned to Julie in disbelief. I glance at Tess, who's staring at her mother in shock. What in the hell?

"It's not my instrument of choice, but yeah." I fill the uneasy silence. "I can play. Not like our lead singer, but I get by."

Julie's eyes water. "Would you play something for us later? The piano hasn't been used in a long time." She lifts her gaze to her husband at the other end of the table.

I look between the two of them, but I might as well be invisible. Some unspoken conversation carries on around the table. I feel like I'm intruding on a private moment. "Sure, if you like. I mean, I'm a little rusty, but I could probably do some Christmas songs."

"No one's played that piano since Paula." Ron's voice sounds hollow and void of any of the strong, authoritative tone he's had since I walked in the door. Now it makes sense. Paula, Tess's older sister who died from a brain tumor, must have played. No pressure at all then to play the piano for her entire family on Christmas Eve. Fuck.

"I know," Julie answers through a shaky breath. "But it's just sitting there, and I thought it would be nice." I recognize the pain in her eyes. I don't think losing a child is something you ever get over. A familiar ache in my chest makes itself known. The harsh truth that my own mother wouldn't have given a shit if something happened to me hits me hard. She probably would've welcomed it. I was an inconvenience at best. Fuck, this was a bad idea coming here.

I turn to the sound of Tess sniffling. It's a glaring reminder not to be a selfish prick. This may be one of the most awkward dinner conversations in history, but whatever I'm feeling is nothing compared to what Tess and her family lost when Paula died.

Ron clears his throat. "We'd love it if you could play, Matt."

I glance at Tess warily, as she wipes the tears from her cheeks. My heart stutters seeing her vulnerable and hurting. I'd do anything not to see that again. "No problem."

"So, you've got a lot of tattoos there." Ron starts back on the cross-examination, and I know he's deflecting, not wanting to show the emotion he's fighting about losing his daughter. "Guess that goes with the territory of being in a band, kind of like a lot other things." His stern expression fixes on me.

There are a few uncomfortable chuckles around the table, but there's no mistaking what he means here. I know I haven't been a saint, but I hate assumptions. I've got tattoos, so I must be some badass delinquent. I'm in a band, so obviously I'm only capable of sex, drugs, and rock and roll. Never mind about the countless hours of preparation we go through to perfect what we do, or how dedicated we are to our fans, or how the Brit gives most of what he makes back to the music academy he attended. None of that shit matters. Perception is reality.

"Dad!" Tess hisses under her breath.

"Not really. Our rhythm guitarist only has one. And I know a lot of guys in the business who don't have any. What about you?" I ask, turning the tables on him once more.

His eyes narrow. "What about me?"

"You were in the Navy. Don't all sailors have at least one tattoo?" I know I'm playing with fire, but I can't seem to stop myself. The room goes silent once more.

Ron pauses for a moment, then slowly pushes the sleeve of his shirt up, revealing a tat of a nautical star. "Touché."

"Guess they don't care about yours, hmm?" I grin at Tess. Her eyes widen in panic before chaos erupts. A barrage of questions from around the table fire at her, and Mason jumps up from the kids' table to rush over. "You have a tattoo, Auntie Tess? Where? Where?"

Rachel shrieks from across the table, above the buzz of everyone else, glaring at her sister. "When did you get a tattoo?"

And my work here is done.

I HEAR THE SCREEN DOOR close as I pace the driveway alongside the Camaro and fight the urge for a nicotine fix. I'm out in the cold under the guise of finally bringing in the wine I forgot about earlier, but I think everyone in that house knows that's a lie.

I just need some air. I'm not used to the family inquisition.

Jim, Rachel's husband, approaches with a glass of whiskey, holding it out for me.

"Thought you could use this."

"Thanks, man."

"Congratulations," he says, lifting his own glass to me. "You made it through the gauntlet."

I laugh, taking a long sip, the amber liquid providing a delicious burn on the way down. "I think the jury's still out on that."

"Ah, Ron's not that bad. Once you get past the 'where did you go to school' bit, he's really just a big softy. Gotta admit, when you asked him if he had any tattoos, I thought I was going to shit myself. That was pure genius."

"Or pure stupidity. Where'd you go to school, just out of curiosity?"

"Yale." He shrugs like it's no big deal at all. "Law school."

I drain back the rest of the whiskey. "Why am I not surprised?"

"Doesn't really matter at the end of the day. As a parent, you're protective of your kids." I feel my jaw set. If only my mother had been protective of me. "But he likes you, and more importantly, Tess likes you. In all the years I've been with Rach, I've never seen Tess with anyone." It's hard not to feel at least a little smug about that. Any of those loser boyfriends of hers in the past were insane to let Tess go. But their loss is definitely my gain.

Opening the car door, I reach into the back seat for the bottle of wine. "Awesome car, by the way." Jim gives the Camaro a look of longing. "Ron would love it." And suddenly, I like Jim a lot more. He's throwing me a bone here, giving me an in with Tess's dad.

"Thanks for the tip and the whiskey."

"Any time. Now, I think you have some Christmas songs to play."

"IT HASN'T BEEN TUNED IN years." Julie wrings her hands together as she stands beside the piano bench.

"That's okay. I haven't played in a while." I try to block out the intense stares of the small crowd gathered around the piano, all wrought with anticipation. My heart thuds against my chest as I gently run my fingers over the keys. I know this is big for Tess's family, and I don't want to screw it up. If I can give Tess something, anything that will ease the pain of not being able to share another Christmas Eve with her sister, I want to do it right.

The first few bars of "Silent Night" are a little choppy, and the piano is definitely out of tune, but none of that matters. Gradually, more voices join my own, and soon the room is filled with song. Lily finds her way to the bench beside me, and I grin down at her as she sings at the top of her lungs, completely off key, but so damn adorable it makes my heart hurt.

I glance up and see Julie slide her arm around Ron's waist, leaning into his side, and borrowing his strength as she sings through her tears. My voice is suddenly raspy and rough, and while I'd like to blame that on weeks of performing three-hour concerts, I know I can't.

I catch Tess's gaze, tears pooling in her dark eyes as I come to the end of the song. She mouths, "Thank you," and the urge to take her in my arms, take away her pain, overwhelms me.

Lily breaks the silence, her voice excited as she yells, "Play Rudolph!" I let out a laugh, turning to Julie as she wipes her tears and nods quickly with a smile.

"Rudolph it is."

TESS LAUNCHES HERSELF AT ME as the elevator rises to the

loft. She could barely keep her hands off me on the drive home, not that I'm complaining. It took everything in me not to pull off the road and fuck her in the front seat, but apparently I like to torture both of us.

My back hits the mirrored wall of the elevator, my hands cupping her sweet ass and a rough growl rumbling through my chest as I taste her lips. Cookies and brandy and fucking heaven. It's rough and carnal, my tongue sweeping over her plump lips before diving into her mouth. Fuck, I missed this. I missed her.

The elevator door opens, and she tries to wrap her legs around my waist. Almost impossible given the sexy length of this skirt that needs to come off right now. I stumble forward into the loft, and she giggles against my lips, gripping my jacket and tugging at it desperately.

An unfamiliar scent of pine invades my senses, and I lean back, glancing into the living room. Tess lets out a little whimper that turns quickly to a small gasp. There's a massive Christmas tree in my living room, probably eight feet tall and lit up with a thousand little white lights.

I furrow my brow at her, taking a healthy squeeze of her ass. "Did you get a tree, Cardinal?"

She shakes her head, her dark hair falling in her face. "No."

Carrying her closer to the tree, I see a note propped up on one of the middle branches.

Wouldn't be Christmas if I didn't get you a tree. See you tomorrow. ~Tom

"I can't wait to meet him," Tess says quietly, her hands finding their way into my hair.

"Mmm." Turning us to the couch, I drop her onto the waiting cushions, and she lets out a loud laugh. Music to my ears. Nothing sounds better. She leans up on her elbows, the heat and raw desire sparking in her eyes as I shrug my leather jacket off and drop it to the floor.

"No more talk about families tonight." Holding my gaze, she reaches down to unzip those little gray boots, kicking them one after the other to the floor. "From now on, it's only you and me."

She nods slowly, trapping that gorgeous bottom lip between her teeth as she leisurely rolls her tights down. She arches from the cushions, and I can't resist trailing my palm up her inner thigh, gripping the fabric of her tights and tugging them the rest of the way off.

"Now you." Her voice is all breathy and full of need. The little tease parts her thighs and blows my mind as she slides her hand up under her skirt.

I fumble with the buttons of my shirt until it finally hits the floor. "Your turn." The weeks of pent-up frustration fires through me. The heat in my veins electrifies watching her. She lifts her ass, wiggling out of her skirt, and tosses it at me with a coy little smile.

Her eyes dart to the patch on my arm and she leans up, tracing her hand over it. "What happened?"

"Nicotine patch. I'm quitting." I lift her hand from the patch, turning it to kiss the palm. "For you."

Her smile makes all the nicotine cravings I've had worth it. I take in every delicious curve of her highlighted in the glow from the tree, swallow roughly as she leans up and tugs the red sweater off, revealing a burgundy lace bra. I step out of my pants, and her eyes widen at the sight of my cock. And then, I'm covering her, drunk off those sweet little groans she gives me.

I'm everywhere, tasting her skin, biting at the curve of her neck, lowering to suck a hardened nipple into the warmth of my mouth once I've freed it from her bra. She digs her hands into my shoulders, traces down my spine, and grabs at my ass.

I flatten my tongue against her sensitive nipple, stealing a glance up at her as my piercing rolls over her heated skin. Her lips part, and I feel her rock her hips forward. Her hand leaves my ass to tug at the lace between her legs. "I missed that. I need . . . Fuck . . ."

Smirking against the swell of her breast, I lean back, slowly covering her hand with mine, and tease where I know she wants it most. "Tell me what you need, Cardinal."

Gliding my lips to the swell of her other breast, I roll my hips forward and groan. "Is this what you want, hmm?" My hips slowly press to hers, and she arches to the sensation, her head thrown back against the cushions, her dark hair falling in a wave over the edge of the couch.

She writhes against me as I work the lace down her legs, letting my lips trail up the column of her neck, lingering under her ear. "Tell me, baby." My muscles tense as she wraps her legs around my waist, and I push the head of my cock against her tight heat.

Her hands claw at my hips as she turns her head to launch her lips to mine. It's frantic and wild, teeth and lips and deep groans, and I can't get enough of her. "Please, please, please." She pants against my ear, her breaths ragged, making any bit of control I had snap.

I grip her hips and tug her forward as I sink into her, punching out a deep, rough rhythm as desperate as hers. It's blinding lust fueling us both, and I lean back to smooth my palm up her stomach and cup her breast, the rough pads of my fingers grazing her nipple and the lace of her bra.

The thought of fucking her tits comes to mind as I feel her heels press into my lower back. "Oh fuck." I drive home faster, sliding my hands along her thighs. I unhook her legs from my waist, tugging them over my shoulders, turning to bite at her ankle.

Her arms stretch over her head as she grips the side of the couch, arching up into me. Her mouth drops open on a gasp, and I feel her tremble, pulsing around my cock. I strum over her swollen clit with my thumb, the erotic sound of slapping skin mixing with her cries as I fuck her harder, deeper, faster, because that's what she's demanding.

"Oh God, I can't." She's a rambling, beautiful mess. Completely wrecked, her hands wildly clutching at my skin. "Matt . . ." I lean forward, pushing her legs back against her chest, my torso pressed against her full breasts as I claim her lips once more.

Fuck, she tastes good. I had forgotten, or didn't want to torture myself trying to remember. No fantasy, no memory can come close to actually being with Tess. Hearing her beg, feeling her hips rock up to meet each roll of my own, burying my face against her neck and breathing in her sweet scent is as close to heaven as I'll get.

My heart hammers with the realization of what she's come to mean to me. I've been lost without her for the past few weeks, and that terrifies me. I've let her into my heart, and I can only hope she wants to stay.

Tessa

I ROLL OVER, SQUINTING AT the early morning light seeping through the blinds, and rub the sleep from my eyes. My hand comes away smudged and I scowl, realizing that I never washed my face last night. Delightful.

Sliding carefully out of bed so as not to disturb Matt, I pad softly into the adjoining bathroom and shut the door so he won't wake. A glimpse of the raccoon eyes staring back at me makes me laugh. I look like an '80s hair band reject. Real attractive, Tess.

I take care of my morning business quickly and then wash

the remnants of last night's makeup away, smiling to myself. I suppose I shouldn't be that surprised—I was insatiable when we made it back here last night. After weeks apart and enduring that interminable, emotional dinner at my parents, I couldn't stand it any longer. I wanted to wrap myself in him and block out everything and everyone else. My heart swells; I guess that's what can happen when you fall in love.

I still haven't told him how I feel, though. At least, I don't think so. There was an iffy moment during an orgasm where I might have accidentally let it fly, but I don't think he heard me. Which is probably for the best. I'm sure it's written somewhere that you shouldn't tell someone you love them for the first time in the throes of some of the best sex you've ever had.

But when, then?

A muffled cry from the bedroom startles me, and I quickly swing open the bathroom door, only to find Matt still asleep. He's curled around my pillow, clutching it to his chest, his expression pensive. He looks so young like this, with pouting lips and long eyelashes that brush his cheekbones . . . except for the myriad tendrils of ink adorning his arms and shoulders.

Concerned, I watch him for a beat, but he seems okay. He groaned in his sleep a few hours ago, enough to wake me, but calmed down as soon as I wrapped my arms around him. It's a reminder that for all these weeks, we've only spent a few nights together. I wonder how often his dreams are disturbed.

Although I'm trying to be just as careful when I slip back between the sheets, his expression becomes distressed. He wakes with a start, his eyes wild. "Shh, it's just me," I whisper, and lean in quickly to kiss him. Instead, he wraps his arms around me and rolls us over until I find myself on the other side of the bed with him draped over me. I can feel his pulse racing beneath my fingertips on his neck. "Are you okay?"

Ignoring my question, he looks at me with concern and slides his hands over my shoulders and down my biceps. "You're cold."

"I got up to wash my face. I'm sorry I woke you."

"It was good timing, actually," he mutters and buries his face into my neck, inhaling deeply. The tension drains out of him, and I smile against his shoulder, loving that I can ease him like this.

Threading my fingers through his short locks, I let my nails scrape lightly against his scalp; I swear he starts purring. "Did you have a nightmare?" Wordlessly, he nods, still hiding his face. I whisper, "Do you have them often?"

A shiver runs though him. "Sometimes."

"Do you want to talk about it?"

"Not really." He pulls back to rest his head on the pillow. "They come and go. Nothing you should have to hear about."

"Don't you trust me?" I try to keep the hurt out of my voice, and I think I'm mostly successful. I know he's glossed over the details of his childhood, and although I don't want to push him, I can't help my desire to know more. He shakes his head and pulls one of my hands up to his mouth, where he places light kisses on my knuckles.

"I trust you more than I've trusted anyone in years," he confesses, and a thrill runs though me at his admission. "It's just that talking about all that crap isn't going to change it. You shouldn't have to listen to me whine about my fucked-up past."

For a fleeting moment, he looks so damn *sad*, that I just want to hug him hard enough to take all the pain away. As I see him mentally tamp it down and compartmentalize it again, I realize that although that might help temporarily—that my arms, my body, my *love*, might help him forget for a while—it's not a permanent fix.

"My family liked you." I squeeze his hand in support, and he snorts in amusement.

"I think your dad still finds me lacking."

I reach up and smooth a worry line from his brow. "I think he likes you fine. I'm sorry he grilled you so much. I've never brought anyone home, so I didn't expect him to be that gruff, I guess. But you held your own and stood up to him. He admired that."

In truth, I've never seen Dad so adversarial. He's always been imposing, but I don't remember him being *that* tough when Rachel brought Jim home the first time. I was so proud of Matt. He didn't flinch, despite how uncomfortable it must have been for him. "It went better after the Christmas carols."

"Thank you again for playing. I didn't want you to feel like you were on display, but it made my mom so happy."

He smiles, his eyes searching mine. "It felt a little weird at first, but I was happy to do it."

"It was good for all of us. Paula would hate that we've let the piano sit there unused for so long."

"Maybe it took someone from outside your family to do it. You know, to kind of break the seal?"

I nod, contemplating. "Maybe so. Speaking of, have you ever . . ." I take a deep breath and plunge in. "Have you ever talked to someone about your nightmares?"

"You think I need a shrink?" His smile tightens a little, his voice challenging, but I continue to look at him calmly.

"It's not a question of need. And it's not for me to decide." I swallow back my almost-admission. "I care for you, and if there's something troubling you, I want to help. I know that seeing a grief therapist helped my family immensely after Paula died, though." I hope he realizes that I'm not judging him. "And I've seen how useful therapy is for the parents of the kids we help through the foundation. Everyone has struggled with something in the past or has something in the present that seems insurmountable. It helps to talk to someone completely disconnected from the situation for a fresh perspective." I smile gently. "One thing I learned after Paula's death, although it's been only recently that I've put the lesson to use, is the past is just that—past. It doesn't have to affect the future."

Pursing his lips, he looks down at our joined hands. "You really believe that?"

"I do."

Suddenly remembering what I have for him, and wanting to change the topic, I roll over to grab my bag on the floor. Quickly retrieving the small, wrapped box, I turn and sit up in the bed, facing him. Holding the sheet up to cover my breasts, I hand him the present. "Merry Christmas."

Matt looks shocked for a moment, and then a shy smile spreads across his face as he sits up. He takes the present gingerly. "I have something for you, too, but it's downstairs. Should I go get it?"

"Whatever you'd like." I bite my lip, my nerves getting the better of me, until he tears off the gold paper and lifts the lid. Wordlessly, he stares at the dark green stone, and then lifts it out of the box by its oiled leather cord. The small amulet is oblong and flat, and I hold my breath as he examines the tribal marking carved in the polished surface. "I found it in a little shop downtown," I babble. "The marking is Maori. It's called a toki, although I'm not sure if I'm pronouncing it correctly; it means strength, control, determination, courage, and focus."

He looks at me in wonder. "Is that how you see me?"

I nod, uncertain how he'll feel about that. I loved the idea of him wearing this close to his heart when I bought it, but now, watching his eyes, I'm afraid he thinks it's too serious. "You don't have to wear it if you don't want to," I add quickly. "I know you don't normally wear any kind of jewelry, but I thought—"

"Why wouldn't I wear it?" He looks confused and a little over-whelmed, but then the box goes flying as he launches himself at me. Pinning me down against the mattress, he entwines our fingers, the amulet trapped between our palms. "I love it. Thank you."

Any nervousness I had dissolves as he presses his lips to mine. He smiles roguishly when he feels me melt beneath him. "We'll get to your gift later, if that's okay."

A FEW HOURS LATER, WE'RE in the Camaro heading south on 101 to Tom's house. It's my turn to be anxious about an im-pending parental meeting. I know how highly Matt regards his adopted father, and I want to make a good impression. Drumming my fingers on the plastic container of cookies in my lap, I look out the window and wonder what he's like. He sounds like a saint from what Matt's said, but he looks like a serious bad ass in the pictures I've seen.

As I look down, my eyes water with gratitude for a second time as I carefully finger the delicate silver filigree butterfly that now hangs from my neck. Poor Matt—he didn't know what to do when I burst into tears after I opened the blue box from Tiffany's and saw the beautiful token, sprinkled with tiny diamonds. It was embarrassing, because I hate crying, but I couldn't help it. He knows what butterflies mean to me, that they're my way of honoring Paula. It's the perfect gift.

"You're not getting all teary on me again, are you?" He's jok-ing, but I detect a little apprehension in his voice, too. He probably didn't expect me to go all girly on him this morning and is worried that I may cut loose again.

I flash him a smirk. "No," I lie, sniffing quietly. "Thank you again."

"Anytime, Cardinal," he murmurs, taking my free hand in his. "I'm glad you like it."

"I love it." *I love you.* I glance down at the shiny thing lying against my skin. "You didn't have to spend so much, though."

"Tess, the very fact that you don't care whether I spend money on you or not makes me want to spend *everything* on you." He squeezes my hand. "Most women I've known have been about two things: being able to say they've fucked a rock star and taking advantage of all the perks that come with it. You have no idea how refreshing you are, how *in-fucking-credible* you are, and that alone makes me want to never leave you."

Although I don't need a reminder about the women he's been with in the past, my heart skips a beat. A yearning hits me that's so intense it takes my breath away. I don't want him to leave, either. This is it—I have to tell him. The words are practically fighting to get out. And, with luck, maybe he won't run away screaming.

"Matt, I—"

"Well, here we are." He pulls up in front of an older, well-cared-for house and gets out quickly. We're not far from the airport, but it seems like a quiet little street. After walking around to my side, he helps me out, giving me a nervous smile. I was so wrapped up in my internal struggle, I almost forgot that this meeting is a first for him, too. "What were you saying?" He grabs the bottle of scotch that is our gift to Tom out of the back seat.

"Oh, nothing." I sigh at the lost opportunity, before giving him a bright smile and gesturing to the house. "Has he lived here long?"

"We moved here from LA not long after he adopted me." He looks back at me and smiles reassuringly. "Don't worry, Cardinal. He's going to love you." With practiced ease, he lopes up the stairs to the porch perched over the garage and knocks before opening the door. Just before we step inside, the revving of an engine draws my attention to a beat-up looking dirt bike a couple driveways down. The helmeted rider is staring at us. A shock of recognition hits me. He looks like the asshole that kept tailgating me that day.

"Tess? Come on, babe; you're letting the cold air in."

I step in, a little shaken by my revelation, and allow Matt to take my coat. I must be mistaken. There are probably a million bikers in the city. Shaking my head, I chalk up my overactive imagination to nerves and smooth down my burgundy sweaterdress. Matt said I didn't need to dress up, but it's Christmas and the first time I've met Tom. The house smells of roasting meat and evergreen, thanks to the oversized tree in the living room.

Matt calls for Tom, and when we turn the corner, I almost walk into a solid wall of muscle. Standing even taller than my dad, Tom is balder than a cue ball, with a thick silver goatee and kind gray eyes that seem to see right through me.

I instantly like him.

"I thought I heard you yelling," he rumbles with a big smile. "I'm not deaf yet, you know."

Matt scoffs and they exchange a manly back-patting hug. "Coulda fooled me, old man." He takes a deep breath and slips an arm around my waist. "Tom, this is Tessa Baker. Tess, my dad, Tom Logan."

"Merry Christmas, Mr. Logan." I smile and hand him the container of cookies. "My mom made these. You wouldn't want to eat anything I've attempted to bake, at risk of losing a tooth."

His laugh sounds deep and smoky as he cocks an eyebrow at Matt, who actually *blushes*. "Now I understand why I've seen less of this one lately." He gives me a friendly hug. "Nice to see he's developed an interest in something other than engines and that motley crew he plays with."

I grin, watching the unspoken conversation bouncing between them, until Matt shakes his head. "Yeah, yeah. Don't scare her off before dinner, all right?"

"Wouldn't dream of it," Tom teases, before giving me a wink. "Well, come into the kitchen, you two. Between the three of us, we should be able to do this pot roast justice. Oh, and Matt? Crack open that bottle of champagne in the fridge." He smiles warmly at me, and I find myself beaming back. "This is a celebration, after all."

chapter twelve

matt

LAUGHTER DRIFTS TO THE KITCHEN, and I add another splash of Baileys to the coffee. Once Tom got over his initial shock at actually meeting Tess, we fell into easy conversation.

I shouldn't be surprised; both Tess and Tom just have a way with people. I owe everything to Tom. Fuck knows where I would be today if he hadn't found me trying to steal his car all those years ago.

And Tess . . . Glancing out to the living room, I watch as she pulls her mass of black hair into a ponytail, a smile etched on her face, while Tom rehashes my late teen years. The things I'm starting to feel for Tess scare the hell out of me. That she's come to mean so much to me so fast has me questioning whether it's real. Wondering when the other shoe is going to drop and reality is going to smack me in the face.

"I want to show you something," Tom starts, and I scowl, carrying in the tray of coffees along with the cookies Tess brought.

"Pretty sure she doesn't need to see pictures of me when I was eighteen, old man."

Tom just grins at me over his shoulder before continuing his search of the bookshelf.

"I'm pretty sure *she* does," Tess says. I set the tray down on the low table in front of the couch before sinking down beside her, taking a firm squeeze of her thigh in the process. Her eyes widen, her face flushing as she darts her eyes to Tom and then back to me.

"You're coming to the gala next week, right? I didn't get your RSVP, must have got lost in the mail." Tom levels me a knowing look. "But I've reserved two seats for you," he casually says. Real subtle.

"Gala?" Tess takes one of the coffee mugs between her hands, blowing over the top. My gaze drops to her tempting lips, and she shoots me a warning look.

"Mhmm. It's for the group home. We do it every year: black tie, dancing, silent auction."

Tom shakes his head, returning with a thick photo album, and sinking down into his battered and beloved leather chair. "Didn't tell her, did you?"

"We've been busy." Tess tries to hide her smile behind the rim of her cup.

"Matty here already gives us half of what he makes, I'm sure. We use that mostly for improvements and upgrades. The garage, new instruments for the music room, beds that are like sleeping on a cloud for most of these kids. The gala helps with the education programs and scholarships. They'd never be able to afford to go to college without them—gives them a chance, you know? Hope for the future, and sometimes that's all you need as a kid. Somebody to have a little hope for you." He glances at me before continuing, "Anyway, it's a great time, and you're both coming."

"Yes, sir." I give him a mock salute, sliding my arm across the back of the couch behind Tess. "How's the situation with Zach?"

Tess looks at me confused, and I give her a brief rundown of what's been happening at the group home, glossing over the confrontation we had. "There're two kids there, probably seventeen?" Tom nods, snagging a cookie from the container. "Zach and Beck. Both of them think they're the big shots in the house, but Zach is cocky, arrogant, and involved with the wrong crowd outside the home."

"Sounds familiar," Tom mutters with a hint of a smile.

"And Beck isn't?" Tess asks.

"Not as much," Tom chimes in. "Fletcher's been by. He's teaching a bunch of them how to play."

I smile over at Tom before glancing back at Tess. "Fletcher taught me everything I know about how to play the guitar."

"Not everything," Tom says. "Some things you can't teach. You don't just play, Matt. It's something different with you, something special."

I shake my head, still not used to hearing anything positive, even after all this time. Tom, being Tom, knows me well enough to steer the conversation back to something that's not going to make me uncomfortable. "Anyway, since the day we called the cops after the fight in the garage, Zach's been pushing it even more. I've had to talk to him a couple of times. I think he's making up for losing face with the rest of the kids when you took him down." He rubs his hand across the back of his neck and lets out an exasperated sigh. "He's a handful. Been taking the dirt bike without permission. He broke curfew again the other night. Had to drag him back at one in the morning."

Frowning, I try to tap down the memories that lurk around the fringes. How many nights did I do that? How many times was Tom the one dragging me back? I wonder if Zach realizes yet just how rare it is to have someone like Tom give a shit about him. "Is he spending time in the garage?"

"A bit. He's better when he's busy. You know how it goes if they've got nothing to do."

I feel my jaw set. "Do I ever. Want me to come by? I've wanted to see how they're doing on the Harley." Leaning forward, I pick up one of the coffee cups.

Tom waves me off. "Nah. You hardly get any time off. Spend it with Tess here."

"I could help." Tess glances at me.

I almost spit my coffee out. "You in a garage with these kids? No fucking way. Talk about a teenage dream." Tom's deep laugh fills the room and Tess's face heats again. "It's going to be bad enough when they see you helping out later."

She turns to me, her voice low. "You don't want me to go?"

I let my hand drop from the sofa to drift across the back of her neck, feeling her shiver slightly under my touch. "Of course I do. Just stay by my side, Cardinal."

"That's the only place I want to be," Tess says quietly, her dark eyes full of desire.

Tom clears his throat, and Tess breaks away from my gaze, her cheeks flushed. Tom cracks open the photo album and lays it on the table. Tess seems just a little too excited to see these black-mail pictures of me as a scrawny, awkward teenager for my liking. "Right. Let's start with when Matt turned eighteen."

"YOU'VE BEEN PRACTICING." I MAKE my way into the music room at the center after I've spent a few minutes listening to Beck warm up his guitar from the hallway. As it always has been around the holidays, the group home is overflowing. Tom and the staff have pulled out all the stops to try to make the day seem a little less lonely. A huge tree in the front room that I know he would've taken them to the lot to pick out, decorations, and lights literally everywhere. He's even got gifts under the tree for them all. It's not much, but for kids who have nothing at all, I know it makes a difference.

Beck glances up from the sheet music in front of him, a smile breaking across his face. "You heard that?"

Nodding, I cross the room and pick up one of the Gibson acoustics from its stand by the wall. "I sure did."

"This guy Tom knows has been giving me lessons," he starts to explain. "Fletch—"

"Fletcher Reid." Beck's eyes widen as I slide the guitar strap over my shoulder, strumming a few chords. "He taught me how to play, too. You're in good hands there."

"He taught you?" He stares back in disbelief.

"Sure did. What's he got you working on?" I nod to the sheet music, laughing when I see the familiar notes. "'Back in Black.' Nice. Three chords that will change your life."

He smiles at me. "That's what he said."

I let the feel of the weight of the guitar in my hands ground me. These last few days have been intense. First, surviving the inquisition with Tess's parents, then her meeting Tom yesterday, and now wanting to help out here, it's all been a bit overwhelming. Having a woman like Tess actually care about who I really am outside of the band has thrown me for a bit of loop. "Imagine that. Let's hear it then."

"I'm not very good." Beck anxiously glances down at his fingers.

"I wasn't either. That's why you practice." Blowing out a shaky breath, his grip tightens around the neck of the guitar. "It helps if you relax; give your arms a bit of a shake, empty your head and just play."

"Easy for you to say," he mumbles, glancing back up at me, unsure.

Instinctively, I rub the amulet on my neck. Tess said it meant determination and courage. It's hard to wrap my head around her actually seeing those things in me. It would be easy to leave Beck here to work this out for himself, but I know all too well how that feels. Whether the kid realizes it yet or not, he needs someone to give a shit. Good thing I've got a few hours on my hands. "None of this is easy," I say. "You just have to want to try."

"WHERE'S TESS?" I JOIN TOM in the kitchen with an armful of plates. Dinner was pure chaos, with drop-ins from all over the city. Kids, now a few years older and in a better place thanks to the group home and Tom, as well as fresh faces he'd never seen before. Word gets around on the street about a place like this, and it's been like Grand Central Station in here.

Tom's up to his elbows washing dishes in the sink while a few of the kids help dry and put away. I squeeze past Amanda, one of the many staff members crammed into the kitchen. "I think she's taking a tour of the garage," she says, turning to shove a container of leftovers into the packed fridge. "A couple of the boys wanted to show off the Harley."

"And you just let her go?" I hiss above the buzz of energy in the kitchen. I know Tess can take care of herself. The woman is fierce, never backing down from anything, but the idea of her in the garage with a couple of these kids carrying around chips on their shoulders doesn't sit well.

Tom glances up at me. "Aaron went with them," he says, his brow furrowed. Still, that possessive streak that grows by the minute when I'm around Tess kicks up a notch.

Setting the dishes on the counter, I motion to the hallway that leads to the stairs and the garage. "I'm just going to check on the bike."

"The bike, sure." Tom glances at me from the sink.

It's a good thing Sean's not here. He'd never let me live this down. More than one of his laws have been broken over these last couple of days.

Pushing thoughts of the annoying Brit away, I turn down the hallway, stopping when I hear commotion at the side door. I see Zach slamming the door against the wall, the sound echoing through the house as I make my way over. "Nice of you to join us," Beck says dryly, folding his arms across his chest, glaring at Zach. "Dinner was over a half hour ago."

Zach looks like he's had a rough night. His eyes are sunken and bloodshot, the leather jacket he's wearing is a ragged disaster, his jeans are ripped, and he reeks of cigarettes. Tom won't be impressed. "Relax," Zach mutters, his voice raspy. "If you would've come with me, I wouldn't be late." His tired eyes slide over to me, assessing, hard. "Thought you'd come to see how we're spending your money?"

"He's cool, man," Beck says defensively.

Zach lets out a huff before heading to the table. "Sure, cool," he murmurs. Kicking a chair out from under the table with his boot, he sinks into the seat and scans the remaining trays of food.

If I had to guess, I'd say he hasn't slept in a couple of days. He's exhausted, in desperate need of a shower and an attitude adjustment. "Nice ride out there," he adds around a mouthful of crusty bread.

"Thanks."

"Looks like it's had work done to it recently," Zach says, a hint of a mischief on his face that I don't like.

"A bit of a paint job." His tired eyes narrow at me, his jaw tense, radiating anger. I know what this is like. I *was* Zach for a while. He feels trapped, his options are slipping away, and there are days when it might be easier just to let yourself go down that darker path. Better the devil you know than the one you don't.

Tess's familiar laugh breaks the mounting tension, and I turn to see her coming down the hall with Aaron. Just the sight of her calms me, making me wish we didn't have to leave for the rest of the tour right after the holidays. Time is flying by, and it feels like we haven't had nearly enough time together, just the two us.

"That's a great setup in the garage," she says happily, stopping beside me. "And the Harley is looking good. They're doing a great job." Zach clears his throat, deciding to make his presence known.

"If I had known we had help like this, I would've showed up sooner." Trying to squelch my anger that threatens to boil over, I turn to glare at him.

Aaron takes a seat beside Zach, and Zach immediately backs off, sagging against the chair. "I see you made it back. You okay?" Aaron nudges him in the shoulder.

Zach shrugs, his eyes darting over to Tess before focusing back on the table. "I'm alive. That good enough for you?"

Aaron nods, reaching for a cookie on the dessert tray. "Works for me."

I feel Tess's hand on my arm and glance back at her. She's white as a sheet, staring at Zach, her dark eyes wary, all traces of her previously happy mood gone. "Hey, you okay?" I steer her back down the hall, away from curious eyes. "What's going on? You look like you've seen a ghost." I push her hair back, unable to resist brushing my thumb over her cheek.

Her eyes search mine for a moment, and then she shakes her head with a bullshit half-laugh. "I think it's the turkey coma. Way too much food today."

"Tess . . ."

That fiery streak of hers is back quickly, and she lifts a brow, challenging me like she always does. "Matt . . ."

"Tell me what's wrong, Cardinal."

She reaches up, gently cupping my cheek, and I close my eyes, leaning into her touch, needing it more than I want to admit. "I'm just tired. It's been a long day," she says quietly, and I know that's all I'm getting. Once Tess has made her mind up, there's no changing it.

"Come on. I'll take you home."

Her smile is back, slaying me, filling up the empty holes in my heart. "By home do you mean your place?" she asks as we start back down the hall.

"I mean wherever you are." Pausing at the kitchen, I smile at her, and she squeezes my hand. A simple gesture, full of promise.

"I think we're going to head out, if that's all right."

Wiping his hands on a dish towel, Tom nods. "No problem. We've got lots of help, right boys?" A collective groan greets him as the kids helping with the dishes continue to work away.

"I'll be by tomorrow to work on the Harley."

"Sounds great," Tom says, moving over to envelop Tess in a hug.

"I'm just going to say goodbye to Beck and Aaron." Tess and I slip back to the dining room, finding them still at the table with

Zach.

"I'm going to stop by and work on the bike tomorrow if you guys want to help." I hope Zach pulls his head out of his ass long enough to join us.

Zach tosses a balled-up napkin on the table. "Whatever," he mumbles. Now I know how Tom must have felt with me. How he probably still feels on a daily basis with Zach and some of these other kids. The man clearly has the patience of a saint.

"Around one or so. Sound good?" Zach shrugs in response. Beck gives me a more enthusiastic nod.

"They'll both be there," Aaron answers for them, leaning back in the chair. "Bring pizza," he adds, glancing at Zach.

"You got it." Somehow, I think it's going to take more than pizza to turn Zach around.

Tessa

THE DRIVE BACK TO MATT'S is quiet, save for his soft humming along with whatever's on the radio. He has the most marvelous voice. Although a higher register than Kennedy's, it's rich and vibrant, and more than capable of bringing me to my knees. I wish he could see how talented he really is.

"Whatcha thinking about so hard over there?" he asks as we wait for his noisy garage gate to open. The screech of the gears could wake the dead.

"I'm thinking that thing could use a gallon of WD-40." I shoot him a look. "Before that, though, I was thinking you should sing a few tracks on the next album."

He huffs in amusement, his cheeks pinking above his scruff.

"Nah, Kennedy and Cam are better suited to singing lead." After we pull in and park inside the safety of his garage, the door begins its laborious descent behind us.

"If you say so." I smile wistfully. "You can sing for me anytime. I love your voice." I would never want to screw with the dynamics of the band, but it frustrates me sometimes how Matt automatically defers to his bandmates, and how he merely considers himself lucky to be a part of the group, as opposed to truly believing he's just as responsible for their success as the others. It was fascinating to watch the four of them interact during the planning for Parker's benefit concert, as well as the show itself. Kennedy, Cam, and Sean all listened carefully to what Matt said and made sure he weighed in before making any decisions. It seemed obvious to me that they believe Matt is an essential part of Redfall. They respect him as a talent and as a man. As for Matt, sometimes it seems that he's just grateful they let him tag along.

It works for them, I guess, and I don't want to push him into something he isn't comfortable doing. I simply wish I could help him see in himself the extraordinary man that everyone else sees.

What I see.

He climbs out and comes around to my side of the Camaro. "I'm partial to your voice, too. Especially when you're screaming my name in the middle of the night."

"Keep it up and your memories are all you'll have." I slip my hands around his neck. He's deflecting, and I let him. Rome wasn't built in a day.

His lips graze my neck, and I shiver reflexively. It's like the man is a drug my body can't get enough of. "You love it when I keep it up." He flexes his hips, letting me feel what's beginning to stir in his jeans. "Shall we go upstairs and give you a reminder?"

"Yes, let's."

Hand in hand, we climb the ridiculous stairway—which takes longer than usual because we keep stopping to make out and grope each other like a couple of teenagers—up to his loft. If he had an elevator from the garage like the one from the main lobby, we'd probably already be naked. He flings the metal door open with a crash, and I giggle as he drags me to the couch, almost colliding into the enormous Christmas tree. Clothing is peeled off between playful yet passionate kisses, and finally I have his smooth, colorfully decorated skin under my hands.

He pulls me to his lap, and we both let out groans of relief when I sink down onto him. The mood shifts; his touch becomes more desperate, and his arms wrapped around me are like steel bands. My head drops back as I savor the feeling of absolute full-ness—it's overwhelming sometimes. He's the total package—a generous heart, brilliant mind, and passionate soul. My heart swells with love and it's on the tip of my tongue to tell him how I feel. But, the sudden vulnerability I see in his eyes stops me.

"Why can't I ever get enough of this, of you?" he mumbles against my lips.

I'm not sure he wants an answer. Instead of using words, I try to show him how I feel with my lips, hands, and body.

I hope he can hear me.

"DO YOU WANT TO MOVE to the bed?"

I shake my head where it rests in the crook of his shoulder. I can't remember ever being this relaxed. We're lying on the floor on a pile of cushions and pillows we pulled off the sofa, wrapped up in a blanket and each other. The scent of evergreen fills the large room. Twinkle lights on the tree are the only illumination, and they sparkle above us like so many stars.

"Do *you* want to?"

He presses a soft kiss to my temple. "I don't want to move from this spot. Possibly ever." He pulls me closer, and I snuggle in with a happy contentment. His hand closes over my left breast and he gives it a gentle squeeze, as if to reassure himself it's still there. Matt has a thing about my boobs. I swear, sometimes it's like he wants to set up camp there, but you won't find me complaining. "Will you tell me what upset you earlier at the home?"

Rats. I was hoping he'd forget about that. Trying to relax as inconspicuously as possible, I hum and trace random circles on his arm. "What makes you think I was upset?"

He chuckles, the sound rumbling in his chest. "Cardinal."

"It was nothing." I duck my face, ashamed of myself, and wish I could take back my earlier weird little moment of déjà vu.

Everything had been fine. Aaron and I had been laughing with a couple of the kids in the garage before coming back inside, and then, there was something about that kid, Zach. The set of his shoulders and the way he tilted his head when he leered at me. The first thing that hit me was that he was the biker that followed me that day Matt's car was keyed. Which is completely ridiculous. Whoever it was wore a full helmet.

Jumping to conclusions, especially about someone who Tom is trying so hard to work with, is grossly unfair of me. Matt had to fight the same type of presumptions when he was growing up, still does in some ways. I know Zach is a handful, and he's giving Tom a major headache, but he needs people to believe in him and show a little faith, not make baseless accusations.

I hate that my mind automatically went there the instant I met him.

"What?" With a finger under my chin, Matt gently draws my

face up to his. His eyes are full of concern, protectiveness even, which makes me feel even guiltier.

"Nothing, really." I smile up at him. "So, you're occupied tomorrow afternoon, it sounds like?"

He gives me a measured stare. When I don't break, he purses his lips and releases my chin. "Yeah. Hopefully we'll be able to make some progress, both with the bike and the kids."

"You don't sound very confident."

"Some of them are tough nuts to crack." He shifts, bringing our heads closer together on the pillows. "I can appreciate Tom's tenacity where I was concerned much more now. I must have driven him crazy back then."

A chuckle escapes me. "Just back then?" My chuckle becomes a shriek, and I try to twist away from his sudden tickle attack. He stops just as fast as he started and pulls me against his chest.

"Do you want to come with me tomorrow?"

I look at him with surprise. "I didn't think you really liked having me there."

"I loved having you there," he says with a touch of exasperation, his fingers gripping my hip a little harder. "But I don't want you to be there without me. Especially in the garage."

"Seriously?" I shift on the cushions and raise my chin in challenge. "Besides Aaron and Tom, there are a bunch of staffers there. What could happen?"

"Tess," he says, realizing his mistake, but not his peril. "You don't know these kids like I do. You're like a red flag waved in front of a bull."

Sweeping a strand of hair out of my eyes, I look down, pretending to be hurt. As I hoped, he raises his arm to slip it around my shoulders. "I should know; you always make me feel—Ah!"

His whole body lurches as I swiftly grab the pressure point

in the soft inside of his bicep, just above the crease in his elbow. I release him just as quickly, and he stares at me with amazement and just a hint of betrayal, rubbing his arm. "Holy shit that hurt."

"You've met my dad. Can you believe he'd release three daughters to the world without teaching them a few things? I can take care of myself."

He chuckles and, somewhat gingerly, slips his arm around my waist. "Point taken."

I trace my finger over some of the swirls of ink on his shoulder. "Back to your question. I'd love to go, but I can't take the time off. There are some things I need to make sure are on track." I'm still very new to my job, and although Abby is very free with vacation requests around the holidays, I want to show that I'm responsible.

He hums in satisfaction. "It'll be quite a shock for some of those high society–types when I show up with you on my arm at the gala. I think they've always expected me to bring a groupie in a slutty dress they can gossip over later."

"Hmm, I'm not sure I own anything slutty enough," I tease. "I'll have to work on that."

He flips me over so he's on top, startling a squeak from me. "Not too much skin, Cardinal." His eyes darken as they bore into mine. My skin heats; I can feel a slow flush spread across my neck. "I don't give a shit what anyone expects. No one gets to see your special places but me."

Everything south of my navel clenches at the gritty sound of his voice. "No worries; I have just the thing." My head lolls back as he starts kissing down my jaw to my ear. I love the dichotomy between the strength in his arms as he holds me captive and the tenderness in his kisses.

"If you were worried about something important, something about you and me, you'd tell me, right? I know that neither of us have had much in the way of real relationships, but even I know we need to feel comfortable talking about the big things if we're going to make a go of this."

My twinge of guilt is quickly smothered by a rush of emotion at the shy sincerity in his voice. I cup his cheeks and gently raise his face so I can look into his eyes. "If it's important, I *will* tell you. Big, small, and everything in between."

As soon as I get the nerve.

THE NEXT MORNING, I'M FLOATING on a Matt Logan high. It's quiet in the office, with most of the staff out until after the new year starts, so I only get a few funny looks as I drift through the halls like a lovesick schoolgirl.

Nadia's assistant walked out with her, so I'm on my own until I find a replacement. Nibbling on my thumbnail, my thoughts are on a certain bass player rather than the stack of résumés I'm sorting. He's just so damn *sweet*. Even in the throes of passion, there's always a tender touch or word to show me he's connected, that he's right there with me, every step of the way. It was hard to leave him this morning. Closing my eyes, I can easily picture his lean, muscled back as he lay in bed, the sheets pooled down around his waist . . .

"Anybody home?"

Startled out of my lustful thoughts, I glance up and beam at the familiar bald man peeking in my open door. "Tom! Wow, it's great to see you." Standing swiftly, I step over to give him a quick hug as he enters my office. I eagerly look beyond him, expecting to see Matt, but there's no one there. Although I'm happy to see Tom, I'm confused as to why he'd be here, unless . . .

"Is everything okay?" I ask urgently, gripping his forearm.

"Where is—"

"Matt should be at the group home by now, probably with a boatload of pizza," he says with a gentle smile. I release him with a mumbled apology, but he shakes his head. "Don't worry about it; in fact, your concern is reassuring."

Puzzled, I finally remember my manners and gesture for him to sit down at the small table I use for meetings. "Well, how can I help you?" I query as I sit down across from him.

He tents his hands on the table. "I'm sorry to show up unannounced. I wanted to wait until I knew he'd be occupied so we could have a little chat."

My eyes shoot open, and my stomach twists in knots. I knew our first meeting went too well. Was this to be the sort of grilling that my dad gave Matt?

I wait for him to begin and steel myself. "Tess, you're a lovely girl, and based on the way Matt was looking at you during Christmas, it seems he thinks so, too." He watches me carefully. "There's a spark in his eyes that I haven't seen in a long, long time. If ever."

I know Matt cares for me, but I haven't allowed myself to believe that it may be as serious for him as it is for me. Hearing Tom's candid assessment is heartening. But my nerves return when Tom runs a hand over his shaved head.

"How much has Matt told you about his growin'-up years?"

"Some," I say quietly, looking down at my hands in my lap. I don't want to be rude, but I'm uncomfortable talking about Matt's past behind his back. "He's told me the basics about his mom and that he was shuffled around foster homes before ending up in the group home. I'm sure there's probably more. But I respect his privacy. I hope he'll tell me someday when he's ready."

He holds up a hand. "I'm not here to tell tales that aren't mine to tell," he clarifies. "But I did want to give you a little perspective."

Stroking his goatee, he gathers his thoughts. "Matt is my son. He's a gifted musician and a celebrity, but first and foremost my son. One I never thought I'd have." His leather jacket rustles as he leans back in his chair. "My wife and I weren't able to have children, so we focused on the kids that came and went through the group home in LA. We tried to give them what we could. It became even more important to me after I lost her. She would've loved Matt." He glances past me with a faraway gleam in his eye.

"Anyway, what I wanted to say is that before he met me, Matt had no one in his corner. Even while his mom was still alive, he was essentially on his own. And the foster system is so strapped for resources, kids just can't get the dedicated attention they need. He was so wary of me at first. He drove me nuts, the little shit." He chuckles, his smile reminiscent. I try to imagine a younger, smart-mouthed Matt, pushing Tom's buttons then like he pushes mine now. "It took me ages to get him to trust me," he continues. "But I wouldn't give up."

"Why not?" The question escapes me before I can stop it, but he doesn't seem to mind.

"Because there was something about him. Something special behind all the bravado and anger and hurt that called to me." Tom's gray eyes seem to laser right through me. "I hope you know what I mean."

I nod, my throat closing up. I know *exactly* what he means. "Tess." Tom leans forward, covering my hands on the table with one of his larger, rougher ones. "My point is that I hope you're serious about this. Believe me, I know his reputation. There have only been a couple girls in his life that Matt's mentioned to me more than once, and you're the *only* girl I've actually met, besides Fletcher's niece back when he was nineteen. This should tell you something.

"I'm not saying you have to get married and have a bunch of babies." My breath catches at the thought, which somehow isn't quite as terrifying as I used to think. "But I hope that it's real. Not some fling you're just trying on like a new dress. You don't *seem* like that type of girl, and I do trust Matt's judgement." He frowns and he shakes his head, as though irritated with himself. "He's had enough disappointment and people using him for whatever they can get out of him. He needs someone besides me and the guys in the band to be in his corner."

I return his steady, probing gaze. "It *is* real. At least, it is for me." I slide my hands out from under his and sit back, crossing my arms protectively. Matt would die of embarrassment to know Tom was saying all this, and I'm sure Tom knows it. It says a lot about Tom's genuine affection and concern for Matt that he'd risk his wrath coming here. Throwing caution to the wind, I finally whisper, "I . . . I love him."

Tom's eyes flare in surprise and he rubs his whiskered chin. "Have you told him?"

I shake my head. "Not yet. It never seems like the right time. I don't want him to feel pressured to say it back if he doesn't." I toy with the button on my jacket sleeve. Saying it out loud makes my excuses sound so childish. Glancing up at him, I see only understanding instead of the censure I expect.

"I don't think there is a *right* time for telling someone you love them. It just happens." He sits back, a smile playing about his lips. "I had just picked her up from a babysitting job when my wife told me for the first time. I almost crashed us into a palm tree."

I return his smile hesitantly. He makes it sound so easy.

A small bird lands on the ledge outside my window, drawing our attention. "Matt told me what happened with your sister," he adds, keeping his eyes on the bird as it hops around. "As tragic as a loss like that is, it can also inspire you to treasure every moment of your life—and the people who are in it."

The bird flies off again, and he returns his gray-eyed gaze to mine. "Yes, it can," I murmur, swallowing down the sudden lump in my throat.

After giving me one more measured look, he nods to himself. "Well, I've taken enough of your time." He slaps his hands on his knees before standing. I spring up and walk with him toward the door. "I hope you don't think I'm an overbearing assho—" He grimaces. "That I'm a jerk, for coming here today."

"Of course not. You worry about him, like any parent should. And you want him to be happy. I want that for him, too. But we've only been together a short time. I don't want to scare him by just blurting it out. Besides, this is new for me, as well. What I feel for Matt is different." I squirm a little at revealing myself before this man I barely know, but who knows Matt better than anyone.

"I understand that now. I think you're just the person—" The sound of a motorcycle revving blares from inside his worn jacket. "Oh, excuse me." With a small grin, he pulls his phone from his pocket and checks the text. His grin evaporates.

"What is it?"

"I've got to go. There's something goin' on at the home." He avoids looking at me, making my stomach plummet.

"Is it about Matt?" His jaw clenches, answering me without words. "Tom, what's happened?"

"Nothing out of the ordinary, unfortunately. Just Zach raising a little hell. Again." He shakes his head and tucks his phone back in his pocket. Seeing my worried frown, he gives my shoulder a reassuring squeeze. "The kids are always getting into scraps. No biggie."

"All right." I fold my arms and try to smile, but I can't help my worry. "I hope it's not too bad, whatever it is."

Tom nods, obviously eager to get moving. "I'm sure it'll be fine." He starts to head out the door, but stops and throws me a teasing wink so much like Matt's, I'd swear he was his biological father. "Besides, you have bigger worries—like how to tell my son you're in love with him."

With that, he turns and hurries down the hall, leaving me gawking in his wake.

chapter thirteen

matt

TWO HOURS IN AND THE garage at the group home is buzzing with energy. Aaron and I have kept busy trying to channel the
erratic behavior of some of these teens. They seemed to be doing
better before Zach got here.

His presence alone changed the dynamic dramatically. What
started out as excitement and an eagerness to learn after they de-
voured the pizza I brought, took a darker turn the minute Zach
walked into the garage. He passes critical judgement with a simple
look, a shrug of his shoulders, or a snide comment about how
lame working in the garage is. Unfortunately, some of these kids
hang on his every word.

When you're outside looking in, it's easy to pick out the lem-
mings, the ones who will follow Zach, no questions asked. Beck is
another matter entirely. He's trying to focus on replacing the rear

brake pads of the Harley—one of the last parts we need to repair before it's road-worthy again—but it's difficult when Zach refuses to leave him alone for more than five minutes.

"You're just the golden boy today, aren't you, Beck?" Zach throws another sneer at him, trying to get a reaction. "Teacher's little pet. What a pussy."

"Enough," Aaron's voice rises again, and he takes a firm stance near the bike. "If you'd just pay attention, maybe you'd learn something."

In a scene that is all too familiar, Zach huffs and returns to polishing the chrome air cleaner cover, surrounded by his pack of wannabe thugs across the room.

"Ignore him," I mutter to Beck as he scowls at the bike.

"I'm trying to."

"I know you are. I also know it's not easy."

"He's a fucking jerk," he whispers under his breath.

"Watch your mouth." Beck glances up at me, looking much older than his seventeen years. "If he knows he's getting to you he'll just keep doing it."

"Remind me about this again." Beck picks up the torque wrench and changes the subject.

"I torque everything to specifications. You need to do it properly. Let's just say you don't want an accident on your hands because you were being lazy."

Beck listens intently as Zach and the rest of the crowd join the fold. "It's one of the areas you don't mess around with. Safety first. Always."

"Guess there's a lot that can go wrong with a bike," Zach comments, picking up the skull brake caliper insert and studying it carefully.

"Yeah, there is. That's why you need to pay attention."

Zach glances at me, his eyes hard and assessing, muscles coiled for a fight. Fuck, I remember those days. So much anger and resentment bottled up and ready to explode. It can consume you. I want to tell him to stop being such an ass, that it does get better, but I know he doesn't want to hear it. The best I can do, the best any of us can do, is just to be there for him, and for any of these kids who've had no one in their corner for far too long.

Zach glances at the bike, moving beside Beck, surprising the hell out of me. "You're the boss. So show me what I need to know." It's a glimmer of hope from Zach, and I'll take it.

An hour later, while Aaron and I are taking the boys through the basics of tire changing, the Brit calls, checking in from across the pond with his annual holiday update. Sean's at home in London, spending time with his parents and his twin sister, Sydney, before we head up to Canada for the rest of the tour.

"Syd's engaged, Grasshopper! Fucking engaged!" He's furious and begins ranting like the fool he is. I have to hold the phone away from my ear as he hollers. "To a bloody barrister. She's known him for about thirty seconds. Wore a proper three-piece suit to Christmas supper."

"Pretty sure I've seen you in one of those," I mutter, moving out of the garage to catch some air. It's cooler today, a dampness settling in, but I know that's nothing compared to what awaits when we hit Winnipeg for the tour in the new year. Minus fucking forty. The Canadian fans are diehards, though. Some of my favorite crowds.

Sean goes on. "He's a wanker."

"Would anyone be good enough for your sister?"

"No. Not since Simon died. But a barrister? Come on. She can do better." He lets out a huff of frustration.

"Mmm."

"Fuck, I wish you guys were here. I need to play."

"So play. You've got your own place there, tripped out with the latest equipment, if memory serves."

"It's not the same." I can practically see the pout on his face, sulking like a five-year-old who's lost his favorite toy. "Tell me about your holiday, then. Get my mind off this clusterfuck. How is the lovely Tess?"

I think about fucking her in the shower this morning. The luscious curve of her sweet ass grinding against me, her soft cries driving me insane as I claimed her over and over. It was intense and raw, frenzied and needy, leaving us both a breathless, quivering mess. Tess has managed to crack me open and plant herself into my heart and soul. What the hell did I do before I found her?

Sean's annoyed groan ends my vivid memory quickly. "Not you, too. Damn it. It's bad enough HRH is writing ballads every other day. I've lost you, too?"

"You'll live, I'm sure."

"More for Cameron and me, then. How is his dad? When I talked to him a couple of days back, things were improving."

Frowning, I pace the side of the garage. When I dropped Cameron off in Boston at the hospital before the holidays, his dad's heart attack had hit him hard. His father is an overbearing hardass who probably wishes Cam had never laid eyes on any of us. Despite all of that, Cameron saw him as invincible. "He's recovering. Too stubborn not to. I think it shook Cam up more than he wanted to admit."

"I saw that one coming a mile away. The man is a walking stress bomb. Probably works eighteen hours a day."

"Probably more than that."

"You think Cam's okay, though? I mean, shit like this rattles you."

I know where he's going. Cameron being clean after his last stint in rehab is relatively new, fragile at best. But with a focus now on getting his dad better, I hope he's got another reason to stay clean. "I think he'll be okay. He's still texting us all a few times a day. It's when he goes quiet that we have to worry."

"You're a wise man, Grasshopper. Good thing we all have you to keep us on the straight and narrow."

Shaking my head, I glance up at the threatening skies. "Jesus, if you're relying on me to keep you in line, we're in some serious trouble."

"Nothing wrong with a little trouble every now and again. Keeps us honest, yeah?"

"CARDINAL! LIMO'S WAITING." I ADJUST the cuff link on my shirt as I wait for Tess downstairs in my loft. It takes a lot to get me in a suit. The gala for the group home is one of the events I'll make an exception for.

It's being held this year at the Bently Reserve. Pretentious as all hell. I'd typically hate going to this thing. I'd operate on autopilot with the stuffed shirts and high society elite, and the small talk that just about kills me. This year, that's all changed. The thought of having Tess on my arm, by my side, has hit me hard. Something protective, territorial has kicked in. This nagging desire to make sure everyone knows she's mine.

There will be press there. Tess and I will have to walk the red carpet and pose for a few pictures. There will be no question after tonight that we're together. I'm not sure if she's prepared for that. We haven't exactly talked about what it all means for her, or how it could change things for us. I know what the pressure can do when the bubble you've put yourself in breaks, and your life is exposed, raw, and open for the world to see.

Turning to the sound of heels on the staircase, my breath stops at the sight of her. Enticing curves poured into a ruby red gown made to fit her in all the right places. Her long, raven black hair falls in waves around her shoulders. She's a walking dream . . . my dream.

She turns around slowly in front of me as I drop my gaze over her. "What do you think?"

It takes a minute for my brain to function. "I think we should stay here. Let me peel you out of that dress, you gorgeous girl."

She smiles—that one I know is meant just for me. "You like it?"

Taking a step toward her, I skim my hand around her waist, feeling the rich fabric of her gown under my palm when I press her against my chest. "I love it. You wore this color just for me, didn't you, Cardinal?"

"Maybe," she says, her voice breathy as she grips the lapel of my jacket.

I can't resist pressing my lips to hers, a deep groan vibrating through my chest as my palm skims up her exposed back. "Cherry fucking almond. You know I like that one."

"You like all of them," she whispers before crushing her lips to mine once more.

My fingers toy with the zipper on the back of her dress, dragging it down. I guess we're going to be late.

Tessa

I BRIGHTEN MY SMILE AND straighten my shoulders, bracing

myself for another inquisition. Matt hadn't been kidding when he said people would be surprised he brought someone to the fundraiser. I've felt the inquisitive gazes all night. But the nearly constant presence of the tall man beside me has made it more than bearable.

"Matt!" A distinguished, iron-haired gentleman approaches. "So nice to see you again. I wasn't sure you'd be here this year because of your tour." Matt shakes his hand, a practiced smile on his face.

"I wouldn't miss it for the world," Matt assures him. He smiles down at me. "Tess, this is Daniel Green."

"Tessa Baker." I shake his offered hand as Daniel explains he's the president of an investment bank. We exchange pleasantries for a few minutes and eventually trade business cards when he learns where I work. His firm is a huge backer of the group home, but he'd also love to help What's Your Dream. It's been like that all evening. With Parker's concert still fresh in people's minds, and knowing how involved Matt and Redfall were in the success of the event, people have been practically falling over themselves to be associated with our future projects.

A woman wearing a gown more appropriate for a woman thirty years younger drifts over to us. It's obvious that she's no stranger to Botox. "My wife, Missy," Daniel supplies. Missy smiles at me, the skin of her too-smooth face stretching unnaturally. The heavy diamonds glittering at her throat and ears stand out against her artificial tan.

"So nice to meet you," she simpers, and I suppress my cringe at her limp society handshake. She gives Matt a sly glance. "I didn't know you had a little sister, Matt. How nice of you to bring her."

I feel Matt's fingers dig into my waist a little. "My girlfriend, Tessa Baker," he says shortly, by way of introduction.

"Oh!" She blinks in faux surprise, looking between us. "But, you're so . . . Oh well, I suppose that's all part of the rock-and-roll image, isn't it? Older men with young girls? Paul McCartney is seventy-something, and his new wife is half his age."

"Uh, nice to see you again Matt, and lovely to meet you, Tessa. I'll have my charity department give you a call," Daniel interjects quickly, his smile now brittle as he ushers his wife away. "Come along, dear."

"Catty bitch," I mutter after they're out of earshot, and then shrug, dismissing her. It's not my fault that she's having trouble accepting her sixties.

"Daniel's not bad, but his wife is a trip. Ignore her. She's just jealous." He reaches up to toy with one of the microscopic straps holding up my gown. "You're easily the most beautiful woman here."

I duck my chin, his compliment making my cheeks heat. "I love this dress. I've been hoping for another opportunity to wear it." It's a copy of a Vivienne Westwood couture that would impress Vivienne herself. My mother did a fantastic job on it; the rich red satin flows into a few graceful gathers that make the most out of what nature gave me. The runway version was ice blue, but Mom happily recreated it in my favorite color.

"It's not just the dress." He presses his lips to my neck, and I shiver. "Let's get out of here so I can show you what I mean. *Again.*"

"Stop!" A giggle bubbles up as I grab his hand at my hip, keeping it from sliding down to my ass. "We don't have time. They're starting to seat people for dinner." I nod to where Tom is standing with a small group of donors, looking supremely awkward in his tux, and scanning the room—for us most likely. We're supposed to be at his table.

Frowning in sudden consternation, Matt steers me around the corner and stops us by a potted plant. "Cardinal, I've never thought to ask if our age difference bothers you." He casts a worried glance in the direction of Missy the Catty Bitch, and the light dawns on me.

"Of course not. There's only seven years between us, Matt." I smooth down his long tie. Damn, the man looks good in a tux. "My parents are eight years apart, if that makes you feel any better."

He slides a hand around my waist. "It does, actually. You once said your birthday is in a couple of months. When, exactly?"

I bite the inside of my cheek. I should've known he'd ask that. "February," I say, looking over toward Tom. "I think we need to join the others."

He holds me fast. "When in February?"

Sighing internally, I look up into his earnest, excited blue eyes. "The fourteenth," I admit, and his eyes widen predictably.

"You were born on Valentine's Day?" The amusement in his voice makes me groan. "How did your folks plan that?"

"I don't think there was much planning involved." I roll my eyes and turn to lead us back to the group and away from the subject. Having a birthday on the biggest Hallmark holiday of the year has always been annoying as hell. All my birthday cards were festooned in shades of pink with frilly lettering and sappy sentiments, the holiday overshadowing everything else. As a tomboy growing up, it drove me batty. It's probably not as bad as having your birthday on Christmas, but it's got to be pretty close.

"I think it's perfectly appropriate," he murmurs, trailing his fingers down my bare arm before falling into step beside me. Holding hands, we join the others moving toward the round tables set up with white cloths and gleaming china in the magnificent room. I've always loved the Bently Reserve. What's Your Dream has held several events here.

"Have you checked out the silent auction yet?" a deep voice asks, and I turn and beam at Tom.

"Of course! There's a great mix of items. Your donor team did well. I have my eye on the private dinner for two at the Top of the Mark."

"Great views from up there," Matt comments, giving me an approving nod. "I haven't been there in years."

"Who says I'm taking you?" I retort, tossing my head and linking arms with Tom, who laughs heartily and claps a hand on Matt's shoulder.

"Sorry, son." He gives me a wink. "The lady clearly has good taste."

"*My* lady," Matt growls, pulling me back to his side. "Hands off, old man."

Tom holds his hands up, still smiling. "Fine, fine. Let's get this dinner started, shall we? I'm starved."

There are more camera flashes around the room as we move among the other guests. From the minute we stepped out of the limo, the evening has been captured on film. I can only imagine what the gossip blogs who follow the band will say about another member of Redfall falling off the list of eligible celebs. Because that's exactly what it's looked like tonight. Matt has stood tall and handsome, his hand firmly at my waist. It's as if he's relishing the opportunity to declare to the world that we're a couple. The thought is both encouraging and a little scary.

Matt holds my chair for me as I sit, and the simple gesture strikes a chord in me when I notice several other gentlemen doing the same for their partners. This is *real*. We're out, in public, showing affection and behaving just like other couples do. Just like other people *in love* do. So what if he hasn't said the words yet? Even if he's not quite there yet, he's certainly close to it. I need to get over myself and just tell him how I feel. I love him. Like Tom said, there doesn't have to be a *right* time. Right?

"Darn it," Tom mutters as he frowns down at his phone and draws Matt's attention.

"Something happen?" he asks, leaning over to see the text message.

"Is it Zach again?" I ask. I know they want to give Zach every opportunity to pull himself out of the anger he's currently wallowing in, but I can't help but wonder if this time their goodwill is misplaced. There's something about that kid that's disturbing.

Tom glances over to me and shoves his phone in his pocket. "Nothing that we need to worry about tonight," he assures me. I look at Matt for confirmation, and he skims his hand over his blond hair before slinging his arm across the back of my chair.

"It's just the same old shit, Cardinal, I promise." He presses his lips briefly against my temple, and then sits back as the well-trained team of waiters begins their intricate dance around the tables with trays laden with food. "Zach isn't involved; he's not even there tonight."

"FUCK." MATT'S GROAN OF RELIEF brings a smile to my lips. "I hate wearing a tux." He throws his jacket on a chair and yanks at his tie like it's strangling him.

"You may hate wearing it, but you looked fantastic tonight." I retrieve the offending jacket and hang it up out of harm's way. His lips quirk in a smile, and he comes up behind me, pulling me against his chest.

"Is that so?" His lips tickle my ear, making me squirm in his grasp. "I'll tell you what's fantastic, and it's what's under this dress." I hold my breath as his skillful fingers draw down the long zipper of my gown. Yards of red satin settle at my feet with a soft rustle, and then I'm lifted into his strong arms and tossed on the bed.

He's on me in an instant, and we're a tangle of lips and limbs. I struggle to undo his shirt buttons, but it's hard to see what I'm doing because he won't stop kissing me. It finally comes free, and I'm starting on his pants when his ringtone for Tom splits the air.

Matt mutters a curse and rests his forehead against mine for a beat, before rolling over with a huff to answer. "Your timing is—" he begins, but stops abruptly. "Seriously? Fuck."

I sit up and hold a pillow over my chest, alarmed at his tone. "No, don't do that," he continues, reaching to take my hand. "Come here. We can pull out the sofa bed for you." He meets my curious gaze and smiles. "We wouldn't have it any other way. Right."

He ends the call and tosses the phone on the mattress beside me. "Someone's vandalized Tom's house. Broke the windows and smashed a bunch of stuff. He was going to sleep at the group home."

"No, of course he should be here," I say instantly. Giving the pillow a squeeze, I let out a chuckle. "Guess I'd better put something on."

He grabs it from me and tosses it aside, making me laugh. "It'll take him a while to get here." He pulls himself over me and smirks. "I can be speedy."

"I LOVE THIS DRESS!" APRIL slaps a newspaper down on my desk. "Do you think your mom could make me one?"

I lift the paper, which she conveniently folded open to the society section. There, among a few other photos of last night's gala, is a shot of Matt and me on the red carpet. We're smiling at each other, and he's gently moving a strand of hair out of my eyes.

I love it.

"Sure, of course she could."

April picks up the paper and sits opposite my desk. "You look sensational together," she declares, looking at the photo. "Did you have a nice time?"

"It was great. They raised a ton of money. Matt's dad was thrilled." I pull out the stack of business cards I collected last night and hand them to her. "I made a lot of good contacts, too."

She shuffles through them, nodding with approval. "How did it feel walking the carpet together?"

"It was a little unnerving at first," I admit and take a sip from my coffee. "But Matt was so relaxed, he made it easy."

"Well, he certainly has experience, considering all the awards Redfall has won." She folds her arms. "So, are you guys living together now?"

I grimace. "Not technically, although I have almost as much clothing at his place as I do at mine. Jada was complaining last week that she's hardly seen me since he's been home." A twinge of guilt hits me again when I picture my roommate's pout. A girl's night with her is way overdue.

"Well, I'm sure it's just a matter of time." She stretches her arms above her head before standing up. I'm about to argue with her prediction, when she continues, "Do you guys have New Year's Eve plans, too? I'm going to a party over on Treasure Island—why don't you and Matt come with me?"

"I'll ask him, but I'm not sure what's going to be on his plate. His dad ran into a little trouble last night after the gala." Tom had been troubled when he arrived at Matt's last night, but he hid it behind a knowing smile when he saw me looking much more disheveled than I'd been a couple hours earlier. He helped me make up the sofa bed while Matt arranged for security for Tom's place until he could get the windows fixed. They both repeatedly assured me there was nothing to worry about, but it was hard to believe them. Especially when I saw the photos Tom had taken of the damage. It wasn't just simple vandalism. It was rage.

"Just let me know. It's no problem to add two more to the guest list." She rises and starts to walk out, when Abby appears in my doorway. She and Kennedy returned yesterday from visiting his folks in Minnesota, and she's in the office today to catch up a little before they venture to her parents' in Napa tonight. She's been in a happy little love bubble all morning. But the stricken look on her face now makes my heart stop.

"Tess . . ." She swallows heavily, her hands gripping the door-frame. "You need to come with me. Now."

chapter fourteen

matt

"WHAT A MESS," TOM GRUMBLES as he wades through the broken glass on the floor in front of the living room window.

Tucker's team of security worked well into the night, trying to get Tom's place back into some sort of order. They removed graffiti from the garage door and installed a new state-of-the-art security system despite Tom's initial reservations. It's a battle he knew he wasn't going to win. One look at the sheer destruction and my mind was made up. The first call I made was to Tucker.

The police have a couple of leads from the neighbors, nothing concrete. I think Tom and I both have a sinking suspicion of who's behind this, even though he's not going to admit it.

"We need to talk about Zach." Tom levels me a look of warning before glancing out to the disaster on the front lawn. It will take more than a couple of days to clean up the damage.

"We have no proof of anything."

I feel my jaw clench with mounting tension. "Seriously? Have you seen his attitude?"

Tom sweeps up more broken glass. "If I had a dime for every kid with an attitude."

"Smart-ass." I plant myself in front of him. "I'm trying to be serious. If something ever happened to you . . ." The thought of something happening to Tom because of one of these kids sits like a dead weight in my gut.

He gives me a half smile, his tired eyes saying more than words ever could. It's rare to see him like this. I know he's worried about Zach, about all of them. This has rattled him more than he wants to admit. "Matty, I've been doing this my whole life. I've seen worse. If Zach was involved—" I scowl and he squeezes my shoulder before continuing, "*If* he was involved, I'll find out. None of these kids are very good at keeping a secret."

"I'd be happy to talk to them for you, Tom," Tucker offers, his arms crossed in that familiar protective way I'm used to seeing.

Tom lets out a laugh. "I appreciate it, but one sight of you and I'll never get anything out of them. What are you benching these days? 350?"

Tucker shrugs, leaning against the wall all smug. "Something like that. Offer stands if you change your mind."

"Thanks. I'm glad this one has you in his corner." Tom nudges me in the shoulder. "He can be a handful."

"Don't I know it. The stories I could tell you."

"That right?" Tom leans against the broom. "I'm all ears."

I narrow my eyes at Tucker. "You wouldn't dare."

"So many choices. Where to start? Mexico City or the Tonga Room at the Fairmont."

I shake my head. "I should kick your ass for even bringing

that up."

"I'd love to see you try. Tom, come with me. Let me show you the security system and we can swap stories."

IT TOOK EVERYTHING IN ME not to confront the kids when we arrived at the group home this afternoon. With the cops dropping by to question the boys earlier, the tension is thick in the air. You can feel it, like a dark cloud threatening to engulf us all.

For once, I'm glad Tess isn't with me. She doesn't need this kind of shit, and if anyone was to step out of line, I don't want to think about what I'd do. My wandering thoughts are interrupted by Tom's authoritative voice as we stand in his office.

"It's just a normal day, got it?" A rare warning from him. "Besides, they've been looking forward to seeing that bike finally hit the road. I don't want to spoil it for them. They've worked really hard on getting it ready."

Fuck, I know how important this is for these kids. How important it was for me finally to be part of something that wasn't tainted, that was your own hard work. Rebuilding all those bikes in the garage changed my life. I know that now, even if I didn't then.

Tom pushes my helmet into my hand. "Aaron did a safety check earlier this morning with them. It's good as new. Probably better, thanks to you."

Words of praise from Tom, from anyone, are still hard to hear. "Take it for a spin and then we'll set up a schedule for the boys to ride it." I give him a mock salute and he laughs. "Remember to take Aaron with you. The boys need to know the rule about never riding alone is one we all follow."

"Even though Zach takes the dirt bike all the time by himself?"

I fire back at him.

"Matty . . ."

"I know, I know. Be nice. I am capable of that sometimes."

"Always knew you had it in you, kid."

Shaking my head, I make my way down to the garage, the smell of oil and rubber drifting to me. A small group has gathered around the Harley, with Zach and Beck giving it an intense looking over.

"I hear it's ready to hit the road."

Zach glances up from the bike, his scowl firmly in place. "So, we did all this work for you to have another toy? Nice."

"No. You did all this work because you should know how to take care of a bike. And because you'll all be riding it." He looks warily between the bike and me.

"Right. Like we'd be allowed to ride this," Zach challenges.

"You can. If you follow the rules."

"I knew it. There's always fucking rules." Zach's voice drips venom, his eyes narrowed as he watches me like a hawk.

Aaron steps beside Zach, clearly not in the mood for any of his shit. "Watch your language. And you all know the rules. Be home by curfew, help around the house, and stay out of trouble." He pauses, looking purposefully at Zach, before continuing, "And never ride alone. You always ride with one of the volunteers. We'll set up a schedule and teach you the basics. That's it. It's that simple."

"Sweet," one of the boys says, excitement evident in his face.

Zach squints down at the bike before his eyes land back on me. "This isn't your bike, then?" he asks suspiciously. So much distrust. The kid's had a lifetime of disappointment. How many broken promises has he heard? Zach and I are more alike than I want to admit.

"We talked about this. It's for all of you. But like Aaron said, you have to respect it, take care of it, and follow the rules of the house."

"Well, Beck here just got his learner's permit." Zach lifts his chin in Beck's direction. "Let him take it first then."

Straddling the bike, I shove my helmet on. "I'll take it. Make sure it's okay, and then, if any of you have a permit, you can go for a ride. How's that sound?"

Zach runs his hand across the back of his neck, giving me a noncommittal shrug. "Whatever."

Beck gives me a nervous smile while the group steps away. The bike roars to life in that distinctive, deep rumble that can only be a Harley. It grounds me like my bass does. It's freedom, a promise, a rush of adrenaline that will always keep me coming back for more.

Beside me, Aaron grins as he revs his own bike, and we give a nod to the boys, accelerating smoothly out of the garage.

The open road has always been a heady call for me. Today is no different. There's nothing quite like riding over the Golden Gate Bridge, hugging the curves in the road, and putting the Harley through its paces.

It handles like a dream with the exception of the brakes that seem a little soft. Nothing a minor adjustment won't fix. The wind whips against my leather jacket as we climb to the Marin Headlands with hills jutting out on one side, and a stellar view of the Bay on the other. Cardinal would love this ride. I can almost feel her pressed up against my back, her arms firmly around my waist, tempting me like she always does.

The winding road is perfect to test the Harley, although not for the faint of heart. Snaking along the edge of the Pacific, I come out of another tight turn, starting to brake for a car that's moving at a glacial pace. They're gawking out the window at the view, some girl in the passenger seat leaning out to take pictures. Never mind that there're a few designated spots up here to do that, let's be idiots and take some ridiculous selfies off the end of a hairpin turn.

I catch sight of Aaron in my mirror as his bike slows, but the brakes on the Harley aren't responding. My heart hammers as the back wheel locks, and I try to remember every safety tip Tom ever gave me.

It's a blur, a whirlwind of spinning chrome and burning rubber as I lose the battle to keep the bike steady. The Harley wobbles and my shoulder hits the asphalt first, pain searing through me like wildfire. The bike slams into the guardrail, flipping me off in a jarring slam down the steep hillside.

I'm thrown and tossed against the rocks, disoriented as I tumble; the sky, the Pacific, jutting rocks and thick brush run in a burning loop that doesn't seem to want to end. My head pounds inside the helmet, my vision blurred when I finally slam to a stop.

Disembodied voices drift down from somewhere up above as the metallic taste of blood fills my mouth. It hurts to breathe; my lungs are on fire, my arms numb. I try to lift my head, but it weighs a thousand pounds.

Opening my eyes is a monumental task, but I can hear Tom's voice in my head, steady if not a little muted, telling me to try to stay awake. Choppy breaths burn, each one worse than the last as I force my eyes open. I catch sight of a small white butterfly hovering near the carnage of the Harley. A sign of life amongst the bent and mangled chrome. The hammering in my head intensifies, and I squeeze my eyes shut to the red-hot heat of pain, until all that remains is darkness.

A JACKHAMMER HAS TAKEN UP shop in my head. It feels

like my eyes are sewn shut. A faint, steady beeping and muffled voices slowly drift to me. I can only make out a few words. None of it makes sense. Why can't I feel my arms? Flashes of light keep blinding me. Distorted faces peer down and then move to make way for the darkness.

"Separated shoulder . . ." I don't recognize the voice. I hear a sharp scrape of a chair across the floor. I fight to open my eyes; my throat feels like it's on fire. "Nerve damage, numbness . . . would be a shame." And then the only voice I want to hear.

"Please . . . I'm sorry . . ." I can feel the light touch of her hand on my side, her breath against my cheek. Cherry fucking almond. "Come back to me." And then there's nothing.

Tessa

THE CAB RIDE TO THE hospital passes in a blur. A choking fear envelops me, and I have to concentrate to keep breathing. All I know is that Matt was in an accident and is being taken to St. Francis's by ambulance. I clutch my purse in a death grip and play with the zipper pull until Abby places a hand over mine.

"He's going to be okay, Tess," she whispers, although she doesn't sound confident at all. It's not until she wraps her arm around my shoulders that I realize how badly I'm trembling.

The cab lurches to a stop outside the unassuming emergency entrance on Bush Street. I'm vaguely aware of Abby handling the payment as I scramble to get out and sprint to the ER door. Matt's name is on a loop in my mind, and I can't get my feet to move fast enough. There's an ambulance in the loading bay, and I wonder if that was the one he rode in.

I'm babbling at the admitting clerk like a lunatic when Abby saves me again. She speaks to the girl in low, calm tones, while I slam my mouth shut and try to calm down. If I don't, they won't let me in to see him. And I have to see him. We're given visitors passes and directed to a waiting area. Despite the soothing colors and cool wood tones, the dreaded smell of antiseptic and bleach turns my stomach. The last time I was in a hospital was when my sister died.

I want to throw up.

We follow the staff person through the crowded ER waiting area and down another hallway to a smaller room. Tom is standing in front of a vending machine, staring at his feet, when we arrive. He turns, and I see everything I've been dreading in his expression: despair, regret, and pain . . . so much pain.

"Tom," I gasp, my knees buckling. He quickly pulls me to his chest in a rough hug and guides me to one of the hard chairs. Kneeling in front of me, he closes his calloused hands over mine.

"Deep breaths, Tess," he murmurs, his voice coarse. It's unnerving to see such an imposing man holding back so much emotion.

"Is he going to be okay? What happened? Is he awake? Is anyone else hurt?" The questions tumble out of me so fast I'm amazed he understands, but somehow he does.

He swallows and takes a deep breath. "No one else was injured."

"Where is he? Can I see him?" I try not to yell, but the fact that he only answered my last question is alarming.

"They just took him back. He needs surgery." Tom runs a hand over his bald head. "I think they might be x-raying him first. I don't know for sure. We don't know how bad it is yet. No one can tell me."

My tears finally spill over. "What happened?" I cling to his hands in my lap. I catch movement behind him, and it's then I see Aaron sitting in a chair across from me. He looks ten years older than he did mere days ago.

"We were testing the bike." Aaron leans forward to rest his elbows on his knees. "We always take a ride first to make sure they're perfect before the kids get on. We took the coast road. There was a car in front of us." I suck in a ragged breath, and Abby slips an arm around my shoulders.

Tom rises from his knee to sit on my other side as Aaron continues, "Matt wasn't slowing down. I saw his bike dip, and then it went sideways. He slid into the guardrail and flipped over the side."

"Oh my God," Abby murmurs, as I stare at them, horrified. I want to scream, but no sound comes out.

"I called 911 and then tried to climb down to him, but the hillside was too steep for me. The emergency crews had to go down with ropes and haul him up on a stretcher," Aaron explains, his voice weary. "Thank God he was wearing a helmet and his leathers."

Tom scrubs his hand over his red-rimmed eyes. "I got there just as they were loading him into the rig. They said something about internal injuries, maybe a collapsed lung."

The door opens and we all turn to see Kennedy and Tucker quickly striding toward us. Abby rises from her seat beside me, and Kennedy gives her a quick kiss before shaking Tom's hand in greeting. "How is he?" Kennedy asks. "We got here as fast as we could." I'm frozen to my seat as they stand and speak in hushed tones around me. My heart pounds, and I feel sick. He has to be all right. He has to be.

"Tess?" My eyes focus on Kennedy's face as he bends down to look at me. "He'll be fine. He's tough. Okay? If these guys can't fix him up, we'll get someone who can. Don't you worry." He gives my shoulder a squeeze in support and I nod, but I can't muster more than that. It's like all the words in my head have flown and my tongue is a lead weight.

Just then, my phone rings and I answer it without thinking. It takes a second for my brain to compute that it's my sister, jabbering excitedly at me.

"There you are! Has Conner called yet? Your newest nephew is on his way!" Rachel chirps. "And you owe me big time, by the way. Since you're not here, I'm pulling babysitting duty while everyone else is at the hospital. When can you fly up?"

Tears spring anew, and I open and close my mouth a few times as my sister prattles on. Since I've avoided hospitals since Paula died, I've always volunteered to watch over my various nieces and nephews when my siblings have had their babies. "Tess? Tess, are you there?"

"Yes, I'm here," I manage, my voice thick, and my sister gasps on the other end, immediately picking up on my distress.

"Tess, are you okay? What's going on?"

"Rach . . ." I take a deep breath, but I just can't. I can't say anything because if I start talking, all my worst fears are going to tumble out. Abby takes the phone from my shaking hand.

"Rachel? This is Abby Walker. Yes, nice to speak with you again, too. Tess is fine, but . . ." Her voice trails off as she walks toward the other end of the room. I close my eyes, silently thanking my boss yet again. Abby's met all of my family over the years, so I know she'll be able to explain what I can't.

"Mr. Logan?" Tom and my heads shoot up to see someone with a hospital name tag holding a clipboard. "I need you to come complete the admittance paperwork for your son."

"How is he?" I ask quickly, standing immediately.

She smiles with practiced empathy. "I'm sorry, but I don't

know. Someone should be able to give you an update soon." She turns to Tom. "Mr. Logan?"

Tom nods and takes the offered clipboard and pen. Numbly, I watch as he begins to scratch in Matt's name. Matthew T. Logan. "What's the T for?" I ask suddenly, embarrassed that I don't know this basic bit of information.

"Thomas," he rumbles, a ghost of a smile on his lips. "He changed his middle name a few years after I adopted him. Shocked the hell out of me at the time."

I give him a watery smile. That's so like the Matt I know, fiercely loyal. "It doesn't surprise me a bit." Tom returns my smile and continues his writing.

"Rachel is calling your parents right now," Abby says quietly, handing me my phone. "She says she'll be down as soon as she can get a flight."

I hate to interrupt what should be a celebration for my family, but I'll be grateful to have my sister with me. "Thanks. I appreciate you talking with her," I begin, but she hushes me.

"Don't even think about it." She glances over her shoulder to where Kennedy is standing in a corner and talking on his phone. "He's calling the rest of the guys. They will all want to be here. I think Tucker is going to arrange more security, too."

"Oh my God, of course." I run a hand over my eyes, the weight of Matt's celebrity hitting me in the chest. Once word gets out, we'll have to deal with the media, photographers. Hell, probably even some fans. "Should we call April? Oh—Nicole will need to know!" Nicole is the band's publicity wunderkind we worked with during Parker's concert. She'll know what to do.

I start rummaging in my bag for . . . I'm not sure what. My head spins, and I can't seem to keep my thoughts straight. I need to make a list of everything we need to do so I don't forget. I must have Nicole's number somewhere.

"Stop," Abby says, her voice both soothing and firm, and gently takes my bag from me to stop my frantic movements. "Kennedy will handle everything. Don't worry about it, Tess."

I take a ragged breath and let it out in a whoosh, forcing myself to calm down. "Right. Sorry." I rub my temples, trying to ease the throbbing in my head. "When do you think they'll be able to tell us something?"

"I'll go ask if someone can give us an update. Are you going to be okay for a few minutes?"

I nod and try to give her a reassuring smile as she returns my purse. "Yep. Sorry for freaking out."

"Perfectly understandable." She waves a hand. "And stop apologizing. I can't even imagine how I'd be feeling if it were Kennedy." Her eyes drift over to him for a moment, and then she shakes her head. "I'll be right back."

A COUPLE OF HOURS LATER, my nerves are at the breaking point. All they've been able to tell us is that Matt is in surgery and it shouldn't be much longer. A television drones on in the corner. Two tall men dressed in black arrived a while ago and spoke with Tucker—security, obviously. One stayed with us and the other stepped back out in the hall. I've kicked my shoes off and I'm pacing along one of the walls. I can't just sit anymore, or I'll explode. Everyone keeps their distance, although I can feel their worried eyes on me. Tom is sitting and staring at his knees, nodding his head slightly as Aaron and Kennedy speak softly to him. Abby brought back some sandwiches from the cafeteria, but they remain on the tray, mostly uneaten.

Wrapping my arms around myself, I pause and stare at one of the mass-produced pieces of artwork that adorn the walls. The questions are piling up in my head, and my anxiety rises with them. What's taking so long? What happened to the bike? Matt's an experience rider. Did the brakes fail? That doesn't make sense, either. There's no way he would've taken it out for a ride if it hadn't been ready.

A harsh snort from Tom catches my ear, and my attention is suddenly riveted. "It *is* my fault. I should've listened." Tom's voice is weary, full of regret. "You and Matt tried to tell me, but I just didn't think, and now look at what's happened."

"You couldn't have known," Aaron argues softly, clapping his hand on his friend's shoulder. "This isn't your fault. And we don't *know*, not for sure. Don't go there, man. The truth will come out when the cops find him."

"Find who?" Startled, they turn to me; their guilty faces are almost as alarming as their words. "Did someone do something to cause this?" I demand, my voice shrill.

"Tess—" He cuts off when the door opens and a tired-looking man in scrubs enters. We all scramble to our feet.

"Mr. Logan?" Tom nods and takes my hand, bringing me to stand with him. I'm holding my breath, equally eager and fearful of what comes next.

The doctor introduces himself and rubs the back of his neck. "Firstly, Matt's out of surgery and in post-op now. They'll move him to the ICU in a while, and then you'll be able to see him. He's in rough shape, but he's stable. Okay?" He looks at us directly to make sure we've absorbed his words, and then nods with a small smile. "Here's what we know so far." His voice holds a practiced confidence as he reads off a litany of ailments. "All the ribs on his left side are broken and he has a collapsed lung. There was some metal debris on the hillside that punctured his abdomen, but it avoided all the major organs. His left shoulder separated, and his arm and wrist are broken. It will be a while until we can tell if there's been any nerve damage."

Kennedy swears softly behind us. The doctor gives us a faint smile, but it doesn't reach his eyes. "He also has a concussion. He's still unconscious, but I don't want you to panic. It's not unusual for head traumas to take a while to wake up. His helmet saved him from more serious injury. It could've been much, much worse. He's one of the lucky ones."

I choke back a gasp. He could've died.

The thought makes my knees buckle and I sink into a chair as the doctor says a few more things to Tom, pats him on the shoulder, and then leaves. He could've *died*. He could've died and then he would never know that I love him because I've been too chickenshit to say anything.

I make it to the bathroom just in time to lose what little I have in my stomach.

♪ ♩ ♪ ♩

ANOTHER INTERMINABLE HOUR OR SO later, a nurse finally comes to say we can see him. Her eyes go between Tom and me. "Only family is allowed in ICU."

"Tess *is* family," Tom says firmly. I squeeze his hand in gratitude.

The nurse purses her lips, but doesn't argue. "Fine, but only one of you can be in the room at a time, and only for fifteen minutes." She looks at us expectantly, and I rest my hand on Tom's bicep.

"You're his father," I whisper. He nods and immediately follows the nurse from the room. I look after them, hugging myself tightly so I don't fly apart. I start to resume my pacing, but the door opens again and I gasp.

Standing in the doorway with Abby is my father.

"Daddy!" I bolt into his arms and immediately burst into tears as I feel his strong arms enfold me.

"There, there, Tessa-bug," he rumbles softly. "It's going to be okay." I cling to his jacket, my tears wetting his shirt, as he lets me cry.

"What are you doing here?" I manage through my hiccupping sobs. "I thought Rachel was coming. What about the baby?"

"Vi and the baby are going to be fine. Your mother is staying there to help them. I wanted to come." I look up at him through watery eyes and return his smile. "Now, tell me what happened." I recount Matt's injuries, taking comfort in my father's quiet strength. He doesn't interrupt. He just takes it all in, handing me tissues as needed.

When I finally take a breath, he kisses my forehead and then fixes me with a look I know well: the serious look of a commander overlaid with the compassion of a father. He gives me the same look whenever I've faced a challenge, whether it was learning to ski, a test at school, or a job interview. It grounds me and helps me find the courage I need. And I need it now.

"He's going to need your help to get through this, Tessa," he says quietly. "It's not going to be easy. But you're strong enough. Based on what I saw at Christmas, I think you both are. You can do it together."

I take a deep breath just as Tom returns. He looks shaken, and his eyes are redder. He looks at my dad and me warily, and I quickly introduce them. They shake hands, a look of understanding passing between them. One father who fears losing his child, and another who knows what that pain is like.

An aide leads me through a maze of hallways. My heart is in my throat. Finally, she slaps a panel and a door swings open to the ICU. I follow her example and take a squirt of the hand sanitizer mounted on the wall. A ring of patient rooms surrounds the nursing station in the center of the unit. She leads me to one of the rooms and slides the glass door open a little further. Taking a deep breath, I move the privacy curtain aside and freeze. Matt's large frame seems dwarfed by all the machines surrounding his bed. His face is pale, and I have to hold back a gasp at the sight of the tube inserted in his mouth. His left shoulder is swathed in wrappings, and his left arm is immobilized in a brace and more bandages. A nurse in scrubs fiddles with an IV hanging beside the bed, and she gives us a quick smile before her eyes return to her task.

"I know the tube looks scary," the aide comments. "We'll be able to remove it soon as his vitals improve. We'll also put a hard cast on his arm and wrist. After he's been transferred to one of the med-surg floors, the visiting rules won't be so restrictive."

Bruises cover every inch of his exposed skin other than his face. His leather clothing may have saved him from road rash, but it couldn't stop his body from being battered in the fall. I sink into the chair by the bed and take his hand. It feels clammy, and my heart clenches when he can't return my squeeze.

"I'll come get you in fifteen minutes," the aide says, and then she and the nurse leave. My eyes can't leave his face. His eyelids quiver, and I wonder if he's reliving the accident.

"Oh, Matt," I gasp, trying to hold back a sob. Now is not the time to break down. I gulp a breath and start over. "Okay. Here's the thing. I love you." I pause but, of course, there's no response, so I ignore my sniffles and plow on. "I hope you can hear me because I love you, Matthew Thomas Logan, and it's about time you knew.

I should've told you earlier. I'm sorry I waited until now . . . until you're lying here broken and beaten and unable to answer. I was afraid to tell you. I was afraid that you didn't feel the same. Or that it'd be too much for you and you'd go running for the hills, and that would've broken my heart."

The muted hum and swoosh of the machines are simultaneously reassuring and ominous. I swipe away my tears and try to calm my stuttering breaths. "But don't worry. I'm going to tell you how I feel about you every day . . . you'll probably get sick of hearing it, but I'm going to tell you anyway. You won't be able to get me to shut up. I promise." I lift his limp hand to my lips and kiss his scraped knuckles as the words pour out of me. "And I promise I won't give up. I won't give up even after you're walking and talking and the casts come off. As far as I'm concerned, you're stuck with me until you say otherwise. Maybe even after that."

I reach out with my free hand and brush it over his short hair, before leaning over and placing a soft kiss on his forehead. "So do me a favor," I whisper, one of my tears falling onto his cheek. "Come back to me so I can start telling you."

chapter fifteen

matt

"*I TOLD YOU TO STAY in your fucking room.*" *It's my mother's standard greeting.*

"*It's time for school.*"

"*You're never going to learn shit there. I don't know why you bother.*"

I can feel my heart race; the constant steady beep falters and stutters beside me. A door bursts open; intermittent voices shout around me. It's too confusing to try to figure out. At least it drowns out my mother's voice.

"I KNOW YOU'RE NOT MUCH of a talker, but this is ridiculous." Kennedy's voice reaches in and tries to pull me from a steady sleep. I'm bone tired. "Should I talk about the Tonga Room? They said talking might help, and if anything can pull you out of this, it's that night."

I feel like I could sleep forever, just keep drifting in this cloud of calm. So, that's what I do.

"ENOUGH OF THIS SHIT, GRASSHOPPER." An uncharacteristic sniffle, and then the Brit's voice is back, booming and invading the darkness again. "I'm pulling out the big guns and going all *Steel Magnolias* on you. I know, I know. It's a chick flick, but Syd made me watch all of them when we were growing up. Some of them aren't bad. Others confirm my belief that woman are impossible creatures to figure out." I can make out rustling, maybe a magazine? A newspaper? I think I let out a groan.

"Anyway, in case you haven't seen it, Julia Roberts, circa the *Pretty Woman* era so you can get an idea of the hotness, is in a coma, and Sally Field plays her mom. She reads magazines to her." His voice fades and I struggle to open my eyes. "Actually, Julia's character dies in the film, but let's not focus on that. The idea is a good one. I've got the latest copy of *Burnt* magazine, and guess whose pretty mug is on the cover? Now that I think about it, it's probably a good thing you're unconscious for this particular portion of your life. You'd hate the attention. We're going to need another room for all the bloody fan mail and flowers."

I try to turn my head in the direction of his voice, but it hurts too much. "Here we go. Page fifteen. Matt Logan, legendary bassist. See? I've always said you were legendary, but now that it's printed here in black and white in one of the finest market magazines, it has to be true, right?" My lungs complain as I try to take a deep breath, so I miss most of what he's saying for a bit until his voice filters back in. "The accident is still under investigation. As it fucking should be."

A tire iron to the head would hurt less than his voice right now. I focus on the white noise, the steady hum of machines that won't leave me alone, and I welcome it pulling me under again.

I WAKE TO A RELENTLESS buzz. Opening my eyes is a chore, and things are hazy, floating. It hurts to turn my head. Why are there tubes up my nose? My neck and shoulder feel braced in some contraption that makes it hard to move.

My throat is dry, burning, begging me for something to drink. What the fuck happened? A blurry, large form slumped over in a nearby chair snores away. It's the only sound over the humming machine in the dimly lit room. My jaw feels locked shut. It's a struggle to open my mouth, and when I do, nothing comes out, even though I want to scream.

I fight to take a breath, but the scent of flowers is suffocating, pushing down on my chest.

A tatted arm comes into view. I recognize those tats. It's something familiar that finally makes sense. I can feel his big hand curl around mine, and I manage to croak out a single word. "Dad." I close my eyes to the raw sound of my voice, to the searing pain.

"Matty, Jesus Christ, kid." I hear the chair scrape the floor, and feel the bed sink with his weight beside me. His warm breath is on my hand before he holds my palm to his cheek. I fight to open my eyes again. "Shit. Nurse!" I grab onto his big, booming voice like a lifeline. "Don't you dare leave me. You're going to be okay. Nurse!"

My eyes open to find his staring back at me, uncharacteristic tears spilling to his cheeks. I try to wet my lips as his hand tightens against mine. "You look like shit," I rasp.

He drops his forehead to our joined hands, and I feel the bed shake a bit as he takes a stuttered breath before lifting his eyes back to mine. I try to lean up, but it's impossible. A steady weight feels like it's holding me in place. "Don't try to move."

"Wha . . . ?" I try to take a swat at the tubes in my nose, but I'm held tight by his grip.

Commotion at the door causes my head to spin, and I squeeze my eyes shut. Voices I don't recognize snap at Tom to move away. His grip just tightens over my hand. "I'm not leaving my son."

"Stubborn," I mutter, forcing my eyes to open to a huddled crowd of strangers. White coats, concerned looks, penlights, and clipboards.

"BP is 160 over 90."

"Can you hear me?" White coat number one is obviously in charge. Her face looms close to mine, her voice a pounding blast to my ears.

"Right here." I'm panting, exhausted from just a couple of words. "Don't have to yell."

"Grasshopper!" Fuck, the Brit is here, too. I'd recognize that annoying accent anywhere. "I don't give a rat's ass what your fucking rules are. I want to see him."

"Get that man out of here, or I'm calling security." White coat number one again. She's annoyed at Sean. I know the feeling. I try to get a look at him at the door, but I'm too weak to move.

"The security here is *ours*! Don't go toward the light, Matty!" I can still hear him ranting away as a door is shut in an attempt to drown him out.

"Where." It's all I can manage before my eyes slide shut. I feel Tom release my hand.

"I'm Dr. Elliott, the attending physician here at St. Francis.

Can you tell me your name?"

"Matt . . . Matt Logan." I take a shuddered, painful breath.

"Good, and how are you feeling?"

I open my eyes to her ridiculous question. "Is she serious? Cardinal . . . Fuck."

"Try not to move too much yet. Do you know what happened?" The sea of nameless faces hovers closer, poking, prodding, and trying to get at me. Memories of a dark alley, of fists and danger run a loop in my head. *No.*

"Get off me." I struggle against the vice-like grip on my arm.

"Matt, calm down." It's Tom's voice that I try to focus on.

"Matt. You're safe. You're in the hospital." Dr. Elliott's words float in, and I try to make sense of them, my eyes darting to the lingering crowd. "Do you remember what happened?"

Glancing back at the doctor, my heart races as snippets burst in confusing pieces. The open road, a curtain of long, black hair, a spinning cloudless sky. "The Harley."

Dr. Elliott nods. "Yes. You were in an accident. You've been in a coma for almost two weeks."

"What?" I try to swallow, feeling panic set in as I search the room for Tom. "No. The concert. Cardinal."

I slam my eyes shut, willing the room to stop turning as the doctor's voice filters back in. "It's normal for patients to be confused when they wake up. The morphine is probably doing the talking."

"How long will he be like this?"

I struggle against the steady hand pressed against my shoulder, trying to push up to the sound of Tom's voice.

"Dad." My throat is on fire and raw, and my tongue feels weird, swollen and taking up too much space in my mouth.

"It's hard to tell. Unfortunately, we still don't know a lot about what goes on in the brain during a coma like the one your son's been in. But he's awake, and that's the best sign we can have. When he's calmed down a bit, we'll come back and run through a few tests."

"Get off me!" I feel my jaw set as a younger man's face comes into view.

"Try to calm down, Mr. Logan."

"He's not usually like this."

The doctor shakes her head at me. I'm being scolded. "He's disoriented right now. He might be incoherent and confused for a while, lash out, or have trouble focusing. It's important you try to stay calm during this time. He'll need that."

"I'm right fucking here!" The burn in my throat threatens again.

"Mr. Logan, it's important you try to stay calm."

"Matty, it's okay."

Turning in the direction of Tom's voice sends a searing pain through my shoulder. "Get him off me!" My arm flails and my fist makes impact with the young kid's nose. Blood, dripping red, and chaotic shouts for more morphine swirl until I'm plunged back into darkness again.

"WE CAN'T HAVE THESE IN here when he wakes up."

"Why the hell not? They said he needs things around that will trigger memories."

"Extra-small condoms may not be the memories he wants, genius."

I hear a quick laugh and then Cameron's voice. "Fuck, that was classic. Tess is all right in my book. The look on his face when Tucker opened that box." There's a round of subdued laughs, but it all sounds hollow. "But seriously, we should donate these to a clinic or something. He'll lose his shit if he sees boxes of condoms in here." Condoms? What the hell are they going on about?

"The hospital administrator tracked me down this morning." That's Kennedy's voice, and I turn my head in the direction it's coming from. "Asked me to tell the fans if they want to help, to make a donation to the trauma center. Said he couldn't have the lawn of his hospital looking like a mini Woodstock anymore, and that they were running out of space for the flowers and these." I hear a soft thud as I slowly blink my eyes open to the harsh light.

Through a shaky breath, I manage a few words, my voice raw. "Would you all shut the hell up?"

"Ah! Sleeping Beauty has awoken! See? The condoms worked!" Sean slides the chair over to the side of the bed, dropping into it and leaning forward. "You look like you've been run down by a truck, mate. Get the nurse, Cam."

I practically growl at Sean's words. "No. No fucking nurses."

"Come on now, Grasshopper. There're some hot ones here. I'd be taking advantage of every single sponge bath that was offered if I were you." He smirks at me, but he looks tired. "Heard you broke one of the male nurse's noses. Badass."

Furrowing my brow, I try to sit up. "I did what?"

"What hurts?" Cameron asks, sitting on the side of the bed.

"My tongue feels weird."

Sean shakes his head. "You've been out for fucking days and the first thing you're worried about is your tongue?"

"You were on a ventilator for a while." Kennedy moves beside Cam. "And they had to take out your tongue piercing."

My head spins in confusion. "My tongue piercing?"

"Yeah, mate. Please tell me you remember how epic that was." Sean shoots Kennedy and Cameron a look of worry before turning back to me. "The bet we had a few years back? If you could survive the tongue piercing, I'd get my cock—"

I groan as the memory slams back to me. "Fuck, stop. That was in Australia. I remember now."

Glancing down, past the dressing on my shoulder, I notice a cast running the length of my left forearm down over my wrist. "Fuck."

"Yeah. About that." I look up to Kennedy, nervously rubbing his hand over the back of his neck. "It's broken in three places. Your wrist, too. You had to have surgery for a collapsed lung, and your shoulder's a mess, but man, finally seeing you awake after almost two weeks is damn fucking good." His half-hearted smile falls flat. Even through the confused haze that seems to orbit me, I can see that.

"How long until I play again?" I grind out, a feeling of helplessness I'm not accustomed to rolling over me. Fuck, for them to see me this way, it just doesn't feel right.

Kennedy glances warily at Sean and Cameron. "Um, I don't think that's for us to explain."

"How fucking long?" I snap.

"Clam down, Grasshopper."

"Answer the fucking question!" Pain cuts through my shoulder like a hot blade as Sean tries to press me back to the bed.

"They don't know," Kennedy blurts. "The broken bones in your arm and ribs, probably a couple of months. But your shoulder . . ." His voice trails and he shakes his head. Kennedy Lane at a loss for words is something I never thought I'd see.

"What about it?"

He glances away, looking desperately at the door. "We should wait for the doctor, I think."

"Don't you dare fucking bullshit me! Not you guys." My lungs burn, my weary body begging me for a break.

"Matty." Cameron sets his hand on my un-casted arm, and I search his worried face. I can't remember seeing any of them like this. Even through the stints in rehab, and Brodie's suicide. "The tests they've done show you've got some nerve damage in your shoulder. A potential brachial plexus injury."

"What is that?" My throat constricts, and my chest thuds.

"Why can't they just speak fucking English when they explain shit?" Sean huffs.

"It's a group of nerves that run from your spinal cord," Cam explains, ignoring Sean. "They control the muscles in your shoulder and arm. It's probably minor, and you'll be fine in a few weeks."

"Probably?"

Cam nods, moving in slow motion to my fucked-up brain. "Yeah. Some physio with Tucker and you'll be good as new."

"And if it's not minor?"

Silence greets me; silence and the incessant hum of the machine beside my bed. I'm so fucking tired. Tired of being confused and floating in a dream. "I don't think we should talk about this right now," Kennedy says.

"What fucking happens?" There's a threatening edge to my voice I don't recognize.

"We won't know how bad it is until we can get you up and into some physio, but some people have a permanent disability," Cameron states. Harsh and brutal and plain as day. My entire life, everything I've ever actually been good at could be gone, ripped away from me.

"But that's not going to be you, Matty." Sean tries to break the mounting tension in the room. "You'll be back up and playing with us in no time."

I glance over to the table against the wall, overflowing with cards and flowers. The scent reaches in and grabs hold. I focus on one of the glittery cards, on the lines of a black guitar that's pictured on the front. The letters above it seem to morph and blur. It makes no sense. The blood pounds harder in my ears. "Get out."

Sean fists the thin material of the hospital shirt I'm wearing. "We aren't leaving you."

"Sean, just for a bit, okay?" Somehow, I manage to bring my eyes back to his. I can feel myself teetering on the edge. "Please."

Sean glances warily over to Kennedy before pushing up from the chair. "It's time for the lovely Tess's shift anyway." He shoves on a pair of ridiculous yellow sunglasses. "She's been here the whole time." And I know that. Somewhere in all the confusion and unknown voices, in the flashes of light and time, I know she's been here. Her touch, her scent, her energy, I can feel it. But to know she's seen me this way, it's another punishing blow to my gut.

"Give me a couple of minutes."

"We'll be back later tonight," Kennedy says, opening up the door.

The door closing behind them is faint. The ceiling seems closer as I stare at it, slowly closing me in, snuffing me out.

Two weeks, Kennedy said. I've been out for two weeks, through New Year's, for fuck's sake. It's just a confusing void of time. I take a glance across the room, over the sea of flowers to the window. It's dark, another day passing with me having no idea.

Closing my eyes, I try to will the relentless pounding in my head to end. I hear her before I see her. Hesitant steps, a sharp intake of breath, the creak of the bed as she sits beside me. "Matt?" She approached as if I'm an unpredictable, caged animal who might attack.

Swallowing back the lump in my throat, I turn my head and open my eyes, and I see it. All the things I never wanted to see:

sympathy, regret, and worry. She's looking at me like I'm a stranger. I'm right back to being that weak, terrified, clueless teenager living on the street.

"Tess." Her dark eyes light up with that one word, and she reaches for my hand, crushing it in her grip.

"You remember." I ache to brush the tears falling to her cheeks, but I can't. Fear grips me, threatening to take over. "They said you might forget some things." She leans forward to rest her forehead to mine. Her scent washes over me, her hair falling in a dark curtain around my face, and I breathe her in.

"Could never forget you, Cardinal." It comes out as a dry whisper.

I can feel a tremble roll through her as she presses her delicious curves against me. I welcome it all—the burn in my lungs, the pain searing through my shoulder as she clings to me. I want to drown in it—in her.

"Oh God, I'm sorry." She pushes away from me. "I shouldn't be putting any weight on you. What hurts? What can I do?" The words tumble from her lips in a rush.

"Just hold me."

♪ ♩ ♪ ♩

Tessa

A HALF-SOB ESCAPES ME AS relief surges. I gingerly slide my arm behind his neck and hold him as tightly as I dare. The machines I've relied on for days to assure me that he's still alive continue their inexorable beeping.

He presses his face against my neck and inhales deeply. "I thought I was dreaming again, but my dreams never smelled this good."

I laugh weakly, my tears threatening again. I've cried so much in this hospital; I'm surprised I have any tears left. "It can't be that good. I haven't showered yet today." I've only left to shower and change clothes a few times since his accident. If it wasn't for Abby and Jada, I wouldn't leave at all. Every three days or so, one of them frog-marches me out to the car and takes me to clean up.

"You smell amazing," he mumbles, wincing with the effort. I try to pull back again, but his good hand has closed around my shoulders, holding me in place.

"Matt, I should move," I argue, although my heart really isn't in it. "I don't want to hurt you."

"You'll only hurt me if you leave."

The raw honesty and fear in his soft voice pierce my heart. "Never." I stretch carefully to press a gentle kiss on his cheek, avoiding the oxygen tubing. "You're stuck with me now."

A faint smile touches his lips, and his eyelids flutter closed. They warned me that he'd probably fall back to sleep quickly, and I shouldn't worry, but panic bubbles up anyway. I promised him something, and I don't want to miss my chance. Taking a deep breath, I blurt it out.

"I love you, Matt."

Holding my breath, I wait, but there's nothing. His breathing is deep and even, and I feel his arm holding me slacken. Damn. I waited too long.

With a resigned sigh, I rest my head on the pillow beside him, allowing myself one more minute to savor his warmth and the relief that he's still with me before resuming my usual seat beside the bed. His whispered croak startles me.

"Best fucking dream ever."

♪ ♩ ♪ ♩

"ARE YOU OKAY?"

Snapping my head up, I look directly into Kennedy's concerned gaze. The security guy standing on the other side of the doorway politely ignores us. There are two other burly men in black—hired by Tucker—standing at each end of the hallway. It's weird to see hired security in a hospital, but they've been worth their considerable weight in gold. For the first few days, it wasn't unusual to find roving bands of Redfall fans—and worse—trying to find Matt's room. A paparazzo, disguised in scrubs and hiding his camera in a bouquet of flowers, would've made it if one of the security guys hadn't recognized him. I can only imagine how much a photo of Matt while he was still on the ventilator would've been worth to a tabloid.

I straighten from where I'm slouching against the wall outside Matt's room and give him a tired smile. "I'm fine. Matt's asleep again."

"Maybe you should get some, too," he suggests, but I shake my head.

"Dr. Elliot said he'd probably be in and out. I don't want to miss the next time he wakes up." My insides churn from the dual relief of finally saying those three little words to him and not knowing if he was coherent enough to understand what I said. No matter, he's stuck with me, regardless.

Kennedy falls into step next to me, and we walk slowly back to the small waiting area around the corner. Tom is there, in discussion again with one the detectives on the case. Normally, I hate that celebrity cases seem to take priority over those of regular people, but I can't deny I'm glad of it this time.

"We'll notify you when we have more information, Mr. Logan. Call us immediately if he contacts anyone at the home again."

Tom nods, his face troubled. "I will. Thank you for all your help."

Kennedy excuses himself to go find Cameron and Sean, but my eyes lock on the detective. The police have spoken with me only once, to interview me about what I knew about the kids at the group home, but I've been able to get some information from Tom and Aaron. The detective rises and gives me a perfunctory smile as he leaves. He doesn't need to tell me what they were talking about this time; I know.

Zach. My blood runs cold at the thought of the little thug who is the number one suspect. After everything Tom, Matt, and the other staff and volunteers have done for him, and this is how he repays them. Underlying my anger is a twinge of guilt; I should've said something earlier about my suspicions regarding Zach and the incident with the Camaro. But who knew he'd do something like this?

I don't know what evidence the police have regarding the crash, but we know now that it wasn't an accident. Someone tampered with the brakes of the Harley after Aaron had given it a last wipe-down before the test ride. Both Zach and Beck fled as soon as news of the accident reached the group home. I know Tom is still struggling with his feelings where Zach's concerned, so I keep my thoughts to myself. But if Zach *is* responsible and I ever run across that punk . . .

Taking a deep breath to calm my rage, I unclench my fists with difficulty and sit next to Tom. He absently pats my knee. "Kennedy told me the guys broke the news to him. How is he?"

"He's asleep again." I sweep my hair away from my face, feeling drained. "We didn't talk about it. He's exhausted." Bracing my elbows on my knees, I let my head hang down to stretch the kinks out of my neck. I really should nip over to Matt's for a quick shower and a change. I was just there yesterday, but the hospital smell seems to seep into my clothes faster these days.

Tom pats my back. "Well, we'll be talking with him about it soon enough. He needs time to process everything. We've had two weeks to adjust to it; he's had about twenty minutes."

I mumble agreement and sit up to find him watching me with that measured look that reminds me so much of my father.

"Why don't you take off for a while and get some sleep—some *real* sleep in a *real* bed, not on one of those spindly cots they've got here." Before I can argue, he says, "I want some time with him when he wakes up again, and then he'll need to see you. And you won't do him any good unless you're rested, Tess." He grins at me through his own exhaustion. "Besides, your father will shoot me if I don't at least try to take care of you."

I chuckle, realizing the truth of that statement. My dad has stayed in town, while my mom stayed with my brother's family to help with the new baby. He's come to the hospital at least once a day to check on me and make sure I'm eating. He and Tom have forged a friendship over bad hospital coffee and the love of their respective children. I've found them several times, sitting and talking in a corner of one of the waiting rooms, long after I thought Dad had left after visiting me. They make a formidable pair.

Surreptitiously sniffing my sleeve, I cringe at the pervasive odor of antiseptic and sickness. Maybe a quick shower and change would be a good idea after all. "Okay. If he wakes up, tell him . . ." I pause, struggling to find the words to express my roiling emotions. Tom just nods and gives me a knowing smile.

"I will."

♪ ♩ ♪ ♩

"WHY DON'T YOU JUST MOVE in with him?"

I frown, but of course Jada can't see me over the phone. "It's too soon," I say defensively, although my stomach flutters at the thought of waking up every morning to Matt's sleepy blue eyes. "Besides, he hasn't asked me."

"He's given you keys to his place, and you're over there ninety percent of the time anyway," she says, a hint of mirth in her tone. "If you move out, maybe I'll finally be able to shack up with Greg."

"You hate Greg. You say he's bossy and arrogant." The hospital looms ahead and my anxiety increases accordingly. Despite Tom's encouragement, I hadn't meant to fall asleep. I sat down on the bed to remove my shoes so I could shower and woke up four hours later sprawled across Matt's bed, still half-dressed. It's almost five now, and my Uber is crawling in rush-hour traffic.

"Yeah, well, that anaconda in his pants might be worth a little arrogance."

I laugh in spite of my nervousness, which was her goal. "We'll see. Hey, I'm at the hospital; I'll call you later."

"Okay. Thanks for checking in. I'm glad he's awake. Hang in there, Tess." I can hear the smile in her voice. "The worst is over." We say our goodbyes, and I thank the driver.

My hair is still damp from my fastest-shower-in-history, so I gather it quickly into a loose ponytail to get it out of the way while I wait for the elevator inside. My shoulder twinges from the weight of my laptop and a few files in my bag. Abby has been a godsend since the accident. In addition to keeping me from imploding those first few hours, she's never once suggested that I should come back to the office while Matt was unconscious. She and April stepped in to handle the more immediate things, while I worked when I could from the hospital. Of course, she's been here, too, with Kennedy and on her own, keeping up to speed while checking in to make sure I'm okay. I'm still so new to my role, another boss might have handled it differently. I'll never be able to thank her enough.

The sight of Sean's concerned face when I get off the elevator sets off alarms. "Tess! Finally!" He quickly links his arm with mine and propels me down the hall. "He's been having a nice chat with his dad, but that hot doctor is back in there now, and you know how well that went last time."

I'm almost breathless by the time we reach his room. My taut nerves stretch even tighter when I hear Matt's raised voice through the closed door. Sean gives me a comforting pat on the shoulder, and I enter as quietly as I can, so I don't interrupt the doctor's narrative. The doctor pauses mid-sentence anyway, and Matt heaves a sigh of relief.

"Cardinal . . ." He holds out his hand, and Tom moves so I can step forward and take it. Matt squeezes my fingers like I'm his last link to sanity, and maybe I am. Sinking into a chair next to the bed so the angle isn't as difficult for him, I squeeze him back. The oxygen tubing has been removed from his nose, and I want to kiss him so badly I can barely stand it.

"Sorry I wasn't here when you woke up again," I murmur, but he shakes his head.

"It's okay. I'm just glad you came back."

I can't help it; I raise our joined hands so I can press my lips to his knuckles. "Of course I came back." His blue eyes search my face, until a throat clearing from the doctor brings us back.

"As I was saying." She gives me a small, polite smile. "Healing your arm and wrist is the first order of business. We won't know if surgery will be required for the damage in your shoulder until we see how you respond to therapy."

Matt's grasp on my hand tightens almost to the point of pain, the only sign of his distress. Dr. Elliott continues outlining the care plan: restricted activity for at least four weeks, extensive physical therapy for his arms and shoulders for months afterward, and stretch bands and pool therapy.

"I don't have a pool," Matt says, his voice hoarse, and drops his gaze to the rumpled blankets covering him.

"I do," Cameron says, and I jump. There are so many damn flower arrangements in here, I hadn't noticed him and Kennedy standing in the corner next to the window.

"Ah, well good. That's good." The good doctor's voice sounds slightly breathless, and she touches her hair as she glances at Cameron. "Pool therapy will be extremely beneficial. Biofeedback may also be helpful," she continues, resuming her confident demeanor, but keeping her eyes on her patient. Cam smirks and shoots a wink my way. I simply shake my head.

Matt swallows with difficulty before trying again. "How long until I'm back to normal?"

A small frown ghosts over her lips. "It's hard to say. It really depends on how you respond to therapy and how much you put into it. You're lucky that you're in good physical shape to begin with." She pauses and cocks her head, considering. "I'd guess six months to a year."

Matt stiffens, and I hear a muttered "Fuck" from one of the men in the corner. Tom nods, looking resigned. Dr. Elliott carries on, ignoring the sudden dearth of energy in the room. "I know that sounds like a long time, but, as I said, it depends on how your therapy goes. Everyone's recovery is different."

After another minute, it's clear that Matt is no longer listening. He stares dully at our joined hands, his thumb running listlessly over my knuckles. With a last glance at Cameron, the doctor excuses herself with a promise to check back in tomorrow morning.

Tom clears his throat and signals to Matt's friends. "We'll go see about getting you something for dinner that's better than what I saw being delivered down the hall." He brushes his hand across the top of my shoulder. "I'll bring something back for you, too, sweetie."

"Thanks, Tom." I smile up at him in thanks. He knows I won't be budging from here again tonight.

"I think we'd better check on what Sean's been up to," Kennedy adds. "One or all of us will be back tomorrow, yeah?"

"Yeah, okay." Matt's jaw tightens, but he doesn't look up. Cameron gives me a wry smile and a tweak of my ponytail, before they all shuffle out.

The muted hum of the IV is the only sound in the room. Despite the long rehabilitation in front of us, all I can feel is gratitude that he's alive and awake.

"How do you feel?" I wince at the ridiculous question. "I mean, do you need anything? Any pain meds?"

"Nah. My nurse hooked me up just before the doc came in. The pounding in my head has lessened to a dull roar, so I guess it's working." He raises his head slowly, as if he's afraid it might fall off, and half-smiles. "She said I'll be discharged in a few days, assuming the latest test results come back okay."

I huff out a breath in relief. "Good."

"Dad said you've been here with him almost the whole time."

"I have. And the band, of course. There's been at least one of them here every day." I reach out and smooth his matted hair back from his forehead. "You should've seen how the staff reacted to them the first few days," I add with a smile. "A couple nurses walked into walls, they were so busy ogling."

A smile flickers on his lips, and then he clears his throat. "It's nice you stayed to keep them company."

"That's not why I stayed." I search his face, but see only turmoil in his eyes. "I was so afraid you wouldn't wake up," I admit, my voice barely a whisper. "They kept saying it wasn't unusual for people with head trauma to be unconscious for a while afterward." I swallow down my fears and manage to give him a shaky smile.

"I was having the weirdest dreams." He grimaces, as if willing away some memory.

The cheap plastic chair creaks as I scoot closer to the bed. "I wondered what it was like for you. If you were in too much pain to dream."

"I'm not sure I can tell you," he says, sounding drained. "At first, I felt like every inch of my body had been beaten with a baseball bat. Then there are times I can remember the dreams, but not the pain."

Looking up at me through his long eyelashes, he swallows. "When I first woke up, and you were here, uh, it was confusing, you know? I think I was still dreaming or hallucinating, because, um, because I thought I heard you say . . ."

"Because I said I love you?" I'm calmer than I thought I'd be. "I do. I love you."

He flinches, almost like he's been struck, and he stares down at our hands. "Oh my God."

My stomach drops, and I turn toward the window to give us both the illusion of privacy. His rejection stings even more than I'd feared, but it's out there now. I can't take it back so I keep going. "I can't remember exactly when I realized it, but I've been trying to tell you for about a month."

He laughs shortly, but there's no humor in it. "I must not be the only one who was concussed."

The thin veneer of calm over my raw emotions bursts, and I stand abruptly, dropping his hand on the bed. "Why? Because I would dare to love you? You think there must be something wrong with me to feel that way about you? Good God, Matt—yes, you had a shitty childhood, and I can only imagine the heartbreak you must have gone through all those years. But when are you going to wake up and see that you deserve every good thing that's happened to you since? You've worked your *ass* off to hone your talent and become one of the best at your craft to give back to those people who have loved and believed in you for years." My chest heaves as the words pour out of me, my exasperation with his inability to see how worthy he is eclipsing my embarrassment over him not feeling the same way about me.

He gapes at me, as I stand with my fists clenched and my chin raised in defiance. I know I should shut up—he *just* woke up—but I can't stop myself.

"Tess . . ."

"You are worth it," I grate out. "It was your idiot of a mother who didn't deserve *you!* You did nothing to warrant her piss-poor treatment. I know you feel lucky that Tom found you, but I don't think of it as luck. I think it was fate. I think you were meant to find Tom, someone who could see you for who you were, give you the love you deserved, and the tools to become all that you could be."

"Tess . . ." He raises a hand, but I shake my head. I'm on a roll.

"So, don't sit there and tell me who I can or should love. I'm not asking you to feel the same." My heart twinges at that. "I never thought I'd feel this way for someone, so forgive me for wanting to share."

He stares at me for a beat. Then he catches me by surprise when he reaches out and grabs my arm, jerking me down to the bed. I'm off balance and afraid of hurting him or of him hurting himself, but he moves his hand to the back of my head, holding me in place. His blue eyes burn with a pain that takes my breath away, before they soften and become glassy.

"Well, since I can scarcely breathe without you, Cardinal, I'd say you don't have to worry about me not feeling the same."

chapter sixteen

matt

"SEAN'S ON THE COVER OF *Burnt* magazine again." Tess calls out from the kitchen as she putters away, making lunch. The toaster pops—a BLT again, one of the few things Tess can make without having to call the fire department—plates clang and drawers are opened and closed. Life just fucking goes on.

For the last four weeks, since I've been home, my schedule has been reduced to waking up in pain, navigating the shower with my arm cast wrapped in plastic bags, and trying to take a breath that doesn't actually hurt. "It's been over a month. You think they would've moved on by now."

From my prime location on the sofa, I let out a dull half laugh. "You would think."

"It's very sweet, what he did."

"Sure." I glare at my faithful bass guitar that taunts me from across the room. It's been six weeks since the accident. Six weeks of not playing the guitar. Six weeks of searing pain and nightmares, of dodging paparazzi who want a money shot, of arguments and tension. Six weeks feels like a goddamn lifetime, and the physio is only just beginning. Most of the time, my shoulder feels like it's being cut with a hacksaw from the inside out. Thank fuck the cast on my arm comes off today. "He just likes the attention."

"He did it for you."

I haven't got a comeback for that. Tess is right. Sean dressing up in a disguise on the day I was released and having Tucker wheel him out of the hospital was pure gold. Him, bundled up in a big blanket and jumping out of the wheelchair, clad head to toe in red leather, was just the distraction the paparazzi needed. He stole the limelight in the way that only he could, and allowed me to escape through one of the back doors of the hospital unseen.

"They're calling him the nicest guy in rock and roll."

"Super." I know my voice is flat. It's been that way since I woke up in the hospital. The guys visit in a blur of stilted conversations that don't even matter. Inevitably, they navigate to the guitars, unable to resist the urge to play. That's typically when I tell them I need to lie down. We've never been awkward with each other until now.

No one wants to talk about the massive elephant in the room that threatens to trample us all. We won't know how long I'll be out until I can actually get to some serious rehab on my shoulder without the cast in the way.

Time, apparently, is the key. Unfortunately, I've never been good at waiting.

Tess tries—fuck, does she try to entertain me. And when she's not here, the guys or Tom are. It's a constant buzz of activity at the loft. Never a moment of silence. It's all designed to make sure

I don't slip down the darker path.

We've all read countless articles on recovering from this kind of injury. On how depression can sneak in. Recovery doesn't happen overnight, and you need to maintain a positive mindset, make sure you keep active, blah fucking blah.

I should focus on the fact that I survived this fucking accident and that surgery isn't required—that if, in Dr. Elliott's words, I was going to have an injury, one like mine is the best-case scenario. But this cast and the unknown it could be hiding is wearing me down day by day.

The possibility of never being able to play the way I did before is like a noose around my neck that tightens with each passing minute.

"Matt?" I turn my head in the direction of Tess's voice, finding her standing beside the couch, the familiar look of pity I loathe etched on her face. I hate that I've put that there. That I'm the reason for the dark circles under her eyes and the tension that now seems to live in her body. She's had to calm me down one too many times; the nightmares have returned with a vengeance. I keep the details to myself. She doesn't need her head filled with memories I'd like to keep dead and buried.

"Mhmm?"

"Did you not hear a word I just said?"

"Sorry. I zoned out."

She sinks to the couch beside me, setting a tray with the BLT and a protein smoothie on the coffee table. "The guys? They're asking what time your appointment is."

My jaw hurts from clenching it so often. "No."

Her dark eyes widen as she leans back from me. "No?"

"You heard me."

"But—"

"No, Cardinal. I don't want them there."

She sets her hand on my good arm. "I really think—"

"You don't get to *really think* about this. It's not your shoulder. It's not your fucking entire life on the line." The harshness of my words, of my tone, hangs in air. I push up from the couch, stalking to the window. I need distance from Tess. Distance from all of them.

"Matt, please don't do this. They just want to help." I can hear the hitch in Tess's voice, and I long for that feisty side of her that six weeks ago would've told me to get my head out of my ass. She's been walking on eggshells around me. All of them have, and that kills me.

This accident has changed everything. It's a dark cloud hanging over us all. The guys in the band all share concerned looks, their conversations abruptly stop when I enter a room, and if I have to hear the words "you're going to be fine" one more time, I may fucking explode.

I glance out the window to the pier in the distance. I'd like to get lost in that crowd. To be nameless for a while. Someone whose face isn't plastered on magazines talking about impending band breakups and long roads to recovery.

At least we know who did this now. The cops are still looking for Zach since Beck returned to the group home and spilled his guts. Beck had caught Zach in the garage, messing with the Harley before I took it out. At the news of the accident, they both panicked and split.

Beck is wrought with guilt about not saying anything and about listening to Zach when he told him they'd both go down for this. The looming threat of prison time is one that I know too well.

Beck broke down when I went to visit him at the group home. Full-on sobbing. Told me repeatedly how sorry he was. I don't blame him. He's not the one who fucked with the bike. Zach's still missing and facing some serious jail time if they ever find him, which will likely only serve to harden him further. Another lost soul who's going to spend the rest of his life in and out of prison isn't what I want. Not for Zach, not for anyone.

Beck at least wants to break the cycle that Zach seems to be stuck in. He's pouring all of his energy into the guitar and the garage, and that's something I can appreciate. Fletcher and I are alternating visits, helping him learn the basics. It's clear the kid has talent, and it's up to him where he lets it take him.

Tom's drowning in his own guilt over this clusterfuck. He's apologized for not giving Zach his walking papers from the group home after the fight he had with Beck. But Tom wouldn't be who he is if he gave up on these kids. It's the reason I'm still standing here, because he refused to give up when everyone else had turned their backs on me.

I feel her arms wrap around my waist from behind, always careful of my ribs. That's what Tess has become now—gentle. No more raw and unfiltered touches, the ones I used to crave. The ones I miss.

She sets her forehead against my back, her sweet curves pressing against me. "You're going to be fine," she mumbles against my shirt.

I hate the word fine.

"TAKE YOUR TIME. REMEMBER, IT'S kind of like a rusty hinge. It's going to take a while to get the kinks out. Try making a fist again."

I lift a brow to Dr. Elliott, before staring back at my hand. The indents from the cast cut into the ink on my wrist, to the tattoo that Tess first asked about. The matrix of double-sided arrows that remind me everything is connected.

Closing my fist is awkward and takes more energy than it should, but the good doctor seems pleased. "Good. Now, bend your elbow."

I follow her instructions, feeling like a child. Raw pain burns through my shoulder, radiating down my arm. "Fucking hell."

Tess flutters closer, fussing over me like a mother hen. "Careful," she whispers.

I lift my chin, meeting her worried eyes, the doctor's voice echoing in my ears. "Try rolling your shoulder. I can give you a prescription for the pain."

"Shit." I wince, my right hand tightening against the edge of the examination table as I try the simple task of lifting my shoulder. "No. No prescriptions."

"It would help considerably."

"We've talked about this, doc. Pills around me and the guys are no go."

"Are you sure?" Tess folds her arms across her chest.

"Positive. I'll pop a few ibuprofens if it gets bad, but that's as far as I'm going." Squeezing my eyes shut from the pain, I take a few shaky breaths before I feel the doctor's hand on my arm. Fuck knows we don't need more stress. We just got Cameron back from rehab, and I'll be damned if I'm going to bring the temptation of prescription drugs around him, or any of them for that matter.

"That's good for today," Dr. Elliott says, and I open my eyes once more. "I'm going to send you home with some more exercises to strengthen your shoulder. You've started physio already?" She rolls her chair over to the desk on the other side of the exam room and flicks on a light.

Illuminated on a backlit screen are a series of x-rays. My throat is suddenly dry. I'm almost afraid to look at them. "Yeah. Tucker's got me on a workout plan."

"Good. Make sure you take it easy for the first little while. The last thing you want is to injure yourself further because you tried to bench press above your weight." The doctor levels me with a stern look as she slips her glasses on.

"Got it. What's all this?" I ask, glancing at the x-rays. I try to keep my shoulder back, but it wants to slouch forward, leaving my arm hanging like a ragdoll. The once defined muscles in my arm seem to have faded into oblivion.

Dr. Elliott points to the first photo, lifting a pen to trace a line over it. "These are the x-rays we took earlier today. Your ribs are healing nicely. You're starting to breathe easier?"

"Sure. If by easier you mean I don't feel like I'm going to pass out with my next breath, then yeah."

"That's good," she says seriously, turning to me. "Look, I know this is hard, but it isn't something that is going to get fixed overnight, Matt. You've had a traumatic injury. It's going to take some time for you heal, but you are going to heal. I have no reason to think otherwise. You're going to be fine."

That damn fucking word again. *Fine.* Tess offers me a tight, fake smile, and then Dr. Elliott starts droning on about the rest of the x-rays. I've tuned her out. I only catch bits and pieces of what she's saying. An uneasy feeling has taken over, an annoyance crawling through me, and I don't like it. I don't like this sense of helplessness. I don't like Tess feeling sorry for me, like I'm some charity case of hers.

By the time the appointment is over, and Tess collects the encyclopedia of information and exercises from Dr. Elliott, the lump in my throat has grown bigger, threatening to choke me.

The only thing I know I need is distance and quiet. I'm drained from this whole ordeal. Tired of answering questions, tired of the constant tension of feeling like I'm letting everyone down.

"YOU SHOULD CALL YOUR DAD back. He's left a few messages." I glance over at Tess, curled up in the chair across from me, reading one of the pamphlets the doctor gave us this afternoon. Her dark hair is tied back in a messy ponytail, and she's wearing one of my old concert T-shirts over a pair of leggings.

The ride home was spent in an awkward silence—something else that's not normal for Tess and me. I can feel the tension simmering under the surface, threatening to boil over.

"I'll call him tomorrow."

She lifts a brow before returning to the fascinating read of *Exercises for Shoulder Strengthening*.

"What? Is that not okay with you?" My words come out harsh and clipped.

Lowering the brochure, her eyes meet mine. "I didn't say anything." It kills me to hear her so guarded.

"You didn't have to."

She folds the brochure up and sets it on the coffee table. She's eerily calm. Another red flag. Tess wears her emotions and her heart on her sleeve—at least she used to. "You want to tell me what this is about?"

I feel my jaw set, and I lean forward. "I'll throw that question right back at you, Cardinal."

I know exactly what I'm doing—baiting her. But I need the real Tess back. The feisty, sometimes infuriating, confident Tess who pushes and tests me.

Uncurling herself from the chair, she pushes up, her eyes

brimming with tears, and the sight cuts through me.

"Tess . . ."

"You know, I'm trying here." She quickly brushes the tears as they start to fall.

"Here's the thing. You don't have to try. Just be you."

Throwing her arms up in the air, she stalks over to me. "I could say the same thing to you."

Pushing up from the couch, I tower over her, watching the steady rise and fall of her chest. "I'm trying, too, you know."

"Really? You call sulking and staring out the window trying?" She props her hands on her hips. I feel the anger spike along with the gnawing pain that won't leave me alone.

"I call it recovering, or did you forget about that?"

Her eyes widen, and I see a flicker of that heated passion I crave. "How could I possibly forget? It fills up this whole place!" she hollers. "You haven't even tried playing. The doctor said—"

"Oh, fuck the doctor!"

"That's real mature, Matt. Way to handle the situation. God! You are the most frustrating man on the planet."

"You want me to try playing, sweetheart? Is that what you're missing?" I brush past her, stomping to the guitars that line the brick wall.

My shoulder complains as I tug my red Fender from the hook. I can feel the adrenaline firing dangerously, masking the pain as I turn back to her. "You want to see me play?"

"Matt, don't. Not like this."

"This is me, fucking playing!" Lifting the Fender with my good arm, I swing it against one of the amps in the corner. The cracking of wood echoes over and over as the guitar shatters against the amp, jagged pieces flying to the floor.

It's cathartic, it's freeing, and it's making me feel something other than numbing pain. I don't stop until the entire Fender is nothing but an expensive pile of firewood on the floor next to the mangled amp. My shoulder is on fire, I'm out of breath, sweat breaks out over my skin, and I welcome it all.

Slowly, an unnatural quiet brings me out of my rage, and when I finally turn back to find Tess, she's gone.

♪ ♩ ♪ ♩

Tessa

I FLY DOWN THE LONG back staircase to the garage, the discordant metallic twanging of overstretched strings and the sound of exploding wood echoing behind me. A sudden silence makes me pause at the bottom. I'm still poised for flight as I clutch my jean jacket that I snatched off the hook next to the door as I left. Did I close the door behind me? I don't think I did.

"Cardinal?" The anger and accusation in his voice drift down to me from above and goad me into action again. I run across the garage and slide behind the wheel of the Camaro, my fingers automatically finding the door opener. My heart thunders as I nervously tap the steering wheel with my fingertip while the damn gate creeps open, creaking like a goddamn fire alarm. The last barrier to freedom finally removed, I cautiously look out into the alley before pulling out. Checking to ensure the gate is closing behind me, I catch a glimpse of his tall figure stepping out from the stairwell before I hit the gas.

I drive around aimlessly for several minutes, letting the deep purr of the engine and the warm leather scents of the interior soothe my jangled nerves. There was no real thought involved in my departure—I just had to leave. I've never seen him so angry before. The arc of the guitar soaring through the air was so unexpected, it didn't seem real; it was the crashing sound when it made impact that shocked me.

My phone rings in my pocket. I ignore it. If he can act like a child, so can I. "Damn it, Matt!" I growl in frustration, banging my fist against the steering wheel. Such a stubborn, pig-headed, immature, mulish . . . idiot! Why can't he see that he's not doing himself any good by just sitting and sulking like a pouty twelve-year-old boy?

My breath leaves me in a whoosh. Twelve-year-old boy. That's what he was when his mom died, plunging him into an even worse situation than he'd already been in. This is probably the worst thing that's happened to him since Tom adopted him. I stop at a red light and stare out the rain-streaked window, a grudging understanding slowly extinguishing my ire. Maybe that's what this is. The stress of the accident and subsequent recovery period is drawing that scared, angry boy he once was back to the surface, like a slow-burning fuse just waiting for a gust of oxygen to make it explode.

And I was the oxygen.

The words he spoke before his doctor appointment come back to me. *"It's not your shoulder. It's not your fucking entire life on the line."* Is that what he really thinks? At the time, I'd thought he was just being dramatic—sometimes the man could be as over-the-top as Sean. I know that the brachial plexus injury isn't anything to sneeze at, but everything Dr. Elliott has said has been promising. His PT is going well, despite not being as fast as he'd like. How can he not see the progress he's made? I've done everything I can think of to encourage him and show him how well he's doing. Why isn't that enough? How can I get through to him?

I grimace at the rough, cold feel of the brake pedal against my bare foot. I'd had just enough thought to grab my coat with the car keys and my phone in the pocket before I went out the door. I wish I'd grabbed my shoes, too. My scowl deepens at the sight of a man walking down the sidewalk with an enormous bouquet of roses and an insufferably cheerful smile. I'd almost forgotten . . . happy birthday to me.

I hate having a birthday on Valentine's Day. I'd studiously ignored the date as it marched closer on the calendar, pouring myself instead into doing whatever I could to help Matt. He hasn't mentioned the date either. He probably doesn't remember my admission during the gala about my birthdate. Besides, he has enough on his plate right now.

My phone pings with a text. Gritting my teeth, I reach into my jacket sitting on the passenger seat and fish my phone out of the pocket. I don't really want to see what he has to say for himself, but I can't stop myself from looking. Scanning the screen quickly, I see his call, but the text listed below is a surprise. I smile as my heart softens.

Happy birthday, little girl. Your mom and I hope your day is going well. Say hi to Matt for us.

The light turns and as traffic starts to move, I hit my blinker. I know exactly where I'm going now.

The house only has a few lights on when I park on the street in front. I get out and walk across the sodden lawn to the kitchen door, shuddering at the feel of squishy grass between my toes. Scraping my feet on the rough welcome mat, I swing the door open and breathe deeply, the scents of home better than any perfume.

"Dad? Mom?" I call to the quiet house. Someone must be home—the door was unlocked.

"Tessa?" My dad looks surprised, but smiles as he comes around the corner into the kitchen, a coffee cup in hand. "What are you doing here?" He frowns down at my crimson-painted toes gleaming against the linoleum. "Where are your shoes? It's raining."

A tired giggle bubbles up. "It's a long story. Is Mom here?"

"No, she had to run to the market. We're having pot roast." He stretches his neck to look behind me, his brow furrowing when I close the door. "Where's Matt?"

"Wallowing in misery, no doubt," I say dryly, moving to pour myself a cup of tea from the pot sitting on the counter. When I turn around, cup in hand, I see he's watching me, his head cocked to the side. Then he leans against the counter opposite me and sets his mug down.

"Okay, let's hear it." He folds his arms.

"He's just so frustrating!" The tea sloshes in my mug as I wave my free arm. "His doctor says everything is going great, which is fabulous news, but it's like he can't stand hearing it!" I begin to pace, gesticulating as I rant. "Tucker is helping with his physical therapy, the guys make sure to include him with all the rescheduling decisions for the tour so he can never doubt his place in the band is secure, and Tom visits him every day to keep him up to date with the police investigation. And the way he acts, you'd think it was all some type of torture."

I set my mug down so I won't spill anymore, and lick a stray drop of tea from my thumb. Breathing heavily, I try to calm down. "When he's not doing PT he just sits around the loft wallowing. I'm doing my best to help, but he keeps pushing me away."

"Okay, so you had a fight." At my hesitant nod, he shrugs as if it's no big deal, but then narrows his eyes at me. "Wait, did he *scare* you? Is that why you're here without any shoes?" He glances down at my bare feet and abruptly stands straighter, every muscle tense, as if he's about to do battle on my behalf.

I quickly move in front of him. "No! Yes, we argued—well, actually, he had a tantrum—and I left because he was being an ass.

But it wasn't *that* kind of fight," I explain, trying to sort it out in my own head. He was beyond reason, so wrapped up in his frustration that he wasn't going to listen, and I was just as upset as he was, to be honest. I *was* shocked by the sudden violence and the sheer stupidity of destroying one of his favorite instruments, but I was never *afraid* of him.

Shoving my hands in my hair, I begin pacing again. "Look, I get that he's not used to all the inactivity he's been forced into, but he's healing really well, and now that the cast is off he'll be able to increase his exercises. But it's like he doesn't believe what anyone tells him. If brooding were an Olympic event, he'd have a gold medal." I slap my hand on the counter, and his mouth twitches at my outburst. "I . . . I just want to scream at him!"

"So, why don't you?"

Startled, I stare at him; he's leaning casually against the kitchen counter, as if we're discussing the weather. "Well, he's still recovering," I stammer, nonplussed. "He's barely gotten his cast off. He's not in any condition—"

"He's fine," he says bluntly. My mouth drops open.

"He could've died!" My stupid tears well again, and I quickly wipe them away. God, I hate how easily I cry now. "I could've lost him entirely." I'm shaking, the choking fear I'd felt while he was lying unconscious billowing up suddenly like a dark cloud.

"Tessa." Dad's eyes are full of sympathy and understanding. He holds his arms out in invitation, and I immediately go into his welcome embrace. His chest is solid against my cheek, a testament to the military workout he's never given up. He lets me sniffle into his shirt for a few minutes, and then takes a deep breath. "Tessa-bug, you didn't lose him. He's going to be all right. I know how much you care for him and that you're worried about how he's handling all this. But when you're worried, you go into hover mode."

I jerk my head back to glower up at him. "I don't hover!"

"Yes, you do, but you come by it honestly. You learned from your mother."

"Are you complaining about how Mom takes care of you?"

He chuckles. "Of course not. However, Matt doesn't strike me as the sort who can abide being coddled for long. Especially when he's feeling sorry for himself."

I open my mouth to defend him and close it. Matt *is* feeling sorry for himself. "Don't get me wrong," Dad continues. "After what he's been through, he's entitled to feel a little sorry for himself. It's a reasonable reaction. I've seen it in men and women I've served with who were injured. From what I saw when you brought him 'round on Christmas Eve, it's obvious the man has courage. He's strong." He clears his throat. "And he loves you."

My heart stutters at his straightforward statement, and I step back out of his embrace, looking up at him through my eyelashes. "How can you tell?" I ask quietly, feeling a tightening in my chest. Although I haven't been shy about telling Matt I love him since my outburst in his hospital room, he's never once said those three fateful little words to me. But it doesn't matter. *I can scarcely breathe without you, Cardinal*, he'd said. That's enough.

I've been so caught up in Matt since then, I haven't thought what anyone outside our bubble might see or think about it.

My father glances at the ceiling, as if seeking strength. "Please. The way he looked at you that night? I might be a crusty old sailor, but I'm not blind. Besides . . ." He coughs into his fist, his ears pinking. "Tom might have mentioned something."

"Tom?" My head snaps up, but my father is staring out the window to avoid looking at me, his lips twisted in a smirk. "Oh my God. So, while I was waiting for Matt to wake up, you two were gossiping about us like a couple of old women?"

I swat his arm, but he merely laughs and pretends to duck. "Not the *entire* time," he protests through his chuckles. A smile tugs at my lips, ruining my scowl, so I give up. He slips his arm around my shoulders.

"Look, honey. All I'm saying is that after the blow he received, it'll be natural for Matt to struggle while he finds his feet."

"I know that, Dad."

"*And* maybe your pampering just keeps reminding him of everything that happened and everything that he fears *might* happen. If you want to help him move on, don't smother him, Tess. That's not what a man like Matt needs. Just be yourself. Smart mouth, bad cooking, and all."

I roll my eyes, and he chuckles again. "So, are you ready to go back and face the music yet? Or do you want to put on a spare pair of shoes so you can help me putter in the garage a while?"

IT'S LATE WHEN I PULL the Camaro back into the garage and shut off the engine. Helping Dad reorder his socket wrenches and clean up the garage also helped me clear my head. Maybe I have been letting my concern for Matt override my instincts. But is it fair to snap back at him with my usual snark and add to his anxiety? He's got enough to worry about without me adding to it, doesn't he?

There are no sounds from the loft as I mount the stairs. I'm sure he must have heard the garage gate groan shut—everyone in a ten-block radius can hear the damn thing. Maybe he left? Or maybe he moved on from the guitar to smash up the entire place? Bracing myself for anything, I open the door quietly and enter. The living room is empty, a single lamp in the corner emitting a soft golden light. The deep dents in the amp bear silent witness to the afternoon's ferocity. The scraps of what's left of his poor red Fender stick upright in the garbage can that's now sitting by the door. Everything else seems as it was.

A noise from up in the bedroom alerts me. I can't see him, but I know he's up there. My steps on the bedroom stairs echo in the loft in time with my heartbeat. He's sitting on the edge of the bed, his head in his hands.

"Hi," I whisper and sit on the edge of the low wall that surrounds his elevated bedroom. He doesn't raise his head but reaches blindly toward me; I immediately move and take his hand. He pulls me to stand in front of him so he can rest his forehead against my stomach. I feel him shudder as his arms encircle my waist.

"You came back." His voice is muffled, but I can hear his relief. I swallow the sudden lump in my throat and gently ruffle his blond hair.

"Of course I came back. This is where you are."

He leans back a bit and looks up at me. His eyes are dark with contrition. "I'm glad. Although I wouldn't blame you if you hadn't."

I brush a fingertip over his lips, and he closes his eyes, as if savoring my touch. "Did it help?" I ask simply. He knows what I mean—a corner of his mouth turns up.

"Yeah, actually it did."

"Okay, then. Next time you feel the urge to break something, though, I'd advise you to call Tucker. I'm sure he has things you can destroy that don't cost quite so much."

He huffs a chuckle. "No doubt." He scans my face and digs his fingers into my waist. "I'm sorry, Tess. Are you okay?"

I nod, resting my hands on his shoulders. "Of course. It will take more than that to drive me away."

"I'm not sure whether that makes you too good to be true or completely nuts." His eyes spark with a sense of humor that I've missed these last six weeks.

"Let's go with the first choice." He laughs in response and positions me back a step so he can rise. He bends over and awkwardly digs into a pocket of his backpack with his healing arm. I fight the urge to move to help him. It's harder than I thought.

Ignorant of my internal struggle, he turns and shyly holds out a small black velvet bag. "Six weeks ago, I had meant for this evening to go differently. Happy birthday."

Oh my God. I gulp and take the featherweight bag. My heart is in my throat as I open the strings and tip the contents into my palm. A thin platinum oval winks up at me in the dim light. "Oh, Matt," I breathe, and hold it up to look more closely. "They're beautiful." Three delicate charms hang from the bracelet: a butterfly, a heart, and a guitar. I look at him with wonder, blinking back tears.

"They seemed appropriate." His husky voice sends a shiver of desire down my spine. "You have my heart, after all."

He's standing too far away. Clutching my gift in my hand, I rush and throw my arms around his neck, startling him. With a soft grunt of gratitude, he hugs me, squeezing as tightly as his shoulder will allow. "I love you, Cardinal," he whispers, and I gasp out a half-laugh, half-sob against his collarbone. I don't *need* to hear those words, but I have to admit they sound pretty damn good.

"I love you, too." I sniff into his chest. "And I'm sorry."

"What have you got to be sorry for?" he scoffs, his arms tightening a bit, as if I might slip away from him.

"I'm sorry for smothering you. I'll try to give you space and won't nag when you do something asinine."

His laugh resonates in his chest. "I'm sorry for behaving like an ungrateful Neanderthal with his head up his ass," he replies, his nose buried in my hair. "I know this whole thing has scared you, too."

My giggle comes out as a gurgle, thanks to my stuffy nose. "Sounds like maybe we both talked to our dads today."

"Maybe so." He cups my cheek, tilting my head so he can see my face. The longing and love shining in his eyes—with a hint of desperation—take my breath away. "I need us to be normal again, Tess. I just want to play my music and love you the best way I know how. And I promise to do whatever I need to do to accomplish both."

"Me, too." I pull his head down to mine, my lips ghosting over his. "We'll figure it out, Matt. It's what we do."

chapter seventeen

matt

I'M A DRENCHED, SWEATY MESS, *caught in a tangle of metal and steel. Tess's broken body is still as stone, unresponsive, just out of my reach.*

"Looks like our work here isn't quite done, boys."

A group surrounds us, their faces cloaked in the darkness of the night. Sadistic laughter, a kick to my ribs, followed by another.

Pain seers through my shoulder as I struggle against the weight of the Harley. I'm pinned, trapped, and unable to move. A shadowed body moves closer to Tess, crouching down beside her. He tosses a sneer my way.

"I think we'll have some fun with her."

I wake up in a cold sweat, arms flailing and heart hammering to another vivid nightmare. Tess stirs awake beside me, her arm sliding across my chest. "It's just a dream." Her voice calms me, and I bury my face in the blanket of her hair.

Just a dream. It's not real. She's real. She's what's real.

Tess. She's everything that's good and right in my life. She's here and she's safe. I repeat it over and over until the harshness of the dream starts to fade.

My arm is on fire with the weight of her draped over me, but I don't want to move.

"Sorry," she whispers, leaning away, but I need to feel her, close and protected. Away from the nightmares that threaten to pull me under.

"No. Don't. I want you here. I need you here."

"But your shoulder."

"I need you, Cardinal."

"I'm right here," she whispers against my neck as I tighten my hand over the delicious curve of her hip.

She seems to know what I want, what I need on instinct alone. Slowly, she straddles me, her creamy thighs brushing my overheated skin. There're very few advantages to having little to no mobility in my arm, but this is one of them. Tess taking control, leading me down the path we both want to ride.

It's sweet torture not being able to tighten both my arms around her, to lift her like I used to, like I want to. Her like this, spreading her thighs wide, guiding my cock to her entrance, watching when she throws her head back as she rides me, takes my breath away.

Leaning forward, I pull one hardened nipple into the warmth of my mouth. She answers on a parted sigh and a gradual grind of her hips. This is what's so fucking perfect about Tess and me: the give and take. She's strong where I'm weak, a breath of fresh air when the darkness threatens to choke me.

I tighten my good hand against the curve of her ass, coaxing her faster. Her slow and steady rhythm quickly becomes raw and erratic. Coaxing my lips back to hers, her fingers tighten into my hair, tugging relentlessly with each intense thrust of my hips. It's like she can't get enough of this, of me.

Feeling her clench around me, heat fires up my spine, and I lean back to watch her fall apart. It's a sight I'll never get used to. I'm right there with her, the arm I can move bracing around her back as my hips slam forward with my own release.

She's a panting wreck, her hair wild and tangled around my face. Her shaky breaths mix with my own as she clings to me. For a few glorious minutes, I don't care about the throb in my shoulder or the stress of not being able to play. It's just Tess and me, and that's all I'll ever need.

She realizes far too soon that despite her best efforts to avoid it, she's crushing me.

"Sorry about that." Her gentle lips brush against my shoulder as she lifts away, tucking herself under my other arm.

"I never want you to apologize for that." Her fingers lightly trace the lines of ink on my chest, and I breathe her in. Pulling my hand through her thick hair is soothing in a way I hadn't expected, but then everything about Tess and me has been unexpected.

"You never talk about your dreams." She glances up at me.

"You don't want that shit in your head, believe me."

"If you won't talk about it with me, maybe you can see a counselor." Scoffing at her suggestion, I shake my head. She leans up, her lips hovering just over mine. "It's eating you alive. I can see it."

"I've been dealing with it my whole life. No counselor is going to make it better." I take a bite at her bottom lip. "You do that already."

"You are the most stubborn person on the planet."

"I thought you had that title." She shakes her head with an amused grin. "If this is about before, you know that's not me. I'd never hurt you, Tess."

"I know that. And it's okay; everybody needs to get lost some-times."

I lean back against the pillow. "That's a really good lyric."

Her answering laugh is exactly what I need. There's no drug they can give me that makes me feel the way she does. "I'm seri-ous." My hand skims along her side, up to cup the underside of her breast. Fuck, if I could stay here like this with her, life would be so much easier. "I've been writing a bit."

I can see her smile in the path of the moonlight peeking through the window. "You have?"

"Mmm. I'm thinking about talking to the guys about it since I'm fucking useless otherwise."

Her leg hitches over mine as she presses against my side. "You're a lot of things, but fucking useless isn't one of them."

"Is that right? Why don't you tell me what else I am then, Cardinal, hmm?" I slip my hand up her back, tugging at the ends of her hair. It earns me one of her sexy little moans. "You have my undivided attention."

♪ ♩ ♪ ♩

A COUPLE OF WEEKS LATER, I'm at Kennedy's front door in Bodega Bay, shifting nervously. My grip tightens on the tablet in my hand. I'm a fucking idiot for calling him and asking to meet. Of all the ideas I've had over the years, this has to be on the list of the worst. The man is a lyrical genius. He's going to think I'm ridiculous. What the hell was I thinking?

I look back to the Camaro, plotting my escape. I shouldn't have come here.

The door whips open as I contemplate my sanity, and Ken-nedy offers me a grin. He looks relaxed, but then again, he's not the one about to spill his guts. "Matty, it's good to see you, man. Come on in."

I step inside, taking a look around. I hope to hell he's alone. "How's the arm coming along without the cast?" He nods in the direction of my shoulder.

"It's a work in progress, Tucker tells me. Slow and steady, you know?"

"I hear you. You're in good hands there. Tucker won't let you be the slacker we all know you are." He leads the way into his massive living room.

Sinking down to one of the couches that face the ocean, he eyes me. "What's up? Not that I mind you visiting. You know you're welcome anytime."

"Is Abby here?" I glance down the sprawling hallway.

"She's at work. It's just you and me, so take a load off, and spill it."

I drop into the couch across from him, my leg bouncing off nervous energy. "What's happening with the tour? Have you guys talked about replacing me?"

Kennedy scowls, silent as he studies me. "You're kidding me, right?"

"I'm serious. Look, man, I get it. You've got commitments, fans, and the entire country of Canada waiting for you."

"No. *We've* got all of those things. How can you think we'd replace you?"

"Don't tell me it hasn't crossed your mind."

"It hasn't." I lift a brow. "Okay, so the record label's been asking, but we shut it down." Shaking my head, I rub my hand across the back of my neck. "Matty, it's not an option. This is temporary. Your shoulder's going to heal, and you'll be back in no time."

My throat constricts, reality spilling out of my mouth. "There's a possibility I may never play the same way again."

Kennedy doesn't even flinch. "I don't believe that and neither do you."

Feeling the frustration start to fire through me, I try to lift my arm. Every day it gets a little easier. The aqua therapy in Cameron's infinity pool has definitely been helping, even if it does come with Sean lounging poolside like the king of the world with a fruity umbrella drink in his hand, barking orders at me. Therapy is a long and painful road in more ways than one. "It's nerve damage, Kennedy. There's no way to predict how it's going to heal, *if* it's going to heal."

"Have you even tried playing yet?"

"If by *try* you mean trashing the red Fender, then yeah."

His eyes widen. "Wait, which Fender? Not the '72?"

"One in the same." He grimaces. "And technically I didn't really try to play it; I just kind of totaled it. Anyway, it's found a nice new home in a landfill."

Kennedy leans forward, resting his elbows on his knees. "You know you can always talk to me. You, the guys, you're my brothers. And what I've always said is still true. The band doesn't work without all of us. We'll figure this out." Hearing any of the guys talk this way always gets to me, even after all this time. I'm still surprised people actually give a shit about me.

"Plus, to be honest," he continues, "the break is nice. Not that I like what you've been going through. I've gotten time to spend with Abby and Mom and Dad."

"Glad I could help you out."

"You know what I mean. It kills me to see you like this. If I could trade places with you, I'd do it. We all would."

My fingers tighten against the tablet as I fight to keep it

together. "Shit. Don't get all emotional on me. I feel bad enough as it is."

"You're stuck with us. You leaving, or whatever else is going through that thick skull of yours, isn't happening, got it?"

Giving him a slow nod, I open up the tablet, my heart pounding. "Since I can't play, I've kind of been sort of writing a bit. I mean, it's not like your stuff, but it's something."

I finally glance back to him.

"Kind of sort of been, hmm?"

"Fuck, I don't know why I'm so nervous."

"If it helps, I'm a wreck every time before I share something new with you guys. What if it's shit? What if they laugh at it? What if we can't find a way to make it ours? A million questions run through my head, you don't even want to know." He glances down to the tablet. "Going all high tech?"

"I know you write everything out old school with notes and everything, but there's a couple of apps I found."

He lets out a laugh. "Jesus. There's an app. Of course there is."

"Welcome to the 21st century. Anyway, it lays down tracks for the bass, even drums, so you can get a feel for it. Obviously, it's not going to sound like it would when you play it."

"When *we* play it," he says pointedly.

"Right. When we play it, but it'll give you an idea."

"You want me to call the rest of the guys? It can be a celebration. A little different than the one we had on New Year's Eve." He pushes up from the couch to start heading down to his studio.

"What happened New Year's Eve?" Following him down the stairs, he flips the lights on. I can feel the familiar rush of adrenaline, glancing at the glass-enclosed studio at the far end of the room. How many hours have we spent down here perfecting a track, fighting over a chorus, playing into the middle of the night? History written right here in this room.

"We had a party in your room." My eyes widen as he continues, "Sean blew up a bunch of those extra-small condoms you kept getting from fans, filled them with glitter." He laughs, lifting one of his Fender acoustics from the stand and pulling the strap over his shoulder. "Fuck, that was funny. We had to wade through them, there were so many."

"Wait, you spent New Year's Eve in my hospital room while I was unconscious?"

"Damn right we did. Party hats, music, sparkling cider at midnight. The whole nine yards. It was pretty fucking epic. The nurses weren't impressed."

"I had no idea."

"Course you didn't." He shrugs as if it's no big deal. "We didn't want you and Tess to be alone."

"Was Tom there?"

He glances at me. "Who do you think came up with the idea?" I stare back at him speechless. What the hell else happened when I was in that fucking coma? "So, show me what you got."

The tablet weighs a ton in my hand. I know as soon as I do this, everything will be different. My voice in the band up until this point has been just that, a voice put to his lyrics. Sure, I add my own spin on the tracks when we record and play live, we all do that, but this? This is something else, something personal. Lyrics that are entirely and completely mine.

Kennedy just waits, sitting on one of the stools behind a microphone. He gives me the time I need until I open up the app and let him hear my soul.

Tessa

MATT STICKS HIS HEAD IN my bedroom door. "Got any more tape, babe?"

"Sure." I toss a roll across the bed to him, and he snatches it with his good hand. "I think there's more on the kitchen counter, too."

"'Kay." He gives me a wink and then ducks back out, the sound of tearing packing tape echoing in his wake.

We've finally decided to take the next step and officially share his loft near the wharf. It's been unofficial since his accident; most of my clothes are already there. This weekend will see the removal of the rest of my belongings from the lovely condo I share with Jada. Some things will go to storage; the rest will find a home nestled among his guitars and assorted bits of sound equipment. And the new keyboard that Matt uses to compose.

With a happy sigh, I grab my spare roll of packing tape and tear off a strip to seal a box of books. Thank God for the Redfall boys. In the weeks since Matt shared the lyrics he'd been working on with Kennedy, it's as if a weight has lifted from him. All three of his bandmates have been incredibly supportive since the accident, of course, but I think the way they were so accepting of his compositions shocked him in a good way. He's still too shy about it to share any of his new songs with me yet, but I've heard him plunking away downstairs some nights when I've awoken to find his side of the bed empty. I try not to push. He'll share when he's ready.

However, thrilled as I am about this new outlet for his pent-up creativity, I'm still worried. I don't think he's tried playing the guitar yet, and his nightmares have gotten worse.

The quiet snick of the latch brings my head up. Jada leans against the closed door, her hand still on the knob. "How you doin' in here?"

"Almost done. When's your next victim moving in?"

"Ha ha," she says dryly and sits on the corner of my bed. "I've decided to keep it all to myself for a month or two. Maybe give Greg an opportunity to become my new roommate."

I shoot her a glance. "Really? I didn't think things had progressed that far." While I've been staying with Matt since the accident, Jada formed a tempestuous friends-with-benefits arrangement with one of the IT professors. Their rumored tryst in the server room has apparently become the stuff of legend among the computer geeks at SFSU.

She shrugs. "What about you? It's not that I don't like Matt—he's grown on me." She chuckles. "Just remember that if things don't work out, I've got your back." Her deep ebony eyes fix on me with a sincerity that touches my heart.

"Thanks. I appreciate it." With a wry smile, I move the box I just loaded to the stack by my window. "This feels right, though. For both of us. We're ready."

"Good." She cocks her head at me. "Have they caught that kid yet?"

I frown at the mention of Zach. "Not yet. Matt says it's not surprising, considering how resourceful street kids can be. He's probably long gone by now anyway."

"He'd be stupid to stay in town." She holds another box open for me to put a stack of sheets into it. "So, this is really it, then. You're really leaving me."

"Yep. Really leaving." I stand on my tiptoes to reach a stack of bedding in my closet, and then turn to see her grinning at me.

"Good. Because what I really wanted to know was if it was safe for me to put the sex trapeze in here."

I burst out laughing, and she easily dodges the pillow I throw at her. She skips to the door and opens it, with a promise to start boxing up my few and rarely-used kitchen implements. We both know we'll remain friends—but I'll make sure to call ahead so I don't interrupt any wild computer geek orgies.

♪ ♩ ♪ ♩

"BE CAREFUL OF YOUR SHOULDER!" I dart forward and take a box from the stack Matt is awkwardly trying to carry in the door at the loft. "You don't have to carry three at a time, you know." Stubborn man.

"These aren't heavy." He frowns. "It's like all they have are towels or pillows or something. Doesn't Jada know how to pack a full box?"

I sniff and set my load down in the corner where we're stacking everything for now. "Don't blame Jada. I was grateful for her help. How much is left in the truck?"

"There're only a few more things for this stop." The rest is going to be loaded into a small storage unit nearby. "Oh, and your brother had to leave to take Mason to his soccer practice. He said to call him later if we still needed help."

I hum in acknowledgement and twist one of the boxes around so I can read what is in it. Out of the corner of my eye, I catch Matt trying surreptitiously to rub his bad shoulder.

"Did you hurt it?" I drop what I'm doing and march over to prod gently at the hard muscle of his injured shoulder. He sighs but otherwise bears my ministrations.

"No, it's just a little sore, Nurse Baker." He laughs when I frown at him. "Honest, it's okay."

However, the blue eyes smiling down at me are tired, and the deep bags under his eyes look even worse in the late afternoon light.

He hasn't gotten an uninterrupted night's sleep all week thanks to the damn nightmares. "Maybe so, but you've worked it a little more than usual today. Why don't you lie down and try to rest a bit? I can bring you an ice pack." I try for a winsome smile. "I don't want to bring the wrath of Tucker down on me for screwing up the progress you've made."

Those formerly smiling eyes narrow in suspicion. "I don't need a fucking nap, Tess," he spits. "I'm not a two-year-old."

I open my mouth to tell him to stop acting like one, but I clap it shut just in time. This not hovering stuff is hard. "Fine," I retort instead, and whirl away from him to calm down. But before I get five steps away, I swing back around, my worry for him bubbling over.

"No, it's not fine." With my hands on my hips, I choose my words carefully, trying to keep my tone even. I can see him getting his back up, and we can't have this conversation if we're yelling. "We need to talk about the nightmares, Matt."

"There's nothing to talk about." He turns on his heel and stalks toward the garage door. "I need to adjust the Camaro's carburetor. Call me when Tom gets here."

"*Hold it right there.*" I'm surprised to hear my father's steely tone of command in my voice, but it has the desired effect. Matt releases the doorknob as if it burned him and turns to face me like a recalcitrant schoolboy. I'm not sure if this is the right time to bring this up, but when *is* the right time? Taking a deep breath, I dive in.

"I'm not going to let you run away this time. Don't try to deny it." I glare at him, and he obediently shuts his mouth. "Because that's exactly what you were doing. Every time Dr. Elliot or I bring this up, you find some way of deflecting. You change the subject or make an excuse to leave the room. I have to talk to you about this. I love you and I'm worried. I'm worried about you. You've made so much progress physically, but you're ignoring the other effects of the accident. And you won't let anyone help. You won't let *me* help."

My voice quivers against my will, and his shoulders slump in response. "You shouldn't have to deal with my bullshit," he growls, rubbing his hand through his hair in frustration. "I don't want it to affect you."

"But it does, Matt. It affects me every time you thrash yourself awake, fighting an invisible foe. I have bruises from it." My hips and biceps—his favorite handholds when I help him exorcise his demons during the night—are peppered with fingertip-sized marks. He ducks his head, avoiding my eyes. "I'm not complaining, just stating a fact. I understand that you don't want to talk to me about them, but you have to talk to someone. You need to see a counselor."

He raises his head at that, bristling. "Will you still move in if I don't?" he challenges. Every inch of his body is quivering in restrained emotion, his chin stuck out, just waiting for the shoe to drop. Always assuming the worst.

"Of course I will." I take a deep breath and relax my shoulders, suddenly realizing how rigid I am. "Ultimatums aren't my style. Getting you healthy is." I move over to my purse and rummage around for a moment, finally finding what I'm looking for tucked in a pocket. Walking up to the brooding figure by the door, I brandish it, startling him.

The business card is battered, frayed at the edges, and bears a coffee stain on one corner. Based on the panic in his eyes, you'd think I was threatening him with a cobra.

"Her name is Sheila Mercer. She helped me—all of us, really—after Paula died. Even my dad went. I thought it was complete crap at first, but Conner and Casey talked me into it, and I'm grateful they did."

"Did Tom put you up to this?" The haunted look in his eyes tears at my heart, but I'm relentless. I stand tall and continue to hold the card out, daring him to take it.

"No. Has he suggested it, too?"

He frowns down at his feet, and that's all the answer I need.

"I was angry at the VA for not getting Paula back on Dad's coverage sooner, at the disease, at Erik for leaving. Even at Paula for dying. Sheila made me see things differently and gave me tools to use to cope. Eventually, I was able to get over the worst of my grief." My recently conquered problem with commitment, which was due to the tragic disappearance of Paula's fiancé after her death, is beside the point.

"I don't need to talk to some quack doctor," he argues, but there's no heat in his voice. He's eyeing the card in my hand suspiciously, so I wiggle it a little between my fingers, enticing him.

"Well, she's a psychologist, not a psychiatrist, so she's not a doctor." I smile, but it fades. "I love you, and I will continue to do whatever I can to help you in whatever way you need it. However, I can't be your cure, Matt. It's not fair to either of us. You need to take control of whatever is fueling your nightmares. This might be a good way to start. Please, just *think* about it."

I hold my breath. He scowls, and I feel a frisson of fear. He doesn't *look* like he's going to explode, but then again I never thought he'd trash one of his prize guitars.

"They're mostly about when I was living on the street." He stares at his shoes, taking a steady breath. "And my mother, if you want to call her that. None of it is pretty." I swallow back the lump in my throat and wait. I thought I wanted to know, but seeing his haunted expression raises doubts. Is it fair for me to ask him to dredge up painful memories of the past? The thought of a young

Matt trying to make it on the streets stabs at my heart.

With a gulp, he lifts his head and takes the card. A relieved smile creeps across my face, and then I'm in his arms, holding on tight. He smells of spice and strong, warm man. We stand quietly, wrapped in each other, and the tension in both our bodies begins to ease. How could I ever have doubted that this is where I'm meant to be? Burying his face in my hair, he takes a deep breath. "I'll call her," he whispers, his hot breath tickling my ear. "I can't guarantee it will do any good, but I promise I'll try."

Tears spring to my eyes. "That's all I ask."

AFTER OUR TUMULTUOUS AFTERNOON, WE'D decided the storage unit could wait. Matt wanted to give Tom a call, and I wanted some fresh air. And some spanakopita. So I took the Camaro and ran down to our favorite Greek restaurant to pick up dinner. One of these days, I suppose I should learn to cook, but—I pluck a stuffed grape leaf from the bag and pop it into my mouth—today is not that day.

At the corner, I notice a motorcycle cop wrapping up a traffic stop. I give him a wide berth and turn down our alley. My mouth waters from the delectable aromas wafting in the car. I jab the garage gate button impatiently, wondering if we have another bottle of that yummy sauvignon blanc left.

The godawful grinding of the gate is punctuated by an even greater noise, before the whole thing shudders to a stop. Awesome—it's finally broken. Now maybe I can talk Matt into getting a better gate.

Grumbling to myself, I get out of the car to see if I can still pop the handle and open it manually. The gate is stuck about only a foot off the ground and . . . what the hell?

There's a short piece of rebar stuck through a gap in the gate and into the track. The opening mechanism strains against the obstruction; if I can pull it out, maybe it will—

"Leave it."

I whirl around, shocked to see Zach standing about three feet from me, and I automatically step back, almost into the gate. He looks like he's been living under a bridge—maybe he has. His holey sweatshirt is stained and hanging off his thin frame, and his jeans are torn at the knee. Lank dark hair hangs into his eyes, eyes that are full of malice and frustration and aimed directly at me.

"What the hell are you doing here?" I demand, my shock giving way to the anger that's been simmering in me since the accident. "Haven't you already done enough?"

"I didn't mean to hurt anyone," he spits out, his words interrupted by a hoarse cough that rattles in his chest. "I just wanted to fuck up the bike. I didn't think he'd be able to get it out of the garage, much less take it on a joy ride. Stupid prick." I'm not sure if the loathing in his eyes is directed at Matt or himself.

"He could've died!" I glare back at him with my fists clenched at my side. The edges of my vision turn red and my body shakes with rage.

"So what if he did!" he screams back, his pale face turning red. "Rich fucking rock star. Who the fuck does he think he is, telling me he 'understands' what I'm going through." He steps closer, penning me in. His rank odor turns my stomach. "He doesn't understand shit! He lives in a fancy apartment with tons of money—what does he know? He's got everything he wants. I bet you'll get on your knees anytime he snaps his fingers, ready to suck his—"

My hand draws back to slap him, but the sudden appearance of a knife in his hand is like a bucket of icy water. My rage evaporates, replaced by cold fear.

"What do you want?" I ask flatly. The adrenaline is pumping as I turn over the possibilities, my father's instructions on self-defense rushing back to me. Can I do this?

He grips the knife like a lifeline, seeming to regain his confidence. "You have to tell him I didn't mean it. Tell the cops I didn't mean it." I take a deep breath as he continues, "Look, I don't want to hurt you." With his free hand, he grabs my wrist.

Okay, then.

In an instant, I twist my wrist in his grasp, clamp my other hand on his firmly, and wrench his arm to the side. The knife clatters to the pavement, and he cries out in pain as I force him to the ground, maintaining the wristlock. I don't stop moving until I have him face down with his arm behind his back, and my knee firmly planted on his tailbone.

I ignore his enraged shrieks and concentrate on not hyper-ventilating. It's not easy. Spots dance in my vision and I want to throw up. I almost can't believe I remembered how to do that. Dad would be so proud.

Glancing around wildly, I realize I'm stuck. Zach's immobile, but now what do I do? I can't call anyone; my phone's in the car.

My question is answered seconds later by a loud command that cuts Zach's screeching short. My eyes snap up to see the stern smirk of the motorcycle cop I'd passed on the street. "Let him go, miss. I'll take it from here."

Matt is never going to believe this.

chapter eighteen

matt

"I'M GOING TO FUCKING KILL him." The tension rises as I glare at Tucker. He's been keeping his spot at my door with his arms crossed, blocking me from getting out for the last few hours. Those hours have done nothing to calm the rage that I feel coursing through me.

It's been chaos outside the loft since Zach was arrested, due to the flashing lights and the ensuing news crews once word got out that there had been another incident involving Redfall. The band and Tucker arrived quickly, only stirring the already boiling pot. Tom's with Tess at the police station while she gives a statement. Tucker had to physically hold me back from going with her.

And there's more. Tess shared her suspicion that Zach was the one who keyed my car when she took it while the band was touring in Australia. Worse, that she thinks he was following her on a dirt bike the day it happened. I'm not sure which I'm more pissed off about—the fact that she kept it from me, or the fact that it happened. I told her when this started, no secrets.

"You're not doing anything," Tucker says, his voice firm and steady as always. "He's in custody. He's confessed. He's going to be spending some serious time in juvy. You need to let it go."

"Don't tell me to fucking let it go! He had a knife!" I holler, pacing the floor.

"And Tess took care of it, Grasshopper. Badass girlfriend you got there." Sean grins at me from the couch in the living room. I shake my head at him and his ridiculous hair. He's got it dyed pure white this week. Some shit about wanting to see what he'll look like when he gets older.

"Shut it."

"Would you have preferred she couldn't take care of herself?" Cameron asks from the kitchen. I narrow my eyes at him. "I'm being serious. It could've been a lot worse if Tess was some wall-flower who didn't have a Navy vet as a father."

"I know that. I know it could've been worse." I move to the window to observe the growing crowd on the street below. Even though the police have packed up Zach and carted his sorry ass away, the fans and the intrusive paparazzi just keep coming.

"She's fine, Matty." I turn to see Kennedy, moving to the line of guitar stands against the wall.

"Would you think that if it was Abby? Would you be this fucking calm?"

"No. Probably not. But you'd all be talking sense into me, just like we're doing now." He lifts a Gibson from one of the stands and slides the strap over his shoulder. "Tucker is right."

Tucker coughs from across the room. "Sorry, what was that again?"

Kennedy glances at Tucker with a half-smile before focusing back on me.

"The kid is going to do his time for what he did. You need to let it go," Kennedy says, lifting one of my Fenders and holding it out to me. "You want to get some frustration out? Play."

An uneasy silence takes over the loft while I stare back at him. Swallowing back the lump in my throat, I stare at the familiar lines of the guitar. "I haven't since the accident."

Kennedy holds the guitar out. "Don't care. Play."

"I don't know if I can." My voice sounds hollow with my admission. It scares the hell out of me not knowing. Tess's famous shrink friend would probably say that's the biggest reason I haven't tried. Fear of the unknown makes you do stupid things, keeps you from moving forward.

"I know you can. We all know you can," Kennedy presses.

"You've been doing the rehab exercises. Tucker says you're stronger than ever," Cameron adds, joining us. I watch as he lifts another guitar from the stand, plugging it into an amp before he strums a few chords.

I look over at Sean as he bolts up from the couch, reaching for my favorite Rickenbacker. He slides the strap awkwardly over his shoulder. He looks ridiculous. "How fucking hard can this be? Honestly. There are only four strings on this one."

A laugh slips out despite the stress of the day. I don't deserve these guys, but after everything we've been through, I know I'm stuck with them. Brothers to the end. I might doubt a lot of things in my life, but I'll never doubt that again. "When in the hell did you learn to play bass?"

"Right the fuck now. That's when. Come on then, Matty, dazzle me with your legendary ways."

"Shit." I reach for the neck of the Fender, feeling it ground me as it always has. Lifting the strap over my shoulder is as familiar as breathing. I let the weight of the guitar settle, the strings taunting and tempting me.

With my heart pounding, I take a look at my bandmates, the years we've spent playing to handfuls in dimly lit bars and then thousands in packed stadiums looping back to me. Memories we will have for a lifetime. It's time to make more. "Okay. Let's do this."

"I DON'T LIKE THIS," TOM says, scowling at me as we sit in the small visiting room at a juvenile detention center just outside San Fran. It's Zach's home for the next couple of years as he serves out his sentence. It's about as bad as you expect. Claustrophobic, depressing, slowly sucking the life out of you.

"I know you don't."

"If I had just listened to you and Aaron—"

"Don't go there. Just don't. If it wasn't me, it could've been you on that bike, and that? That would've killed me."

Tom huffs and shakes his head. "He just needs to do his time and get on with his life."

"I know that."

He pins me with one of his stern glares. "You could've died, Matt."

"But I didn't. I could've also ended up like Zach. That could be me in there. You're the reason I'm not. You gave me a chance. Hell, you gave me dozens."

"And talking to him is going to do what exactly? Nothing I've said or done so far has made a damn bit of difference." Tom drums his fingers against the worn wooden table.

"Maybe this won't, either. Maybe he doesn't really give a shit.

But I want to try. I need to see him. Call it closure."

His expression softens, a hint of a smile replacing the concerned frown he's been wearing since we got here. "When did you get to be so smart, kid?"

"Learned from the best."

The steel doors opposite the table open up, and Zach shuffles in with a burly guard. Gone is the cocky air of defiance Zach used to wear like a badge. He looks like he may have gone a few rounds with a prizefighter and lost.

Glancing between Tom and me, he drags out a chair from under the table across from us, scraping it over the linoleum floor. He winces as he sinks down into it. He's beaten and exhausted. His head's been freshly shaved, and he's sporting a few good cuts.

An awkward silence hangs in the air until I break it. "Guess I don't have to ask how you're doing."

No response from Zach. He just scowls at the empty beige wall on the other side of the room.

"You need to eat at least," Tom says, his voice clipped.

Zach's sunken eyes dart between us. "Why do you give a shit about me? What? Cameras following you around again? Good photo op?" The words come out of his mouth flat, like he's lost his fire.

"No cameras. No bullshit. It's just us."

Zach folds his arms across his chest, shaking his head.

"You like living this way? Looking over your shoulder all the time? Sleeping with one eye open?" I lean forward.

Zach slides his hand over his shaved head, and then down across his face. "I've never stopped doing that."

There's a hint of desperation I'm sure Zach regrets in his voice. It's obvious that the past few weeks in here have taken a toll. I know how this works. The new kid is typically the punching bag, bottom of the established pecking order. You have to earn respect. In the group home, Zach was on top—King Shit. In here, he's nothing.

"They offer programs in here you should probably take a look at. Job placements to get you on your feet when you're out." Tom's voice fills the room as it always does. I've learned over the years to listen to him. I may not always like what he's had to say, but the man commands respect.

Zach eyes both of us warily. "I don't get it. What's in this for you?"

"I want to know what you were thinking, Zach." There's a disappointment in Tom's voice. I've heard it more times than I care to remember.

Zach slumps forward and, for the first time, I see the cracks in his armor. "I didn't think," he mumbles, eyes fixed to the table. Tom glances at me with a subtle shake of his head. "I screwed up. I never meant to hurt anyone."

"You could've said something. I've always had an open-door policy and you know it," Tom's gravelly voice shows signs of breaking. This has rattled Tom more than I realized. It's more than just me getting hurt. It's Tom's entire life's work; his faith in these kids and the system he's put in place has been rattled.

"I thought I could fix it." Zach grinds his hands together. "Doesn't matter."

"Would you at least think about the courses? It would help pass the time if nothing else." I watch his jaw set as he considers what Tom's saying.

He gives a noncommittal shrug, slouching down further in the chair. "I'll take that as a yes." Pushing back from the table earns his attention. He lifts his head to glance up at Tom and me, and I can recognize the panic in his eyes. The last thing he wants to do is go back inside to whatever nightmare his daily routine has become. Unfortunately, it's his reality for now.

Tucker's right. Zach needs to do his time, and I need to let it go. Nothing is going to make him miraculously turn a corner unless he wants to do that himself. "Take care of yourself in here," I say, gripping the back of the chair.

"You're going to be okay, right?" Zach's eyes dart to my shoulder.

"I am. You will be, too."

Zach huffs, shaking his head. "Whatever. You're not the one in here."

"Listen to the guards, do the work, and if you're lucky, this will be the last time you're in a place like this."

I don't know if Zach hears me or not. If he believes me, or if he's so far gone that he just doesn't care anymore. At this point, I've done all I can.

"ARE YOU SURE YOU WANT to go for a ride?" Tess asks as I steer her downstairs. My Victory custom sits in the quiet garage, gleaming under the overhead lights.

"Oh, I'm very sure," I whisper, pressing my lips against her neck. It earns me a hitch of her breath, and one of those laughs I live for.

"It's just that you haven't been out since the accident, and you're leaving for the tour in an hour." The tour is back on, six months almost to the day of the accident. The weeks and months I've put in with Tucker and in Cameron's pool with rehab exercises, and the countless hours spent playing into the middle of the night, have been painful and at a lot of times frustrating, but they've made a difference.

It hasn't been without adjustments to the band.

Three-and-a-half-hour concerts are going to take a toll, so I'll be at the piano for a few songs to give my shoulder a rest. Kennedy calls it the next evolution of our sound. It's a little more introspective, but the guys are all on board with it. My recovery has given us all a much-needed break from the grueling schedule of touring, and now, we're itching to get back on the road.

"I know. But I love to ride, Cardinal. You do, too. We're making time."

"Look at you getting all philosophical on me."

"It's time with your favorite shrink, Sheila Mercer. She's a woman of many talents," I tease. She narrows her eyes in response.

Over the last couple of months, I've started seeing the therapist Tess suggested. It's awkward and draining, but I also know I need to do it. The nightmares still loom large, and probably always will to some degree. At least now I have an outlet that doesn't involve me going off on Tess or Tom. I've never been someone who believes the psychobabble you hear about. Sheila isn't like that at all. She's no-nonsense, direct and to the point. I get the feeling she doesn't put up with a lot of shit, which I fully appreciate.

She's challenged me to look at things differently. To see that what happened with my mother was her fault, not mine, and that the choices I made to survive on the streets are things I can't change, and that I can't let them define me. I still believe the past affects the future. I wouldn't be who I am without it, but a little perspective is a good thing.

We've only scratched the surface in the sessions we've had. Old wounds that never really healed are cut open and allowed to bleed, maybe for the first time. I know it's progress. Slow and painful, but progress.

"She's sixty, and unless you're into something I don't know about, I'm going to assume I don't have to worry about those talents," Tess says, lifting her helmet from the handlebar.

"You never have to worry about anything with me, Cardinal." I grip her luscious hips as she straddles the bike. "My heart is yours and always will be."

"Smooth talker. And you're stalling." She flips her hair over her shoulder, and I straddle the seat, facing her. Her eyes widen as I cup her face between my hands, my thumbs brushing over her cheeks.

"Are you sure you can't come with me?" Those dark eyes stare back at me, and I can see the want, the aching need we share.

"I can't. You know I have to work with Kennedy's brother on the NASCAR event." I know Tess is excited about starting on this particular dream fulfillment. Kennedy's brother Adam, a star on the NASCAR circuit, is helping out giving a little girl with MS her dream of spending the day at a racetrack. I know it's for a good cause. I'm ready for the tour, but playing for the first time since the accident to our die-hard fans also scares the hell out of me. Tess has a way of calming me, bringing me back to reality. I guess she's going to have to do that from a distance.

"You're adorable when you pout," she teases.

"I'm not pouting." I lean forward, nipping at her bottom lip, skimming my palm along her thigh.

"Sure you're not," she whispers against my lips. "And I thought we were going for a ride."

My hands slide up under her shirt, feeling her warm skin as my fingers tease higher. Her helmet falls from her hand, landing with a loud thud on the floor of the garage. "We are, Cardinal. We are."

"GRASSHOPPER! KISS YOUR GIRL AND move your arse!" Sean's voice bellows from behind the door as I spend my last few minutes with Tess.

"I hate that he's rushing me," I mumble against her neck. "Two more minutes, right here." I breathe her in, feeling her press against my torso. Fuck, I'm going to miss her.

"You have to go!" Tess swats my ass as she pushes away from me. "Before he breaks the door down."

"Don't make us use the spare key." Tucker's threatening voice drifts through the door.

"I'm coming," I growl, turning to open the door.

"That's what they all say." Cameron leans against the wall beside the door. "Plane's waiting, Casanova."

"Make yourselves useful." I roll over my suitcase to Tucker, passing Sean and Cameron a few guitar cases. The others will already be loaded with the rest of the equipment en route to Montreal, the first stop on our tour.

Tess smiles as she leans out to the hall. "Make sure you look after him."

"Always do, Tess. Don't worry." Tucker gives her a salute.

"You know, I can look after myself." I tighten my arms around her waist.

"I know that, but it's nice to know you've got people in your corner. You always will."

I gently brush her dark hair behind her shoulder. "Always?"

She looks at me with all the promise and hope I never thought I deserved. "Always, Matt."

♪ ♩ ♪ ♩

Tessa

"SHE'S SO EXCITED, I THINK she could power a small city!"

I look over at April and mirror her enthusiastic grin. We've been like that all day. Amanda Blakely, a twelve-year-old from Folsom whose dream was to spend a day at a racetrack, has gotten much more. She's been the special guest of Adam Lane, Kennedy's brother, for today's NASCAR race at Sonoma Raceway. She visited the pit and helped the crew, and then watched the rest of the race in one of the VIP boxes with her family. After he'd won, he'd taken her for a victory lap in his car, which sported an enormous Redfall logo on the hood, snuggled amongst his other sponsors. I thought she would explode from happiness.

Although the entire day has been carefully documented by our photographers, Amanda and her family were now posing with Adam and a few of the other drivers by their cars. As April says, you can never have too many pictures.

The day has been an adventure for me, as well. I've never been to a race before. As breathtaking as the actual event was, the organized chaos afterward is just as amazing. Pit crews and techs haul equipment, and carriers stand ready to load the precious race cars. Fans, groupies, and autograph hounds swarm everywhere. In fact, I think there are as many groupies here as there are at one of the guys' concerts. April and I found a spot at the foot of the now mostly empty stands where we can be out of the way and still keep an eye on everything happening on the track.

Smells of exhaust and gasoline are heavy in the warm air. I spy Abby standing at the edge of the track, looking for us among the swirling mass of bodies, and I wave to catch her attention. Her relationship with Kennedy made this an easy dream to fulfill, but that didn't mean we haven't been busy with months of planning, negotiations with the raceway's own charity, lodging details for the whole Blakely family, and the press, of course.

It's all helped keep me occupied so I don't dwell on missing

Matt. Which I do, desperately. It's the first time we've been separated by more than five hundred miles since the accident. I had
to fly to LA for some meetings a month ago, and it felt like I was
missing a limb. Now, sometimes I miss him so much it's hard to
breathe. I don't know what I'm going to do when he has to fly to
Europe or Australia again.

But I have a job to do, too, and I want to do it well. I'm still in
my first year as giving director. Abby and the board of directors
were incredibly supportive while Matt was recovering, and I don't
ever want them to think I'm taking advantage of their generosity.
Plus, I love what I'm doing. Seeing the look on a child's face when
they receive their dream has always been wonderful, but now
that I'm more directly responsible for the arrangements, it's even
better. I have a goal to increase the number of dreams we're able
to fulfill by ten percent in the next two years, and I'm going to get
there, by God.

My phone chimes with a text. I pull it out and laugh at the
photo of Sean dragging an obviously reluctant Matt and Cam into a
fast food place with *poutinerie* in the name. More gastric adventures
with the Brit, it seems. I sigh and smooth my hair away from my
face. The first concert in Montreal was a triumph, according to the
press, and the second stop in Toronto was just as good. They're in
Winnipeg tomorrow night before continuing west. They should
be home next week. I should be able to last that long, right?

Right.

"Congratulations, Tess!" Abby gives me an enthusiastic hug
when she reaches us. "Everything has gone off without a hitch.
Fantastic day."

"Thanks. I have a great team." I gesture toward the causeway,
where my assistant, Hal, and a couple of my Giving staff members
are chatting animatedly with the catering crew. A warm feeling

infuses my chest, as I recognize the words I've heard a million times from Abby's lips fall from my own. I do have a great team, and I learned from the best mentor a girl could have.

My boss gives me a knowing smile. "So do I." April and I both laugh, nodding in acknowledgement of her praise. We stand for a few moments, looking out over the happy scene, and enjoying the feeling of a job well done. The joy on Amanda's and her family's faces is a welcome reminder of why our work is worthwhile.

Seeing that the photos are winding down, April leaves us to go corral the photographers. I glance at Abby. "Are you going to join Adam and his wife tonight, since Kennedy's gone?"

She smiles a secret smile. "No, I had something else in mind." Before I can ask what that might be, she asks, "What have you got on deck for tomorrow?"

"Well . . ." I sit on the edge of the short wall that surrounds the track and mentally recount my schedule. "I have to write the after-action report from all this," I begin, gesturing to the scene below us. "I need to call Barry at Nintendo; I have a Skype meeting with Brigitte at—"

"How about a quick trip up north?"

My head snaps up. Her hazel eyes twinkle with mischief, and my heart leaps. "Are you suggesting what I hope you're suggesting?"

A smile tugs at her lips. "Why not? You can do all that on the way, right? We can see the Winnipeg and Edmonton shows and fly back Monday morning in time for the staff meeting."

I jump to my feet, and whatever she sees on my face makes her laugh. "Who am I to argue with the boss?" I grin absurdly and brush a smudge off my suit pants. I want to race out of here and start packing, but April is waving at me to join her down below, reminding me of my obligations. "I'll wrap this up, and then we can book a flight."

"No need; I had Hal do it this morning. He's got us booked out of SFO tomorrow at eight a.m., with a short layover in Minneapolis. My treat—and don't argue. I have a ton of air miles to use." She slips an arm around my shoulders and guides me toward the stairs leading to the track. "We should get to Winnipeg in plenty of time."

"You've been planning this since this morning?" A laugh bubbles out of me as we walk down the steps and begin to navigate through the crowd. "My, aren't you the devious one? What happened to the all-work-and-no-play Abby Walker I used to know?"

"Oh, she's still about the work. But you can't be in love with a Redfall man and not know the value of play, too." She gives me a wink. "Now, let's go say goodbye to Amanda and the Blakelys."

OUR PLAN GOES ALMOST SMOOTHLY. A traffic accident on the highway in Winnipeg means our car pulls up to the artist entrance to the MTS Centre just after the guys take the stage. Tucker meets us with a broad smile, watching as we eagerly climb out of the SUV.

"Kennedy and Matt are going to freak when they see you two," he comments, his deep voice rumbling in his chest. "How did you keep it a surprise?"

"It wasn't easy," I mutter, sharing a glance with Abby. We'd both ducked calls from our men, having to claim via text that we were in meetings where we couldn't pick up. In reality, we'd been in the busy Minneapolis airport, penned in by wailing children and pissy travelers, with no hope of hiding where we were.

He hustles us inside and, after getting our VIP passes from a staffer, shuttles us down a labyrinth of hallways. "Well, whatever you did made them act like sulky teenagers denied the car keys.

Pathetic!" He chuckles. "But it fired 'em up, too. They're killing it tonight."

The dull roar emanating from the utilitarian block walls grows louder as we walk, bursting into an echoing cacophony when we step out into a vast blackness. Disoriented, I halt and thrust out my hand, feeling like I'm going to pitch forward. My eyes and ears adjust as I feel Tucker's strong hand on my elbow and I grin, recognizing one of Sean's drum solos.

Abby and I stick close together as we pick our way behind Tucker. It's hard to see the dim flashlight bobbing ahead of us. The floor vibrates in sync with the sounds from the stage. Tucker was right. The guys *are* tearing it up tonight, and considering the constant roar of the crowd, it sounds like the good citizens of Winnipeg—Winnipegites?—feel like they're getting their money's worth.

We mount some rickety metal stairs, and my hands sweat at the feel of the open blackness underneath us. But when we reach the stage level, the darkness gives way to the light bleeding through the backing curtains. Tucker positions us in the wings at the edge of one of the curtains just as they finish a song. "Don't touch the curtain," he whispers in my ear, and I nod. At least, that's what I think he said. It's hard to hear over the screams of the audience. I feel him move to stand behind us, and then promptly forget him. All my attention is on the tall form in front of me under the lights. My heart is pounding and it's hard to breathe. His back is to me, but he's close enough that I can clearly see the sweat soaking through his gray T-shirt between his shoulder blades. I wipe my damp palms on my hips and swipe my hair over my shoulder. Holy damn, he looks good.

Handing his bass off to a roadie clad in black, he stalks past Cam to take a seat at the grand piano. The spotlight hits him, turning his short blond hair into a halo. Kennedy swings around and backs up a little to give the stage to Matt, and in doing so, spies us in the wings. His face lights up when he sees Abby, and I hear her gasp in response. I give him a cheeky little wave, and he smirks. Returning my gaze to Matt, it's obvious he hasn't seen me. His eyes are trained on the keys, and then close slowly, his head tilting back, and he begins to play.

She binds me to this earth,

silken touch as strong as steel

The crowd hushes as his rich tenor soars and bends the notes to his will. After a moment, Cam and Kennedy join in, their guitar lines swirling in the air around the piano. It's surreal to see Matt at the grand instead of Kennedy, but the joy I feel at hearing the lyrics I've only heard bits of when I've woken at night in the loft now out in the open . . . It's indescribable.

Blazing red, she soars above it all

crashing through the monotony

She is life and light, heat and sweat

she's all the home I'll ever need

and I'll be damned if I turn away

His eyes open and meet mine across the stage, wide with shock. I can't breathe; the intensity of his gaze paralyzes me. Then a brilliant smile lights his face, and I gasp, my legs feeling like jelly. My face aches from smiling.

They finish the song and Matt stands as the crowd goes wild, but it seems distant, a vague roaring that fills the space around us as he stalks toward me deliberately. Then he's grabbing my hand and pulling me into his arms.

In the sudden glare of the spotlight, all I can see is his face, inches from mine. My pulse thunders in my ears as his lips descend, and everything vanishes except him. His soft mouth is warm and demanding, claiming me in a way that only he can. Then he pulls back, leaving me trembling in his arms, his eyes soft with love. Love for me.

"Well, it's about time, Cardinal. Did you like your song?"

Tears spring to my eyes as my heart swells with love for this brave, determined man. He's overcome the nightmare of his childhood and the hardships of his dangerous youth to emerge as this strong, gifted, generous man whom I love with every fiber of my being. I don't know where the future may take us, but if I have anything to say about it, it'll take us there together.

The Redfall adventures continue. A sneak peek at "Chase the Dream," book three of *The Refall Dream Series,* coming in 2018. *Content subject to change.*

chapter one

cameron

"STOP SLOUCHING, CAMERON." THREE WORDS from my mother guaranteed to make my thirty-seven-year-old self feel like an awkward teenager again. "All those years hunched over your guitar haven't done a thing for your posture."

"Lovely to see you too, mother." I lean in for the obligatory kiss to both of my cheeks—clean shaven as requested in the formal email sent from her assistant earlier in the week. The familiar scent of Chanel swirls around me as she leans back with a scrutinizing gaze, looking for flaws.

"You always did look so handsome in a suit," she starts in a rare compliment. "This isn't the Armani I sent over, is it?" She purses her distorted lips in disapproval. The collagen and countless facelifts have been putting up the good fight. Not a single wrinkle on her sixty-year-old face, dripping in diamonds and vintage Versace, hair perfectly styled and sprayed to within an inch of its dyed blonde life, she still manages to commands the room. The poster model for the billionaire's wife.

The crowd at the Chapman Center for the Arts buzzes around her, all sharks in the water, quietly waiting for their turn to take a bite. A few minutes with Victoria Chapman, the reigning Queen of Boston's elite first, and my mother second, can rocket you to elite status. You can almost smell the desperation on the high society wannabes lingering around the fringes.

Cameras flash around us, though this time in a welcome change, they aren't for me. It's the elitist event of the year in Boston, put on by my parents in support of the Arts Center, one of the many charities who benefit from my family's influence and power. Hell, the building is named after them. But, even if this is a massive publicity stunt, it's for a good cause. It may be the only thing that actually doesn't turn my stomach about being dragged here.

The money raised tonight and throughout the year supports the arts center that provides opportunities for talented musicians that otherwise wouldn't be available. Everything from programs like the one my band Redfall played in Sydney that offers chances for child prodigies to train with symphonies around the globe, to an all-day private high school focused on the arts, and a fully funded daycare for the musicians who are part of the symphony. I know how much time and dedication it takes to play at this level. It also takes money—something these musicians don't have.

"I stopped wearing the clothes you picked out for me when I was sixteen." She shakes her head slightly before flattening her hand down the lapel of my dark blue suit jacket. "And it's Tom Ford," I add just to rub it in.

She takes a step back as if standing too close to her son is a crime, her eyes narrowing. "Armani cuts a better suit. How many times do we have to have this conversation?"

"In your opinion."

"My opinion is the only one that matters, dear." She links her arm around mine and turns to flash her practiced smile for the cameras before gliding us through the lobby. The masses part for her as if she's some holy relic to be revered. "There's someone I want you to meet."

I frown, glancing down at her. "I do just fine getting my own dates, thank you."

"Yes. We know." She flashes me a warning glare before her public mask snaps back into place. "Darcy Hamilton." I barely manage to bite back a groan. "Recently single," she continues on, just loud enough for me to hear as we merge into the line for the theatre. She nods and gives a finger wave to a few people along the way. "She was dating Benjamin Knight, you know? Of the athletic company? Shoes, apparel."

"I'm familiar," I murmur. "Isn't he worth a few billion?" Sometimes, it's fun to annoy her. She scoffs slightly, taking a program from one of the ushers standing outside our private box seats.

"Please." She leans closer, her voice dropping lower. "He had a gambling problem. Lost half their earnings in one night. It was quite the scandal. I'm surprised you didn't hear about it."

Shaking my head, I lead her to our spot above the mezzanine. Only the best box seats for the Chapmans. "I've been a little busy."

She pats my chest lightly. "It's cute that your hobby can keep you entertained. While you've been gallivanting from city to city with your little band, your father has been working himself nearly to death."

"I hate to break it to you, but he's been doing that his whole life. And I don't gallivant."

She waves the program in front of me, clearly not wanting to hear a thing I say. "Anyway, Darcy is lovely. Long blond hair, thirty, on the board at the Hospital Foundation. She was Miss Massachusetts a few years ago, you know. I think she does Pilates at the club.

I've seen her there when I meet the girls for brunch on Thursdays. Her parents own Hamilton Jewelers," she rattles on, sinking down gracefully to a seat at the front of the box.

"You going to tell me how much she weighs too? Jesus. It sounds like you're trying to sell me one of the horses." Unbuttoning my suit jacket, I take the seat beside her.

"Watch your language, Cameron."

I smell her before I see her, a cloud of Clive Christian wafting over me. It's an expensive scent I grew up with, being surrounded by high society women who wanted to make sure they not only looked rich, but smelled it too. They all have a certain air about them—something that screams refined, sophisticated, elitist.

"Ah, Darcy, Elizabeth . . ." It's hard not to roll my eyes. "You made it." My mother should have been an actress. She actually sounds like she cares about these people. She stands and extends the customary kiss to the cheek greetings, and I stand as well. Even after years in what is considered a raunchy and highly unpredictable rock and roll band, the manners that were drilled into me come back easily.

"Cameron, of course you remember Elizabeth." My mother motions from Elizabeth to me as if I'm on display. I don't remember Mrs. Hamilton. Too many carbon copies of her have passed through our doors over the years. None of them are memorable. But I lie, because it's what's expected of me.

"Mrs. Hamilton," I greet her, earning me a few brownie points. Yes, mother. I remember every single thing you and your legion of nannies taught us. Elizabeth looks her fill of me, her eyes widening as I take her offered hand. She can hardly hold it up with the ice rink sitting on her finger—a given when your husband owns one of the biggest jewelry franchises in the world. "Lovely to see you again."

"Oh, you've grown into a fine young man, wouldn't you agree,

Darcy?" At least Darcy lives up to the hype my mother was spewing. She's striking in that manufactured, beauty-queen way. I wonder why her mother doesn't have her married off already. Talk about trophy wife material.

Almost as tall as my six-five in her stilettos, she's rocking a form fitting white sequined gown that barely conceals a pair of fake tits that probably put a significant dent in Daddy's pocket book. Perma smile plastered on her face, model worthy pose beside her mother, looking at me like she'd like to pounce. She's got so much make-up on, I wonder what she actually looks like underneath it all. Darcy too, is dripping in jewelry—some huge sapphire monstrosity locked around her neck that looks like it weighs more than she does. Jesus, woman. Eat a cheeseburger.

"I would absolutely agree," Darcy purrs, holding her hand out. Freshly manicured nails, painted blood red, bling on her wrist and fingers, except notably the finger she's desperate to put something on. "Darcy Hamilton." She's about as subtle as a brick to the head.

"Pleasure to meet you. Cameron Chapman." Her nails trail a light circuit over the inside of my wrist as she bats her big eyes at me, looking a little stunned. Maybe it's all the mascara weighing her eyelids down. Her nails scrape my skin. It feels like she's staking a claim, and I don't like it. I move to the side, motioning for them to sit.

"I downloaded your latest album last night," she purrs brushing past me, her voice all breathy. "It's brilliant."

"Yeah? Well, you can thank Kennedy for that. He wrote it."

She giggles at this—the appropriate response for all of these ridiculous women who don't have a fucking clue how to carry on an actual conversation. Underneath all that glitz and glamour, she's not as far off from the groupies as I'm sure she thinks she is. I wonder if she even knows who Kennedy Lane, our lead singer is, if she listened to a single thing we've done before she found out our mothers were trying to set us up.

Her hand snakes up my arm. "Maybe you could play something for me sometime." I let her blatant pick up line hang in the air as she lowers elegantly into the seat. She makes sure the high slit of her dress opens to reveal her endlessly long legs. I curse the no-sex bet I made with our pain-in-the-ass bassist Matt Logan again. I'd actually like to fuck that smug look off Darcy's face. She thinks I'm a done deal, and judging by the expectant looks on our mother's faces, so do they.

sneak peek

Gable (The Powers That Be, Book 1)
By Harper Bentley

Summer, two weeks before class:

YOU KNOW THAT FEELING YOU get when you meet someone and feel as if you've known them for a lifetime? As if you're just connected in some way?

Yeah, that didn't happen the first time I met Gable Powers. Matter of fact, I didn't like him one bit.

Oh, I know about all the Powers boys now. I actually knew about them by the first day of school since it seemed as if every woman on campus couldn't stop talking about how each brother was just as gorgeous as the next, and things like, "Omigod! The Powers brothers are *so* hot!" or "Aren't they just *the* cutest you've ever seen?" were proclaimed almost everywhere I went the entire first week of school. From listening in on these chicks wax rhapsodic over these brothers, if they were anything less than Nick Bateman clones, well, then I'd be highly disappointed. But from their conversations, I learned the Powers were from Seattle, all of them went to Hallervan, Zeke was a senior who played on the football team, Lochlan was a freshman who was some kind of computer genius, Ryker was a sophomore wrestler and Gable was a junior. I had yet to figure out what his superpower was, but I can honestly say that when I first met him, I couldn't have cared less.

My up-close-and-personal with Gable Powers left me less than thrilled, and when I finally figured out who he was and said something later about it to my new roommate, I got a stare of disbelief which made me roll my eyes.

So here's how it all went down.

I'd answered an ad in the *Seattle Times* for a roommate. On my way to meet Amy (fellow sophomore who'd eventually become my new roomie), I'd had a flat tire and had to pull over in an area of the city I was unfamiliar with—hell I was unfamiliar with the entire friggin' place—and, of course, it'd been raining. As a farm girl, I knew how to change a tire, had no problem changing a tire, but per Dad's instructions, I called AAA and stayed in my car waiting for someone to show up, kind of feeling like a wuss for doing so. I knew I could've done it and been on my way in no time but I decided to let Dad parent me for a change. Not that he wasn't a good father; it's just that I was majorly independent.

Needless to say, I was a little surprised when a black pickup truck stopped behind me and a guy got out, almost immediately after I'd hung up with the auto service. I mean, I'd heard AAA was fast, but come on. The guy had come to the driver's side and when he'd tapped on the window of my little Honda, I'd seen the full sleeve tattoo on his muscular arm and my eyes had bugged out.

See, I'm from a small town in Idaho where everyone thinks tattoos are Satan's markings, which I know is ridiculous and is one of the many reasons I couldn't wait to leave that shitty little place, but I regret saying that when I'd seen his arm, I'd been a little on edge. The guy had stood there in the pouring rain while I contemplated what to do as I checked out the rest of him. He appeared to be over six feet tall and his entire body was ripped. Dang. I could see his abs all bumpy and defined through the wet white t-shirt that clung to him, and his rain-soaked jeans were stuck to what appeared to be muscular thighs. I'd then felt bad for ogling him as he stood there getting drenched, so I finally rolled my window down an inch and he'd bent to ask if I needed help.

And, my God, was he beautiful.

I stared at him as rain dripped from his straight nose to the ground. It drizzled down his high cheekbones where it met his strong, stubble-covered jaw, trickling to his chin before finally slipping off. The long curls of dark hair that framed his tanned face were dripping wet also, but it was his light brown eyes that held my attention, so expressive and soulful, lined in long, sooty lashes that were spiked from the rain. Damn. He was a total friggin' hunk.

"I've called Triple A, so no, thank you," I'd yelled over the rain through the cracked window.

He'd given me a sexy half grin, which made butterflies bounce off the walls of my stomach. "I could probably have it fixed before they even get their truck started."

I'd twisted my mouth to the side not really knowing what to do. I mean, if I agreed to let *him* fix it, *I* may as well just do it. "Uh, that's okay."

"Seriously. You wouldn't even have to get out, Rebecca. Just pop the trunk and I'll take care of it. You won't even have to lift one of your pretty, little fingers." The smug look he'd given me made me frown. A lot.

"Rebecca?" I asked wondering what he was talking about.

"Of Sunnybrook Farm. You know, all clean and wholesome. Prissy," he'd replied with a twinkle in his eye as he grinned fully now, his straight white teeth making him even more attractive.

What the hell? I'd grown up with two older brothers and I

was anything but prissy. I could drive a tractor for chrissakes! "No, really, it's fine," I said through gritted teeth.

"Oh, c'mon. Can't have a helpless little lady like yourself out here all alone, you know. What are you, like fifteen?"

I blinked at how rude he was being which was when Kim Kardashian, Jr. had walked up holding an umbrella and wearing the shortest shorts I'd ever seen. The crop t-shirt she wore had so much cut off that I could see her braless boobs hanging out from under it and couldn't help but gape at how provocatively she was dressed. Then she'd whined, "What's going onnnnnn, Gable? God! These helpless little Daddy's Girls are so annoying! *I* could've changed the tire by nooooow! Leave the rich bitch alone and come onnnnnn!"

And that was the precise moment I think steam had shot out of my ears. I reached down and jerked up on the trunk release because *fuck that*. Then I'd thrown open my door and saw the guy jump out of the way. I walked to the back of the car, raised the trunk, pulled back the carpet and removed the jack then went to the side where the tire was flat, put the jack down and started loosening the lug nuts with the tire iron.

"Whoa! What do you think you're doing?" Jerkface asked, having come around to the side of the car where I was.

"Well, *Prissy Rich Bitch* here is changing her tire if you haven't figured it out," I muttered glaring up at him. And my eyes got great big when I saw that *both* his arms were covered in tattoos. Whoa. And why that made him even hotter, I had no idea.

That was when Kim, Jr. huffed and called the guy an asshole (with which I couldn't disagree), then she called me a stupid cunt (with which I totally took offense) and my mouth fell open as I watched her stomp back to the truck in her strappy wedge sandals, her ass cheeks totally hanging out from under her shorts. Wow. Classy babe.

"At least let me help you with that," Tattoo Guy said, ignoring his girlfriend.

The glare I'd given him had him holding up his hands to his sides in surrender, his eyebrows raised as he grinned at me. I know I must've looked like an idiot with my long, blond hair soaked and hanging in my face, my cute, white cotton romper, which was sticking to me everywhere and was now probably ruined as I'm sure were my very awesome, white ankle-high gladiator sandals, but I'd be damned if I was going to let him help me now after he'd made me out to be some helpless female.

When he hung around, I muttered, "Go away," as I positioned the jack and twisted the handle. Once I got the car jacked up, I realized he still hadn't left so I stood and turned to him, putting my hands on my hips. "What?"

The perusal he gave me made the butterflies kick up again. Stupid fucking half grin. I frowned at him then moved back to the tire and proceeded to take off the lug nuts. When I went to remove the tire itself, he stepped in, took it off the wheel and rolled it to the trunk as I followed, telling him I had things under control and that he should just leave now.

"Can't have you getting yourself all dirty, now can we?" He'd looked me up and down appreciatively and that's when I realized he could see everything through my outfit.

Shit! I hadn't bothered wearing a bra because the romper had a built-in shelf bra, and I'm sure I was giving him quite the show, knowing my nipples had gotten perky at his heated gaze. But now I had to own it. So taking a deep breath, I leaned into the trunk to remove the spare, but he pushed me aside gently and reached in for it. And, God, he smelled good, all fresh rain and hot man. Damn it.

"I can handle it. Really. Why don't you and Luscious take off?" I mumbled.

He set down the tire, appearing confused, then asked, "Luscious?"

"Your girlfriend. Isn't that her stripper name?" I smiled sweetly at him hoping that'd make him mad and he'd finally leave, but instead, he'd barked out a laugh then proceeded to roll the tire to the front. I sloshed through the rain behind him then watched as he finished changing it, none too happy about it.

"That's it," he said when he finished, putting everything back in its place in the trunk. Then his eyes landed on me, once again moving up and down my body making me want to cover myself with my arms but refusing to do so, and after wiping his hand on a rag held it up for me to give him a high five. "Nice working with you."

A high five? Really? Maybe he did think I was fifteen. "Uh, yeah," I replied moving my hand slowly up to touch my palm to his.

He ended up grabbing my hand during the high five, and I swear, this is so cliché, so stupid chick lit banal, but I honestly felt a damned jolt go through me when we touched. I think he felt it too because he looked at our hands, scowled for a second before scrutinizing me closely then let my hand go.

His honey-brown eyes stared in thought into my green ones for a moment before that sexy grin hit his gorgeous face again. "Well, Miss Priss, I might be seeing you around."

"I'll be waiting breathlessly until that moment." At my sarcasm, he grinned again. I rolled my eyes and said, "So . . . thanks for the help." I'm pretty sure he heard the muttered, "Jerk" I tacked on, but to his credit he didn't say anything as I closed the trunk and rounded the car to get inside, but before I could pull my door closed he was there holding it open.

"You go to Hallervan?" he'd leaned down and asked, and, God, those eyes, that face . . . that body. My lord he was hot.

"Starting this semester," I answered still trying to pull my door closed.

"Maybe you'll get lucky and see me." He winked then walked away.

"One can only hope," I'd mumbled, rolling my eyes again, before closing my door and driving away.

It was then I looked down and saw my ruined outfit and sandals only then remembering I had an old pair of Keds and a raincoat under the passenger seat. Great.

acknowledgements

TO OUR FAMILIES. THANK YOU for your love, support and patience.

Much love to the Facebook Dream Team. Your support and continuing visuals are a constant source of inspiration.

To the super-talented Jada—thank you for your vision. You're simply amazing, and we're in awe of your beautiful talent.

To Lauren and the Write Divas, thank you for your continued guidance.

Christine, thank you for making this beautiful. You're incredible!

To our wonderful pre-readers—Mandy, Patty, Corinne, and Tami. Thank you for taking the time to read, and for your suggestions along the way!

A million thanks to the community of authors and their on-going support including Melanie Moreland, and the incredible Harper Bentley. Harper, our spirit animal is throwing glitter and rolling around in it as we speak!

Much love to the bloggers, Twitterloves, Facebook friends and groups, and review sites who support and inspire. It's a ride we wouldn't take without you.

To you, the reader. Thank you for taking this journey with us. We hope you enjoy it as much as we enjoyed writing it. Rock on, friends. Rock on.

about the authors

A LITTLE OVER SEVEN YEARS ago, a Canadian vegetarian and an American carnivore bonded over their mutual love of purses, cocktails, and swoon-worthy story telling.

Leslie Carson lives in Ottawa, with her busy family and three cats. She's at the rink so much, Zamboni drivers know her name.

From her home near Portland, B.B. Miller spends her days with friends and family in search of the perfect pear martini.

Together, they enjoy visiting random vineyards and writing about the romantic adventures of good and bad boys.

They would love to hear from you:

The Dream Team

www.ingramcontent.com/pod-product-compliance
Lightning Source LLC
Chambersburg PA
CBHW061929170626
46813CB00006B/2347